Praise for *The Family Chao*

"A Dickensian drama of family conflicts and intrigues; an insightful comedy of the American immigrant experience, and of a small town's inner workings. Lan Samantha Chang's creation of characters through dialogue is worthy of a great playwright."

—John Irving, author of *Avenue of Mysteries*

"Imagine *The Brothers Karamazov* set in a Chinese restaurant in the Midwest, imagine the characters of various passions from Dostoevsky's novel stepping into a century where politics, economics, racial and cultural conflicts, and many botched American dreams are accentuated by the floodlights of modern journalism and social media—here we get Lan Samantha Chang's superb novel, *The Family Chao*. Chang is a virtuoso with situations and dialogues, and has a delicious sense of humor and a sharp eye for the absurdities found in a close-knit yet incongruous society. In this symphonic novel, Chang gives us a multitude of souls lost and found: the gregarious are isolated, the ruthless are hunted, the voiceless scheme with hidden power, the innocent suffer from murderous desire. This is one of the finest and most ambitious novels about America I've read in recent years."

—Yiyun Li, author of *Must I Go*

"I loved Lan Samantha Chang's *The Family Chao*, at once a brilliant reimagining of Dostoevsky and a wholly original and gripping story about the passions, rivalries, and searing pressures that roil a singular immigrant family."

—Jess Walter, author of *The Cold Millions*

"An indictment of the asphyxiating myth of the model minority, *The Family Chao*, an intoxicatingly bold and capacious wonder, is a compelling murder mystery, a love story, a legal drama, a meditation on internalized racism, an examination of fraternal bonds and filial burdens, and a wrenching vivisection of race. This provocatively honest novel illuminates the inextricable ties between family and society, exposes the pain of being an eternal outsider, explores the array of ways in which bigotry smothers the spirit, and lays to waste the polite lie that human experience is universal in a country with such a particular history. We are fond of saying that while anyone is oppressed, no one is free; *The Family Chao* reminds us that some are freer than others, reminds us that public discrimination amplifies private dramas, reminds us that our shared history haunts our homes, and yet, bears witness to the enduring power of love and family. Written in graceful prose and with astonishing perception, this novel is a must-read, a campaign against indifference, a journey into the heart of the American Dream, and a page-turner. Candid, penetrating, refreshing. Give a copy to readers of Dostoyevsky, Baldwin, Viet Thanh Nguyen, Celeste Ng, or to anyone who cares about what it means to live in twenty-first-century America."

—T. Geronimo Johnson, author of *Welcome to Braggsville*

THE FAMILY CHAO

ALSO BY LAN SAMANTHA CHANG

All Is Forgotten, Nothing Is Lost

Inheritance

Hunger

THE FAMILY CHAO

A Novel

Lan Samantha Chang

W. W. NORTON & COMPANY
Independent Publishers Since 1923

Printed in the United States of America
First Edition

Book design by Patrice Sheridan
Production manager: Julia Druskin

Library of Congress Cataloging-in-Publication Data

Names: Chang, Lan Samantha, author.
Title: The family chao : a novel / Lan Samantha Chang.
Description: First Edition. | New York, NY : W. W. Norton & Company, [2022]
Identifiers: LCCN 2021037009 | ISBN 9780393868074 (hardcover) |
ISBN 9780393868081 (epub)
Subjects: GSAFD: Mystery fiction.
Classification: LCC PS3553.H2724 F36 2022 | DDC 813/.54—dc23
LC record available at https://lccn.loc.gov/2021037009

W. W. Norton & Company, Inc., 500 Fifth Avenue, New York, N.Y. 10110
www.wwnorton.com

W. W. Norton & Company Ltd., 15 Carlisle Street, London W1D 3BS

In memory of James Alan McPherson

1943–2016

PART ONE

They See Themselves

FOR THIRTY-FIVE YEARS, everyone supported Leo Chao's restaurant. Introducing choosy newcomers by showing off some real Chinese food in Haven, Wisconsin. Bringing children, parents, grandparents not wanting to dine out with the Americans, not wanting to think about which fork to use. You could say the manifold tensions of life in the new country—the focus on the future, tracking incremental gains and losses—were relieved by the Fine Chao. Sitting down under the dusty red lanterns, gazing at Leo's latest calendar with the limp-haired Taiwanese sylphs that Winnie hated so much, waiting for supper, everyone felt calm. In dark times, when you're feeling homesick or defeated, there is really nothing like a good, steaming soup, and dumplings made from scratch.

Winnie and Big Leo Chao were serving scallion pancakes decades before you could find them outside of a home kitchen. Leo, thirty-five years ago, winning his first poker game against the owners of a local poultry farm, exchanged his chips for birds that Winnie transformed into the shining, chestnut-colored duck dishes of far-off cities. Dear Winnie, rolling out her bing the homemade way, two pats of dough together with a seal of oil in between, letting them rise to a steaming bubble in the piping pan. Leo, bargaining for hard-to-get ingredients; Winnie subbing wax beans for yard-long beans, plus home-growing the garlic greens, chives, and hot peppers you used to never find in Haven. Their garden giving off a glorious smell.

You could say the community ate its way through the Chao family's distress. Not caring whether Winnie was happy, whether Big Chao was an honest man. Everyone took in the food on one side of their mouths, and from the other side they extolled the parents for their sons' accomplishments. Heaping praise upon the three boys who grew up all bright and ambitious, who earned scholarships to good colleges. Commending them for leaving the Midwest. Yet everyone was thankful when the oldest, Dagou Chao, returned to Haven. Dagou coming home to his mother, moving into the apartment over the restaurant, working there six days a week. Dagou, the most passionate cook in the family. Despite the trouble between Winnie and Big Chao, everyone assumed the business would be handed down fairly, peacefully, father to son.

Now, a year after the shame, the intemperate and scandalous events that began on a winter evening in Union Station, the community defends its thirty-five-year indifference to the Chao family's troubles by saying, No one could have believed that such good food was cooked by a bad person.

DECEMBER 21

Fa—mi—lee

"*PLEASE HELP, YOUNG MAN.*"

Through the crowd at Union Station, slipping in and out among the travelers, the frail voice reaches James Chao's inner ear. A first-year college student, James has lost his Mandarin, forgotten the language as a toddler with two older brothers teaching, loving, and tormenting him exclusively in English. Only from time to time, when he's not expecting it, will a spoken phrase of Mandarin filter to this innermost chamber of his ear and steal into his consciousness.

"*Please help.*"

James turns. He's looking into the face of an old man. The stranger might be in his seventies, close to his father's age, but he is altogether more frail than Big Leo: he clutches an ancient blue traveling bag in one hand, stooping with the weight of it, and his eyes are milky with time. He's seen through the cataracts, can see beyond James's generic jeans and hoodie to recognize another Chinese man. Can the familiarity be also in their movements, something in the way they look at one another? Is it in the stranger's way of gripping his luggage, mirroring James's grasp on the greasy paper bag of vegetable jia li jiao he's bringing home for his mother?

"I'm sorry," James says. "I don't speak Mandarin." Here's a liability of his: he always wants to help, but his ignorance makes him useless to his own kind. Not just to this man, but to every lost Mandarin-speaking traveler fumbling in mid-transfer who mistakes him for a helpful guide.

James can't tell if the man has understood his English. He shakes his head, then retreats a few steps. But the old man holds up a finger to say, "One minute!" and reaches into his coat pocket.

"I can't help you," James says. "I—" He's interrupted by an announcement for the California Zephyr. The crowd streams around them, everyone hurrying to make the train.

Standing stubbornly in place, the old man pulls out a U.S. airmail envelope addressed in Chinese characters, from which he extracts a photograph. He and James lean in and study it together.

It's a posed color snapshot of a solemn-faced middle-aged man and woman seated with a young girl of about ten, her black hair cut into heavy bangs across her forehead. She grasps a small, muscular beagle on her lap, and the animal gazes balefully, red-eyed, into the flash. James doesn't know why he's being shown this, but as he studies the photo shaking in the man's hand, he senses that he knows these strangers. He's never met them, but he can tell that they are recently arrived to the U.S. He can recognize the feelings in their mute, level eyes: defended, skeptical, yet somehow filled with hope.

"Fa—mi—lee," the old man says. "Fa-mi-lee Zhang." The crowd has trampled through; he and James are alone now. He points at the photo, then to himself. "Zhang Fujian."

"Family Chao," James says, putting a finger to his chest. "Chao—" He could never pronounce his given name, Li Huan, correctly.

The old man flips the photo. On the back is written, in slightly smeared blue ballpoint, an Illinois address. James feels the lightening of relief. The town is near a stop along the same Amtrak line as his own stop, Lake Haven. The track is on the upper level.

He points across the station to the metal stairs. "Follow me," he says.

The man's wrinkled face splits into a brilliant smile of fake teeth.

James adjusts his backpack and duffel. He can do it, he will lead the stranger up out of this dark abyss of bending tunnels to the next step of his journey. He's singularly moved by the idea of the old man traveling from afar—from the other side of the world, perhaps—to be united with his family, as James himself is traveling to his own family, coming home from college a thousand miles away, for Christmas.

James makes his way at an intentional pace toward the platform, glancing back at the man who shuffles along several steps behind. They reach the metal staircase. James can see a single light above the uncovered tracks, and beyond this light, the violet-gray underside of the evening sky heavy with snow. He nods, gestures toward the stairs, and takes the steps slowly, listening through the noise of the station, the low grumble of an approaching train. There are the old man's footsteps, tentative but determined. *Tap. Tap. Tap.*

Near the top, he senses a slight reverberation on the steps under his feet. There's no cry, no thud, but he can tell by the sudden absence of the tapping that something is wrong. He turns.

The man is lying at the foot of the stairs. It's as if someone picked him off the steps and flung him down at an unnatural angle. James sees a spreading stain of urine darkening the concrete floor, spreading past his bag, which has flown, or been bumped, to the side.

James hurries back down the stairs. He drops his duffel and bag of jia li jiao, strips off his backpack.

Through his mind runs the drill of CPR class. The first step: Call for help. He pulls out his phone, dials 911, and shoves it back into his pocket. The paramedics will track the call. He kneels beside the man.

James opens the withered mouth and looks past the gate of dentures, checking the tongue. He unbuttons the rough coat and puts his ear to the man's chest, pressing his cheek against the shirt. No heartbeat. He examines the face. Wrinkles gone now; the bluish skin melted back against the bones.

He lays his ear against the man's chest. No pulse.

It's absurd that he of all people is the one to try to save this man. But no, not absurd. He's not a random stranger. He's a premed, he's taken two

CPR classes. Though his arms feel weak and rubbery, though he's terrified, he knows what he's supposed to do. He positions his hands as he has learned, locks his elbows, closes his eyes, says a silent prayer, and makes the initial push, almost a punch, into the frail rib cage. *One, two, three, four, five*. At thirty, he checks for pulse, for breathing. Nothing.

He'll try the rescue breaths, make sure to do it right. He gulps air and puts his lips over the old man's mouth. A sour-sweet taste, like cranberries, spreads over his tongue. He struggles for another lungful of air. He's already sweating. He listens for the heartbeat: nothing.

Will the paramedics come? James looks up. The station is empty now. There's only one person within earshot, a plump man sprinting to catch the train.

James resumes CPR and puts his back into it. Hears, senses exquisitely, an agonizing crack. He's learned about this, reminds himself that such a crack is not always a bone breaking, but simply grinding, loosening the chest.

Minutes pass, with James alternating breathing and pumping. He's tiring, slowing down. His shoulders ache, his arms are rigid. The man is a shapeless bag of bones and cartilage, as lifeless as the plastic-and-fabric practice mannequin, but more uncanny than the mannequin, more remote.

Someone's tapping his shoulder. He clutches at the body, but strong hands pull him away.

"Thank you," someone says. "We'll take over now."

A team of EMTs moves in with a stretcher. James huddles to the side on hands and knees. He can hear the EMTs conversing in quick, confident terms he should remember from his classes, but he can't focus enough to understand. He's unneeded. Someone else is pumping at the body and he knows that, by now, they're also probably unneeded. Cold with sweat, sore all over, he stumbles to his feet. The scene, the train station, seems unfamiliar. Snowflakes drift over the stairs, sparkling in the light from the lamp above.

An EMT is next to him.

"Are you a relative? A grandchild?"

"I—no," says James. "His name is Zhang Fujian. My family name is Chao. We were just—fellow travelers. How is he?"

"I can't give information to unrelated—"

"Please."

She looks at him for a moment. "He's unresponsive," she says. "We can't pronounce him dead, it's done at the hospital. We'll continue CPR until we get him there."

"Should I come along?"

"There's no need." Her voice is sympathetic. "You did the best you could. But the chance of bringing someone back with CPR is very small."

He recalls the photograph. "Check in his pocket. There's an address."

"All right, thanks."

Without knowing why, James grabs his greasy paper bag and hands it to her. "For his family."

The medic takes the food and walks back to the stretcher, where the others are still pumping. In seconds, the body is gone.

James is alone. Gradually, he becomes aware of his own heartbeat, his thoughts. They assumed he was related. It was too complicated to explain. For half an hour, he *was* related.

He reaches down for his backpack and duffel, and that's when he sees the old man's ancient traveling bag. He hurries in the direction of the EMTs, but they are gone.

James hears the low whistle and squeak of his approaching train.

What else is there to do but pick up the traveling bag and bring it with him? When he gets home, he'll look inside for ID; if he can't find any, he'll try to find the man's family, the Zhangs. He tries to visualize the address on the back of the photograph, the smeared *Illinois*. He'll mail the bag to them. Boarding the train, he puts the bag with his own luggage onto the rack above and sinks into his seat.

He remembers the old man, frail and light, like a hollow-boned human bird, falling back as silently as a feather falls, but a mortal being, not at all light, so consuming to pummel and to hold, solid, stubbornly organic. Why did he give the jia li jiao to the EMT? The jia li jiao was going to be a present for his mother. Instead, he handed it off, as if a gift of food would make up for a human life. He'll go home and tell Dagou. Dagou will understand. He pulls his hood over his face. The train rocks slightly, bearing him deeper into the country, toward Dagou and the city of Haven.

Be on My Side

"They don't eat seafood at the Spiritual House," Ming Chao says.

His connecting flight brought him to an airport closer to Haven. There he rented a car and picked up James from the train station. He's now taking his brother the final thirty miles to their father's restaurant. Ming Chao, Ming the Merciless, middle child and most successful of Leo's sons. Math whiz and track star, he left home for good to work in Manhattan.

Years ago, Ming swore to everyone that he would never again spend Christmas in Wisconsin. He would never again deplane into a white tarmac of nothingness; never again slog knee-deep without boots across the airport rental lot under the frigid sky. Never again lay eyes upon his childhood street in winter, with its modest houses feebly outlined in strings of colored lights. He told everyone he would rather spend the holiday in New York, alone in his apartment, than return to this godforsaken heartland of deprivation.

So he wouldn't normally be here this late in December, but for his mother's personal request that he attend the luncheon tomorrow at the temple. Because she's asked him to pick up James and make sure his brother gets something to eat, he's now embroiled in the kind of family conversation he hates: charged and futile. James has blurted everything that happened at Union Station. He's described a photograph: a man and woman, a girl with bangs, a beagle. He's described the exhausting, terrifying process of performing CPR. Ming has no desire to dwell on his brother's trauma of having a man die under his hands. He can't stand to hear James describe his sense of piercing solitude, his shame. He steers the conversation toward the jia li jiao.

"There might be fish oil in the curry," he says. He skirts the south end of the lake, turns off the freeway, and steers past the big box stores and then the office buildings, toward the local businesses. It's all even more insignificant than he remembered. "Ma quit seafood this fall, when she moved in with the nuns. So it doesn't matter you gave away her present."

"I wanted to do something for his family," James persists.

"They don't eat anything with eyes. Even their dogs are vegetarians." Tiny flakes whirl down; Ming switches on the wipers. "You shouldn't involve yourself in other peoples' private lives," he says. "Not even out of the best intentions. You've never performed CPR. That family could track you down and file a lawsuit."

Ming steers the rental into an alley. This is also the kind of route his father and older brother take—circuitous and perverse, pointlessly sneaky. And Ming has inherited the Chaos' intense physicality, with his greyhound leanness and the aerodynamic way he carries himself, putting the tip of his nose forward over the wheel.

"You don't have to stop at the restaurant," James says.

Ming thinks of his mother's instructions. "You haven't had dinner."

"You can just drop me—" James's pocket buzzes as if something is trapped inside.

"Who's that?" Ming asks.

But he knows it's Dagou. Thrilled that James is coming home, Dagou must be pelting him with texts. Not that Ming is being left out. James, the sad-sack poker player, is holding the phone so anyone can see it. Ming peers over, and indeed, the text is from their older brother.

O, James! My heart is a fucking rose in bloom!

Now their phones buzz together. It's a group text, also from Dagou. Each looks at his phone, then at the other's.

Tomorrow, at the Spiritual House. Please be on my side.

"On his side about what?" James asks.

"He's on the warpath." How could Ming explain? How could anyone describe the chaos that had descended on the Chao household as soon as James left home for college? Four months later, their mother was living with Buddhist nuns and Dagou had bulked up by thirty pounds. "And he's crazy," he tells James, unable to stop himself from adding, "How he manages to stay engaged to Katherine is beyond me."

Ming can't figure out how Dagou has attracted the devotion of a woman like Katherine Corcoran. Too smart for him, too attractive, too accomplished, and too good. Too much of a good thing, and Dagou unable to avoid fucking it up. Dagou, falling in thrall all over again with Brenda Wozicek, that pansexual demon of his high school days. Brenda Wozicek, who in her junior year slept with every boy and girl on the cast of *Jesus Christ Superstar.* (She had been chosen, inevitably, to play Mary Magdalene.)

"What do you mean?" James asks.

Where to start? Way back in high school, when she'd inflicted lasting damage on their brother by not giving him the time of day? "I think it started to go bad last year when Dad hired Brenda as the new server."

"No." James defends their brother's long-term relationship, and no wonder: Dagou and Katherine are like parents to him. They've been dating since college, when James was in the third grade. "Brenda was just a high school crush. He told me about it. She was always, um, with other people. And white guys. Like that football player, Eric somebody."

"Eric Braun. Her stock has dropped since high school. Now she's a denizen of Haven, a waitress, a hopeless villager. She has tattoos. She has blue hair," Ming says. But Dagou has never gotten over those six months, in high school, when Brenda was a blonde. In Dagou's mind, she's still on prom court.

"Dagou loves *Katherine*," James insists. Of course, James, who's obviously still a virgin, believes it's Katherine who has made Dagou's heart into a rose in bloom.

"Like father, like son," Ming says. He turns back to the wheel, avoiding James's expression of confused naïveté. How is it possible he and his brother were born of the same parents, grew up in the same house, witnessed the same fights? The tumultuous conflicts over food and women, from which Ming recoiled, have turned James into an obedient son, a good little premed, close to Dagou and their mother, even to their father. James is a sap. This is a tragedy, but Ming prefers to see it as a comedy.

"Ma asked me to fly home for this special luncheon at the Spiritual House tomorrow," he says. "So I called Dagou, made him tell me what's been going on. It turns out the place is a madhouse. Dagou's sleeping with Brenda Wozicek, and he's raving like a nut. All of a sudden he's saying Dad *owes* him. I tell him, 'If you wanted Dad to give you a cent, you should have gotten it in writing.' He doesn't listen. Instead, he's sponsoring this community luncheon tomorrow. He has a showdown planned, with Dad, in front of Ma and everyone they know. He asked Gu Ling Zhu Chi to adjudicate."

"What good will that do?"

It will do no good—no good at all. "He has this crazy hope that Dad will obey Gu Ling Zhu Chi because she's the head nun," Ming says, "or abbess, whatever. If he thinks she's going to take his side, he's in for disappointment. These Buddhist types live on handouts. Ten-to-one they support whoever has more money."

This Ming has believed ever since he gave the grateful nuns the dowry for his mother's living expenses. He supported Winnie's sudden decision to leave his father and take refuge at the Spiritual House. But the thought of her absence from home makes him uneasy. This is the real reason he's staying in a hotel.

James says, "Isn't Ma still a Christian? Won't she want Ba to be charitable to Dagou? To enter the Kingdom of God?"

"Ba would more easily go through the eye of a needle than enter the Kingdom of God." Ming squints at the windshield. The air is chill, the sky is moonless: gray, thick level clouds lower to meet the earth. What's that feeling in the air? Both quiet and disquiet. It's going to snow a lot more.

"Your problem is that you love everyone too much," he says. "But things have taken a steep downhill around here since you left in August.

Stay out of it. Don't get involved, and go back to school right after Christmas. You're young, James, there's still hope for you. You stay away from Dad and Dagou. You listening?"

"Is Alf all right?" James asks, reaching for the one remaining source of comfort.

"Alf is fine. You need to bring him to the luncheon tomorrow. Ma wants Gu Ling Zhu Chi to pray for him with all the other dogs."

"Holy Alf."

"We're here." Ming turns into the parking lot. It's ten-thirty and the restaurant is closed. Upstairs, in his bachelor apartment, Dagou's lights are out. Downstairs, the small, shabby dining room is deserted. Only the red neon sign is still lit: FINE CHAO.

"Get something to eat; Dad is here. He'll bring you home." He pulls his rental into a space next to their father's Ford Taurus. Leo has kept their mother's car, the Honda, which she renounced along with the rest of her material goods. Now Leo has two cars. But Ming has rented his own vehicle. It is an ignominy to return to Haven, the site of shame, torment. He won't add to it by borrowing a family car, eating at the restaurant, or sleeping in his childhood room. He wants to be beholden to their father as little as possible. "I'll meet you and Alf tomorrow, at the Spiritual House, around eleven. Ma will be happy to see you." He pops the trunk. "Don't forget your luggage."

James gets out and moves his things into their father's much larger, fuller, messier trunk, where they'll be lost among the packages, the dumbbells, and the snow shovel. Sitting behind the wheel, Ming checks his phone. He reads his brother's reply to the group text: *I'm on your side. Love, James.*

The Dog Father

Entering the Fine Chao Restaurant through the back door, James passes, on his left, the stairs to the basement, and on his right, the restaurant office with its old television murmuring. Next is the kitchen, where nothing has changed in fifteen years. There's the bulletin board covered with scraps of paper, yellowing with age. These are notes Leo and Winnie Chao wrote to each other over the decades. When they fought, these missives were a primary method of communication. (The other was to use the children as messengers.) The notes are written sometimes in Chinese and sometimes in English in order to confuse the workers. There's also a schedule, now eighteen years old, of Dagou's high school orchestra rehearsals. From a time even before then, from before James was born, there's a list of frequently requested items in English and Chinese:

Egg rolls
Wontons
Pot stickers
Crab rangoons (*What are these?* Winnie, their mother, annotated in Chinese. Their father wrote underneath, *Wontons filled with cream cheese.*)
Beef with broccoli

Following a scattershot statistical analysis, Winnie also compiled a list of things Americans liked:

Large chunks of meat
Wontons and noodles together in the same soup
Pea pods and green beans, carrots, broccoli, baby corn (no other vegetables)
Ribs or chicken wings
Beef with broccoli
Chicken with peanuts
Peanuts in everything
Chop suey (*What is this?* Leo wrote. *I don't know*, Winnie wrote.)
Anything with shrimp (*The rest of them can't eat shrimp*, she annotated. *Be careful.*)
Anything from the deep fryer

Anything with sweet and sour sauce
Anything with a thick, brown sauce

And there is, of course, the list of things the Americans *didn't* like:

Meat on the bone (except ribs or chicken wings)
Rice porridge
Fermented soybeans

In a small fridge for employees, there are containers of stir-fried vegetables kept separate by O-Lan, the woman from Guangzhou who is one of three outside kitchen employees, and who doesn't eat meat; beers for JJ, the second chef, and for Lulu, the other server (who after years of silent courtship have unexpectedly gone to San Francisco together over the holidays); and Dagou's personal stash of pork with jiu cai and noodles. James heats a pile of pork and noodles on the stove. He's starving.

As he transfers the food into a bowl, a pounding noise comes from below. It's the sound of his father, Leo, Big Chao, coming up the stairs—footsteps that reverberate and thump with the authority of a man larger than he actually is. To these footsteps is added deep and resonant grumbling, profanity growing more audible until, when he reaches the top of the stairs, a full question detaches itself and sings into the kitchen in a ringing baritone:

"Who the fuck is coming to clean up half an hour after close?"

James abandons his dinner, edges into the hallway. "Baba, it's me."

He's the only son who still calls Leo "Baba," which Dagou shortened to "Ba," and Ming changed to "Dad." Sometimes his brothers refer to Leo as "Aw, Gee, Pops"—this is one of the only jokes they share.

"Oh, it's you!" Leo yells, emerging into the hall. "I smelled those disgusting jiu cai noodles and thought it was your worthless brother. But it's you."

He grins, delighted, and claps James on the shoulder.

He's a sturdy, vigorous man with tadpole eyes and a dark, strong-featured face thickened by food and living. James catches a whiff of cooking grease, pipe tobacco, and stale clothes.

"Your hands are cold," he says, pushing away an image of the man in Union Station.

"I was in the basement, freezer room! Picking out something for tomorrow." Over Leo's shoulder is slung a restaurant delivery bag.

"You shouldn't go down there when no one else is in the building." The freezer door locks automatically. "It's not up to code, Baba."

"It's fine," his father says. "Jerry Stern worked his magic with the city inspector. I told your big brother, study law, but he doesn't listen, majors in music. Now Baby Mozart's paying off his loans cooking for Americans." Like the rest of the community, Leo uses the term "American" to describe any outsider. The term is half ironic, half utilitarian.

James is disappointed Dagou isn't here to welcome him home. He doesn't dare ask his father where Dagou is, doesn't want to provoke him.

But Leo, guessing his thoughts, says, "Your worthless brother's making out with his new girlfriend. Or getting ready for his big showdown at the nunnery tomorrow." He gestures to the hall. "Come to my office! I got something strong for you."

The office is crammed with detritus from thirty-five years of business, including an ancient adding machine and a naked fake Christmas tree. James sits in his mother's old chair, his father in the recliner. Leo catches James's eye, shoots him a flare of approval. Despite all Ming has just said, James feels a metabolic, answering spark of happiness, kinship, recognition.

"Try this." Leo Chao holds out a tumbler to James.

"Did you get this from those guys you know in Chicago?" James asks, eyeing the unmarked bottle on Leo's desk.

"Yeah, this is real thing."

As James lifts the glass, a hideous, pungent odor of fruity, rotten socks pervades his sinuses. He squeezes his eyes shut, sips, and lets the awful taste spread over his tongue.

"Ha, look at that!" His father gestures at the television.

There's nothing on the screen except a fenced patio with an open gate. Then an animal lumbers onto the patio, sniffing at the fence. It's a yearling bear, burnished brown—there's no mistaking its thick, furry body, the bulk of its rear end, its heavy yet clownish, rolling walk.

A small, stocky black creature torpedoes down a staircase. The creature barks wildly, growling and snapping at the bear, which, after a moment's stunned confrontation, rises up on its hind legs in dismay. Like a black streak, the dog chases the bear up and down the patio, lunging and nipping at its heels. Panicking, the bear clambers over the fence. The dog, tail up, remains in the patio.

"Ha!" Leo emits a deep belly laugh. "You see that? Just like Alf. French bulldog, best breed in the world!"

James hands him back the tumbler. "Baba," he says, "you know Dagou isn't worthless. He can really cook."

In the pause that follows, James wonders if he's angered his father. But when Leo Chao speaks, his tone is genial.

"Maybe not worthless," he says, "but he has an inferiority complex. You American-born Chinese so timid and brainwashed, will do anything for a woman who'll give you a good lay."

Did his father just change the subject, or is it all part of the same argument? James doesn't know. Leo hands the tumbler back; James takes another tiny, terrible sip. He *is* timid with girls. Is this why he's halfway through his freshman year in college and still a virgin?

"All you ABCs! You think since you're not here first, since you have different eyes and dicks, you're not good enough for fucking around. You got it *backwards*. We came to America to colonize the place for ourselves. That means spreading seed. Equal opportunity for fucking. You know what's the biggest disappointment of my life? Seeing my oldest son pussy-whipped by one white woman."

He frowns at the TV; its dim light flickers over his features. "My stinking son. Brainwashed by his mother and teachers. They say, 'You're special,' *ha*! 'You can do anything you want!' *Nobody* can do anything they want. Do you think I want this dog's life? No, I do what I have to do. But my oldest son? He's trying to *find himself*. What's to find? Decides to be *musician*. Then he leaves the East Coast with his tail between his legs. He's wasted years of life."

"He's amazing in the kitchen," James says. They watch images move across the screen. "Baba," he says, "if you can *be* anything you want to be in America, then why can't you *do* what you want? And what if you don't want to be big and rich? What if you want to be small?"

"Is that what *you* want?" snorts Leo.

James struggles. How to explain to his father what he wants? It's something he has only just begun to put into words, and only to himself.

"I'm not ambitious like Ming," he says. "I don't want to be super-rich or buy expensive real estate. I'm not ambitious like Dagou, either. I don't need to be as creative as he is, or to make people happy. It's not that I don't want to be interested in my job. I *do* want to help people. But I mostly want—I want to feel small. To be a small piece in the big mystery of everything." He stops to think, trying to explain his own curious desire. "I want to get married and have kids, and a dog. I want to walk the dog in the morning, go to work, and come home at night. Mostly what I want is—well, an ordinary life."

"An ordinary life." Leo smiles in the half dark. *"Blood sacrifice!"* he yells, startling James. "I came over in nineteen seventy-*two*; a pioneer, breaking land. I sacrificed myself—all so my sons could be magnificent! I did all this—only to be dog father. Is anyone grateful?"

"We're all grateful."

"I'm going to die dog father. *I'm going to die!*" Leo yells, glaring up at James. His bellow thins to a theatrical mew. "How is it possible I'll die so far away from home?"

The face of the man at the train station appears before him. James closes his eyes. "Don't say that, Baba."

Leo huffs; invisible sparks fly toward the television. "Don't worry," he says. "I'm not going to die."

"No, Baba," James says. Although he knows this is impossible, he believes it. "You'll never die."

"Not me." Leo smiles. "Ah, James. My good boy. Not my most accomplished boy, not my most talented boy, but you're *my* boy, you love me."

DECEMBER 22

At the Spiritual House

JAMES AND LEO, along with Alf the dog, arrive at the Spiritual House an hour before the luncheon. The sky is heavy with impending snow. Sleet is falling, tiny droplets cling to Alf's bat-like ears. As they approach the red double doors, the ears twitch. Faint barking echoes from inside. James scoops the dog into his arms. Thirteen inches at the shoulders, Alf has the confidence of a much larger animal. James must keep him from fighting. Also, he must be on Dagou's side. What will that require?

The moment the door opens, Alf wriggles expertly out of James's hold and leaps to the floor, collar jingling.

They're standing in the former gymnasium of an old elementary school. This is the Spiritual House, purchased by Gu Ling Zhu Chi a dozen years ago, when the city shifted its resources to larger educational facilities. Nobody knows how much she paid, or where she found the money; Leo claims the school district was glad to off-load the shabby building at a bargain price. The gym is small, with a stage at one end and doors on either side. Several men from the community and a dozen women, half of them robed in brown, chat in clusters on the wooden basketball court still marked with its colored lines and semicircles. In the center of the court is a table displaying a three-foot porcelain figure of Guan Yin.

While Leo stands grinning, adjusting the strap on his delivery bag,

James searches for Dagou. The half-dozen temple dogs circle him and Alf in a delirium of barking, clicking paws, and waving tails. They're mixed breeds, smooth-haired, ears neither floppy nor exactly pointed, and a few with the long legs, fleet feet, of racing hounds. Two are from the Humane Society. Two are rescue dogs from a meat restaurant in South Korea.

"Some spiritual house," Leo says, offhand. "More like an asylum for women and dogs."

Alf stands his ground in the middle of the untidy pack, chest ruffled. He lets himself be sniffed. He begins to growl.

"No, Alf—"

But Alf doesn't go into battle. He shoots back out from the pack of dogs, whining with happiness.

In the same instant, James is swept into a hug from behind. His mother's new smell, of wool and incense, suffuses his nostrils. Her hug is so firm and loving that he almost panics, struggling to detach himself. Alf yaps frantically. James manages to get free and turns to greet her.

"Hi, Ma—Alf, get down!"

In only a few months, Winnie has transformed. From a plump and pretty woman, she has withered into a puckish novice, her hair shorn to a salt-and-pepper prickle.

"Sister Yun!" Leo exclaims in mock reverence.

"Come here, James," says Winnie, tugging his sleeve. James can feel her not simply ignoring his father but bracing herself against him. Even the wool of her robe seems to stiffen when he speaks.

But Leo won't leave her alone. "You remember me?" he croons, leering over James's shoulder. "You remember me, Sister Yun? From the big, bad world outside the temple?" He slides his gaze from her to James. "So much love," he says, his voice tinged with irony. Or is it envy?

Alf whines. Leo's face lights up in a prepossessing smile. He's suddenly decades younger than his wife, ages younger. He's the man in the photo taken just after he arrived in the U.S., a cigar clamped between his square teeth.

"Horndog," he scoffs at Alf, who is still trying to leap into Winnie's arms. "Player. You forget who feeds you now?"

James is still searching for Dagou. He glimpses Ming near the stage, out of place in his navy blazer. Following his mother, with Alf at his heels, James makes his way across the small gym, passing the table with the toddler-sized statue of the bodhisattva, clothed in robes of gold, surrounded by small dishes of food and pots of burning joss sticks. Nearby, there's a bowl of sesame candy. Winnie picks out a piece and hands it to James, who puts it in his pocket. Then, taking his arm, she leads him past the stage. They leave the gym. They're standing in a school hallway, near a window.

"Your hair is wet," she says.

"Only a little."

"It's going to be big storm. Gu Ling Zhu Chi said so. Now, let me see you." Her thumb and forefinger cup his chin. The light, brightened by snow, dazzles his eyes, and he can't see the other women who speak nearby.

"He looks like you, Winnie," someone says.

"Nonsense. Look at his nose. He got that nose from the father."

His mother says, "You're studying too hard. You need to take deep breaths. Breathe."

James breathes. The strong smell recalls his mother's incense table at home. She raised James and his brothers as Christians, and even wore a little gold cross on a fine chain around her throat, but she never gave up Guan Yin. Her Pu Sa stood on a small table in a room upstairs. Before the statuette, she burned incense in a squat holder made of a peanut butter jar covered with tinfoil; next to this, she kept a glass of water in case Guan Yin might suffer from thirst.

She's the heart of everything, James thinks. She's the heart of the family, just as Ming is the brains, and Dagou is the lungs, and our father is the spleen. Why has she left home, left us?

"Ma," he croaks. "I miss you." Then he blurts, "Are you happy here?"

"I'm fine. Gu Ling Zhu Chi says I only need to work on my tranquility."

Winnie won't reveal the nature of this threat to her tranquility. James broods over her health. She is ten years younger than his father, but at the thought of her falling ill, he finds himself back in the bowels of Union Station. Fresh sweat springs to his palms. He searches her features for signs, symptoms.

"Don't worry, James," she says. "I'm all right."

They're joined by three of the Haven community: Mary Wa and her children, Fang and Alice. Mary Wa owns the Oriental Food Mart, where Leo buys supplies. She is Winnie's best friend; and Fang is James's. In a girl-heavy peer group, they're the only boys. Fang is an oddball. He didn't get along at school and he shows no sign of getting along now. Although Mary still claims that Fang is going to enroll at UW–Madison, he's not even at the community college. Today she has persuaded him to dress up for the luncheon. His denim sports jacket splits around a wide paisley tie resting on his belly. His face is like a larger version of his mother's—peach-cheeked, with a mild plump mouth and wire glasses—but whereas Mary's eyes are serene, his gleam with a fanatic intelligence.

"These people aren't real Buddhists," he tells James, pulling him aside as Mary and Alice chat with James's mother. "They're just a random group of bodhisattva lovers. This is a woman's group and a cult of personality, not a temple."

"How do you know?"

"There are how many Chinese in Haven?" Fang goes on, ignoring him. "Out of forty thousand residents, there are several hundred Chinese, total; maybe six hundred of us including children? There's not enough money here to support the real thing. It's a community center. And a humane society. And Gu Ling Zhu Chi isn't a real teacher of sutras. She just lets them call her that, informally. She knows it," he adds, glancing at the "head nun" or abbess. "That's why she calls it the SH, not a temple. She's not arrogant."

James thinks of his brother Ming, warning of opportunistic "Buddhist types." "But what *is* the real thing?" he asks. "Is there a rule book or something?"

"I know what I'm talking about. I've been to Chicago. My mother took Alice and me last month, and we went to visit a temple. Alice thinks I'm right," he says, beckoning to his sister. "Don't you, Alice?"

James tries not to turn around too quickly. He's been in love with Alice Wa for years, since the childhood they spent outdoors together while Fang stayed inside, glued to his PlayStation. James must have spent a hundred afternoons with Alice, crouching over anthills, watching the insects burrowing, excavating, dragging corpses of fruit flies and houseflies and even dragonflies into their heaped-up tunnels, glistening wings moving along the sidewalk in an iridescent funeral procession. Although they attended different high schools, they intersected, also, as child laborers, James running errands for the restaurant and Alice at the register of the Oriental Food Mart.

Until they were thirteen, Alice was what you might call a "natural beauty": smooth-skinned, with light brown eyes behind corrective glasses and a nose so small it could be drawn on paper with two dots. She didn't go to the gym or play a sport, and since the Was never vacationed, she was in every way untouched by American leisure: the pale princess of her mother's grocery, thin-wristed, her black hair uncombed around her shoulders. But around fourteen, Alice began to grow, soon surpassing Fang by inches. Her little nose also grew longer, dipping down with the ferocity of the Was' Manchurian ancestors. James saw her at the store with decreasing frequency. She made no eye contact; her hands shook as she gave out change; her sentences—never complex—trickled away. No one was surprised when, after high school, Alice, too, stayed at home.

Now, standing close to Fang, Alice slides a glance at James, her glasses magnifying her long eyes and soft, caramel-colored irises. If only she would not stoop, but she does. He has a penetrating, hallucinatory double vision of her as some caged, exotic predatory bird. Green-feathered, yellow-eyed, hook-nosed, clawed, and horned. A wing clipped.

Ask her out. It's Dagou's voice he imagines. *Ask her out, you noodle-dick.*

"How is college, James?" Alice half whispers, and the sound of her voice—sweet and silvery, with a strange, rich, low undertone her mother instructs her to conceal by raising it to its highest register, like a small girl's—pierces him. When they were thirteen, she let him look under her shirt. Only once. At the memory, painful feathers sprout up on the flesh of his arms, the back of his neck. Sweat soaks his sleeves. Where are Fang and their mothers?

"Okay," he says. "Listen, are you at the store later today? I may come by to—"

Alf yips and whines at Alice.

"Stop it, Alf!" More yipping. James tries his father's command. "Ting! *Ting?*" Like many dogs, Alf understands two languages, but sometimes listens to neither. He leaps on Alice. She drops her purse.

When James struggles to retrieve it, he and Alice narrowly miss bumping heads, and he catches unexpectedly the smell she's carried with her since childhood, a combination of cheap shampoo and dried goods—mushrooms, seaweed. There's also something that affects him so viscerally his hand slips on the purse. He clears his throat.

"Be right back," he croaks, and hobbles away, Alf at his heels.

In the little men's bathroom, James bolts the door. He pulls down his pants, sits on the toilet in the left-hand stall, closes his eyes, and takes hold of his penis. Alice, naked, straddles him and pushes his head against the tank. Alice's vivid caramel eyes lock onto his as she smiles a predatory smile and kisses him, thrusting her tongue deep into his mouth. Her powerful wings flap once, twice as she hovers above him. James ejaculates into a wad of toilet paper. He breathes.

Alf barks.

James opens his eyes. "What the fuck, Alf? Can't I have some privacy?"

Alf barks again. He stands directly in front of the toilet: bat ears, bright button eyes, heart-shaped nose, and small, slightly quivering jowls.

James stands, flushes the toilet, pulls up his pants. Alf puts his front paws on the toilet, dangles his head inside, and begins to drink.

James pushes him aside, closes the toilet lid. Alf whines. James turns on the faucet and hoists Alf to the sink. His pink tongue laps sloppy circles into the stream of water. The dog's solid weight in his arms, and the clean, harmless water running calm him. He sets Alf back on the floor and turns off the tap.

Someone knocks at the door.

"Just a second."

Another knock. He opens the door. It's his father.

"Almost done," James croaks, gesturing at the sink.

Leo's face splits into a knowing grin. "Beating off for Buddha? Ha, ha! Sorry to disturb you! It's time for you to get out of here. Gu Ling Zhu Chi is coming."

The Abbess

Backstage, Ming and Winnie are already waiting. Up to now, Ming has managed to avoid wasting his morning. He woke early, went for a run, showered, and drove to the Spiritual House. He made some calls for work and skimmed a document. He checked in with his mother. But now the day has come to an inevitable bottleneck. They're stuck in a group of people, waiting backstage for their audience with Gu Ling Zhu Chi. Dagou still isn't here.

Gu Ling Zhu Chi's public appearances are rare and unpredictable. Because Dagou sponsored the community lunch, she's promised to adjudicate his case. Dagou couldn't keep his mouth shut, and so there are several other visitors waiting for consultation. They're mostly women whose American lives have grown too bitter for them to eat more bitterness, or too morally confusing for Confucius. For years, they've been coming to Gu Ling Zhu Chi for spiritual guidance.

Ming has a grudging admiration for the old abbess. Whatever her Buddhist qualifications, Gu Ling Zhu Chi is the only person in town Leo Chao might listen to. Leo respects her, in his way, because of some mysterious backstory Ming doesn't know. Ming examines his father; Leo waits with uncharacteristic taciturnity, his hands in his pockets and a restaurant delivery bag slung over his shoulder.

Gu Ling Zhu Chi and her handler walk onto the stage.

The old woman is so small her elbow fits right into the fingertips of the handler, an Amazonian nun whose beautifully shaped, silver-blond buzz cut shines like that of a towheaded boy. The Amazon, An, was once Chloe North. Years ago, she appeared early one morning at the front door of the Spiritual House, a high school sophomore, dressed in only a torn Totoro nightgown, clutching a kitchen knife, with bruises on her chest and arms. Next to An's creamy skin and pale blue gaze, Gu Ling Zhu Chi's face is brown and shriveled, her pouched eyes calm behind thick-lensed glasses. Even Fang says she's inscrutable.

The first people to come forward are Mr. and Mrs. Chin, mechanical engineers. Everyone knows the reason for their consultation. Their middle daughter, Lynn Chin, a college sophomore, has changed her major to journalism. She has been seduced by words in a language they don't like to speak. She's refusing to take pre-law classes. If not for their resistance, she might be majoring in English.

Lynn herself stands nearby, with Fang and James, and Alf. She is a dusky, bespectacled young woman who's almost always clutching a book.

"What was your old major again?" Fang mutters to Lynn.

She scowls. "Data science."

While Mr. Chin, tall and sheepish, shuffles his feet, Lynn's mother leans toward Gu Ling Zhu Chi. Ming edges offstage. Despite his admiration of Gu Ling Zhu Chi, Ming scoffs at the idea that she can foretell the future. He believes in free will. Moreover, he possesses enough cultural knowledge to see through this fatalistic drivel. He's had four years of intensive Chinese, and he can read the newspaper in both complex and simple characters. He's the most literate in Mandarin of his Haven generation. From his college history course with a world-class scholar, he knows that Gu Ling Zhu Chi and her group are small eddies at the edge of the great river of twentieth–century change: they're cultural leftovers from not one but two or even three revolutions ago. Truth be told, he is repulsed by Winnie's prayers; growing up, he often closed the door in order to avoid the sight of her on her knees, forehead to the floor. Of course, Dagou was never a skeptic; their mother's prayers filled Dagou with proper guilt and shame. He's an unreconstructed sinner, stupid with the burden of having grasped neither Eastern nor Western moral teachings.

Still, Ming can't avoid eavesdropping on Mrs. Chin. In Mrs. Chin's dream, Lynn is near campus, sitting in a tea shop, drinking matcha bubble tea through a bright pink straw. Mrs. Chin is outside, knocking on the window, but Lynn can't see or hear her.

". . . doesn't she know that college is more than just four years of bubble tea? That she's slurping up her higher education—hurtling toward a terrible future?"

Gu Ling Zhu Chi's eyelids flicker as she speaks. "The dream isn't about this life, but about the afterlife." She reaches out to hold Mrs. Chin's hand. She is praying now, in an inaudible murmur. Ming checks to see how Lynn is taking all of this. She has her nose buried in an Elena Ferrante novel.

Ming has wondered why his mother is just now bringing him and his brothers to Gu Ling Zhu Chi. It occurs to him that he might have it backward. It's possible that Gu Ling Zhu Chi is the one who asked to see the three of them. Maybe the old abbess wants to speak specifically to him, to Ming. Ming, who has paid his mother's dowry. Does she want more money? As if he can sense Ming's apprehension, Alf leans against his leg, comforting and solid. Alf's bright eyes follow Winnie's footsteps as she shuffles up to Gu Ling Zhu Chi, who bends toward her slightly, gazing through her thick glasses.

A quarter hour goes by before Winnie comes to fetch him. "We're going to start without Dagou."

Ming and his mother walk to the little platform. Everybody else has politely gone backstage, except for James and Fang, that bilingual snoop.

"Sons," Winnie says. "Greet Gu Ling Zhu Chi."

As he has been taught, Ming ducks his head and mutters, "Gu Ling Zhu Chi." James copies him.

"James first. Stand here," Winnie says. "Ming, over there." She gestures Ming away. Does she not want her sons to hear each other's fortunes? He steps away, but leans toward them, listening.

"Hold out your hand, James."

James goes red. Ming grins. His brother must be wondering how much Gu Ling Zhu Chi can see. Can she tell that James wants to make out with Alice Wa? Can she foretell his grade in freshman chemistry? There are other things she might advise him about, Ming considers—such as how to recover from his failure to save the old man at the train station. But James doesn't have the Mandarin to communicate with her.

Gu Ling Zhu Chi examines James's palm. She bends his fingers, examining the lines, and murmurs something to his mother, tracing out a shape. She presses his fingertips, squinting through her glasses as the blood flushes back into them over and over. As she does this, she unloads on Winnie a fantasy of James in twenty years: James as a great man. Probably she's only telling Winnie what she wants to hear. Although, who knows? It might be true. It might be that when they were handing out Leo's flaws—miserliness, dissipation, lechery—James was passed over.

Winnie nods at Gu Ling Zhu Chi, hopeful, proud. She turns, pats James's arm. "Okay. She's done."

"What'd she say?" James asks.

Winnie shrugs as if it's not important, but Ming can see that she's decided not to tell. He can always read her. "Good things," she says, but he knows something is bothering her. "You're fine. Now go, James." She gives him a little push. "Ming, your turn."

Ming makes his way back and shows Gu Ling Zhu Chi his most deadpan face. She studies him, her pouched eyes magnified by her thick glasses.

As she did with James, Gu Ling Zhu Chi examines his palms and his fingertips, pressing the tip of each to examine the flow of his blood. Her own hand is surprisingly warm and supple.

"You're not well," she says to Ming.

The expression on his mother's face ripples like the surface of a pond.

"Interesting," says Fang's voice from somewhere behind them. "She says Ming is sick."

Gu Ling Zhu Chi fixes her eyes on Fang. "Get out of here," she says.

James and Fang back away.

"You're about to become very ill," Gu Ling Zhu Chi says to Ming. "You should seek tranquility immediately." Her voice is colorless and deep. She continues to discuss his health, his habits, and his diet. Ming knows she's full of shit. He's given the Spiritual House a lump of money, and now the old lady is trying to scare him into giving her even more money. Upsetting Winnie is a part of the plan. Winnie is staring at Gu Ling Zhu Chi, stricken. Gu Ling Zhu Chi bends toward her in a concerned, attentive way. Only Alf seems not to notice anything amiss. Instead, he yips with joy and bounds off the stage toward the door.

At last, Dagou has arrived.

The Fortune You Seek Is in Another Cookie

From his place on stage, Ming is among the first to see Dagou across the gymnasium. He isn't happy that his brother has shown up to find him with his hand outstretched, ready to receive his fortune-cookie fortune. But Dagou, wrapped up in his own turbulence, doesn't pay attention. He strips off his coat, revealing a pink dress shirt, and makes his way toward the stage.

"Hey, everyone," he says, reaching down absently to tousle Alf between the ears. His voice sounds both higher and deeper, huskier and more sonorous. His gaze settles on Ming; they nod politely.

Ming still hasn't gotten used to Dagou's changed physical appearance. Every part of his body has been blown up from the inside into a heavier version of itself. His shoulders are twice as thick as the year before, and his feet seem to point out slightly. Flesh hangs even from the lobes of his ears. Only his eyes are familiar, dark and quickly moving. ("Restless," James once described him. "Horny," Leo corrected him.)

"Hey, Snaggle." Dagou walks straight over to James and tousles his hair, too. James stands there with his mouth curled up at the corners like a child. Cuff links flash as Dagou opens his arms to embrace their mother. Then Dagou takes a visible breath, chest swelling, and faces their father. Leo Chao's face grows both brighter and darker. Younger, with his edges more defined, he seems to recognize another man in Dagou, someone from long ago.

"I'm here," Dagou announces. "We can start now."

"Where were you?" Ming can't help pointing out that after making them all show up, he's an hour late.

"At the restaurant."

"It's Monday. The restaurant's closed."

Dagou shrugs. " 'Cause JJ's gone, Ba asked me to go through the supplies with O-Lan."

"Where is Katherine?" asks Mary Wa.

Dagou hangs his head. "We broke up."

This is a surprise, and they all stare. Ming drops his gaze. The idea of Dagou dumping Katherine is insufferable.

"What happened?" asks Mary Wa. "I thought you were going to get married."

Dagou shrugs. "She wouldn't agree to a prenup."

Nobody laughs. It's a good thing most of them don't know what a prenup is, because Dagou making a marriage joke about Katherine is offensive.

"Well," says Mary finally, "some girls very shy. You boys want it bad, you need to wait. Sometimes it take one year after marriage, maybe more, for her to get used to the idea."

"Give up, Ma," Fang says.

"We ended it two weeks ago," Dagou says, "because I wanted to give her time to make other plans for Christmas."

There's a murmur of disappointment. Yet no one but Ming notices Dagou's lack of consideration. Two weeks to make new Christmas plans? Dagou is an ass.

"Well," says Mary. "These things run their course." The course of the relationship was twelve years. "It's better to break up before having kids. Once you have kids, you can never change your mind."

"Until they go to college," puts in Leo Chao, smirking at their mother.

"What if she signs the prenuptial agreement?" someone asks.

"That was a joke." Dagou looks around hopefully. When no one laughs, he hangs his head. "I just don't want to marry her," he blurts. "The more I thought about it, the more I knew I'd be making a terrible mistake."

"Let's talk to Gu Ling Zhu Chi," Winnie says. "Come here."

Ming is dismissed. At last, Gu Ling Zhu Chi is done decrying his goals, his health, his work habits. Gu Ling Zhu Chi said one thing, in particular, that Ming finds laughable. She said Ming needs to "return" to his family. As if detaching from his family—the most significant accomplishment of his life—is not the primary reason for his survival. This is what Katherine does *not* know, since Katherine is, maddeningly, drawn to Dagou in part *because* of his family, because of Winnie. As ever, the thought of Katherine's attachment to Dagou, to all of them, fills Ming with an unaccountable irritation.

"Gu Ling Zhu Chi, you know William, my oldest."

Dagou bends humbly toward the old woman in his coral-pink dress shirt, like a jumbo cooked shrimp.

Their father has disappeared. Aside from An and Winnie, most of the nuns have also left the gymnasium, presumably to help with lunch. But everyone else has now edged onto the stage, venturing closer, in order to hear. Winnie and Gu Ling Zhu Chi whisper to each other. Ming peers at his older brother, who is listening intently. With the exception of their mother, Ming has never seen Dagou care about what anyone told him to do. Could Brenda Wozicek be the cause of all of this? Then Dagou faces Gu Ling Zhu Chi and begins to mutter in his childish, flat Mandarin.

"Thank you for agreeing to talk to me. It is very, very important.

"I have been working at my father's restaurant for six years. It started when my mother got run-down, got pneumonia, and my father asked me to come back to Haven. I didn't want to leave New York. Ba promised me that after Ma was better, I could have a choice. He would give me a lot of money to help me resettle in New York. Or, if I decided to stay in Haven for good, he would make me a partner.

"Now six years have passed. I want my half of the restaurant. Half ownership, half of the profits. What is your advice?"

The old woman shakes her head and says a few words in Mandarin. Ming makes out "Xiaoxin."

Winnie raises her hands up to her face.

Dagou fishes a handkerchief from his pocket and offers it to her. "Hey," he exclaims. "You're upsetting my mother!"

Gu Ling Zhu Chi fixes a severe stare upon him. "William, you may stay for lunch," she says, clear and strict as a schoolteacher. "But then *you go to your apartment*. You stay home until after the Christmas holidays. *Be careful*. You are getting in 'hot water,' as the Americans say. If you are not extremely careful, something very, very bad will happen."

Dagou meets her gaze with a frown, a severity of his own, that surprises Ming. "I was hoping you would help me," he says. "I'll stay for lunch, but then I'm going back to work."

"Don't work," Gu Ling Zhu Chi says. "Stay away from that restaurant. You're inserting yourself into a story you don't know. Now go away," she commands, as if Dagou were a pesky child. "I want to talk to your mother." She turns abruptly to An. "I'm tired." An takes hold of her right elbow, and Winnie the left. Ming follows at a discreet distance, listening. The three women make their way out of the room, murmuring about Dagou's spiritual jeopardy, ignoring James and Fang, who wait at the door.

"Ming, what did she say?"

"It's his soul." Ming shrugs. "She says his soul is more important than the restaurant."

At that moment, Leo Chao's shout breaks brightly through their conversation. "Time for lunch!"

The Hunting Blind

The nuns seat them in a row: Dagou, Ming, and James. The handsome son, the accomplished son, and the good son.

Under the long table, Alf settles at their feet with his bottom wedged against Ming's new Ferragamos. The temple dogs stay on the far side of the room. Ming suspects they're tired of vegetables.

He himself feels uneasy around so much food. His face is sticky from the steam rising off the vegetable dumplings arranged in perfect spirals, savory garlic stems bright green beneath their translucent skins. To his left is a platter heaped with pressed tofu skin, sesame lima beans, and black mushrooms. Set evenly along the center of the table are platters of mock meats: a sleek mock fish, its shining surface slashed into tic-tac-toes, and a helmet of golden brown mock pork, patterned like medieval scale mail. Ming puts a few mushrooms on his plate, but doesn't eat them. He's sworn off big meals. He's sworn off carbs. But he especially swore off Chinese food, long ago.

Five minutes into the meal, Dagou nudges his right arm. "Hey, Mingo," he mutters. "I put a month's salary into this food. Why aren't you eating?"

"I don't eat lunch."

"But these su cai jiaozi are really good," James pipes up.

"It's over-the-top," Ming mutters. "Think of the woman-hours they put into making this 'plain food.'"

James gapes at his half-eaten dumpling; it's clear this hasn't occurred to him. It hasn't crossed his mind that somebody—perhaps the two novices seated opposite them—worked for an entire morning in the cafeteria kitchen soaking, cleaning, and slicing the massive quantity of dried mushrooms. Someone spent an afternoon combining the xianzi of the mushrooms, garlic sprouts, bean threads, and greens; and someone rolled the dumpling skins by hand. The SH claims its labor is communal, implying an advanced anarcho-communism, but it's easy for Ming to imagine that Gu Ling Zhu Chi works the nuns as dictatorially as his father works JJ and O-Lan. The place is actually precapitalist: exploiting unskilled labor, redistributing the surplus in the form of vegetarian delicacies designed to please the palate of its ruler.

Dagou goes back to work at his full plate. He's planned out every detail of the menu, but he doesn't seem to know that he's about to be the real meal here: he's the main course.

Their father, seated near one end of the long table, smiles broadly. "Pass the vinegar, please!" His voice is so deep and loud that everyone turns to watch him. Holding a steaming dumpling in a large porcelain spoon, he drips a bit of sooty vinegar on top, greedy and focused. He picks up a sliver of ginger, using his chopsticks with the precision of a surgeon, and places it over the dumpling's puckered nipple. He raises the spoon to his mouth and takes a bite.

"Hmm. It's good," he announces. "But I like my dumplings made with pork. Hot meat juice gushing into my mouth at the first bite. Hot, greasy, delicious pork juice!"

Dagou's chest swells. "You know they're vegetarians here."

"*You* prefer plain dumplings?" their father shoots back.

Dagou doesn't answer. He and their father favor meat in all of their food.

"I have nothing against 'plain food,'" their father says, addressing the community at large. "Winnie says it's sinful to eat living creatures, it amounts to killing, it's an act of violence, especially because the choice is an act of will, because we can decline to eat meat, because it's okay—and maybe even healthier, Winnie says—to eat only vegetables. She says people who stop eating meat have long life, and people who eat only vegetables have the longest life. Yeah, yeah. But, Your Elderliness"—he nods at Gu Ling Zhu Chi—"I, Leo Chao, would rather be dead than stop eating pig. I will be ash and bone chunks in a little urn before I don't eat juicy pig."

It's because of people like their father that communism will never succeed. Because of simple human graspingness. Ming watches Leo beckon with chopsticks. A pimpled novice staggers from the kitchen with an enormous platter of freshly stir-fried young pea leaves. They've been painstakingly stripped from the stems, then soaked, washed, air-dried, and cooked quickly in hot oil with salt and garlic shavings until wilted to a steaming mound. If Leo Chao must eat vegetables, he will devour the most delicious, labor-intensive vegetables.

"Why no meat? Why 'cessation from desire'?" Leo continues, heaping pea greens on his plate. "I love my desires. They belong to me, and so I listen to them, I believe them, and if I were a smart guy, like Fang here"—he shoots a glance at Fang, who blinks behind his glasses—"I would take notes. I want them to flourish and multiply. So, if you think the point of life is 'cessation from desire,' then you and I are mortally opposed. Of course, there's no need to worry about you because you don't believe in violence. So, you and I might as well be friends as enemies, except"—and here he grins, exposing a green stem stuck in the gap between his front teeth—"I don't make friends."

He turns this green grin to Gu Ling Zhu Chi, at the head of the table. If she's annoyed, she gives no sign of it. She's regained her tranquility. Maybe her harsh words earlier, to Dagou, were inspired by an empty stomach; then again, Ming thinks, there is no truth like the truth of what is said on an empty stomach. In vacuum veritas.

"I have a bone to pick with you," his father is telling the abbess. "You seduced away my wife! She talks to you at one party, becomes your friend, and loses interest in meat, in *sex*. All of a sudden, she gives it all up!—the restaurant, the house, even the dog!—and moves into this temple. Are you too good for me, Your Peacefulness?" He pauses, momentarily distracted. For a moment it seems possible—it's almost believable—that he's actually hurt, that he begrudges Gu Ling Zhu Chi for stealing away Winnie. But then his features break open with laughter. "My wife—Winnie, or

Sister Yun—at one time, you know, she would enjoy a good pork hock. She had juicy hocks herself!"

Ming doesn't frown or laugh at this; he's transcended all reactions to their father. But Dagou glowers, outraged on Winnie's behalf. Although Dagou, too, is a dog. A dog in knight's armor! Ming has heard him say worse about Katherine. As for Winnie, her suffering is unbearable. Yet Ming has long ago grown out of defending or protecting her. He is as loyal to her as any son, but nobody forced her to stay with their father for thirty-six years. Long ago, Ming vowed he would never marry a woman like his mother. He has never dated an Asian woman.

Now James leans toward Dagou, gazing at him in love and support. James has vowed to defend him. And Dagou nods at James, grateful for this vow. Ming sits back.

Dagou sticks out his chest. "Dad," he says, "I invited everyone to lunch today for a conversation that will affect the whole community."

Self-important words, surely. But a hush falls over the table. Ming can tell that everyone is waiting to hear what will happen next. Dagou's fate doesn't affect their livelihood or their own families. And yet the fate of these fellow Chinese parents, and these American sons, is everybody's fate.

"Six years ago," Dagou says, "when Ma got sick, you asked me to move back to Haven. You said when I finished helping out, you'd pay me fifty thousand bucks to resettle in New York. But if I stayed in Haven for good, you promised to make me a partner in the restaurant."

The room has grown still. Only a few people continue to lift cautious chopsticksful of pea greens to their mouths. Ming waits for his brother to expose himself. It won't be long.

"For six years, I've worked in the restaurant. I've upgraded the menu, fine-tuned every dish. I've developed a small but significant clientele who can handle a more authentic cuisine. I've invested my life's passion into this place! And I've made a decision," Dagou announces. "I want to be a partner at the Fine Chao, and settle down here in Haven."

James says firmly, "That's a great idea, Dagou."

Their mother is smiling. Her friends regress into a momentary happiness, nodding and patting her sleeves. In the last decade, everyone has given up hope that the community in Haven might continue past their generation. With the exception of misfits like Fang and Alice, the next generation has reasonably left the wretched town to seek their fortunes in more cosmopolitan places. Now here is Dagou vowing to live at home, modeling filial piety to his age group.

"It will be nice to have a young person here in Haven," says Ken Fan. With his thick, graying hair and gift for genial small talk, Ken is a silverback and the informal community leader. He adds, "Maybe you could get MBA, online degree."

The whole group turns to Leo Chao, filled with hope that one of their children should be loyal to them—want to stay with them. But Ming knows that nothing between Dagou and their father was ever so simple.

Leo shakes his head. "I let you come home," he says, "but you're expensive."

"*Let* me come home? Ha. You *begged* me to come home."

"That was when Winnie got that bad pneumonia," Mary Wa stage-whispers to her half of the table.

"I pay your salary," their father continues. "I let you eat for free and live over the restaurant. But I can't support a partner."

"Now, Leo," says Ken Fan affably. "That can't be true."

"I'll prove it to you. Show you my tax return."

"Of *course* your tax return makes you seem broke," Dagou fumes. "Of *course* on paper you're barely breaking even. You never report cash!"

Everyone suspects that Leo siphons off the cash. But everyone also knows it's stupid of Dagou to bring it out in the open.

"Look at my son," Leo says. "When he was little, he thought his father could make it rain. Now he thinks I'm a rainmaker. Thinks I'm sitting on a big pile of cash."

"You promised me!" Dagou yells back.

There's an almost imperceptible rumble from their father, a flicker in his jaw. Ming holds his breath. Beneath the table, Alf sits upright, pushing his butt more securely into Ming's loafers.

"In fact, *you* owe *me*," their father is saying. He surveys the table. "Yes, he owes me rent for all these years he lived here for free!"

Dagou's wide neck flames red. "You *offered* me the apartment! You—"

"I say nothing all these years. But since you bring it up, every year you are a bigger liability. One thousand per month in rent I could be making for a nice two-bedroom apartment over the restaurant. A nice, spacious two-bedroom home—the place where our own family lived until you were eight years old. I could be renting to another family! Making more than seventy thousand dollars! Not counting interest! You're living there for free! And since you mention, there's the extra food. You are not a small guy. I give you room and board. Compounded over six years, that comes out to over one hundred thousand dollars."

Dagou squirms. Ming's lips twitch. Here is the irregularity in Dagou's model of filial piety: if Dagou is truly a filial son, an obedient, selfless son, as he so clearly thinks he is, then he shouldn't assume anything more in return for his labor.

"And now the dog wants a bigger house!" Leo continues. Ming wonders what his father is talking about. "You finally want to settle in Haven like your father! You were too good for it before. Now that you're a failure—"

"That's not true! He's *not* a failure!" James pipes up, challenging Leo.

Genially, Leo waves him off. It was stupid for Dagou to think their brother's help would make a difference. With his skinny face and his college hoodie, not to mention his God-knows-why affection for every one of them, James is not a serious adversary.

"You think I'm a loser!" Dagou yells. "Am I a loser for keeping us alive when all the decent places are moving to the strip? I keep your business going. You pay me almost *nothing*. My salary is a *joke*. I want an equal share of the profits."

"Big man," sneers Leo.

Ming knows Dagou will turn to Winnie a second before he does it. He always runs to their mother.

"He grown up now," Winnie says. "Let him have his share."

"You stay out of this! You gave up the business when you left it for this menstruation hut!"

The table erupts. "Lay off it." "Don't talk to her like that!" "This is a Spiritual House."

Leo pushes back his chair.

Standing, he has the look of a beast on its hind legs: hairy, primitive, his long arms hanging almost to his knees. It isn't just the dark, unshaven hair sprouting in patches on his cheeks. There is something hungry yet remote in his close-set eyes. Everyone can see it. Some of them shrink back and turn away. Ming knows this eerie quality well. It has been there in his father for as long as he can remember. Long ago, he learned to escape its worst, to allow other members of the family to confront it. Now he climbs up into a place of refuge in his mind. A kind of hunting blind, where he can watch and wait.

From above, Ming watches his brother. Dagou has the blank expression of someone who is only just becoming aware of what he's done.

"'*Don't talk to her like that,*'" their father jeers. "Mama's boy! And *you* . . ."

He grins wickedly at Winnie. Despite her vow of tranquility, she appears ready to bolt from her chair. The nuns seated on either side hold on to her arms.

"You think he's still your diaper-filling lamb. You have no idea what a dog he is. Ask him why he needs money now. Ask him. *Ask him.*"

Dagou looks around the table. "It's true, I've fallen in love," he announces. "My *whole life* is changing." He pauses importantly. People stare at their plates.

"Christ," says their father. "All this fuss over a decent fuck."

The nuns gasp. Now Dagou's chair creaks, and he also rises to his feet. He is enormous and he swells with rage. His shoulders tense. He points at his father and his finger is shaking. It could be that he has decided, once and for all, to take down Big Chao. As the Sons of Liberty rose against King George. As the sons turned on Chronos, as he himself turned upon Uranus. So it will be in the family Chao.

Dagou opens his mouth to speak. Closes it. Opens it again. No sound comes out of him. His cheeks are trembling. He stands at the long table, opening and shutting his mouth.

James turns imploringly to Ming.

From his position above the fray, Ming shrugs.

After half a minute, Dagou produces a noise: a kind of squeal, the yelp of a dog that has been struck.

"What are you saying?" teases their father. "Speak up, I can't hear you!"

Dagou inhales one more time, but what comes out of his mouth is just above a whisper. *"Don't you talk about her like that,"* he manages to squeak out, and then, more deliberately, *"you asshole!"*

Their father laughs. It's a big sound of pleasure, amused and sensual, a man's laugh, a timbre of laugh that has possibly never been heard in the Spiritual House. The two novices across the table stiffen as the laugh releases itself, ringing out, then settling down gradually, followed by a long intake of breath.

"Apologize!"

"Never!" Dagou screams back in a voice that cracks as shrill and high as a small boy's.

"Apologize before the Christmas party, or else you're fired!"

Dagou balls his hands into fists. Lines of fury are drawn across his face. His jaw works, his chest heaves. Spittle flies from his mouth. For a moment, even from his safe distance, Ming is afraid.

"William."

Gu Ling Zhu Chi is struggling to stand. An grabs the old woman's elbow, helping her raise herself, gradually, over her end of the table. When she speaks again, her dry voice holds absolute authority.

"William. I told you. Go back to your apartment."

A silence follows. Everyone waits.

Dagou pivots almost frantically from their mother to the old nun and back to their mother again. But Winnie will be no help. Ming knows this about their mother. Her inability to stand up to their father has always shamed him.

Winnie, her face so enragingly heartsick that Ming can hardly watch, gestures toward the door.

Dagou pushes back his chair and picks up his coat.

James is staring miserably at his plate. Clearly, James feels he has failed to be a good brother. Ming himself has no such regret. It is many years since he has tried to help Dagou, longer yet since he has admired him. It's hard to remember a time when he ever looked up to him.

Still, when Dagou nods at him in farewell, Ming nods back.

Passing James's seat, Dagou bends down to him, puts a hand upon his shoulder. "Snaggle," he mutters. Ming leans in close to hear. "Come by later? My place around three o'clock?"

James nods.

The room is silent except for Dagou's disappearing footsteps. The front door closes almost timidly.

Gu Ling Zhu Chi is still standing, with her steely, blue-eyed handler at her side.

"Leo Chao," she says. "Big Chao. You are the boss. But it would be to your own advantage to watch behind you. You know what I am talking about. You're in danger of a bad death."

Her dry voice, crackling with certitude, is followed by expectant quiet.

Leo only shrugs and picks up his delivery bag. The novices across the table sigh. They think it's over. But Winnie is still alert and watchful in her chair. Ming doesn't leave his hunter's blind. He's waiting for a parting attack: Leo Chao seldom fails to get in the final word. Now he makes his way across the gymnasium, not seeming to care. He's almost reached the doors when he stops, opens his bag, and takes out a bulky package wrapped in white paper.

"You can't say I don't come ready to give," he calls out. "I brought special treats!"

He throws the package in the direction of the big gray mutt nearest him.

Ming feels Alf, below the table, raise his head.

The other dogs jump at once to their feet. It's as if Leo's thrown a magnet into a box of filings. Ears perk, nostrils twitch, and a high, starved howl breaks into the air. The room explodes with desperate barking. Alf charges out from under the table.

The dogs fight over the bloody package. Their snarling snouts seek out the paper, their teeth snap on air. Their tails whip and brush and dance. Those who can't get close stand back and whine. From the table, the nuns cry out in protest; the dogs ignore them.

Someone is rushing toward the fray. It's Winnie, all tranquility forgotten, frantic yet determined to rescue her beloved Alf. Brown robes flying, she plunges into the melee. She seizes Alf by the collar, but Alf wriggles free, and Winnie is left holding the leather band. As Leo Chao opens the doors to step outside, a German shepherd mix seizes the meat and dashes into the swirling snow. Alf rushes after him.

"Alf!" Winnie cries out.

But Leo stands by. "Let him have his fun!" He grins and leaves the building, slamming the doors behind him.

"A Big Fish in a Small Pond"

James remembers it this way: The winter after Ming went east, to college, their mother, now working too hard, came down with a bad cold that turned into pneumonia and sent her to the hospital. Dagou left New York, where he'd been living on kitchen jobs and gigs as a bass player, returned to Haven, and moved into the old family apartment over the restaurant. James's big brother was in town again, charismatically uncombed and unshaven, loquacious and needy, pressing James into assistance as he cast extraordinary spells of pungent, savory magic in the restaurant kitchen. Reminiscing about New York, dispensing guidance about the world at large. The two of them spent hours and hours watching football and playing video games in the apartment. It was Dagou who took to calling James "Snaggle" (a joke on James's crooked front tooth and a play on the transliteration "Sangou") and Dagou who nicknamed their puppy "Alf" (a joke on "Arf"; his given name was Bruce Lee

Chao). Dagou took up enough space for two brothers. Although there remained, whenever James thought of Ming, a wordless space, a question mark, a pause.

In midafternoon, as James climbs up the snowy steps to Dagou's bachelor apartment, he remembers it as a place of refuge. He opens the door with anticipation and nostalgia.

"Snaggle," his brother's deep, husky voice emerges from the other room. "Check this out."

Leaving his wet shoes in the kitchen, James passes the old family bedroom now redone with a luxurious king-sized bed draped with a faux-fur blanket. He enters the old living room, now a darkly glowing, carpeted space, a cave, with walls warmly painted brown, and dimmed wall sconces. From one side hangs a stuffed boar's head; and on the other side is mounted a screen, slowly humping through a spiral of rich colors. Dagou's tall bass looms magisterially in a corner. The rest of the room is dominated by an overstuffed leather couch and a glass coffee table with legs of burnished metal. On the table are piles of cookbooks in two languages, and a fortress of electronic equipment, including a mysterious black box.

Dagou, a barefooted bear in a cave, hunches at his laptop, its glow lighting up the high, ruddy contours of his face. James is reminded vividly of their father, sitting with his glass of baijiu in the dark. But Dagou is typing away at the laptop with an air of furious industry.

"Hey, Dagou."

"Hey, Snaggle!" Dagou moves a pile of red stationery from the couch. James lowers himself into the empty space, and the smell of leather suffuses him; it's like sitting in an enormous baseball glove. A glass is put into his hand. James sniffs a strong odor of alcohol. Beneath the leather and the alcohol, he can sense the comforting interest his brother has always taken in him, the generous interest of a larger, stronger animal nudging a youngling.

"Come on, try it. Tell me what you think," says Dagou, pointing at the glass. "I'm bringing out the best stuff for you."

James takes a sip. "It's—strong," he says, his throat burning. It's not as strong as his father's baijiu, but he doesn't say so. He picks up a sheet of red paper.

YOU ARE INVITED TO THE
ANNUAL CHRISTMAS PARTY!
DELECTABLE DISHES!
AND SPECIAL LIBATIONS BY DAGOU CHAO!
FINE CHAO RESTAURANT
DECEMBER 24, 6 P.M.

Dagou sticks out his chest. "This year, Ma asked me to take over the food for the Christmas party. Well, I'm planning the best fucking party ever. Ba doesn't want me as a partner? I'll show him!"

James remembers the old woman's warning to Dagou: *Stay away from that restaurant. You're inserting yourself into a story you don't know.* "Who did you invite?"

"I sent these paper invites to Ma's friends. But now I'm thinking I'll invite everyone!" Dagou waves his arm in the direction of the equipment on the table.

James peers at the tangle of wires; his brother calls himself an "audio-gook." "What's this box?"

Dagou grins. "This is an *illegal transmitter.* I bought it for a few hundred bucks off of a guy who convinced someone to drag it here from China in his suitcase. I wait until it's dark and put it in the attic." He nods at his laptop. "I'm making notes for tonight. Tune in to 88.8 between one and two a.m. tonight for pirate radio! FM 88.8, a lucky number! I've been broadcasting for weeks. I don't know if anyone listens, but I don't care. I'm going to invite the whole world to my party!"

"I'll tune in," James promises, making a mental note. "It's great to see you," he says. "I came to the restaurant last night. Where were you?"

Dagou closes his laptop. He gestures for the tumbler and James hands it to him. "It's a long story." He takes a gulp. "I'm in a kind of jam."

"Are you going to talk to Ba?"

"Never." Dagou takes another gulp. "I *would* tell you all about it, James, but it's too depressing."

"But you're picking fights with Ba. You're drinking in the afternoon. What's going on?"

Dagou sets down the tumbler. "You're full of questions, aren't you, Snaggle? Well, you know my old dreams of living in the city? Of living as a small fish in a big pond until I make it as a musician? Well, I'm done with that. I've given up, I'm ready to settle down for good in Haven, to be a big fish in a small pond. But the problem is—I'm not big enough to do it!" He buries his face in his hands.

James feels a surge of love for his brother; Dagou never hides what he's going through. "Is this why you broke up with Katherine?"

Dagou sighs. "Are you disappointed in me for breaking up with her?"

James shakes his head.

"Then you really are on my side. Because, of course, everyone else loves Katherine more than they love me!

"There's a kind of woman, Snaggle, who is *above all* a good woman, such a relentlessly good, upstanding person that it's impossible to be in love with her. That's Katherine! She even looks like a pillar—such smooth skin, so straight and pure with that long neck—and understanding and forgiving! and solvent!—all of it!—and yet why is it such a struggle to love, to feel an essential tenderness toward her?"

"Didn't you love her?"

Dagou considers. "I think I admired her, Snaggle."

James's thoughts, questions, crowd each other, but he can think of no reply.

"Are you wondering, how is it possible to have sex with someone out of admiration? Well, the answer is, it's not hard at all."

"She's pretty," James says, now red in the face.

"She's exceptionally good-looking. And good. She's way *too* good for me, that's the problem. It turns out, I want a woman who is equally as bad as myself."

Dagou straightens up and frowns at his toes again, wiggling them thoughtfully.

"The question is not why I slept with her, or even why we went out for so many years, but, why did I get engaged to her? How did that happen? How did we go from perfectly cordial dating, which had been going on since God knows when, best friends, every day as pleasant and uneventful as the one before, to pledging to spend our lives together?

"She *is* my best friend. Since she took that job in Chicago and followed me back to the Midwest, our romantic life has slowly evaporated. But it didn't really matter until the last year or so."

"Dagou, what's going on?"

Dagou reaches down, digs his right finger between his smallest toes and twists it around. He brings it out, examines it, and sniffs it.

"So maybe we were engaged for so long it became more and more obvious that we were never going to be married. But words were spoken. *Promises* made. When we were barely out of college, I gave Katherine Ma's old ring. It was from Ba's side of the family, I guess, and when I started bringing Katherine home, Ma gave it to me. You've seen it, do you remember it?" James tries to recall. A green stone, the color and clarity of lake water, shimmers from somewhere in his memory. "A big chunk of super-rare jade with a complex gold setting, some Asiatic panther with spots of diamonds wound around the jade—it's the only thing Ba brought from China, it was the one thing he ever gave to Ma. I honestly don't think he inherited it; I figure he won it somehow, gambling, during those years he spent in Macau. Ma told me there were still a lot of old things tumbling around Macau, left over from the gold and jewelry people brought out of the country and saved and gambled and lost.

"Anyway, I gave her the ring. We were serious at the time. Words were spoken, promises made, unborn children were imagined and named! We were twenty-two years old. We get engaged, everything is fine, and then—well, a *decade* goes by. I don't even know if it's just one day or gradually, but it's not fine. I realize I don't want to be married to Katherine. I ignore this. Because I'm a shit. I don't want to be the bad guy. I want her to break up with *me,* throw *me* aside, so I can come across all clean *here in Haven* to Ma, Ken Fan, Mary Wa—why do I give a flying fuck about what they think? Anyway, this goes on for years, me torturing myself, back and forth, and Katherine—well, I think she *knew.* I believe she knew I was waiting for her to break up with me and so she just . . . *didn't.*

"Then it happens. One day, someone walks into the restaurant, and my life is changed. And it's imperative, crucial, that I break up with Katherine *and* get the ring back."

"Who is it?"

"Hold on. So, I try. I have no dignity, I beg her to break up with me and give me the ring." Dagou twists the tumbler in his palm. "She won't do either thing, of course. You may think breaking up is unilateral. It doesn't take two people to break up. But you're not dealing with Katherine. First of all, she *knows* everyone we know; they call *her* whenever they need to find me, *she* talks to Ma every week on the phone. It's like she's their daughter, and I'm the shitty son-in-law! I can't even forget her birthday, they're all reminding me. They want to know the present." He imitates Mary Wa's quack: "'What did you buy for Katherine?' And this is because they know the truth: She has no reason to stay with me! She could find someone else in a *snap.*" He tries to snap his fingers. "So why doesn't she?" he moans. "Why doesn't she just fucking find someone else?"

He breaks off and stares at James imploringly.

"I don't know," James says.

"Because for Katherine, a promise is a promise. Words are not only words, they are as real as real. Those imaginary Han children, they are real children.

"So what do I do? I sleep with someone else. I fall in love! But secretly. Because I can't bear to have everyone think I'm a cheating scum. Now I *really* need the ring. So what do I do but go back and say the most humiliating thing possible."

In the long silence that follows, James wonders how Dagou thinks he's keeping his relationship with Brenda Wozicek a secret, when everyone seems to know about it.

"I'm telling myself, I'm not a creep because I'm not just going to *take* the ring from her. And so I offer her ten thousand dollars."

After a startled moment, James clears his throat. "Wouldn't that make her feel, well, undignified, Dagou? Wouldn't she believe that you assumed she could be bought?"

"No shit. Of *course*. Of *course* it's ridiculous, and humiliating, and rude, and awful. I don't know why I did it. I was desperate, I was a crazy man! Here I am, entirely without dignity, begging her to let me give her ten thousand dollars so she'll understand we're broken up and give me back the family ring."

He stops for a moment, lost in thought. "And of course she won't take it. She doesn't need the money. She's gotten through that fancy law school, and she's working at this evil accounting firm in Chicago. Katherine is rich."

This is undoubtedly true. Yet there remains one central question about Katherine, separate from the ring and even from the money. "Why won't she let you go?"

"Because she says I'll change my *mind*. She says she *knows* I'll change my mind, that I *really love* her, and anyone else I ever want is just a fling I need to get out of my system, because we got together so young. She'll wait, and I'll come back to her."

"Um, do you think it might be true?"

"No. There's someone else. I'm not even sure *Katherine* thinks it's true. It's more like an oath, it's what she tells herself because she's *decided* it's true. I don't think she loves me anymore. She smiles at me and I'm afraid she's going to slap me, but she still smiles, she smiles."

Surely it can't be that bad. "Of course she doesn't want to slap you."

"Wait a minute, Snaggle. It gets worse."

He stops, gathering his strength to speak. James waits with a sinking heart.

"Do you think I went to Katherine with a bag of cash and tried to buy the 'family ring' outright? That would be bad enough, right? Well, what I did was worse, Snaggle. I didn't have ten thousand dollars, I didn't have *two* thousand dollars. I went to her empty-handed and told her, I need the ring right now. I told her, I'd buy it back but—I'd have to *owe* her."

James flinches. "Don't tell me any more."

"I have to tell somebody! And who else will listen, who else could love me after I finish this story except you, Snaggle? So, now she knows, Snaggle—she *knows*."

"What do you mean?"

"*She knows I don't have any money.*" Dagou's face is wrung up in misery. "I've been keeping up an elegant lie, telling her Dad pays me well, driving down to visit her in Chicago, blowing my salary on dinner. She thought she was engaged to a bustling restaurateur. But she figured out I don't have the ten thousand dollars, and she's not a fool, she knows if I don't have ten thousand dollars, I don't have a cent to my name. So then, to make it *even worse*, she . . ."

A half minute of silence passes. What did she do? James waits, determined to hear his brother out, but Dagou won't finish his sentence.

James prompts him. "Why do you need the ring so much?"

Another silence, even more prolonged and obdurate, this time for longer than James can bear. He blurts, "You're in love with Brenda Wozicek."

An intense flame of yearning opens up Dagou's heavyset features. Then, almost as quickly, a scowl battens them down. "It's not what you think! I don't want to give the ring to Ren. Ren doesn't even care about the ring. She wouldn't want it."

"Why do you want it back? For the family? For Ma?"

Dagou hunches his big shoulders. "I want to *sell* the ring, to these obsessive Qing antique collectors from Taiwan. Because Ren wants to live rich. Money is more important to her than anyone in the world." He lowers his voice. "I haven't told anyone—I signed a lease on this swanky eighth-floor penthouse across town, over in Lakeside. Starting January first. I'm going to surprise Brenda with the penthouse, ask her to live with me—"

James recalls his father's words: And now the dog wants a bigger house! "Did you tell Ba about the lease?"

"I had to! I can't afford the rent. I asked Ba for more money. He said to break the lease, but I can't—it would hurt my credit. Ba just laughed. He says, You tried to bite off more than you could chew! So I set up the luncheon, to ask him for the partnership."

"Do you have to live in Haven? Does Brenda want to stay here?"

"Probably." Dagou shakes his head. "I'm tired of focusing on geography. It's a family obsession. There is no perfect place. It's just that, for people like us—"

"What do you mean, 'like us'?"

"We Chaos, who are full of passion and inner chaos! None of us can bear to be in our present lives. We're charged up with unrelenting ambition for the future; it's why Ma and Ba came to the States. Or we're sad about what might have been. Ba says he wishes he hadn't left China. Ma's trying to get back to a time without Ba. I'm thirty-three and I want to be nineteen again. We want to travel back in time, but we can't, and so we want to go to a new place instead. Place is what we have instead of time. No. Not true. Money is what we have now, instead of place *or* time." He exhales. "Time is money. Place is money. Love, love is money. And power is money. You'll see."

"I don't want to be like that," says James.

"Ah," says Dagou. "But you are. You heard what Gu Ling Zhu Chi said to you."

"No, I didn't."

"I forget you have such bad Chinese. Well, Ma told me all about it. Gu Ling Zhu Chi read your *I Ching* and your palm. Then she stood there and told you your fortune. Do you want to know what it is?"

James is certain he doesn't want to know. But more urgent than this certainty is the desire to know. "If you and Ma know what it is," he says, "then so should I."

"Okay. Well, she said you're going to come into a lot of money, Snaggle. You're going to find and lose more money than some men make in a lifetime. You'll live a big, important life, you'll grow up into a powerful man. You're going to have adventures—expansive, challenging adventures; you're going to live in many places. You'll remember everyone you ever knew, and you'll take on their burdens for them. Love is going to matter to you, more than anything else, and the love of your life is going to be unrequited."

"What do you mean."

"Unrequited. That means, 'not returned.'" Dagou lifts the tumbler and drains it. "All I know is, kid, when you get your big, important life, when you're making your deals, don't forget about your old brother here."

"Dagou," James says, "it's Alice. I want to sleep with her."

"Give 'em up," says Dagou miserably. "Women are crazy, Snaggle."

"But—" James tries again. "Does 'unrequited' mean . . . that I'm not going to have sex with her, Dagou?"

"No, Snaggle." His brother's voice is sad. "It doesn't have to, Snaggle."

"Dagou. What Gu Ling Zhu Chi warned you about."

"To stay away from the restaurant."

"Is she right about that? Is it true?"

"Yeah, Snaggle. It's true."

Big Chao's Blood

"What can I do to help with the party?" James asks, putting on his jacket.

Dagou fishes under the pile of invitations and pulls out a spiral notebook. James is skeptical; his brother almost never plans anything. He reads in Dagou's big, jagged handwriting: *As far as parties are concerned, there are many kinds of greatness. There is greatness of tone, of style; greatness of setting, of occasion, and of the guests. Most important, however, is the food.* Dagou flips the page. James reads: *A perfect, simple winter meal in honor of our closest friends.*

"Let's see," Dagou says, poring over a list. "I've got it planned out. An awesome meal for Ma's friends. I can get most of this myself tomorrow. But why don't you take this list"—he rips out a sheet of paper—"to the Oriental Food Mart. Tell Alice to put these items aside, I'll come pick them up tomorrow. Get me eight bunches of hollow-hearted greens, I need to snag them early. Charge them to the account. Oh, and one more thing," he says, as James turns to leave.

"What?"

"One of the nuns called me. Ma is really upset. She went straight to her room after the luncheon, with a pounding headache."

"Should I talk to her?"

"She needs her rest. But I got a text from Brenda." He gestures at his phone on the coffee table. "Somehow, Alf ended up at her house in Letter City. Can you go pick him up? I'll text you the address. It would make Ma feel better. She loves that dog."

"Got it."

"And when you're at the store, talk to Alice. Ask her out!" Dagou says, as James heads to the door. "Don't wimp out on me. It's time you got laid."

The afternoon is raw. The clouds lower, pale and unrelenting, sealing everything under a colorless vault of winter. Mary Wa's store, a quarter mile south, lies on a slight incline. At the bottom of the rise, James begins to jog. At first he watches carefully, trying to avoid the puddles and slick, marbled ice, but when freezing slush floods his sneakers, he stops making an effort and simply gazes at the shabby homes and businesses. He passes an insurance agency, a spiraling barber pole, and the tropical fish store, half-hidden behind steamy plate glass.

He watches Alice through the window of the Oriental Food Mart. She's on a stool behind the counter, hunched over her sketchbook, knees drawn up under her shapeless gray sweater. She focuses as if she isn't in the store. When the door bangs, she darts a glance at James and folds the book against her chest.

"Hi, Alice."

"Hi."

With a rush of gratitude, James reaches for his brother's script.

"Would you please put these things aside for the party?" he asks, handing her the folded page from Dagou's notebook. "Dagou says he'll pick them up and pay tomorrow. And I need eight bunches of hollow-hearted greens. He said to put it on his credit."

Alice reddens. "I'm not supposed to give Dagou any more credit."

James stands rooted to the floor, feeling the blood recede from his own face and neck.

"I'm sorry," Alice says.

"No, it's okay. I've got cash." James reaches for his wallet, trying to think of something else to say. "You have to help me find them, though," he adds, inspired. "I get them confused with pea greens."

Alice slides her sketchbook under the counter. She leads him over to the cold room. James follows a pace behind her. He's close enough to watch the tendons flicker as she flips the ponytail back over her shoulder. He sniffs cautiously at her cheap shampoo and then, unexpectedly, his dick stiffens. The sap of aggression, Big Chao's blood. He wants to grab her from behind. Alice, somehow unable to hear the pounding of his heart, examines one bunch of greens, then another.

"Here," she says. "This batch came in from Chicago two days ago. They should be all right." She counts out eight bunches and leads him out of the cold room, shutting the door carefully.

"Alice," James says, "when did Dagou start running up so much credit?"

Alice tries the door again. "Sometimes the latch gets stuck open or closed."

James repeats his question. "I won't tell anyone," he says, although he doesn't know if this is true. He must find out, must persuade her to tell him everything, even though this isn't the way he would have chosen to prolong their conversation.

She shakes her head. He's known Alice long enough to recognize when it's impossible to talk her into doing anything against her mother's instructions. But he can never predict when she'll take it upon herself to disobey. There was that Sunday afternoon, when they were thirteen, when she raised the corner of her shirt and let him see a budding breast. He still often trips over this stuck moment in his memory. The line of her narrow torso and then the aureole, the pinkish quirk of flesh, the delicate nub of her nipple. "I want to see it again," he said breathlessly, the following Sunday. She never showed him again.

They're already at the cash register. "What're you drawing? Can I see?"

He expects her to say no. But now she's holding out the open sketchbook for him to examine.

He's expecting nothing special, perhaps wispy penciled images of their surroundings: low metal shelves holding neat, meager rows of canned goods, small piles of Asian pears. He's prepared for something tentative, or perhaps even skilled, but incomplete, a beginning—something to encourage.

Instead, the page is dark with ink. James sees an elaborate drawing, covering the entire sheet except for one corner. He makes out a series of chambers, long rounded rooms. Inside them, a community exists—one room has rows and rows of tiny beds, another laundry lines with identical dresses, tiny hats, clipped onto clotheslines. The chambers are populated with figures, not human shapes, but animals. Rabbits, badgers, rats, weasels. There are adults and children. Playing, conversing. There's a playroom filled with little swings, slides, dragon-shaped riders on coils. There's a coatroom. And here—James is sure of it—is the Fine Chao: dining tables outfitted with tiny lamps; a kitchen with hanging pots and pans. There is a pantry in which James can make out roots, leaves, and sprouts. And a room for cold storage, filled with shelves of what seem to be enormous seeds, kernels, or grains, organized by type, still encased in their protective hulls, and shelves of various-shaped but similar objects that prick upon his memory: insect wings. Glittering wings of all shapes and sizes, drawn in detail, so thinly inked they appear transparent. Toward the top of the page there is a horizontal line, and above the line, a mound.

"Wow," says James. "This is—" He stops. He can't share the peculiar sensations that have welled into him. He's been given a glimpse into a world belonging to Alice, utterly private, but designed and arranged according to a pattern curiously personal to himself.

"I was going to include a library," Alice says, "over here." She points to the blank corner.

"It's so strange," he says, without meaning to say *she* is strange. Maybe she doesn't care. "I love it," he says in a firm voice.

"Sixteen dollars," Alice says, now red-faced, pushing some buttons.

James shuffles through his wallet again and finds a ten and two fives. He gives them over and watches her count out the change. Her hands move with practiced confidence at the cash drawer. But when she gives him the money, her fingers shake.

"Alice," James says, "would you go on a date with me? Hypothetically, I mean—"

"I don't know."

"So you won't go?"

"My mother would probably want me to."

"Don't tell your mother."

She looks up. Her light brown eyes are unreadable, but he knows he's said something to interest her.

"I'll text you," he says, holding her gaze for a moment before it slides away. But of course she doesn't have a phone. He struggles for a plan. "Let's just plan to meet tomorrow, later in the afternoon. Five o'clock. I'll come here."

"No," she says. "My mother will be here."

"Then meet me at the restaurant. No, wait, not the restaurant."

There's nowhere in Haven they're guaranteed to be alone. Work and home, both Leo's. But there's a heady likelihood his father will be at work. "My house," he says with some pride.

Leaving the store, he peers back through the window. She's seated on the stool again, opening her sketchbook. He stands on the sidewalk, watching as she bends over the pages.

Alf's Secret

Walking down the avenue, James remembers long-ago scenes private to him and Alice. It's winter, their mittens are cold and stiff from making a snow fort, and they're picking their way through slushy ruts in the back alleys of childhood. It's a summer afternoon, they're scrambling up to the train tracks, Alice giving James a penny to place on the track and James scurrying away, pulling her with him as huge, dirty freight cars thunder by. These memories transfix his mind; he can't visit them with anyone else. Now he imagines the two of them on a date: standing in line together at a movie theater, Alice wearing a short skirt and a turtleneck sweater, dark wool tights. Does she own these clothes, would she even like going with him to the movies?

He's left behind the hollow-hearted greens. Does he have time to retrieve them? He checks his phone for Dagou's text, studying Brenda's address.

A snowball slams into the back of his head. Icy water trickles down his neck. His phone slips from his hands and skitters into a puddle.

"Ching, chong, fuk choyyyyyyyy!"

Scrambling for his phone, he twists to catch a glimpse of his assailants. Two middle school boys, small but fierce. Their skinny faces, bright with trouble and accusation, are familiar. He knows them by their brilliant, slanted light gray eyes and Scandinavian cheekbones. It's Zack and Cody Skaer. The Skaer cousins have been bullying the Chao brothers since James can remember. Trey, the worst of them and Ming's middle school nemesis, has inherited the family diner; he claims the Chaos compete with them for customers. Zack is his nephew.

"It's okay," says Zack. His pale eyes glitter at James like shattered glass; his freckles stand out even in the dead of winter. "You can fix it. You know how to fix a wet phone? Put it into a bag of rice! *Ching, chong!*"

"Listen—" James begins.

"C'mon, let's get out of here," says Cody.

Voices, friends and other cousins, are calling. Zack and Cody run off.

James turns off his phone, takes out the SIM card, and puts the pieces into his pocket. Then he straightens to watch them all run down the avenue, little Zack trailing the fleeter, taller boys.

In ninth grade, James and Don Skaer came to a truce. James let Don copy his homework, and Don offered James his cigarettes, plus once an actual blunt, which James tried to smoke, because he enjoyed standing with someone behind the school on a November day. The difference between himself and Ming, he thinks, is that Ming was once enraged by the fake kung fu sounds and he himself was not. Maybe James wasn't angry because he couldn't understand Chinese any better than these boys; it was all Greek to him, as Ming said. It was Ming, fluent in Mandarin, who was infuriated, ashamed, and, therefore, a true target.

James plods through the snow, searching for Brenda's house. Letter City was once inhabited by the working Czech community of Haven. Now it's the kind of neighborhood where some residents stay put forever while some move in and out so frequently that you can't keep track of who lives where. There are narrow backyards abutting narrower alleyways. The houses are quite small, but each has its own porch and small front yard, close to the sidewalk. Now and then James passes a bungalow lavishly festooned with Christmas lights, but most are dark. The unplowed streets are almost impassable. He turns into a windless back lane, unnamed and rarely used. The snow is shallower here but there are no paw prints. Why did Dagou send him on this errand? His thoughts are interrupted by clear chimes, the bells of the nearby church, St. Ludmila.

James remembers he's been here before.

He must have been eight or nine years old. He came this way with Leo on Mondays off. He recalls his father beckoning him with a jerk of his chin and the two of them heading out, hand in hand down the alley. James closes his eyes. There's the sound of church bells, the odor of melting earth, old dog shit, and rotting chestnuts. He and Leo standing at a back gate. His father's hand twitching around his, his breath whistling through the warm spring air with taut anticipation. They had come to visit his friend Sharon, a woman with curly yellow hair and ringing laughter. James understands, just now, that the woman, Sharon, was one of his father's lovers. It was the dog in him. He wonders how much his mother knew about Leo's wanderings. She must have known. James makes his way through the snow, down one block, then the next. It's barely possible to recognize the back side of some houses by their size and color, glowing faintly in the snow: peeled white, slate-gray, dull brown, blue siding. The colors are the same in back as in the front, but the back sides reveal bulky additions, sheds, cellar doors, air-conditioning units, satellites, and laundry lines; they are the secret sides of the houses.

He turns left into a parking area held in common by two somewhat shabby gray bungalows. He checks the address, steps onto the porch, and knocks on the door.

Footsteps, quick and firm. The door opens and fills his eyes with soft gold light. A dog darts from this radiance. James bends toward him and with a yip, Alf leaps onto his snowy knees.

Alf, warm and starry-eyed, wriggles up to lick him. James leans over with relief to grab the wagging dog. The door opens wider. A rush of warmth, the scent of spiced candles. A musical voice cries, "James!"

James is face-to-face with Brenda Wozicek.

The lamplight glows on her pale skin and the soft red yarn of her sweater. She has light eyes fringed with thick lashes, and a full red mouth. Her dark hair has a wide, vivid streak of a deep turquoise.

Alf squirms in James's arms. His collar is, of course, missing, and with it his tag, shaped like a bone, with the Chaos' home phone number. Now he jumps to the floor and cavorts around Brenda. He lets her scratch his ears; he pants, grinning, tongue rolling, frantic tail whipping his buttocks vigorously back and forth. James, still dazed, hears an echo of his father's voice: "The tail is wagging the dog!"

Brenda stops scratching; Alf's tail droops. Brenda hoists him up, and he lolls happily in her arms. "James, you're soaked. Come in and dry off."

James is arrested by the beauty of her heart-shaped face. Ming might call her small-town, might talk ironically about her dye and tattoos, but she is undeniably sexy.

"Take off your coat," she says, nodding to the coatrack. "You're shivering. You need to dry off. Put your wet shoes here."

Now he's stuck, shoeless, in her house. Struggling to breathe normally, conscious of his sodden jeans, and—could it be?—the tears in his eyes.

"Sweetie," she says, "you've gotten so big." James feels the blood rush into his cold cheeks. "Did you come looking for me?" Brenda speaks softly, with surprise, as if it would please her more than anything if that were true. For a moment he wants to say he did.

"Um, no," he says. "Actually, I came looking for Alf. Dagou said he was here." Alf and Brenda regard him quizzically. "Do you—I'm just wondering, does Alf come here a lot? You two seem super attached."

"No, I just really love dogs."

"How did he get here?"

"Maybe he's got a girlfriend somewhere in the neighborhood."

Like man, like dog. Embarrassed, James changes the subject. "This is a nice place. I like the way you've fixed it up."

"Thanks!" She shrugs, pouting. "It's put a dent in my credit cards." James steals another look around him, half expecting the room to waver and dissolve in arrears, but the lamplight is as warm as ever.

Alf jumps down, trots purposefully into the other room, as if someone else is there. Brenda glances behind her. James watches the soft line of her throat. She tucks a curl behind her ear in a furtive, restless way that confuses and excites him. Her small ear glows against her dark hair. Her movements are graceful and deliberate, but there's something unpredictable about her—not quite impatient, not rebellious, but wakeful and resistant.

"Dagou sent you here?"

"Um, yeah." She's frowning. "What's wrong?"

"Nothing's wrong," Brenda says. "But I texted him to come and get Alf himself."

At this moment, he's startled to hear a light footstep from somewhere farther inside the house. Self-consciously, he pulls his gaze away from Brenda.

Katherine Corcoran is standing in the doorway, Alf at her side.

"Katherine." James swallows hard, wishing for Dagou. "Why're you here?"

Katherine smiles. "I could just as well ask you that."

"Looking for Alf. Dagou said—" He stops, struck by the recognition that Brenda texted Dagou to come over right when Katherine was visiting. Had Brenda planned an accidental meet-up of herself, Katherine, and Dagou? Whatever her intentions, Dagou has, by sending James, made a narrow escape.

There it is, the elaborate setting, the luminous bright green jade on Katherine's finger.

"How are you?" he stammers. "I didn't know you would be in town. I thought—"

"I'll be in Sioux City at my parents' on the twenty-fifth, but of course I still came to visit. I've been coming to Haven during Christmastime for so many years."

She knows he knows this; she stayed at their house, cooked in their kitchen. Katherine in an apron, learning from his mother how to wash the rice, how to let the oil get to just the right heat before throwing in the vegetables. She's like an older sister to him. She even *looks* like his sister, with her dark hair and Asian features. She was adopted from a rural orphanage in Sichuan.

"Everyone here is family," she says. "It's so good to see you, James! How long has it been—since your high school graduation?"

Remembering Dagou's fear of her smile, James has a sudden desire to run from the room.

Katherine gestures to Brenda, who nods graciously. "And Mary Wa has told me all about Brenda. It turns out we have so many things in common. We've been having a good talk—we've been planning the decorations for this year's Christmas party!"

Brenda says, "James, what's wrong with your hand?"

"That? Oh—it's fine," he says, trying to recall the origin of the scrape. It must have happened when he dropped his phone. He remembers the dismantled phone in his pocket and is anxious to go home. "Do you have a ziplock baggie and dry rice?"

"No. When I want rice, I get takeout from the restaurant."

"I should go."

"Hold on."

Brenda leaves the room, Alf trotting behind her. She brings back ointment and a bandage. As she dabs on the ointment and applies the bandage, James can feel some tension or pain ease under her fingers. He sniffs her perfume—something woodsy, faintly sweet—and the combination of her touch, her nearness, and her scent is disorienting. Whereas Katherine is perfect, like an etching, Brenda's beauty is multidimensional. Just being near her is making him uncomfortable. He can't stare at her for one more minute, but he can't stop staring.

"Come into the living room," she says. James is led to the soft red sofa and lets himself sink into it.

Katherine leans toward him from a wing chair.

"James, help us with the party," she says. "Your mom wants us to keep up the family traditions. She wants continuity. She told me all about the first party, the year the restaurant opened, before Dagou was born. All they could afford was noodles. They made eight different noodle dishes!"

Hers eyes are very dark, shining into his. He turns away, ashamed.

"I was thinking, this year, something special, in honor of your mother? We could decorate the restaurant with wreaths and fir branches? And red napkins and tablecloths, of course: everything red for good luck and longevity. A real Christmas tree? We can retire the fake one. We could make it all vegetarian, in her honor. Even though she won't be there."

"Vegetarian Christmas lamb," says Brenda sweetly. "What do you think, James?"

"Yes, James," echoes Katherine. "What would your mother like?"

James turns from Katherine to Brenda, then back to Katherine. Both women are watching him. "Um," he says, stalling, "Ma is definitely a vegetarian now. But the Christmas party was always, well, kind of a meat free-for-all. So, I don't know."

The parties all began with readings from the gospel, but they devolved to food, drink, loud talk, and laughter, children running, shrieking, breaking things, chaos, more chaos, his father getting drunk with Lynn's father, engaging in a round of camaraderie and insults, and his mother darting in and out of the kitchen—"like a chicken with her head cut off!" Leo Chao said—until everyone had eaten themselves into a state of food-drunkenness, and drunk themselves to the brink of palpitations, and staggered off into the night.

Alf is snoozing with his head propped up on Brenda's lap. Brenda is eyeing James as if they share a secret.

Katherine is saying, ". . . tea candles, mistletoe, really *good* party crackers with—"

"What about Dagou?" James interrupts. His mother was always indifferent to candles, wreaths, miniature lit villages, and fresh-cut spruce trees. He recalls Dagou's notebook. "I think Dagou's been making plans. He wants a simple meal—"

"In honor of your mother's friends," Brenda finishes.

In the silence that follows, James hears the clear and mystical sound of a single chime. Brenda slips a phone out of her pocket, checks it. She leaves the room. Traitorously, Alf follows again.

James and Katherine sit listening to Brenda's half-audible murmur from the kitchen. Katherine twists the jade ring on her finger. She meets his eye and smiles. James feels an answering smile fade from his face. He does not possess emotional self-control anywhere near as strong as hers. And yet, as she becomes engrossed in her own phone, he sees something desolate in the privacy of her bent neck. They can still hear Brenda's voice. It's like listening to an unknown woman talking and laughing through a bedroom wall.

Katherine puts her phone into her purse. "Dagou has been honest with me," she says. "He's caught up in the idea of pursuing a friendship with Brenda. Mary Wa thinks Brenda is trying to steal him away from me. But, of course, that can't be possible. She's not a femme fatale. We've been making friends. She turns out to be a lot like me; she's an ambitious woman who grew up in the middle of nowhere. The minute she leaves Haven, she'll see the opportunities available to her. She'll forget about the restaurant and the things she's doing now. She'll be caught up in the professional opportunities of a city."

Over Katherine's shoulder, James sees Alf enter the room ahead of Brenda, whose pace is dreamy. He gestures to Katherine, but she continues, determined. "And Brenda has so many ambitions that have nothing to do with Haven. She wants to move to Los Angeles!"

Brenda takes her seat, patting the cushion next to her. Alf jumps up. "Actually," she says, "that idea is something you kind of made up as you were talking before. I don't want to move to Los Angeles."

"You did theater in high school," Katherine points out. "You said you'd like to pursue your interests."

"I'm a small-town actor." Brenda shrugs. "My plans aren't professional. I'm not hung up on the superiority of a professional life, or living in a big city. I don't need to go anywhere."

Katherine nods and smiles, but James can tell that Brenda's lack of ambition has caught her off balance. She's tried to empower Brenda, to elevate her future in a way that Brenda couldn't care less about. Brenda has slipped out of this plan, shrugged out of it.

"What *are* your interests?"

"I'll remodel my home. I'll go to the gym. That's the kind of woman I want to be."

James's laughter catches in his throat.

"It's true, James. I don't want to work," Brenda says. Her confidence is superb. James believes her. It's as if he's never seen her fill a pitcher of water or burn her hand on a hot dish. "My long-range goal," she says, "is to marry into wealth. And for that, there are opportunities right here in Haven."

Katherine's tone hardens almost imperceptibly. "If that's what you want, why don't you go after Ming?"

"If you don't know why," Brenda says with a chilly smile, "then you're dumber than you look, Katherine."

James changes the subject. "Dagou's not wealthy," he points out.

"Not now," Brenda says. Again, in the smug curve of her red lips, James glimpses a surety that would be absurd if it were not for the beauty of her mouth.

"And he's not going to stay in Haven," Katherine says. Although he's always believed Dagou *would* leave, James has now heard the truth from Dagou himself. Katherine's certainty of the opposite—self-deception?—makes him uncomfortable. He grew up in a shouting house. He doesn't know what to do about manipulative empowerment or chilly smiles.

"He came here to help out his mother," Katherine continues, "but he doesn't belong here. Isn't that right, James?"

"I've been working at the lab this fall," James says. "I've been really busy and haven't had a chance to check in with him." He feels pressured to keep talking. "Today at the Spiritual House—" He knows he's said the wrong thing. "What I mean is—"

"Mary Wa told me what Dagou said. It's true: we're taking a break," Katherine says, to reassure him he need not feel awkward.

"Okay," James mumbles.

"But we're not broken up—we're on hiatus." Katherine nods at her left hand.

"You're still wearing the ring," Brenda says. Next to her, Alf snorts in his sleep.

"Isn't it beautiful?" Katherine holds up her hand. The panther setting looks crude on her slender finger. But the jade glows with an almost unnatural green, and James understands it must, indeed, be very valuable.

"It's a priceless ring," Katherine murmurs, gazing at it. "A family ring. A symbol of the old country."

"Dagou wants to sell it," says Brenda conversationally.

Katherine flinches. "That's not true. He once told me the ring isn't about money. It's about the value of family, the value of history. It's to be given only, not sold, and given out of affection." She turns to Brenda and a sudden rush of emotion comes into her voice. "I'd give the ring away, if someone really wanted it, but I would never sell it to anyone, not even—"

"That's very generous of you," says Brenda. "I'd assumed it was a symbol of your relationship with Dagou. An engagement ring."

"Dagou and I have history," Katherine says, and James can hear again, in her voice, what could be love, or pride, or hope. "We practically grew up together. We don't—*I* don't—need a piece of jewelry to represent our bond."

"If you don't need it, then will you give it to me?" Brenda asks. Stretching out a hand, opening a soft, pink palm.

Alf looks up.

"I'll give it back to Dagou. I know Dagou wants it back," Brenda says, continuing to hold out her open hand. "He wants to sell it for a down payment on a place here in Haven."

The weather in the room has shifted. Alf jumps off the couch and comes over to James. He reaches down to pet the dog, but cannot take his eyes off of Katherine. She looks very young, fingering the ring.

James believes Katherine might give the ring to Brenda. It might matter more to Katherine to be able to give the ring away than to possess the ring itself. But she's visibly incapable of making up her mind. The ideal thing to do in this moment would be to laugh Brenda's question away. But Katherine continues to finger the ring, to bite her lip. Even James can see that Katherine wants the ring in a way so visceral and so personal she can't bear to give it up. The struggle goes on and on. James can sense in the air, as vital as oxygen, Brenda's restless cruelty. She is making Katherine reveal something about herself that she would not, in a million years, have wanted to reveal: that she wants nothing in the world as much as this ring.

Brenda is smiling.

"I would never take the ring if it means so much to you, Katherine," she says softly, and James hears beneath this softness another kind of cruelty that makes his blood tingle. He can bear it no longer. He stands up.

"I don't think either one of you loves Dagou!" he shouts. "This isn't even about Dagou, for either of you."

He hurries through the kitchen toward the back door, desperate to leave. He shoves his feet into his wet shoes.

"Come on, Alf." He pushes the door open, and the cold air swirls inside.

For a minute, Alf stays at Brenda's feet. He doesn't want to come. Then, all at once, he wriggles away and shoots past James.

"Alf!" James stumbles onto the porch.

Brenda says, "Come back, James."

"I've got to go after him!"

"You need your coat," she says. "Don't worry. Seeing you reminded him to go home. I bet he's halfway there by now."

She's holding out his coat. He spares a crucial moment to grab it. Then he turns and rushes down the snowy steps.

"Alf!" The narrow street is an unrecognizable landscape of shapes and shadows. There is no sign or sound of the dog. In the light from Brenda's porch, he makes out a set of paw prints, which he traces past a neighbor's house and into the back alleyway. James follows the paw prints east, toward home. Snow is drifting up against the back porches and garages, making the alleyway a tunnel of white. The prints are filling with snow. He hears the church bell again, but faintly. His lashes, frozen stiff, press together as he squints into the swirling white. Alf's trail is gone.

The Doghouse

An hour later, inside his father's house, behind the closed door of his room, James seals his phone into a plastic baggie of dry rice. He props his wet sneakers against the heating vent. He tunes the radio to FM 88.8. Outside, snow swirls thickly against his bedroom window. Leo, downstairs in his chair, grunts something at the television set. The house is emptier, lonely, without his mother. And Alf—after a long and unsuccessful search, James did not find him safe at home. Where could he be? Perhaps, returned to Brenda's. At this very moment he might be curled on her soft red couch. Brenda might have texted James; it's possible this reassuring text is simply locked in his nonfunctioning phone.

James opens his laptop, checks his email. A thousand miles away, a deep freezer has malfunctioned in the laboratory where he worked during the semester. Several years' research is in jeopardy and his supervisor wants to know when he can return to campus. An undergraduate ski club is being organized for January. His suite mate wants to know if anyone is still in the dormitory; he's left a charger in his room. At the thought of his suite mate, an Oregonian with a surfer haircut and a beard, James feels a part of his mind rekindle almost physically; he's almost forgotten the dorm, the laboratory. Going to college has split him cleanly in two. There's no overlap between his college self and his identity as Snaggle, the third Chao brother. Is it possible for either of these two parts to fade away, disappear? Is it necessary to choose between them?

He puts his laptop away, turns out the light, and buries his head in his familiar, musty pillow.

He's woken by the sound of static. Cacophonous, otherworldly, tooth-jarring static. James dives for the volume knob on the radio and, before he can master it, Dagou's deep baritone fills the room.

"This is FM 88.8, the Doghouse." There's stock audio of a dog barking. "Music, news, bad metaphors, and original broadcasting."

It's like seeing Dagou from outside his window, glimpsing him alone at night in a lighted room.

"And now a word from our sponsor. Are you bored? Tired of boiled string beans? Tired of *turkey*? Searching for strange flavors, ethnic exoticism, a little family hostility, immigrant anxiety, served up with a heady dash of self-hatred? Then come to the Fine Chao Restaurant! I'll be your waiter and chef, and I'm happy to provide you with all of that. That's D-A-G-O-U, Big Dog in Mandarin, for those of you who know me and were always wondering.

"And now back to our regular evening show: *A Dog's Life*.

"Let me begin with a story—let's say it's one of my fondest childhood memories."

The Package

In his hotel room, halfway across town, Ming is tuning the clock radio, setting the station to rouse himself for an early morning conference call. He has trouble sleeping in Haven, and trouble getting up. He doesn't trust the hotel's wake-up system, and his phone alarm is too quiet. He's searching for a station with especially irritating music, slipping from a sermon to pop, when a familiar baritone speaks into his inner ear.

"It's about twenty-five years ago . . ."

Ming stops his fingertips against the dial.

" . . . and I'm about six years old.

"I'm standing in the Haven Post Office with my father. You might remember me from those days: I'm the stout boy at the restaurant, black hair sticking out like a puffball, nose in the kitchen. In case you were wondering how my hair got like that, my mother buzzed it on setting three and it grew out in all directions. I never had a professional haircut as a kid."

For about a minute, Ming doesn't move. Dagou's radio project, a complete surprise, is also inevitable. It's like a blog, except that a blog is recorded online, forever; whereas this pirate radio project is unrecorded, spooling fugitive words into the dark, impermanent and fleeting, words that *might as well have never been*, unless they're overheard. The project is so Dagou, talking into the reeds: indiscreet, self-absorbed, self-destructive, and a waste of personal resources. Not to mention under the table; Ming is sure the equipment is contraband. He lets go of the clock radio and sits back in the bed, letting his brother's story fill his ears.

"There's something you need to know: As a kid, I really do believe my father knows how to make it rain. I believe he's the biggest, the strongest, the most magnificent man in the world. The *only* man in the world.

"So I'm five years old, and I'm with my father. Ba has to mail a package. I have no idea what's in the package or who it's going to, but I can sense it's important. He announces to the clerk, 'This is going to China.'

"She's a tight-mouthed, prissy type, and I can tell right away she doesn't like my father one bit. Most people don't. For one thing, he's *bigger* than the average Asian guy, and also he's *dark*. I'm like him, too, big and dark; it's Ming with the alabaster complexion; and my youngest brother, Snaggle, is 'just right.' But for another thing, Ba is *crude*. He's checking out the clerk in a way I don't understand because I'm six years old, but I now get that he's undressing her. Considering her possibilities. She's not young and she's not pretty. But he's an equal opportunity barbarian.

"She says, 'Excuse me, but this package *smells*. Is this perishable?' and I *know*—because I watched him sealing the box—that instead of using packing peanuts, he's filled the empty spaces with dried mushrooms.

"Even at the time I wondered what else was in the box. Was it a gift? To whom? What did my mother think? Did she even know about this package?

"There's a pause. She leans toward him just a little, in part, I suspect, because of his undeniable Oriental magnetism, and in part because she thinks he doesn't know much English. And as she's leaning forward, my father opens his mouth and says, in a carrying voice, right into her face, 'None of your business.'

"She straightens up and says, 'Excuse me, mister. Answer my question.'

"He says, 'I told you, none of your business.'

"She says, 'I'm getting the manager.' Suddenly there's this fat-faced guy staring over the counter. My father stares back. The crackle of hostility is hair-raising. I try not to listen. But even though I put my fingers in my ears and la-la-la, I can hear their angry exchange. At some point, my father begins to punctuate all of his sentences with 'you,' like, '*Back off*, you!' I know I should stand by him, but I have started backpedaling, I edge away from the counter. I'm not the only person doing this. There's another Chinese guy in line, Ken Fan—he's turned away, staring out the window as if he's memorizing the license plates of every car in the parking lot. Then Ken Fan *sneaks out of the post office.* Why? Because he's embarrassed to witness this behavior from someone who looks like him.

"The manager yells, 'I'm calling the police. Susan, call the police.' And she picks up the phone.

"My dad takes his package off the counter. 'William,' he says—that's me—'we're leaving.'

"That's when I hesitate. I don't want to follow him out. I want to pretend he's not my father. He gets to the door and he can sense my pause, because he barks, in this deep-throated Mandarin, my name: *'Dagou.'* You should know that all of us have dog nicknames, given by our parents: Big Dog, Second Dog, Third Dog. They must have wanted another kid, maybe a girl, who would have been 'Little Dog.'" Dagou plays the same audio cue of a dog barking. "Humble nicknames mean we're precious; our parents are protecting us from hubris, from malevolence. But like all nicknames, they also mean: You're *mine.*

"I follow him trying to act like I'm not with him. He grabs my arm with the vise grip of someone who's at the wok all day. On the sidewalk, he's yelling, 'You sniveling, disloyal coward! You should be ashamed of yourself! You're my son and you stand by me!'

"I walk along, filled with shame.

"He yells, 'If you hate me, then you hate yourself!'

"He yells, 'Apologize to me! *Coward,* you owe me an apology!'

"I say nothing. I can't speak.

"And right then, while I'm standing at the passenger side, he gets into the car and, quick as anything, locks my door! Then he starts the engine. Pulls away!

"And what do I do? I'm six years old. I don't even know how to get home. In two seconds, I'm running through the parking lot, chasing the car. I catch up at the red light. I'm banging on the door, bawling and groveling and yelling, I apologize, I'm sorry, I'm sorry."

Ming hears the unmistakable sound of Dagou taking a gulp of something. "And in today's news . . . despite my six years of great work in the kitchen, six years of cooking the freshest, most subtle versions of sad-sack menu items—six years of bringing an authenticity to the food that he can appreciate!—my dad just gave me an ultimatum: 'Apologize before the Christmas Party, or you're fired.'

"He thinks I'm still a child, and he's not wrong. I won't be an adult, I won't be able to live my life, until after he is dead.

Dagou lowers his voice. "Yeah, sometimes I lie awake thinking of the different ways that he could go. He could slip on the greasy kitchen floor and crack his head open. He could fall down the stairs. Or the best way, the easier way, would be for him to get locked into the freezer room. That room is older than he is, and totally not up to code. There's no way to get out except with the key we keep on the inside wall. Say the key is missing. He'll be locked inside, gone for good. Wouldn't it be amazing? To wake up every day and know my life is my own."

Ming snaps off the radio. He can no longer bear to listen. Does he hate the self-absorption, the woeful self-aggrandizement of Dagou's performance? Has Dagou relayed a story that reminds Ming of his own humiliation by Leo? No, it's something else. Ming is a child, standing by Winnie's side, listening to the conversation of the community women. He's watching his mother's face. It's not the only time he's registered this particular distress. The pain of it, searing, infinitely private. He knows Winnie's pain as he knows a first memory. To what other woman had his father planned to send the package? Sitting in his hotel room, years later—decades later—Ming clenches his hands.

DECEMBER 23

Passion

IN THE MORNING, Haven is buried in fourteen inches of new snow. Along the avenues crawl aging city plows, woolly mammoths making slow furrows in the glittering white. Into this sparkling, frigid tundra, James struggles alone, protected by a hood, face mask, puffy coat, gloves, and plastic bags pulled over his sneakers and taped at the ankles. After only a few blocks, his jeans are already soaked through and frozen stiffly at the knees.

Approaching the restaurant, James can hear the engine of Dagou's small Toyota pickup with the plow attachment, rumbling from the parking lot. Snow has been pushed up so high the parking lot itself is hidden from view. Dagou, laboring within this fortress of white, can't be seen. James slogs around the walled lot and into the driveway.

Dagou has gotten out of the Toyota and is using a big shovel to heap snow atop the high mounds. He works easily, lifting heaping shovelsful as if they're nothing.

"Hey, Snaggle. You're late."

"I couldn't get to sleep—"

"Oh yeah?" Dagou grins, and James is struck again by his resemblance to their father. "Well, you woke up right on time, noodle-dick—I'm basically done with the snow."

"Sorry."

"S'okay. You're ahead of Ming. He said he'd be here a half hour ago. Lunch is going to be slow, so I'm depending on you both to help prep for the party!"

"I'll do it," James promises. "Go out, run your errands." Gu Ling Zhu Chi warned Dagou to stay away from the restaurant.

"Thanks, kid. I'll go check up on Ma. She's still in bed, her temple friend Omi says. Rough day for her yesterday."

"Dagou—" James swallows. "Don't tell Ma this. Alf got away from me again last night. In Letter City."

Dagou stands, frowning, overheating in his winter jacket. His creased cheeks glow red; he looks hot enough that his feet could melt through the snow. "Well, he knows the way to the house, and the way here," he says. "Someone probably found him and brought him home. They'll call the number on his tag."

"His collar and tag are gone."

A puff of steam escapes Dagou's collar. "S'all right, Snaggle," he says, patting the top of James's hood. "He'll find his way back to us. Like Ba says, he knows who's feeding him."

It's as if the uncontrolled bitterness of his radio rant never happened and his anger never broadcast itself out into the snowy night. James swallows, waves goodbye, then lets himself into the restaurant.

Entering the back door, he has a sudden need to use the toilet. He removes the bags from his shoes and hurries down the hallway.

Only O-Lan is in the kitchen, entirely forbidding, even more intimidating than he remembers. Nicknamed by Leo "The Orphan," she first arrived at the restaurant two years ago with no connections, no family, and no plans. Winnie took her in, noticing her pinched face and her hair reddish with malnutrition. She insisted O-Lan be given temporary work, to get her back on her feet. O-Lan has been at the restaurant ever since. She's carved out her preferred kitchen tasks, defending this territory against JJ, even against James.

Now she barely glances up, as if he hasn't been away for months. She's a woman of indeterminate age—big boned, wary eyed. Sometimes she looks like a plump teenager; at other times, with light from an open window on her face, she appears to be a person who's already lived through a beginning, middle, and end, a story enclosed, known only to O-Lan if she cares to remember it. Her actions in the kitchen are ruthless and efficient, the actions of a person who wishes to remember nothing. Older and indifferent, not wanting to like or be liked, O-Lan is alpha dog to James. She terrifies him. He waves. She doesn't respond.

The bathroom is roomy enough for three people to enter and converse—or argue. Here, Winnie once vehemently scolded James and Fang for sneaking flavored toothpicks meant for the customers. James thinks about the thousands of hours he's spent at the restaurant, doing his schoolwork at a back table in the dining room, or sitting in the office on an old MSG box, rereading Ming's battered *Werewolf* comic books. Perfect child care: the child never out of sight. All three brothers growing up, learning a work ethic here, how to be responsible. While Dagou hung over Winnie's shoulder during off hours, tasting ingredients, Ming was more interested in the contents of the register. He once saved them a hundred dollars when a large family tried to decamp without paying. Ming raced out the door and down the avenue—"O. J. Simpson!" Leo said later—returning with the bills clutched in his hand. But when Ming turned thirteen, his enthusiasm slackened. He no longer spent his downtime industriously folding napkins, snapping beans. His interest in the money lasted longer, until one day he lost patience with even that.

"This place is a dump," he exclaimed. "We work like dogs six days a week. We're making egg rolls from scratch."

"They taste way better than frozen egg rolls," Dagou pointed out.

"The point is, we're investing our labor on a product that is consumed immediately and brings in small change."

"Big Shot!" their father said. "You rather spend your precious time jacking off? Then shoot your wad about your own business and not mine."

For several months after, Leo referred to Ming as Big Shot. Ming didn't respond. As a freshman in high school, he won first place in a math contest. He kept the prize money and invested it on his own. He joined the track team (four-hundred-meter relay) and ran every day. Leo hired JJ, who (until he fell in with Lulu) did whatever Winnie told him to do, and whose greatest flaw was his tendency to sing off-key in the kitchen. For the rest of his time in Haven, Ming clocked in minimal hours at the restaurant, and then withdrew except in emergencies. Leo, for whatever reason, let him do this.

James checks his watch: it's ten past eleven.

In the front room, O-Lan stands behind the counter while a man orders takeout. He wears a baseball hat, and his jaw moves ceaselessly and nervously in a way James knows means he's quitting either drinking or smoking. He booms out his order as if he's at a drive-through: "Sesame peanut noodles and fried rice. And some extra soy sauce packets."

O-Lan doesn't meet his eye, pushes the button on the cash register. "Sih. Doerrr. Fittty. Sih. Cen."

"Did you hear me? I want sesame peanut noodles and an order of rice."

O-Lan spits out, "Sih. Doerrr. Fitt—"

"Be right there!" James hurries to the register, dodging tables and chairs. But O-Lan and the customer are locked in mutual hostility, ignoring him.

The man works his jaw. "Can. You. Understand. Wh—"

The front door flies open and Ming appears against the backdrop of brilliant snow, wearing his cashmere overcoat and again looking, James notices, entirely out of place. His authority is palpable. He strides directly to the register. O-Lan moves aside.

"May I help you?"

"What's wrong with her?" The man fumes at Ming. "I placed an order. I asked for sesame peanut noodles and fried rice."

Ming says, "One order of sesame peanut noodles and fried rice. That will be six dollars and fifty-six cents."

The man hands over a ten-dollar bill. "And extra soy sauce. Seriously, what is it with her? Is she deaf?"

"She can understand the orders, but she can't speak English."

"Then she should go back to where they speak whatever she speaks."

Ming's voice is a shade higher than usual. "She knows what you ordered and how much it costs. She was filling in for me. I was late because of the snow. My apologies. Here's your change. Your food will be ready in ten minutes."

Even Ming knows he must apologize.

In the kitchen, James struggles through the man's order—unlike Dagou, who is a natural, James has never been confident at the stove—and runs into the storeroom to search for more soy sauce packets. Returning to the kitchen, he finds O-Lan, bent low over the open take-out box, working the muscles of her face, licking her teeth. Her lips part in a quick grimace as she aims a gob of spit into the man's noodles.

"What're you doing?" James tries to keep his tone neutral.

O-Lan ignores him. He swipes the order from the counter. He's about to throw it out when a hand pulls it roughly from his grasp. He flinches, turns. O-Lan is putting the order into the staff refrigerator. Then she returns to the cutting board.

Following this incident is the lunch rush—smaller than usual due to the snow and the impending holidays, just the regulars. The regulars are all men. They come only on workdays, as if punching a time card. They sit alone, they almost always order the same thing, and they shovel fried rice into their mouths as rhythmically as swimmers. Only a few of the regulars, whom Winnie calls the "taste buds," are genuinely interested in the food.

James waits on the customers. He's known most of them for years.

In the kitchen, Ming argues with O-Lan. James assumes they're discussing her behavior toward the sesame peanut noodles man, but he doesn't have enough Chinese to navigate the conversation. Even Ming's four years of A's in college Mandarin and his fifteen weeks of studying abroad do not make it easy for him to talk to O-Lan. O-Lan's Mandarin is a mystery to everyone. Ming claims she's from a southern city populated by newcomers from the countryside, and her sentences are inflected with a mysterious vernacular—neither Cantonese nor the country speech of Toisan. "She's the Orphan, in between dialects," Ming once told James. "She has no native language."

Now, as he snaps beans for the party, James struggles to decipher O-Lan's conversation with Ming. They don't seem to be talking about the sesame peanut noodles man. "Snow," Ming says. Ming has a flight back to New York this evening. They trot through a few exchanges—Ming's ironically inflected voice and O-Lan's dry one, curiously similar in tone—until it grows clear to James that Ming is defending himself. But why be defensive, when they're discussing the snow? Next, James hears "United" and "Chicago" and "eight o'clock." "Snow." Now Ming is gesturing with his hands and saying words James knows from Alf's commands: *"Stay. Go. Stay. Go."* "Go? Stay?" O-Lan gestures toward the front window, where they can see a snowbank and a scrap of gray sky.

There's a sense of alteration in the air, the faintest twitch in the room's atmosphere. Something is about to happen. Things are about to change. James recalls the man in the train station. He's listening, waiting for it to happen again.

Minutes pass slowly. The lunch shift is over, and James flips the sign on the door to CLOSED. O-Lan eats the man's spat-upon noodles. She adds hot sauce, stirs the dish into a peppery sludge, and chews methodically. James finishes the beans, takes them to the kitchen sink, and floats them in the big stainless-steel bowl. He tries to focus on his upcoming date with Alice, five o'clock. But he remembers his mother isn't well. When he tries not to brood about this, he starts to worry about Alf. Is he hungry, is he somewhere warm?

Bells jingle, the door opens, and Leo Chao enters, followed by the lawyer Jerry Stern. They stamp their feet and scatter crumbs of snow on the carpet. Leo smiles his gleaming smile. James has often noticed he is not like his self-proclaimed totem animal the dog, but like the Cheshire Cat. His grin is a beam of light over the room.

"Hullo, hullo!" Leo shouts as if to many listeners. "I know, lunch shift is over! But you guys need to break the rules, get off of your asses, get this man some food!" He claps Jerry on the shoulder. "He's going to spend an hour with me going over papers, pro bono work. He's starving. Hey, get him a beer."

James opens two bottles of Qingdao. Jerry is the closest thing his father has to a real friend. A chowhound, he can be found at a back table every day since his divorce, digging his chopsticks into a clay pot red with spice. Jerry is also a suit. As Leo Chao's attorney, he's the sole American who matters at the restaurant. It's Jerry who keeps Leo out of trouble. The last favor Jerry did for Leo involved the restaurant's ancient freezer room. James never knew exactly how, but Jerry helped Leo emerge victorious from the scrape with the city inspection unit. He calls Leo "you sly dog," a reference to something James suspects has nothing to do with the restaurant. It's as if Jerry has married into the family—he will never truly understand it, but he's committed.

Now Jerry mops his forehead with a napkin, takes a draft of Qingdao, and sighs with relief.

"Don't get too comfortable," Leo Chao says. "Come help me with these papers." They disappear into the back.

"One of these days," Ming mutters, "Jerry's going to take a trip to China. He'll get a whiff of the real breadth and depth of Chinese cooking, legendary dishes. That chicken wrapped in lotus leaves he's read about. Authentic peppers from Sichuan, fresh as hell. Then he'll leave the U.S. for good, retire to Asia, and Dad's going to have to cough up real money for a lawyer."

"He says he can't go to China until he's finished paying for his daughters' educations."

"I guess until that happens, Dad is his source." Ming's phone buzzes. "Gotta take a call."

While James struggles to put together Jerry's clay pot pork, Ming steps into the supply room, presumably to discuss the big deal he's mentioned with some bank in Phoenix.

Another jingle at the door. It's Katherine Corcoran. She's snow-dusted and pink-cheeked, wearing a black overcoat, red scarf, and slender black leather boots.

"Hi, James," she says. "Are you getting ready for the party? I stopped by to check in about the decorations."

"Hi," James says uneasily. He's not sure how to behave around Katherine after last night. Does she still see him as her future brother-in-law? Or is he just a waiter? He's more comfortable in the latter role, but she smiles at him as if he's still a future relation. "Um, have a seat," he says. "Sorry it's so chilly in here. Something to eat or drink?"

"How's your mother?" Katherine's voice is warm. She won't let him off the hook. He has the distinct impression she's thinking about the scene at Brenda's house and she wants to make sure he still likes her. He feels a desire—a need—to reassure her that he does.

"She's not doing so great."

Her smile fades. "I know she got upset yesterday. Can I do anything?"

"It'll just take a while for her to get her tranquility back. Dagou just went to see her. And I think Ming talked to her this morning, you could check with him."

"Ming is here?" She looks suddenly severe.

"He's on a call, I think. He'll be back."

Katherine sits at a table for four. She's a defensive diner, with her back to the wall like Al Capone. James asks for her order. Tea. Spicy tofu. Does she want it with, or without, pork? She wants the pork. Would she like brown rice? No, she says, brown rice is an affectation of Dagou's, not authentic. White rice is fine. Whatever her complications, James thinks, they're played out in the real world, not in her palate.

But Katherine's appetite for Chinese food is hard-won. She's learned to love it, after an initial aversion, followed by disinclination, and finally, exploration. Everyone knows she grew up in Sioux City eating peanut-butter-and-jelly sandwiches, carrot sticks, and "ants on a log" (celery sticks smeared with peanut butter, then dotted with raisins). Guzzling orange juice for breakfast; learning to make omelets, pancakes, waffles, and French toast. On holidays, family dinners of an enormous standing rib roast served with cheesy potatoes, mashed potatoes, and sweet potatoes with marshmallows, Brussels sprouts with pecans, creamed spinach, corn casserole, and homemade cranberry sauce. Baking, with her mother, Margaret Corcoran, Christmas cookies in the shapes of music notes, jingle bells, and double basses. Learning to roll piecrust. Yet her immersion in these skills, taught by her devoted mother, have over time created a hunger for another culture. James can see it in the focused way she examines the shabby restaurant. He can see it in the way she looks at him. It's a clinical look, a look of data collection, but also of loss. Why doesn't she do her research in China, where her biological mother lived and died? Because she works so hard at her demanding job in Chicago. In the meantime, the Fine Chao will have to do.

"James, where is Dagou?" She knows all of Dagou's shifts.

"Um, not here today. He's at home testing some recipe, getting ready for the party. Ming and I—"

At that moment, Ming walks into the room.

He seems agitated, younger than usual. Maybe he's afraid of Katherine. She's five years older, and, although they both have the same kind of good looks—clean-cut and self-possessed—she's better-looking than he is. Moreover, she's not generic. Her coat is too expensive to be artsy, James thinks, and yet she doesn't quite have Ming's corporate uniformity. You could just as well imagine her very high up in a special charity for rich people—something righteous, supporting the disadvantaged. Now she turns on Ming with an expression of familiarity and intensity. James feels sorry for Ming.

"What are you doing here?" Ming's voice is cold. He's not afraid, James sees suddenly; he's angry with her. Why is he so angry?

"This restaurant is open to the public, or so I've heard," she replies with equally icy precision.

Ming frowns. "You shouldn't have come to town. Dagou told us about your 'hiatus.'"

"That's none of your business." She's so pretty and so terrifying that for a moment James is almost worried for Ming, or would be if he didn't know his brother's knack for evaporating from difficult situations. "I'm here to see Dagou," Katherine says.

"He's not here." Ming keeps his voice as cool as ever. But there it is: although Ming tries to hold himself completely still, to not move a feature on his face, he blinks.

James blurts, inaccurately, "I can text him—"

"We can all text him," Ming says. He pulls out the chair opposite her. "James, I need to discuss something with Katherine. Will you run to the kitchen and help O-Lan?"

James retreats to the kitchen. There is a fairly fresh pail of soapy water sitting near the door, but O-Lan is nowhere to be seen.

James busies himself chopping garlic for the party. Ming and Katherine are arguing in heated murmurs. They sit facing each other like mortal enemies, or life partners. From where he's standing, he can almost hear them, but not quite. Ming has sent him to the kitchen because he knows (as all of them know) the exact distance that a normal conversation can carry from any point in the empty restaurant. Katherine is flushed. She and Ming are rigidly self-contained, yet as they talk, James can sense a kind of tilt under his feet, as if the carpet has become sand.

In the next moment, Ming and Katherine are shouting, their voices carrying across the restaurant as cleanly to James as if he were beside them.

"I'm not saying it's my business!" Ming says. "It's just hard to stand and watch as—"

"Butt *out*! This is between Dagou and me!"

"You don't get it! Listen to me. Just *listen*. You guys are *over*. You are *finished*. You're embarrassing yourself. Get *lost*! We are not your family! You live in Chicago! You need to leave town and forget about it *for your own good*!"

"You don't know shit about what's good for me!"

"I know more than you think!"

Katherine is weeping.

James senses movement at his shoulder. It's O-Lan, wearing the expression of a cat in a window, a private, hungry gaze, as if she's lapping up every scrap and drop of passion in their conversation. That's what it is, James sees all at once: it's passion. The very air shakes with it. James edges toward the bathroom, that place of refuge. He's about to make a run for it when the telephone rings.

Ming moves automatically to the front counter.

"Fine Chao Restaurant." He listens for a moment. "I don't know," he says at length. "He's not here. I don't know."

There's something in Ming's voice. James approaches.

"Hold on." Ming leans closer to James. "Listen," he says, pressing his palm on the receiver. "Some woman named Chang, an ABC, I'm guessing, is missing a piece of luggage. This woman is calling every Chao within two hundred miles, she says, to search for it."

James stands still, his mind abruptly cavernous, echoing with the distant screech and roar of underground trains.

"Lost item?" Leo Chao returns, ostensibly to get another couple of beers. But he can't do anything subtly. There is something charismatic in his movements—even in the casual way he reaches out to wrest the phone from Ming—that makes them all look over at him, even Katherine, who no longer weeps, but watches.

Ming grabs an order pad and scribbles on it. As he walks back to his seat opposite Katherine, he hands James a slip of folded paper.

Leo listens, then barks into the phone, "A bag? What color bag? How big is it?"

James opens his mouth. He must tell his father what he knows—he's on the balls of his feet—but Ming shoots him a warning glance.

Leo adjusts the phone at his ear, concentrating. An intent and vivid glint comes into his expression. James has seen this before, most recently at the Spiritual House, as his father picked up the slivers of fresh ginger and placed them atop the dumpling. A glint of greed. Leo says, with atypical politeness, "I'm sorry, but no one's turned in anything like that." He listens for another long moment.

James unfolds the note. On the one side, in Dagou's handwriting, is a receipt for crab rangoons and a large wonton soup. On the other side is scrawled a note:

Meet ASAP, at the Other Restaurant. Leave separately.

The Other Restaurant is their name for Skaer's Diner, down the street, which Trey Skaer inherited and runs now. James has never eaten there. He's surprised Ming would set foot in the place, after being bullied by Trey throughout childhood, into high school. Whatever Ming wants to discuss, it must be top-secret if he's willing to go to Trey's diner.

Leo's voice is casual and friendly. "Nope, you're barking up the wrong tree here. Try Chicago? There's got to be a hundred listings for Chao or Chow in that area. We don't try to save people in train stations, or steal people's luggage." A pause. "Okay. There are a lot of towns in that direction. Try farther north, try Minneapolis. Sure. Good luck." He clicks the phone back into the receiver.

"You know what that means!" he announces to the room. "It means they lost his Life Savings! She was tricky, she wouldn't reveal the contents of the luggage. But an old man like that, nine times out of ten he walks around with his Life Savings in hundred-dollar bills. Hell, I'm going to search! It's possible that someone's Life Savings is lying around! If there's any bag of money here, I want to find it. Definitely me, and not that no-good son of mine."

"Don't talk about Dagou that way!" Katherine cries out.

Leo Chao turns his gaze on her. Though he's still smiling broadly, James is afraid. His father's cruelty is also quick as a cat's. But when he speaks, his tone is light.

"Kath-erine-Cor-coran," he says. "You are an attractive woman. Not sexy, but very attractive. I have nothing against you spending your time here. It brings in customers! But you are too good to wait around for a guy about to lose his job. Take it from me. You need someone with more resources, someone who knows how to appreciate you. Someone with experience!" His grin widens. Brandishing the bottle opener, he heads back to the office.

Ming's hair is sticking up on top. He appears absolutely beside himself. "I told you to get out of here."

Katherine's small features are tiny with rage, but she's glaring at Ming, not Leo.

Ming seizes the sleeve of her sweater. His hand is shaking. "You always think the best of him!" he says. "You don't understand—you need to understand—"

"Understand what?"

"To understand the men from our family," Ming says with finality. He lets go of her sleeve.

To James's surprise, Katherine doesn't respond. They are all silent. Katherine pours each of them a cup of tea, but no one drinks anything.

The Other Restaurant

Twenty minutes later, when James arrives at Skaer's, the diner is almost empty. With its plate-glass windows, fluorescent glow, and stark counters, the place is reminiscent of the Hopper painting, but James is fairly certain this effect is not deliberate. He peers through the window; under bright light, a few lonely afternoon owls of Haven who don't eat Chinese food hunch over the counter as if posing for the artist.

Inside, the restaurant is pleasantly warm. From a booth on the far side, someone waves at him. It's Ming.

Ming has hung his overcoat on a rack near the booth. He's smoothed his hair. A small, expensive-looking suitcase defends his side of the booth, and James remembers again that Ming has a flight this evening. Nobody reproves him for this, or insists he spend Christmas at home. He became independent long ago.

"This is like that riddle about the town with two barbers," Ming says as James approaches. "You go to a small town with only two barbers. One of the barbers has a bad haircut. If you and I want privacy, we're doomed to a shitty meal."

"The food can't be that bad."

Ming shrugs and checks his phone. "There's one good thing on the menu, and it's the fish sandwich." He waves his hand at the other side of the booth. "Sit down and order. Go crazy. Supper's on me."

James sits. A young woman brings him a menu, laminated in plastic, illustrated with colorful photographs: an open-faced sliced turkey sandwich with gravy and mashed potatoes; a jaunty cheeseburger and fries. James's mouth waters. He loves American food. Although he's been eating at the dining hall for a semester, it's still exotic.

Ming says, "I have to eat anyway before I get on the plane. Last flight to Chicago. How's it going, little brother?"

James remembers something. "Yesterday I ran into some of the Skaer kids."

Ming speaks without emotion. "Lucky you."

The server reappears with Ming's plate. She's about twenty-four, with a messy bun of wavy orange hair so flame-bright the filaments seem transparent.

"Here it is," says Ming. On the plate is a fried cod fillet sandwich, a lettuce leaf, and a slice of pickle.

"Have you decided," she asks James, "or would you like more time?"

"I'll have the breakfast special, with scrambled eggs and bacon, please. And hash browns."

"Look at that," Ming remarks, when the server has gone. "Real red hair. It's hard to find a genuine redhead now. Too much interracial breeding." He lifts the top bun and peers underneath, then replaces the bun and takes a bite. "Crisp, and light on the tartar. Perfect."

"Ming," says James, "why were you so mean to Katherine? What's she ever done to you?"

"Katherine?" Ming clears his throat. "Nothing. No, not nothing. It's just, she enrages me. She should get away from us, for her own good—but she won't leave. Because she was adopted by well-meaning white people and raised apart from her kind, she's stuck on *us*. She's *fetishized* us.

She wants to *be* us, for God's sake, and what she should really do is accept who she is: a highly intelligent, beautiful, very lucky, well-brought-up young woman who just happens to *look* like us."

"You're insulting her *and* us."

"Katherine and I are strictly business," Ming continues. James can tell that this statement, for Ming, is both true and not true. "She and I talk, we even have a coffee now and then when she's in New York, although she has to order *tea*, because it's more *authentic*—" He frowns at James. "Why? You've got something to tell me?"

Has Ming forgotten that he's the one who's called this meeting? Has he forgotten the phone call at the restaurant? But since Ming's older, James obeys. He leans forward, ready to speak, prepared to pour out all the events of the day before: Dagou at his laptop, adding names and addresses to his list of invitations to the Christmas party; the confrontation between Katherine and Brenda Wozicek; Alf's second disappearance; Dagou's broadcast.

But he finds himself unable to speak to Ming about Katherine or Brenda, or Alf. Or, for that matter, the phone call.

"Ba seems upset with Dagou," he says instead.

"That's because Dagou was his favorite. *Their* favorite. *Still* is."

It seems perverse, given how different his parents are, to imagine that any of their sons could be the favorite of them both. Yet, as usual, Ming speaks with authority, as if relating an established piece of history. Ming can remember. Six years older than James, he has had firsthand experience of things James will only hear about. James has the crushing sense that he was born too late to understand the real story of the Chaos—that the great passions, the bedrock promises and betrayals that formed the basis of whatever lies among the members of his family, have long since taken place. Does their father disdain Dagou because he once had such high hopes for him? Surely their mother doesn't feel that way.

Ming says, "Whatever else you can say about her, Ma is just as traditional as Dad. Dagou's their oldest son. He was supposed to be the crowning achievement of their lives in the U.S."

He takes a bite and chews calmly, observing James, assessing his reaction. James stares at the table.

"Think back thirty-five years," Ming says. "They've moved to this lousy town, they hate their lives, they hate the *villagers*, they hate the *weather*, they hate each *other*—but their oldest son? He's going to be a winner. You can tell by the way Ma talks about how Dagou was as a baby. The way her voice will sweeten. The way she says he was 'such a precious baby.' Her '*baobei*.' So bright. So *large*. So *talented*. Of *course* he would grow up and prove their lives were worth something. And Dagou *is* large. And smart. But he's turned out to be such a disappointment."

As usual, James cannot read Ming's eyes, flinty, fathomless, deliberately still. Ming seems even more detached than usual. Or has the scene with Katherine made James forget the exceptional nature of his middle brother's superpower: his impenetrability?

James picks up his fork, testing its weight. He spreads the dark green napkin on his lap. He slides his hand into the pouch of his hoodie, touches the piece of candy from the temple and a tiny slip of paper he's certain is an old fortune cookie fortune. Lamely he says, "He's really excited about the Christmas party. Maybe he's satisfied with how things are now. Who says he has to—"

"*Is* he satisfied? With the way he is now?"

The server arrives, carrying James's plate of eggs. "Can I get you anything else?" she asks perfunctorily.

Ming asks for another cup of coffee. When the server leaves, he murmurs, "I don't know, *can* you?"

James forks a bite of egg and crisp potatoes. It's delicious. He tries again. "Maybe he's working on something—not the party, but another, bigger project—and he'll show us someday, and he'll surprise us. Or he could be thinking of applying to culinary school—"

"Don't you understand, James, he's never going to change? It's too late for him. Too late."

Dagou's words come back to James—*It's as if none of us can bear to be in our present lives*—and James feels a sudden constriction in the area of his heart and lungs. Is it really true, he wonders, that there might be, in any human life, a certain window of time that matters more than any other? That he could be passing through it now as he sits holding a forkful of eggs, glimpsing it around him, as through the window of a train, and then leaving it behind, irretrievable, disappeared?

"I don't believe it," he says aloud. "It's impossible that a person could get to be thirty-three and have already lost his hope for the future."

"Almost thirty-four," Ming says. "Youth is over at thirty-four. By then you've lost the gleam and possibility of youth, and most Americans couldn't give a shit about you.

"There are only certain times in life when emergence is possible. The life strategy for children of immigrants, starting with nothing, is to use that time to build social, educational, and financial capital on which to ride out the rest of their lives. Dagou has blown it. He's now interested in salvaging his middle age by becoming a member of the petite bourgeoisie. But he doesn't have the capital to be a member of the petite bourgeoisie."

James sets down his fork. He feels, to his confusion, the pressure of tears against his lids, but Ming is checking his phone and doesn't notice. "It's no surprise," Ming says, putting down the phone. "Of course he would decide to settle down, to make 'a commitment to Haven.' He has most of what he needs here: a place to live, a job. People to love and hate."

"A job? But the restaurant isn't really his career. It's just where he's working now, until—" James's words catch in his throat.

"Don't be a snob, James," Ming says mildly. "Of course it's his career."

"What I mean"—James casts about—"is, Dagou must still have other plans."

"If you're as close to him as you think you are," says Ming, "you'd have noticed a while ago that he really *doesn't* have other plans. Oh, at first he used to say he was practicing to audition for the Cleveland Symphony Orchestra or whatever, and then for a while he was talking about moving back to New York, or to somewhere *warmer,* like *Austin,* and opening up a *record store.* But now, after six years, I think he's gotten used to the idea of being a villager, working at the restaurant. Dagou's given up. He's even found some kind of *pride* and *honor,* some *dignity* in giving up: he's telling himself he's helping Mom and Dad, he's their only truly filial son. He thinks the time he's putting into the restaurant is a kind of payment for the sacrifice Dad thinks Dad's made, something Dad thinks Dad deserves. But of course he can't settle for having the most filial piety: he wants Dad to recognize him as a *partner* in the business. What Dagou doesn't understand is that, even if he settles here, Dad is never going to let him get his hands on the restaurant *or* on the pile of cash he's no doubt hoarding. At least, not while he's alive."

James asks a question he has never thought about before. "Does Ba have a will?"

"He's too confident to make a will." Ming grins. "According to state law, everything will go to Ma when he's dead. Anyway, Ba would never *give* anything to Dagou."

"But Ba *needs* Dagou." As he speaks, James knows this is true. "And Dagou's been putting everything into the restaurant for six years."

"That was a self-destructive decision on his part. And he's nuts if he thought Gu Ling Zhu Chi was ever going to side with him. I told you, these spiritual types side with the cash. I get a New Year card from the abbess, every year since I started working in New York."

"*How's everything tasting?*" At the sound of the server's voice, they both start.

"I asked for a cup of coffee," Ming says.

When she's gone, they put their heads together again.

"He should have negotiated a deal with Dad in writing," Ming says. "It's his fault if he didn't."

"But it's in Ba's interest to keep Dagou in the business," James says. "How can Ba keep up his share of the cooking when he gets old? It'll have to be Dagou."

"He's not old yet. Just sixty-nine. Says he's in his prime. No major health problems, and still full of beans."

James struggles against his brother's relentlessness. "Then Dagou should get out of town. Dagou must escape!"

"If you haven't noticed," Ming says, "Dagou's not going anywhere."

For several long minutes, James works on his breakfast. Ming isn't eating anymore.

Fifty Million Dollars

"Three brothers," Ming says. "All three intelligent, promising, and strong, but born into unspoken disadvantages. One: born to immigrant parents, newly arrived in a new country, with nothing but their foreign names; two: born Asians in a community of white Americans; three: born with strong Asian features, genetic markers of their nothingness, slant-eyed, yellow-skinned, gook-faced—"

"Ming," James says. He speaks as gently as possible, because of the bitterness in his brother's voice; and below the bitterness, the self-hatred and the torment.

"*Let me finish.* Four: *born*, moreover, to a singular man who is despised by the community. The other Chinese immigrants hate him because he's depraved, unstable, a crook. The other business owners, mostly whites, hate him because they see him as a squalid laborer, an illiterate, a chink. And his white neighbors hate him because they think he's a usurper, greedy, and a chink. They would consider him a criminal, too, if they paid him the slightest bit of attention, but they've already dismissed him as a buffoon.

"And yet, despite being born to this man, the three sons grow up with looks, intelligence, and charisma—all this because their father, despite being a bullying and unscrupulous man, possesses a mysterious and undeniable force of character.

"He's a heathen. His long-suffering *wife* is a churchgoer—for years, she's been desperately faithful, a believer of the miracles of the Gospels—but he believes in nothing but the urgency of his will, the superiority of his seed. Why be concerned about the afterlife when you have three sons? All physically intact, intelligent, ready to carry on your legacy, your blood, your name? Why believe in eternal life if you're never going to die?

"Because he does not believe in *death*. Death for others, yes. But for himself? It's not happening to him." Ming glances up at James. "What?"

"Yes!" James exclaims, unable to take his eyes away from his brother. He envisions Ming presenting in a corporate boardroom, emanating all the strength, the gleam, of their father. He recalls Leo's reassuring voice, *I'm not going to die.*

Ming goes on.

"The first son is raised to be the savior of the family: the bringer of justice, the righteous achiever who will justify each year of labor and sacrifice, the primary motive for their living in this isolated town, the sanctifier of their miserable marriage, the human answer to the questions waking them up in the night: *Why am I here?* Why am I required to speak a language that can express only a shadow of my intelligence? Why, asks the father, do I squander my natural gifts by feeding people who don't appreciate the food? Or, in the case of the mother, why do I stay with this bully, why do I continue to have sex with this abominable man?

"And yet, despite this favoritism, perhaps *because* of it, the first son fails to thrive. He is a failure. In American terms, he has 'character flaws.' He 'lacks initiative.' He can't 'pull himself up by his bootstraps.' In truth, it's his parents who ruined him. He's spoiled, raised by them as an emperor in a society to which he's invisible. He hasn't been brought up to know *how* to be invisible, he expects everyone to see him and adore him. And so when he comes of age, and is catapulted into American society, he falls back to earth, crawls home to live, not a king now that his inadequacies have been exposed, but a servant. Instead of a savior he becomes nothing more than a dog to kick around."

Ming takes a deep breath.

"But this isn't the story of the father or even of the first son, that dissolute failure, but of the second son. Perhaps because they are already disappointed, the parents overlook the qualities of the second son, who was born possessing intelligence, and above all, *reason*. This advantage, a brain, has been given to no one else in his family. The rest of the family is all spleen and heart and guts—but no brain.

"This second son has never been the favorite. He doesn't own a single article of clothing that wasn't once worn by his older brother. He isn't given a single new toy. He's left alone.

"He has a rich fantasy life, this second son. Having no advantages at school or at home, he develops his ability to dream: in classes, where he excels; between classes, when he is bullied in the halls; and after classes, on the bus. Especially on the bus, where no one will sit next to him, where he's called names, and boys throw spitballs and worse at him, and girls giggle and hold their noses"—Ming mimics the gesture—"and enjoy watching this happen—on the bus, the second son envisions another self, impervious to all of this. Oh, he knows he's alone and surrounded by jeering children. But in his imagination, he's not being bullied. He's watching. He can't feel strangers' fingers twist the corners of his eyes, mocking him. He's invulnerable.

"In his mind, he stays on the bus as it goes past his house, past his neighborhood. The bus continues toward the edge of town, where the houses are larger and the cars sleeker. The second son imagines that the people he calls Ma and Ba are not his real parents. How could they be? Because in his heart of hearts he believes his real parents are white. They could be teachers, dentists, even mill workers. But they have craggy features, pink skin, and light eyes. They eat food as bland as their hair and skin color, and they gave birth to him, making him *generic*—this alone he desires, and wishes so much he believes it—possessing true potential, possessing the ability to truly become anyone and anything!

"Because America is not a democracy, it's not a place of opportunity, he knows, if you can't choose to be white. And because the second son despises these people he calls Ma and Ba, he doesn't obey or honor them; he breaks a fundamental tenet of Confucianism and one of the commandments as well—and oh, he's not so dumb, James, he knows this means he despises himself. Self-hatred is his meat and drink, self-hatred is the fuel of his emotional life, his life in the world, his soon-to-be adult life!

"And yet he thrives, James. He becomes an achiever. You may be wondering how he manages to thrive while burdened by so much self-hatred. How can he succeed, how can he *make it*, if he fundamentally doesn't think he should exist?

"It's because he manages to see above the wall of this disadvantage. Because self-hatred is as galvanizing as ambition. He develops the ability to see *above* his deprivation and to realize that, in reality, he's lucky. Because he isn't cherished, he's allowed to aim beyond his parents' petty goals. He can leave all of them behind.

"He earns a scholarship to an elite university on the East Coast, where, because of assumptions about his name, some believe he's the descendant, many times removed, of a foundational historical figure in his father's native country. Because of this misunderstanding, a lie of omission—for it can't be for any other reason, although they say it's for his *wit* and his *sangfroid*—he gets chosen to be a member of a finals club in his senior year. There he plays squash in their secret squash court and wears their not-so-secret tie. He eats the food cooked by their chef, a Chinese chef, "Mr. Louie," a man actually from Vietnam who has trained as a pastry chef in France, and he adopts his club mates' condescending gratitude for Mr. Louie's labor. While eating the meals of Mr. Louie's, he makes a number of friends whose connections enable him to find a job in 'the City,' where he goes with no illusions about owning it or *being* it. He knows 'the City' seduces people, dazzles them, and burns them up, but he knows not to believe and not to be betrayed. Every week he puts a sum of money away where nothing can touch it.

"The second son pays very careful attention to appearances. Because he knows that in our outer lives lie success. Because the balance sheet is a fingerprint of fortune's favor. Because only in the numerable, the countable, can you find certainty, and only in certainty can you find truth."

"That's not true at all," James hears his own voice butt in stubbornly. "Our inner selves exist. They're unique, and they're meaningful and mysterious, even if they are secret sometimes even from ourselves."

Ming nods. "You're thinking the second son is mistaken," he says.

"You may believe he has a special malady, a peculiar and uniquely individual malady of the soul. Certainly *he* thinks it's possible he doesn't have a soul. Although he doesn't think it makes sense to believe in such a thing. He's living in the twenty-first century."

"He has a soul," says James firmly.

"It's possible." Ming frowns. "And yet, who can be sure? He suspects—not believing, only suspecting—that that which feeds *something like the soul*—the *vestigial* soul—is missing, and perhaps as a result of this, he is inconsolable. Life, any kind of life, any small portion of any day in life, is unbearable for him. The little things of life others enjoy—choosing a new pair of sneakers, eating fancy donuts, going to see the opening of a superhero movie—are so baldly insignificant he can't find pleasure in them. The more annoying details of living—getting stuck in traffic, making conversation with some stranger on the plane—are intolerable. Ordinary life or extraordinary life, neither holds meaning; he's tried them both.

"Yes, there's still something missing. He isn't *certain* of this, because he knows that he's dealing with the invisible realm, but he believes something is missing, and it can't be found through ordinary means. He's tried sex. He's tried relationships. He steels himself against the rejection of his Asian features, makes repeated efforts until he finds white women open to dating him. And he's come to dread the moment when a woman says to him, 'We have so much in common.' Are her parents laborers? Do they spend their days working with their hands, physically carrying and slicing and arranging and transforming *food*, no less, at the order of others? Do her parents make a hundred meals a day for people who think of them as semi-human, a smiling Asian couple like a pair of garden gnomes?

"Were either of her parents, for as little as a year, a month, ten days, *five minutes*, ever in such straits—such financial and situational and familial arrears—that they decided to throw it all in, trade in what assets they had, and their identities as citizens in another world, to become aliens in this one?

"Has she grown up keenly observing, scrutinizing the children around her as if she were researching the most intricate sociology report: their clothes, their games, their television shows, their preferred methods of cruelty, their figures of speech? Has she sought invisibility among them, hoped they would not notice her, because the least bit of attention could transform into physical cruelty?

"He *has* had these parents. He *has* done these things. How else could he have become such a success at finding cover, speaking in code? The fact is, she's nothing like him. And if she thinks she *is* like him, then she doesn't know him at all. And if she doesn't know him, it follows that her proclamations of love are meaningless. It's almost with relief that he understands he can be alone again, can be desolate again. He breaks up with her, remembering that, for him, none of this has ever been feasible because his heart, such as it is, is inconsolable!"

Ming raises his hand, signaling the server.

"Ming," James says again. He has never known what his brother's relationships were like, and now that Ming is telling him, he can hardly bear to listen.

"I want a cup of a coffee! Did you hear me?" Ming shouts. "A cup of coffee!" When he turns to James, he is wearing their father's furious, starving stare.

James winces at his brother's expression. And yet, hasn't he always known this about Ming? That beneath his superiority and charisma, his hyper-competence, his high achievements, there existed this inconsolable self-hatred?

"He understands," says Ming, "that through all of this, he's been seeking solace from a source where it can't be found.

"He searches for a new answer to his questions. And he discovers it. It's hiding in plain sight; it's something he has known since childhood: that all of the stress and discomfort, the dullness and insignificance of his daily life, the only life he has—can all be undone by money. The more money he has, the more his troubles can be undone. Why has it never occurred to him before, despite his immersion in spreadsheets, in other peoples' monetary deals? Why has it not occurred to him that with a large sum of money, all of the problems in his life can be transformed into tiny, insignificant data points, and he can forever be free of them?"

"Really?" Is it possible? "How much money?"

"Fifty million dollars." Ming peers sharply at James. "Hear me out. Invested at only five percent, that equals an annual income of two-point-five million dollars. Fifty million dollars would mean complete freedom. And I wouldn't be the only Chinese man who's put my hopes into my 'Life Savings.'"

Ming signals to the server. "We should order dessert. Just so they know we're still paying customers. But James, little brother, if you can find or earn enough money, you never need to squeeze onto a crowded subway car. Never eat at a bad restaurant. Never worry about anything that can be solved by purchase or payment. I'm working on a deal in Phoenix that'll make my career, I'm aiming for managing director."

James asks cautiously, "What about dating an Asian woman?"

"You know I never date Asian women." Ming raises his hand. "Pie! That's what we need right now." The server approaches the table, and he raps out, "Two slices of pie. What do you have? Apple? German apple? All right. Listen, James," he says when the server is gone. "Here's why I invited you here to talk. Your good deed hasn't gone unpunished. The dying man you gave CPR to? He was carrying his Life Savings. In his luggage. His relatives somehow know the money has disappeared. Instead, they were given a gift of jia li jiao."

Their two pieces of pie arrive, warm, each with ice cream. Ming scrapes the ice cream off of his pie and sets it to the side. He fixes his heavy-browed gaze again on James.

"The man in Union Station was apparently carrying some money — not a huge sum of money, but quite a great deal for him. An EMT told his family about the nice boy who tried to help him. She remembers the boy's name, Chao. What on God's earth made you tell her your name?"

"I picked up his bag," James says. "I was going to check inside for his contact information but forgot about it. I'm almost positive I switched it from your rental into the Ford when you dropped me at the restaurant. Do you remember me putting it in the trunk?"

"It was dark," Ming says. "I was on the phone."

"Where is it? What do I do now?"

"Finders, keepers."

"I have to give the money back to the family."

"Then whatever you do, don't tell Dad. You need to find the bag before he does. Check at home. Check inside the Ford. He took the other car to work today."

James stares at his plate. "Ming, I'm scared."

"What's to be scared of?"

"What if it turns out that, entirely by accident, I stole someone's life savings?"

"Fair exchange for trying to save his life."

"What if Ba finds it first and won't—won't let me give it back?"

"Well, then, make sure you make Dad give you half." Ming shrugs. "Don't look at me. I'm getting out of here. I have a flight tonight. I want to beat the snow."

James remembers the snatches of Ming's conversations with O-Lan. "Is that what you and O-Lan were talking about?"

Ming appears startled, then impressed, as if he's surprised James can eavesdrop. "She warned me a storm was coming," he said. "She said if I left tonight, I might get stuck in the snow. I told her it was fine, I'd rent a car and drive back to New York if I have to. I don't want to be stuck here for Christmas."

"What're you doing for Christmas?"

"I'm going to take the day off. I just don't want to do it here."

"Do you hate it here that much?"

Ming looks directly into James with his implacable black eyes. James averts his gaze. Ming says lightly, "I've gotten over it. Dad and Mom, the house."

"The restaurant?"

"Especially the restaurant. I've gotten over the fact that we—you and me and Dagou—were raised to work at a restaurant in a hellhole in the middle of nowhere, that as children we had less than we deserved. I've gotten over that we were given no resources and no head start on the world. That we were, in fact, starting with a serious disadvantage. That we were bullied—look, I pay the bullies here to make dinner for me now! We have our intelligence, our talents and ambitions. We work hard. And if we come from a place to be ashamed of, *I got over it.*"

He pokes at the back end of his pie, breaking the crust with his fork. He takes a small bite. "And if I were you, I'd get over it, too," he says. "There's hope for you, if you give up on Dagou." He shakes his fork slightly at James. "Your ice cream is melting all over the place."

True enough, the ice cream has slid off of the pie. He spoons up a bit, but he's lost his appetite.

"They've made their choices; you're not responsible. You must live your life." Ming signals to the server. "Our meeting here is done," he says, pointing at the clock. "I've got the check. I've got to catch my plane, so you get going, kid."

James looks at the clock; his heart skips. It's after four. He's supposed to meet Alice in less than an hour. He has to take a shower; he has to change. "Thanks for dinner, Ming. Safe travels. Merry Christmas."

"Sure."

James leaves the diner and walks away, down the snowy street.

During his time at college, he's forgotten he never had to pay for a meal when one of his brothers was around. The habit is engrained in them: the older family member taking care of the younger. It goes all the way up to Leo and his restaurant. James has never thought to break free of it. Walking wearily toward his father's house, he wonders how this idea of family love—this hierarchy of responsibility and of obedience—has helped to create Big Leo's kingdom. The elder takes care of the younger, and in return, he is obeyed. The father, above all, obeyed.

In one of James's earliest memories, he is standing outside, in the backyard—close to this very street—with his mother. The backyard is surrounded by a fence—they have no dog, at that time, but they bought the house and put up this fence with the understanding that someday they would have one. He and his mother stand at the clothes-line under the afternoon sun, next to a basket of soap-smelling, cool wet laundry. *James, please count for me three clothespins.* Bending to the bucket of clothespins and counting one, two, four. Winnie, smiling down at him, taking the wooden clothespins from his hand. *One, two, three.* Ming can say everything he wants, but James knows that he himself was once, and is, specifically, very much loved.

Leo's Ford waits in the snow-covered driveway.

James stops for a moment by the car, distracted. There's something Ming told him to do. He can't remember; it'll come to him later. He lets himself into the house. Upstairs he showers, puts on a clean shirt, and goes back down to wait for Alice.

A Nice Chinese Boy

In the months since Winnie's departure, the first floor of the Chaos' house has taken on a resemblance to a catacomb. The pile of dog bones in the corner of the living room has grown to the size of a gopher mound. Most are long shank bones from the restaurant; here and there, oxtails gnawed to pointed disks poke from the pile like the snouts of giant bats. In the light cast over Leo's solitary chair, you can see a worn path around the clutter where the carpet has been burnished by the ceaseless energy of Alf. The dog trail runs to Leo's chair, around his piles of Chinese magazines and videotapes, and up the carpeted stairs.

James and Alice leave Leo's light on, over his chair. But they're careful not to turn on any other lights. The house has glass doors and many windows, making its first floor easily spied upon. They don't want to be seen from the outside.

They enter James's room. He looks self-consciously at his possessions. A nearby streetlamp casts a silvery glow over his poster of Bruce Lee. There's a little flock of trophies at least ten years old, from the year when he begged his parents to let him stay after school to play chess and soccer. Just for a year. Even then he sensed that something made him different from the other boys in the after-school program, but he did not understand what it was until the end of the year, when these activities were abruptly discontinued and he went back to the restaurant, where he folded napkins and ran errands. It was Ming, considered too smart-ass and lazy to work, who joined the math team, the track team—"anything to shut his mouth," said Leo, "Mr. Know-It-All." It was true Ming had spent a good deal of time telling their parents how they might save money, increase business, and update the place. He had talked endlessly about the newer restaurants near the big-box stores out on the edge of town. His sophomore year, when Ming officially left the restaurant, he became a school celebrity, earning larger and more legitimate trophies for his brainy prowess. James is glad that Alice won't see Ming's old room.

"It's messy," he says. Alice sits on the bed—*does this mean she wants to sleep with me?*—and James also sits, immediately, next to her, searching her profile. A glow from the window outlines her nose, her chin, and the curve of her cheek, but the eye is in shadow.

"The way he spoke about your mother at the Spiritual House," Alice says.

When James doesn't reply, Alice continues. "My mother thinks that was why your mother got away—I mean, why she wanted to live at the Spiritual House. Because she didn't want to be around him anymore."

"Maybe." She must be right. "Maybe she waited until I left for college. It *was* that, I think." How can he make his mind large enough to accommodate both his father and his mother? "But it was more than that," he says into the dark. "I think he was only a part of what she wanted to give up. There was something in herself."

"My mom says your mom needed a break."

"Something like a break," he says. "Maybe from possession, from possessiveness. She let go of the restaurant, my dad, the house, even Alf."

"My mom called it generous. Do you remember how your mom used to bring food, whenever you came to visit? After my father left, and before we started the store."

James remembers helping his mother haul the plastic bags, whenever they went to visit Fang and Alice's. "My parents fought about how my mom used to be," he says. "I guess you could call her extravagant.

There's this story my dad tells about how when they first came to Haven they were super-broke, but my mom still wanted to buy three kinds of meat for soup."

"What meats?"

"Pork and chicken, and fish, I think. She used to like to make a chicken soup with a ham bone and seafood. She used to love meat, especially pork." He pictures the greedy pucker at the corner of his mother's mouth. Maybe his mother and father are fundamentally alike, and their three sons are bound to be the same. Dagou, Ming, and himself: there is no hope for them.

"Do you think we'll ever talk about anything except our parents?"

"I don't know," James says truthfully. He thinks of what his father always said. "They gave up everything for us."

"Sometimes I don't think I know anyone else." Alice shifts position. "So much of what I know is tied up with my mother. And I wonder if that's bound to—to freeze some part of me in place."

James envisions a science project from fifth grade. The teacher brought into school five blue chrysalids of monarch butterflies. Four hatched on schedule, bravely pumping up their wings, and these were let go into the field. But the fifth butterfly got stuck somehow in development, so one of its wings would not stretch taut, but beat feebly back and forth like a sheet of crumpled paper.

"That won't happen," he says. "You've already changed, grown up a lot, since I left for school. You're beautiful." He's grateful she can't see him blushing.

"You went to college and left us," she says.

"I didn't mean to!"

"It's okay," she says, and her warm fingers curl around his. "We won't always be together."

"Why not?"

She doesn't answer his question. "My mom thinks you'll come home to Haven, to your mother."

"She thinks I'll be like Dagou?"

"No, she says you're a nice Chinese boy. She thinks you'll go to medical school and come back to Haven to be a doctor here. She says that out of all you brothers, you are the child who really loves his parents."

"That's harsh on Dagou."

"Yes. But everyone knows he has a hard time with your parents. My mother says, 'too much.'"

"Too much food, maybe. Dagou's planning like crazy for the Christmas party. He says if he pulls off a big bash, it'll impress Dad."

There is a tiny tick-tick of a pulse in the muscle at the base of Alice's thumb.

"Alice," he says. "Why do you think your mom would like it?" He stops, his mouth dry. "Why would she like you going out with me?"

"There are several reasons," says Alice, sounding a bit like Fang. "You're a nice boy, you're a hard worker, and you're going to be a doctor. And I think she thinks this would mean she won't be alone, that I won't ever leave Haven because you will c—"

"What do you mean, 'alone'? What about Fang, isn't he here? And *do* you want to leave Haven?"

"I never thought about it before, until talking to Ming at the Spiritual House. He says he knows some people in New York who hire artists part-time for dog-walking, housekeeping, babysitting."

James jiggles his knee. He wants to wrest the conversation back and start it again.

"Ming asked me if I had any interests," Alice says, "and I told him I was interested in art."

"Yeah," James says, now on solid conversational ground. "You're great at art."

"Do you want to have intercourse with me?"

James turns to look at her, but she's staring at the ceiling. He feels watery in all of his joints.

"You should know I've never kissed anyone," she continues, as if she thinks it sensible to lay out the facts. "What about you?"

"I made out with Shelley Achetel a lot. A long time ago, junior year. She used to come to the restaurant and we'd go into the office."

"Then what?"

"Then she graduated and moved to Waukegan. No one knows about it. Are you sure you want to?" He needs to ask her if she wants to make out with *him*, specifically, or if any boy will do.

"It was my idea."

"Alice," James says, "do you even like me that way?"

"I feel safe with you." She releases his hand and puts her warm fingers on either side of his face.

James leans toward her. For several minutes, he struggles to kiss her, but he can't relax. What if she doesn't like to be kissed the way Shelley Achetel taught him? What if she hates it? Is his tongue too big, does his breath reek of eggs and bacon? What if he is ruining her first kiss? She tugs on him lightly and the world goes sideways, and soft. He opens his eyes. They are lying on his comforter in a faint patch of light. Alice's eyes are closed and she is wearing a look of concentration. James tightens his hold on her. He is seized by a bolt of urgent, desperate desire. It's over in a moment.

"My fault," he says.

"What happened?"

"I came in my underwear," he says sheepishly. "It's over."

"We can try it again sometime."

In the bathroom, James wipes at the stickiness. He goes back to her, relieved they won't have to try again until the future. He slides an arm around her, and they lie back on the comforter, as naturally as if they always had.

"Alice," James says. "How did Dagou start running up credit?"

"I think I'm starting to feel desire now."

"You want me to kiss you?"

"No."

James waits for a moment or two, then repeats his question about

Dagou. "I want to know," he says earnestly, although this is, in many ways, a lie; he doesn't want to know—can't bear to know.

Alice often takes a while to answer factual questions. It's as if she is coming from far away, traveling through elaborate corridors of her mind, to reach the question; then, having reached it and registered it, returning to some interior room of her own, for the answer.

Finally, she says, "When Dagou took over, after your mom left, he started running up the bills. He had a plan to serve better food—fresher food, more authentic. But he couldn't get more money from your dad. And so he started paying more slowly, running up a tab. My mom let it go at first, mostly because Dagou didn't want her to tell your dad. But it's gotten to the point where we can't afford it."

"Is she going to tell my father?"

Alice is quiet for moment. Then, "Not yet. No. But she says she can't give Dagou any more credit."

"What do you think—" he stops, his chest tight.

"I want to make out again, James. Only this time, could you take off your shoes? It's dirty to wear your shoes on the bed."

James obeys. Alice lies back experimentally and lets him lean over her. He feels intense desire again, but this time the desire is less sexual in nature and more a kind hunger. He wants to consume her somehow—her eyes, stubbornly open this time, and her lips, now softer from being kissed, and the bridge of her curved nose, and the coarse strands that grow from the exact center of her hairline. He kisses all of these things. They kiss until they're both thirsty.

"I'll get a glass of water," James says.

"No, stay here."

It is some time before he becomes aware that the phone is ringing, in bouts, again and again. Someone is calling his father's landline over and over.

James stumbles out of bed and down the stairs. He grabs the wall phone and stands in the dark kitchen, surrounded by windows, peering out. It is a moment before he notices the tire tracks on the glittering, snowy driveway. Someone must have been to the house while he and Alice were upstairs. The Ford is gone.

"Hello?" His tongue feels thick and strange.

"James," says a woman's voice. It's Mary Wa. James's hair rumples all along the back of his neck. How can she know what he and Alice have been doing?

"James, where have you been? It almost eleven o'clock! We're texting and calling your cell phone for one hour! Your mom not good. We think it might be stroke. You hurry to hospital."

The Hawk and the Lure

It is Dagou who has taken the Ford Taurus. Has parked his truck and plow on the street, switched to the Ford, and driven off. He makes his first stop at the Spiritual House, where the usual quiet has deepened with the night. The temple's public face is hidden now; even the dogs are asleep. He follows a brown-robed nun down dim corridors to his mother's little room, where he sits helplessly on her wool blanket while two women pack a bag with clothing and supplies. Forgetting to say thanks, he grabs the bag and hurries back to the Ford. He restarts the engine, trundling, revving, and slipping over the unplowed roads toward the hospital.

Dagou parks in the almost-empty, snowy lot. He grabs the bag from the trunk and hurries through the automatic doors. Flowers—he must bring flowers. But the gift shop is closed. In the lobby, there are dozens of poinsettias clustered at the information desk, on end tables, and all around the Christmas tree. Dagou scoops up a large pot of scarlet blooms. He can't arrive both late and empty-handed. He makes his way into the hushed and darkened inner units. The night hospital is a netherworld, its general bustle reduced to the whoosh of machines, the beeping and flashing of monitors. It's the perfect time, everyone knows, for a human soul to slip away from notice, to hover for a moment before vanishing from this world.

He joins the small crowd waiting for news. His father and a few of

Winnie's friends stand outside the visitors' lounge, consulting anxiously with Corey Chen, a boy from Ming's high school class who has gone through medical school and is now doing a training shift in Haven. Of course, they're all dying to talk to Corey, a doctor, even though he's a baby doctor living at his mother's house for eight weeks. No one notices Dagou, or cares if his own mother might be dying. They're all busy looking up to Corey, except for Mary Wa, who, always practical, is looking to God. She's bent over her phone, texting the bad news to everyone and begging them all to pray.

Ken Fan, the diplomat, detaches himself from the group and comes to talk to him. "How are you doing?" He grips Dagou's arm. "Those flowers are beautiful! You're a good son."

"What took *you* so long?" It's Leo.

"You know where I was! You texted me to close up the restaurant!" Dagou sputters. No matter how much he's expecting his father's accusations, they're always unforeseen and outrageous. "I did everything you told me to! Then I had to drop the truck off at the house. Then I went to the Spiritual House to pack some clothes for Ma—"

Leo frowns. "You took my Ford?"

"I had to. The truck still had the plow on it."

Leo's face becomes impassive. Anyone who knew him would almost think he'd been transported to a poker game. Then, as if turning on a switch, he brings himself to the present. "I came straight here," he announces. "I got here first, but I stepped out for a smoke. It was only a smoke! I watched from outside. I saw a doctor walking by, like death, all in white. I couldn't believe he was coming for her. I thought he was coming for someone else! Some other person, a loser. I thought, She's too strong for them. She wouldn't do this to us. So instead of going inside, I had another cigarette. I was on my third, maybe, when the nurse came and found me. She had to repeat herself a lot, because all of a sudden I couldn't hear. I kept thinking, I left her in there to die alone. I left her in that horrible room to die alone."

"*Shh.* She's still alive." Ken Fan points to the door.

"Stop being so literal, you moron. Then when I went in to talk to her, this other nurse came and told me to leave! This ugly, menopausal—"

"How's she doing?" Dagou asks.

No one answers for a moment. "She's awake," Ken murmurs. "We've been letting her rest while we talk to Corey. He says your mother had a transient ischemic attack. At the Spiritual House. Mary was with her."

"Can I see her now?"

"Of course," Ken Fan says.

Leo Chao repeats, "I was here first." But everyone knows Winnie wouldn't want to see him. Ken Fan, his lips set, moves Leo off into the lounge.

Following the darkened, hushed corridor toward his mother's room, Dagou imagines a future menu for the night nurses. Winnie always said, "A little food never hurts." These nurses might like the basics: chicken and broccoli, shrimp with pea pods, garlic eggplant, and house special lo mein. (But for his mother he will concoct a special bone soup with a beaten egg white, seaweed for iron, and black wood ears for lowering the blood pressure.) The nurses might take special care of Winnie if he feeds them, chats them up, and flirts them up, because a little flirting never hurts; maybe respectful flirting will make them respond more quickly when she rings her call button in the wee hours. Maybe they'll turn a blind eye at mealtimes and let her have the special food he brings her. If he cooks and flirts attentively enough, Winnie will get well. She can't *not* get well. He urgently needs her candor and her company, the safekeeping of her warnings and instructions. Without her, he's lurching headlong into peril and uncertainty.

But when he sees his mother, Dagou shudders. He shoves the bag of clothes into the closet, gets on his knees, and tries to fit his big face into her bony shoulder. Hers is not the worst case, according to Corey Chen, but her force of life is flickering. He can sense it in her pale color and her fish-eyed expression. He isn't ready for this. It can't be possible that the future must come at such expense.

She murmurs something unintelligible. She's wearing an automated blood pressure cuff that makes mechanical sucking sounds. He leans closer.

"Christmas party—tomorrow," she mumbles.

"Not without you, Ma."

"You—you have to do it. You take it over." She must have forgotten Gu Ling Zhu Chi's warning.

He takes hold of her cool hand. "I'll make all of your favorite things," he promises. Is that a hint of a smile? "I'll make a red stew, and fish with ginger, everything I can get my hands on. For you."

She murmurs again, and he leans closer, ready to do anything she wants.

"Your father."

"Ma—"

"Apologize to him."

His breath seizes. Specks of color swim before her face. "Let's not talk about it. Ma, I can't apologize to him. You have to understand."

"Zhu Chi shuo le," Winnie mumbles.

"I can't. No matter what she says. I can't take it anymore. I don't know how you ever did."

This confession—or more like a plea for permission; no, an accusation—is followed by a long silence. Dagou stares at his mother's skinny chest, watching it rise and fall slightly under a white cotton blanket. He's waiting her out. With him, of all her sons, she never hides her grievances.

"You look down on me," she mutters at last.

"Of course not." He's struggling to keep the emotion out of his voice.

"You think I was . . . blinded by duty."

Dagou blinks through a sudden spurt of tears. "Yeah, I did. I guess I did. I guess I thought you should have left Dad a long time ago."

Winnie winces slightly. In her wince, he sees something both entirely worn out and also pained. It's like a shrug, an attempt to disregard the suffering that had driven her out of her own house. His chest heaves. He's sobbing now despite himself, with rage and shame and sorrow.

"How could you keep forgiving him?" he bawls.

"I didn't," Winnie says, louder now. At his display of misery, even now, sick, malfunctioning, she's back in control. "I didn't really forgive . . . I just—*tried*."

"Tell me, Ma. Tell me why you did that."

She's the last person on earth. Someday, if not now, she'll leave him for good. She'll fly away from him and never come back. She's getting ready, she's taking flight; but even now she turns to him the way a hawk, once trained and then escaped into the wild, will sometimes turn in the sky and plunge back to the lure. He knows he's the one who will never break free of her.

"You must love your father," she says.

Dagou shakes his head violently, trying not to listen.

But she persists. "If you don't love your father, how can you begin to love the world?"

He struggles to speak above the roar in his ears, above the hiss and push of her blood pressure cuff. "And if I can't begin to love my father," he asks, "or the world?"

"You still have to obey him."

"I can't. I just can't! The whole time we were growing up. You worked way too hard, you wrecked your health because he wanted to make money! You used to fight all the time—about him cheating. Don't tell me that was love."

But it was, it *was*. His mother loved his father, even though she had left him. Perhaps, he perceives, it was *why* she had left him. She'd fled her love. Or, if it wasn't love she felt for him, she was so fundamentally fused to him that her emotions weren't a necessary part of it. Something must have happened. Something had finally shaken even this foundational core—and she had fled.

"That was a long time ago," she whispers. "Forget about it now. None of it matters—forget about possession. I don't believe in it. When I die, I'm leaving everything to the Spiritual House."

"Of course it matters!" Dagou insists, ignoring the thought that she might die. "It matters to you. You set us an example. I remember everything!"

Winnie shuts her eyes.

"I'll get James," Dagou mutters. He's been calling James all night, but James hasn't picked up.

He presses his fiery lips against her forehead. He leaves her room and makes his way down the dim corridor of colorless light.

James is nowhere to be found. Corey Chen is now talking to Mary Wa and Fang. Leo is entertaining Ken Fan and the Chins. Leo is cheerful again, because even Winnie's grave illness can't long shake his unwavering self-dedication. Dagou can't bear to confront his father again. Still, he can't turn away. There's a smile playing around Leo's mouth. He's saying, "No need to worry about her! She'll find another job. If she needs help, she only has to come to me and ask!"

Who is he talking about? Is it O-Lan? Is it Lulu? Or is it the only other female employee, could it possibly be—surely, it cannot be—?

Leo turns to him, eyes bright with anticipation and a kind of hunger. "How's your mother?" he asks. "Is she happy now? After dragging us out here in the middle of the night, just to get a little attention?"

Dagou struggles against the light-headedness of sudden fury. "Shut up," he manages. "You have no right—"

Leo sniggers. "Look at you. Tears in your eyes!"

"You're the one who put her here!" His voice shakes. "You couldn't help tracking your shit into her temple! Even there, you had to torment her!'

"Mama's boy!" Leo sneers, his face grotesque and knowing.

Something shatters in Dagou's mind. He lunges at his father, fingers reaching for his windpipe. "You deserve to die! I hate you. I'm going to kill you!"

Leo is pushing back. He's a strong old man, but Dagou has not been working out for nothing. Dagou brings his father closer, tightens his grip on Leo's throat. A woman is shouting, giving orders, but Dagou can't listen. He feels his father's pulse: hot, human. Leo's eyes bulge. Then Dagou is jerked away. Someone has him in a headlock. It is Corey. Panting, he tries to fight off the men and nuns who close in upon him, seizing his head, his arms and shoulders. He is forced to let go.

All He Needs Is Money

Here is Dagou Chao, ten minutes later, steering his father's Ford down the vacant boulevard, away from the hospital, streetlights flashing by. For several blocks, the traffic lights holding green. Catching the edge of yellow, Dagou pulls through an empty intersection, past the Jiffy Lube, the Red Owl, the bright, empty Taco John's. Only the McDonald's is open. Dagou tightens his grip on the wheel. At the next light, full red, he screeches to a stop. He makes out, above the engine's hum, his own ragged gasps of panic. He puts the car into park, lets go of the steering wheel, and hammers his fists upon it, feeling the car bounce softly.

He hears the echo of his own voice: *I'm going to kill you!* An almost visible miasma slips into the car, an unfurling ribbon of acrid smoke. Darkness presses into him, pushing him against his will toward the dream, that very darkest dream, the source of violence and hope and absolute peace. It's always there these days, beckoning patiently. In his very worst moments, he has only to open the private chamber of consolation, comfort. He's descending into the basement of the restaurant. He's at the bottom of the stairs. His father is there, in the room. Dagou reaches inside.

He stabs blindly at the window switch, gulping in the frigid air that fills the car, clearing away the dream.

Who was Leo talking about, in the hospital? Was he talking about Brenda; is Brenda about to be in some kind of trouble?

At the next red light, Dagou pulls to a stop. The avenue is clear, but the cross street is badly plowed, blocked with pale-blue snow. He thinks with longing of this morning, plowing the parking lot. Nothing but fresh snow and work to be done.

Dagou turns around and drives, more slowly, away from the city. This time the McDonald's is closed. Near the entrance to the highway is a gas station and convenience store. The parking lot is empty but Dagou can see, in the lit store, a single clerk, a boy. Dagou pulls into the lot.

He walks into the empty store, hushed and humming with refrigeration units. The clerk sees him, pales slightly against the wall of cigarettes, tobacco tins, and liquor.

"A bottle of Jack Daniel's," Dagou mutters. "And give me"—he thinks desperately—"twenty Powerball tickets."

The clerk is older than he appeared from outside. He has a blackbird's wing of dark hair, empty flesh around his chin, and tiny old craterous acne scars. He brings down the bottle of Jack Daniel's and scans it.

"Have to ring them up separately," he whines. "Jack Daniel's is twenty-four dollars. Powerball tickets three dollars each."

Dagou gets out his credit card.

"Have to pay for the Powerball in cash."

The clerk rings up the Jack Daniel's. Dagou opens his wallet, adding the bills that tumble out. There are two fives, eight ones. He begins digging change out of his pockets. There are three dollars and ninety cents' worth of quarters and dimes. He recounts the quarters, hands shaking. His entire body is convulsing so violently that he bites his tongue and tastes the tang of blood.

"You don't got it," says the clerk, smirking.

Dagou doesn't answer.

The clerk leans over the counter. "Do. You. Understand. What—"

"Shut *up*!" Dagou thunders, and slams his fist on the counter. Coins jump. He counts the nickels in his sweaty palm. There are only six. His hands are still shaking as he totals up the pennies. He cleans out both pockets and takes out his wallet to make sure something hasn't dropped between the cards, folds. Miraculously, a quarter. Then the entire wad of papers shoots out of his hand and spills across the floor. The clerk is reaching under the counter to press a button. Dagou pushes the tickets back at him, grabs the edge of his jacket, scoops up bills, change, receipt into this makeshift pouch, and hurries off.

On his way out of the door, he runs smack into a stocky, older white woman. Change, bills, receipts fly in all directions. Recoiling, he tries to barrel past her, but she stands her ground. "Watch where you're going!" she says.

"Screw you," he mutters.

She hisses, "Have some manners, you big—"

"Fuck off!" he shouts, checking her with his left hip. There's the wheeling sensation of a heavy person losing balance, but he doesn't care. He takes off running. He reaches the Ford, slams the door, and guns away as fast as he can. As he turns onto the avenue, he catches a glimpse of the woman on the pavement, the clerk emerging from the door. He runs the red light at the intersection, turning left without a pause and then onto the highway, where he takes his place among the other cars, hoping to be invisible. They can't give chase; they don't have his license number. He remembers they have his credit card information. He remembers he left the Jack Daniel's behind.

Who can he talk to? Who is there to tell? Not his mother, who no longer has the strength. And despite her yearning toward detachment, she's still a Christian in her heart: "Love your father." Some Christian love, Ma, more like martyrdom! In the end, even *you* gave up, exhausted, and opted for peace. How can you tell me to keep trying, after what it did to you?

"I can't do it!" he hollers into the night.

If only he could talk to James. He pulls out his phone and dials. But the call goes immediately to voice mail. He hangs up. Anyway, how can he tell Snaggle? Snaggle looks up to him, Snaggle believes he is a man.

He makes a U-turn at the next intersection and heads back into the older neighborhoods, toward Letter City.

He thinks about the afternoon when Brenda appeared at the restaurant, drawn by the HELP WANTED sign or driven in by the rain. Brenda emerging out of a summer storm after more than a decade, her dripping dark curls clinging to her face, her wet lashes and blue-gray eyes gleaming with curiosity and hardness. Ordering only white rice and eating it with a spoon. Not even a fork, a spoon. From the kitchen, he stood noticing her lush body and those alive, oddly resistant eyes. Feeling an old tug of want, deep in his plumbing. The sight of her hurtled him back to senior year of high school. He'd been infatuated with her, but unsuccessful: a skinny Asian orchestra nerd while she was with the captain of the football team.

"You want that girl to eat your Chinese cock?" His father taunted him weeks later, after she was hired as server. "Why so slow? If you don't make a move, I will!"

They were already fucking. Turns out that was—is—not the real problem. In college, after a well-spent summer at the gym, he found a small rainbow of women willing to try him on. Quietly rebellious girls, raised in comfortable homes, happy to trade their good intentions for a big, exotic music major who knew how to make a very good cup of coffee. For a while, anyway. He's not afraid of white women, not the way his father thinks.

The problem was, and is, that he can't afford to keep her. "I want someone to take care of me," she's always said—she's never hidden it from him! "I want someone who can give me the life I always wanted." She has described, to him, that life. Membership at a country club. Two boys and a girl. A house with a four-car garage in the new development, Southlake, and a second home in Marcos Island. "I'm over sex," she's said to him. "I'm over sex for the sake of sex, that is. In two years, I'll be thirty-five. My goal is to secure a comfortable life through marriage."

"I understand," Dagou has said. He can't buy her a *first* home. He's blown most of his stash on the two months' rent and deposit for the penthouse. Unless Leo comes to reason and ups his salary, he won't be able to make any more rent.

How has he found himself enraptured, enthralled, by a woman to whom he's only an Asian fuck boy who can cook? It just happened. He let it happen. He loves her! His heart is a rose in bloom. For the last month, he's found it hard to look into her eyes when they're together. He's afraid of what she'll see. A man tortured by desire. Not a rich man, not even a good man; only a man who is, for her, willing to entirely give over his life.

The windows of her house are dark and rimmed with snow. The car is not in the driveway. She's out tonight, with a group of friends from high school, home for Christmas. He can see the faint tracks where she pulled out of the driveway and into the street. The city plows haven't touched her street for days—this misbegotten neighborhood is not a priority.

Dagou pulls over and jumps out of the Ford. He stands on the rickety front porch and knocks. Rings the bell. Knocks again. Paces. His feet grow numb with cold. What now? He frowns at Brenda's snowy driveway, recalls the shovel in the Ford. With relief, he heads back to the car and pops the trunk, paying no attention to the various objects there, and grabs the shovel. He wedges the backward blade into the trampled snow on the top step and goes to work.

He digs out the steps and the front path, starts on the driveway. It's a cracked, narrow driveway, and the sharp-edged blade gets stuck on chunks of frozen weeds remaining from the summer. Her house is filled with warm colors, soft cushions, and glowing lamps—she's even painted inside—but her awful landlord lets the property go to hell. Well, she won't have to put up with it much longer. For a moment he allows himself to envision the two of them pressed up against each other in the gleaming penthouse, gazing out a wall of windows at Lake Haven. If he can only make the rent!

With his mind eight floors over Lakeside, heaving snow with the force of a train, Dagou huffs with panic and desire. The shovel slams into a crack, jarring his hands. Dagou spins the shovel over frantically and hacks out a section of impacted snow near the corner of the apron.

Seventy years old! If *only* he would retire, then their problems might be solved. But Dagou knows, more than anyone, that his father is beyond mortal time.

Headlights prick his eyes. Her snowy car turns into the shoveled driveway. The lights go off, the door opens, and she steps out.

She looks tired, and not happy, and although she doesn't seem disgusted by his sweaty presence there in her driveway, her eyes don't light up when she sees him. There's a single poinsettia flower pushed into the top buttonhole of her coat. "That's nice," he says. "Where did you get it?"

"I went to fill the tank," she says. "I bumped into Ken Fan. He told me about your mother. I'm sorry, Dagou."

Dagou doesn't want to talk about his mother now. "I went to see her. I can't think about it. Listen, my Dad said something tonight, at the hospital, and it made me wonder if he was talking about you. About you and the restaurant. Are you thinking of quitting your job? I was going to just text you but I thought I would come by and—"

"Shovel out my driveway?" Is it a flicker of affection on her face? Or concern, or merely distraction? "No," she says finally. "I'm not leaving my job. Not yet. But, Dagou, I'm so tired of being broke. Thank God somebody bought the drinks tonight. For all of us."

Rounds of mixed drinks for half a dozen people, hundreds of dollars. It *must* be an old flame, home for Christmas. "I'm going to help!" he says. "Give me more time."

Her smile is a little sad. She does not invite him into the house.

Driving away, Dagou agonizes. Hands clutching the wheel, squinting through the tunneling drifts. Tires churning in the snow; around the car, galaxies whirling. Someone was there tonight. Someone was trying to impress her in front of all her friends. Undoubtedly a man, a competitor. He must hold on to her. He must show her who he is, what he can do. And there's a chance for him, tomorrow, at the Christmas party. All he needs is cash.

Dagou parks the car behind the darkened restaurant. He gallops up the snow-filled stairs, slipping, flailing, almost falling. His key pierces the keyhole. He throws open the door and races through the kitchen, leaving big wet tracks on the floor. He darts into the bedroom, kneels at the foot of the king-sized bed, and digs cold hands under the corner of the faux-fur. There it is, the remainder of his secret stash. It's a stone in his gut, a secret kept even from James. No one knows, except for Katherine.

He'll spend it all tomorrow on the Christmas party. He'll show her at that crucial and momentous event. He'll show the whole community—Brenda, his father—what a man he can be. Everyone will see that he, Dagou Chao, is the true source of generosity, of power, of magnificence. Kneeling over the remainder of his stash, Dagou understands he must plan the Greatest Christmas Party anyone has ever seen.

DECEMBER 24

A Simple Winter Meal

IT'S TEN PAST midnight. Dagou finds his notebook and scans his entries. *A perfect, simple winter meal in honor of our closest friends.*

How many have said they're coming? There are the Was, of course—and well, Katherine, because his mother would insist on her—and also Brenda. Brenda must not work that night, but be a guest. Then there are Mr. and Mrs. Chin and their daughters, and Mr. and Mrs. Fan—maybe six more. Plus the hangers-on, like Jerry Stern. Of course they're coming; they always come, they would be terribly hurt if they ever learned about the party after the fact. Winnie loves outsiders. She believes in reaching out. That makes twenty people. He must invite more of Winnie's friends, make it more like two dozen, more like thirty. And it will be important to include enough food for a few extras, just in case—imagine if they ran out of food. Imagine if a stranger came, assuming the restaurant was open, and found the place lit up and everyone inside. Would it be right to turn away a hungry stranger on Christmas Eve? To turn away an angel in disguise?

So, dinner for thirty-five, forty people. Dagou flips through his notebook. All of his earlier plans now are meager and uninteresting, except for the fresh ducks brining in the refrigerator. Brenda has never eaten Peking duck. He imagines her biting into the finest, most crackling chestnut skin. Enjoying, in addition, a few banquet plates to keep it company. Cold chicken, and the hollow-hearted greens. Plus the stew he promised Winnie. And chicken. He's already reserved the chicken, but his mother believes in combining flavors, she believes in many meats. He has promised her seafood—he can go to the seafood truck. For shrimp to accompany. There must be a shrimp dish—shrimp with mounds of diced ginger and scallions, or salted shrimp in the shell—or both, perhaps. Also, a second seafood dish. To serve only shrimp would be petty and small. Shrimp themselves, so very small. What else? Fish, of course—he's been planning to have fish all along. Soft-shell crab? He imagines how Brenda will glow when he serves platter after platter of soft-shell crab. Of course, she's never tasted it—he knows this because every bit of Chinese food she's ever eaten came from his own hands. He imagines her crunching through the crisp shell. But soft-shell crab isn't in season. He'll be forced to rely on the seafood truck. Although it's not from lack of generosity that they won't have crab, but because he has high standards and will not, simply won't, use frozen soft-shell crab. Scallops, then. Very large, tender scallops. Will scallops be in season? There's a moment—only a few weeks—when they're not available, in the winter. What if they're not available?

Who will work the kitchen, with JJ and Lulu in California? James will help. O-Lan will help. And there must be someone else. Leo won't set foot in the restaurant until the party. He must only be impressed. Of course, impressing Leo will require an extreme purchase of liquor. Dagou will figure it out. He knows it'll work out. Even if it requires desperate measures. It will, it must be done. At this thought, a rushing, cool relief reaches to his fingertips.

At one a.m., he broadcasts the news on FM 88.8. "I'm going to throw the Greatest Christmas Party ever! Six-thirty on Christmas Eve, that's tomorrow, everyone's invited! There'll be liquor and libations! There'll be unimaginable Chinese specialties! There'll be high spirits and fellowship and good cheer!"

He spends the rest of the night downstairs in the restaurant kitchen, preparing a strategy for every dish. Checking on the duck. Making quantities of sweet bean paste. His family thinks he's lazy and disorganized; they don't know what he can be like when he's inspired. Every dish will show the community that Dagou is the bigger man and the most gifted cook: stronger, more generous, more enterprising, more forward-facing, the future of the Haven Chao dynasty. For those who notice such things and who have loyalty to give, he'll be stronger. For those who come only for free food, he'll provide better.

Shortly before the sun is up, he posts a hand-lettered sign on the restaurant door: CLOSED FOR PRIVATE PARTY. Closing the restaurant is the kind of thing Leo Chao never approved unless it was his idea and his party. Dagou tapes the sign with duct tape.

He removes the plow from his Toyota, swaps the Ford for his truck, and drives from one business to the next. In his mind, he's already in the kitchen, making dinner. He's not thinking much about the proprietors he's speaking to, or what they say, or the money he spends.

At six a.m., he's knocking at the front door of the Shire poultry farm, where everyone has been awake for at least an hour. Dagou pays with a hundred-dollar bill for eight chickens. He's at the local food coop when the door opens at seven a.m. He purchases, with cash, every stick of asparagus they have, and a quantity of oranges besides. Back at the Fine Chao, he makes gallons of chicken broth. The kitchen windows steam; a delicious smell of broth escapes into the wintry morning when he leaves the restaurant for more shopping.

He's waiting at the door when Mary Wa arrives to open up the Oriental Food Mart. He shoulders past her into the store with barely a hello. He runs back and forth, consulting his list and piling vegetables on the counter. He piles up baby bok choy, plus package after blocks of noodles, a number of boxes from the freezer section, blocks of pressed tofu, giant bottles of sweet fermented rice concentrate, and pounds of red beans. It's enough to fill two grocery carts.

"I need you to call the seafood truck," Dagou says, as he returns to the counter moments later, his arms filled with ginger.

"They won't come out this far," Mary says. The truck, which drives fresh seafood up from Louisiana, is generally intercepted in Chicago.

"*Make* them come this far."

"It's not worth the money to them," she says.

"I'll make it worth the money," Dagou growls, and opens his backpack. From this he draws forth a large stack of bills. Mary Wa's eyes bulge. She can see inside the backpack a half-drunk bottle and still more money.

"Where did you get all that cash, you unfilial child?"

"None of your business, Ma Wa," Dagou says. "I want to buy five pounds of fresh shrimp with the heads on, ten pounds with the heads off. I want ten live lobsters, three pounds of crab, five pounds of jellyfish, all you have of sharks' fins, and"—he pauses, peering at the ceiling—"abalone? I suppose they won't have the abalone. Find out, and if she does, get it for me. I need 'em to come out here now. I need it all by about one o'clock at the latest." He pauses again. "Also, don't tell her it's for me. I don't want my father to know about this."

"Dagou, I'm worried you are heading for big trouble," Mary Wa says, as she goes to the back room.

"That's none of your business," he calls after her.

As Dagou storms out, he stops in front of Alice, who has taken her seat at the stool, a little pale and sleepy. Dagou looks her over. She's small-breasted, hook-nosed, with long arms and legs, long fingers, and a long, gracefully curved neck. Not bad. "My brother wants to sleep with you," he says. "You should make him happy." He sees her little mouth open, her features loosen in surprise. He shoots her a lewd grin and leaves the store.

The cab of the Toyota gives off a strong odor that reminds him of his father: the smell of alcohol and stale sweat. He remembers, without meaning to, Leo Chao in his loose working clothes, arms swinging at his sides, shouldering his way into the restaurant after a night away from home; Leo counting bills with his outsized hands.

He texts Brenda, to remind her that the party is at six-thirty.

From the Was', he drives straight to the American liquor store. He walks in and orders cases of wine, beer, gin, vodka, mixers, and more whiskey, paying in cash.

"No, on second thought, double the liquor. I want to get everybody drunk," he says to the proprietor, who helps him move case after case into the truck (already loaded with groceries from the Was', plus oranges, lemons, limes, and maraschino cherries). "I want to get everyone especially drunk. But not as drunk as I want to get myself. You're invited. Can you come?"

"I'm working late tonight," says the proprietor. "Holidays. Sorry. Hope everyone has a good time. Merry Christmas."

Late in the morning, Dagou signs in at the hospital as a visitor to Winnie Chao, bringing a thermos of broth with seaweed and a beaten egg white, a bouquet of balloons, and a Christmas card. Winnie's voice is stronger; she has more color in her face. She beams as Dagou gives her a full report about his plans for the party. He tells her he's invited his father. He's done it indirectly, taping an invitation to the front door at the house. He wouldn't disobey his mother, but he won't speak to Leo.

Back in the truck, he texts Brenda for the second time: *Party is at six-thirty. Don't forget!*

Early in the afternoon, two of the Skaer nephews and their friends, Tyrone and Freedy Davis, arrive at the restaurant with a largish package wrapped in butcher paper. He and James greet them at the door.

"What's this?"

Cody Skaer shrugs. "It's ten pounds of stew meat. My dad heard on the radio that you're having a big party. He's sending this meat along, compliments of the family."

At his side, James flinches. "Dagou," he whispers, "Ming says—"

Dagou notices Tyrone and Freedy examining the restaurant menu. Ming has always said the Skaers were racist bullies, but Ming has always been paranoid. Can the Skaers really be racists if they have Black friends? Dagou unwraps the package. "Mutton!" he says. A gift from an unexpected source; the generosity and forgivingness of Christmastime. This would be the red stew. He asks James to chop a lot of ginger and five bunches of scallions to go with it. He tells Cody, "You're all invited to the party!" He doesn't believe the Skaers will come—he knows that they, mysteriously, hold something against him. But he wants to make sure they know they're invited.

He prepares some takeout to send with the nephews back to Trey Skaer: a quart of wonton soup, a large order of chicken with broccoli, and a large order of orange beef.

Tyrone lingers near the kitchen, observing with curiosity the crowded counters, the enormous, steaming pots of broth. "What's all this for?"

"It's gonna be the best meal ever," Dagou says. "You like Chinese food?"

"My family moved here from Houston. Lots of Chinese food. I love it."

"Are you interested in restaurants?"

"I'm going into the business."

Perfect. "Listen, would you and your brother want to come back? Could I hire you to help with the party? I'll pay you, and I'll show you some tips, fifteen dollars an hour, each. Cash."

In half an hour Tyrone and Freedy are back. Dagou gives them aprons and sets them to chopping vegetables.

For the third time, he texts Brenda. *Did you get my texts?*

After several minutes, his phone beeps with a reply. He has to read the message twice before he can comprehend the words.

Sorry, Eric Braun has unexpectedly come back to town. Hope it's okay for me to bring him to the party.

The Greatest Christmas Party Ever

As far as parties are concerned, there are many ways to greatness. There's greatness of style, of setting, of occasion, and of company. There's greatness of food. But behind the most magnificent parties—the spirit, the festivity, the celebration, and the meal—there must beat a generous heart. Dagou's skills in the kitchen are a gift from God. But his heart is Winnie's. Her lavishness, her extravagance flowing from a need to share, to please, and to heal.

Now, as the first guests enter laden with Bibles and wrapped presents, they gaze about and gasp; the small dining room has been transformed by Katherine into a Christmas gift. Tiny lights outline the ceiling and the walls. The red tablecloths sparkle with glitter and glow with lit centerpieces. The faded scarlet lamps are delicately garlanded with ribbons and real holly berries. Suffusing the scene is a mouthwatering blend of succulent and savory smells. Proudly, Katherine welcomes everyone by name. Dagou has given her the role of hostess. He's in the kitchen, setting out the courses and preparing for the final, torrid stir-fries; neither he nor James can long be spared to stand at the door. Brenda is nowhere in sight.

Katherine shows the guests where to put their Christmas presents. She seats them near the twinkling fir tree. Everyone smiles and nods, trying to make their love palpable, making sure she feels the warmth of belonging. Mary Wa presses a wrapped gift into her hands. This is something Winnie used to do—in the years before she renounced possessions, Winnie always gave Katherine a gift at the party.

"Thank you," Katherine says, tears pricking her eyes.

When they are settled, Mary Wa puts on her reading spectacles and opens her Bible.

"'At one time,'" she begins, in Mandarin, "'we too were foolish, disobedient, deceived, and enslaved by all kinds of passions and pleasures. We lived in malice and envy, being hated and hating one another.'"

"'But when the kindness and love of God our Savior appeared,'" Ken Fan continues, "'he saved us, not because of righteous things we had done, but because of his mercy.'"

"'He saved us,'" reads Lynn's mother, "'through the washing of rebirth and renewal by the Holy Spirit, whom he poured out on us generously through Jesus Christ our Savior, so that, having been justified by his grace, we might become heirs having the hope of eternal life.'"

Katherine wipes her eyes. Returning to the door, she greets the Chens and their son, Corey, the doctor who helped care for Winnie the night before; he's brought along a plus-one, a young man from Taipei. Next to arrive are the latest newcomers, an architect with his American wife, who smiles at Katherine over the heads of their brown-haired children. Fang and Alice arrive, dressed up as Christmas elves, Alice in a loose-fitting green velvet thrift-store tunic, and Fang in a red-and-green-striped hat.

James darts over to stand near Alice for a moment, then rushes off to fetch her a Sprite with an orange slice and a maraschino cherry.

"Thanks, James," says Alice. Together, they duck into the hall. Near the office, she kisses him.

"Alice," James begins, his heart knocking against his apron, "tonight, after the party, do you want to—"

"Ho, ho, ho! Merrrrrrrry Christmas!"

Leo Chao tromps in through the back door, crowned in the Santa Claus hat he has worn every year for as long as everyone can remember. Removing his coat, he's resplendent in an eye-watering lime-green and scarlet plaid Christmas sweater, decorated with small, obnoxiously jingling bells. Following him are his winter poker buddies, three men in Carhartt jackets smelling of stale sweat and cold. Seeing James with Alice, Leo slaps James, hard, on the back. "Go get it, son!" Then he heads to the bar, where he introduces his buddies to Jerry Stern, and to Jerry's plus-one, Maud Marcus, a woman running for town council. The poker friends can't stay for dinner because they have Christmas Eve at home, but they take stools at the bar, laconic and content.

Back in the dining room, Katherine checks her phone. "It's Ming again," she tells Mary. Ming has been texting her all afternoon. The blizzard joined to a nor'easter on the previous night, creating a pile-up of flight delays. She's told everyone the story of Ming's texts over the last twenty-four hours: how long he sat on the plane, how many times the pilot changed the length of the delay. The number of times the plane circled before diverting to another city. After landing in Hartford, Ming rented a car, and all day he's been driving back to Wisconsin, driving through the snow. He's changed his mind; he wants to be in Haven, he wants to see their mother. He wants to attend the party. Mary tells Katherine that the party is going to last late into the night, and Ming might still make it, but they both know he won't.

Dagou, in a bright red apron, emerges from the kitchen and urges the guests to be seated. He checks each section of the room: the pitcher of water for the readers, who have moved on from Titus to Matthew; the supply of whiskey for the farmers at the bar; and, especially, the door. He's glaring at the door when it opens to reveal Brenda with a tall, good-looking, dark-haired man. Brenda makes contact with Dagou's glare. Then she introduces everyone to Eric Braun.

There's a lull in all conversations, even the reading, as everyone inspects Eric. With his square jaw and penetrating brown eyes, the man is unmistakably a rival to Dagou. Dagou turns and stalks back into the kitchen.

For an hour, there's nothing to eat but shrimp chips with soda, beer, wine, and liquor of every type procurable in Haven. This is Dagou's social strategy: to get everybody drunk; and although Leo, Lynn's father, and the poker friends are the only true drinkers among them, the sheer amount and variety of alcohol inspires everyone to get tipsier than usual. Around six-thirty, the farmers, somewhat reluctantly, return home to their own family celebrations. Leo tends bar. In the kitchen, O-Lan frenetically rolls out pancakes for the duck, and Dagou cooks them in two pans. James sneaks out, searching for Alice. Near the tree, Katherine is encouraging the new half-Asian children, who have been silently watching, to join in with the other children. At last, they put down their Sprites and enter the ruckus. It's a moment before James spots Alice. She's sitting with her brother and Lynn and with Brenda and her guest, near the corner. James waves at her, making his way around the guests toward her table. Pink spots come into her cheeks.

As James reaches the table, Alice is asking Lynn how her journalism class is going.

"Horrible." Lynn shakes her head. She explains she's not lively or assertive enough to reach out to other human beings. "I wake up filled with dread," she says, "whenever I'm supposed to conduct an interview, make a deadline, or turn in an article. My parents were right. I'll never make it as a journalist."

Fang points at her with a shrimp chip. "It's impossible to write about the truth from within an institution. You say you can't do journalism, but in reality you can't figure out how to get an A."

"But I have to get an A," Lynn says. "Getting an A is the first and only step. I'm a terrible grade-grubber."

"Ice!" Leo yells, signaling to James from the bar. "More ice!"

James leaves Fang, Lynn, and Alice. He makes his way down to the basement, the party tumult dimming, until he reaches the freezer room and there's only a faint sound of cheering from above.

Entering the freezer, he reaches for the string to the single bulb, and the room jumps brightly into place around him. It's an ancient unit, and one James himself rarely enters. He hasn't been inside for almost a year. There are brick walls, and a crumbling brick layer along one side that's only partially repaired and repainted; there are old metal racks where his father stores the meat, wrapped in variously shaped packages, and miscellaneous frozen foods he doesn't recognize. There's the extra ice bin in the corner, and a veritable army of vodka bottles. James shivers, reminded of Dagou's broadcast. He leaves the door open, and, as he has been taught, he checks for the exit key before going farther into the room. There it is, on its shelf. It's a large brass key with a square head. He hurries to the bin and seizes two bags of ice, hauls them upstairs to the bar, where Leo welcomes them with a nod.

In the kitchen, Dagou checks the clock. It's six-fifty p.m., time for the first course: shrimp with heads on, spinach and pressed tofu, sea cucumber, cold jellyfish. Over at Brenda's table—Dagou avoids looking at Eric, but he can't help seeing Brenda—she waves to him, points at the kitchen, but he shakes his head. She's not allowed to help.

He's given James a muttered rundown of the facts: Eric Braun was captain of the football team in high school, when he and Brenda were involved. Homecoming king, the big man on campus, always an asshole. He went to college at Northwestern, majored in business, and made a lot of money in a northern suburb selling commercial real estate. He also married, had a son, and divorced. He's returned to Haven for Christmas, and in the last twenty-four hours he's taken Brenda out for drinks and lunch. Now he's her guest at the party.

Dagou avoids Brenda's eyes as he and James, Freedy, and Tyrone pass around small plates of tender cold chicken, and braised gluten.

At seven-fifteen, asparagus, pork belly, and soup with seafood dumplings.

Now comes the Peking duck. Dagou has directed a man or woman in each group of six to carve the ducks, which are served properly with scallions, plum sauce, and one pancake per person. The dish takes a long time to serve, but each duck is perfectly tender and the skin crisp under its mahogany gloss.

"Let me help!" Brenda pipes up, grabbing James's sleeve.

James glances at Dagou; Dagou shakes his head. James has been instructed to make sure Brenda does no work tonight.

James makes his way to Brenda's table and passes on his instructions. For a fleeting moment, watching Brenda's face, James is certain Dagou isn't letting her help not only because she's a guest of honor, but because she has hurt him.

What does Dagou have in mind? James wonders. He can't tell what Brenda's thinking or feeling, but he notices she's wearing more lipstick and eye makeup than usual. Is it possible, James wonders, that Dagou knows this one thing about Brenda she doesn't know about herself: That she actually *wants* to work? Loves the swinging doors, the hectic insanity of the kitchen? Loves wooing, cajoling, and pleasing the customers?

Near Eric Braun, Alice sits dreamily over an untouched plate of Peking duck. James brings pancakes, but she doesn't want any. He promises her the most mouthwatering dish will be a mutton stew.

"No thanks," Alice says. "I've decided to be a vegetarian."

"It's eat or be eaten," says Lynn. "Mutton stew, yum."

Fang turns to her, grins, and shakes his head in some mysterious warning.

Eric Braun seems confused by their conversation and this restaurant: by its crowdedness and unusual smells, by its cacophonous conversations, many in a language he doesn't know, by so many black heads, slanted eyes. Sitting next to Brenda, he peers around the room and straightens slightly, defensively, as though he's surrounded by goblins. It's not until Fang engages him on the subject of alternate currencies that Eric begins to relax into his cups. James watches very closely. There it is, in Brenda's posture: relief. James doesn't know how he knows this—what unfolding instinct has enabled him to read her. But he's sure of it. Brenda excuses herself. She stands up, takes off her cardigan, and moves toward the kitchen in her snugly fitting red dress. She's going to serve, permitted or no.

It's a simple stir-fry of hollow-hearted vegetable, dressed up slightly with tiny dried shrimps.

"Ren," shouts Dagou, from halfway across the room. Together, he and James, Tyrone, and Freedy have finished lugging out tureens of soup. "You don't help tonight. You're a guest of honor!"

Brenda straightens up, vibrant, gorgeous. "Of course I want to help," she cries. "It's an honor to help such a marvelous chef. This meal is an achievement!"

And as the words leave her mouth, everyone knows what she says is true. Their bodies are lighter, their souls expanded. It is a breathtaking meal created by a truly gifted chef, a man who has reached for and has grasped the power of his life's possibility. They will remember it forever.

Dagou is elated. He shines like the sun. Beams of happiness and sweat rise visibly from his collar. For a moment, just long enough to snap a photo, he and Brenda glow at one another.

"Chip off the old block!" yells Leo Chao. "Look, I can sit in my own restaurant, do nothing, and get served banquet food by a beautiful woman!"

Dagou ignores this. He, James, and Brenda retreat to work on the next course. Behind the kitchen doors, Dagou reaches, leans toward her. James tries not to listen, but his brother has no interest in keeping his feelings a secret.

"This party is really for you. You're a guest of the family," Dagou exclaims. "I wanted it all for you. Are you going to get together with that bozo, or what?"

Smiling, Brenda shakes her head.

He nudges her toward the dining room. But neither of them moves; they stand holding hands. Something's burning on the stove. When James passes them a moment later, carrying extra spoons, he backs off slightly from their radiance. They look as if they are aflame with beauty. He can almost see the stream of happiness flowing through them. Dagou beaming, handsome. Brenda a torch of dazzling light.

They wait until the guests have polished off the greens and the entire soup dish. Then they collect themselves in time to serve the red stew.

This is the mutton, deep and spicy, meat slipping from the bones, so tender and so flavorful that everyone wants seconds. It's the meat the Skaers delivered, and although they'd sent a generous amount, there isn't quite as much of it as there is of everything else.

Eric Braun is entirely taken by the mutton dish. He's consumed a good-sized serving and now he reaches with his fork over to Brenda's plate. He's the only person at his table who is eating with a fork. Carelessly, Brenda pushes her own portion to his plate with chopsticks. Then she stacks the platters, making space on the table for the crispy noodles covered lavishly with seafood.

The Bibles have long been put away. Near the Christmas tree, Mrs. Chin, her anxiety over Lynn's journalistic ambitions forgotten, is making a video to send to Winnie, while, in the corner, Lynn herself is deep in conversation with Fang about whether to switch her major back to data science. Corey's mother is taking a photograph of Corey and his plus-one under the mistletoe, and Katherine is texting at top speed. In the middle of this, James becomes aware of a woman in the corner, talking to a couple of nuns. She's looks Chinese American, around Dagou's age; she's a plump woman wearing red-rimmed glasses, her hair cut into bangs across her forehead. ". . . my grandfather, my junior year abroad," James hears her say, "and we kept in touch." The nuns are calmly nodding. She finishes speaking, rises, heads in the direction of the bathroom.

"Do you know who that is?" he asks his brother, pointing.

Dagou shrugs. "No idea. A stranger. A stranger appears! She must have heard the invite on the radio." He slaps James on the back. James grins. But he puzzles over the unknown woman. He has the sense he's met her somewhere before. While collecting another round of empty plates, he sees her looking over at him and he hurries into the kitchen. When he comes out, she's talking to Mary Wa.

"I'm a vegetarian," Alice says again, when Fang points out she's eaten no meat.

"May I get anything else for you?" James asks. "We made some plain dishes for the people from the Spiritual House." He leans close to her, ostensibly so she can hear him, but actually because he wishes to be near. He speaks into her ear. "After the party, should I come over to your house?"

"Yes, please," Alice says.

Now the room is filled with warmth and light.

Dagou is bringing out bottles of champagne. He leads Brenda to her seat, gives her a little bow, and uncorks a bottle for her.

On the other side of the room, Leo Chao in his Santa Claus hat has sent the stranger back to the nuns' table, dismissing her questions with a few loud, cheerful remarks. He's now popping corks and passing out bottles, talking and laughing. He stands, straightens, like a bear on its hind legs. There's a hush; everyone turns to look.

Leo nods around the room. The bells on his sweater jingle as he holds up his glass.

"My wife, Winnie, would tell me to shut up. But she's in the hospital! So I'll talk!"

There's some nervous laughter at this. Near James, Dagou shifts his weight.

"Winnie would disagree," Leo goes on, "but what can I say? We disagreed about many things! She was always dragging me to church, even though she was a Buddhist. Always hoping some kind of spiritual teaching would rub off on me. Christmas party! Even from the hospital, she wants to remind me about the life of Jesus Christ."

In the moment that follows this undeniably true statement, motionless but for the slight shiver of bells, Dagou clears his throat. He puts a hand on James's shoulder. He's touching him for strength. James looks around at him, concerned. Dagou's sweating, swelling like a bullfrog, glowering at Leo.

"Why don't you listen to her, then?" he shouts. "Just listen to her, for once!"

"Because she's crazy. It's all chemical!" Leo bellows back. "You're younger—you don't know about that time of life. It starts in her fifties, when a woman dries up. She does and says whatever she wants." James almost smiles. Menopause doesn't sound too bad, to hear his father tell it. "She drops womanhood like an old sock. There's no reason to please anybody anymore!"

"You leave my mother alone!" shouts Dagou.

"Get some tranquility," shouts Leo, a grin splitting his face. "Calm down and apologize!"

"I'll never apologize!"

"Well then, time's up. I told everyone, at the hospital! I'm selling the restaurant, and you and your girlfriend are going to have to look for new jobs!"

He points at Dagou, and the bells on his sweater sparkle under the lights.

Dagou is pale. James's own hands grow cold. It's hard to keep listening, though some deep instinct is telling him to be alert, for his own sake as well as for his brother's.

Ken Fan's voice comes clearly through the hush. "You're sure you can't sell it to Dagou?"

"Are you kidding? No, I'm selling it to some guy from the mainland, this guy I know in Chicago. Cash on the barrel! This guy, he wants it as an investment. He knows nothing, he wants to turn it into an 'all-you-can-eat' food factory. You know, unlimited ice cream, crab-legs Sundays, I don't know how those places ever turn a profit, it's probably money laundering, but it's not my problem!"

Dagou is edging from the room. When James turns to follow, Dagou motions to him: *Stay there.* James knows he must stay and pay attention to what else is said. He doesn't quite believe Leo; yet he almost wishes to believe him, wishes Dagou were on his own, free of the restaurant.

"Yeah, it's time for me to move on to new things! Business abroad, business in Shanghai—I'm not selling my house, but I can't be tied up here in Haven every day. This is our final Christmas party here, so drink up! And to my son, our host, the big spender? Good luck with your new job. *You're unemployed.*" Leo raises his glass. "To the future!"

There's some troubled murmuring.

Ken Fan calls out, "To Winnie's health!" and more people cheer.

"Winnie is better!" Mary Wa chimes in. "They release her to rehab next week!"

There's a great deal of clapping and shouting at her words.

"To Dagou, generous man!" chimes in Mrs. Chin.

"To Dagou," echoes Alice Wa across the room, her face a mottled pink.

"To my brother," says James, raising a glass, "who taught me everything I know!"

"To the Chao family, a part of our great town and our community!" declares Maud Marcus.

"To the Chaos," pipes up Fang, red-faced under his striped hat. "To the Chinese brothers! For this surfeit of extravagance, and with warning!"

At the words *the Chinese brothers,* James cocks his head. Fang is referencing something. James senses an echo of, back to childhood, but he can't place it.

"What do you mean?" James asks Fang. The toasts are in Mandarin now, going on over their heads. Eric leans politely in to listen. "This is a surfeit of good food, and it's an extravagance, but what's the warning?"

"Read the bones," says Fang.

"To Winnie!" someone yells again. "To Winnie's health!"

"What bones?" James asks, with Eric and Brenda listening.

"These bones." Fang points at Eric's plate. "Maybe they don't know what they're eating."

A hush of fear comes over James. "The meat was a gift."

"To Mary Wa, for her help over the years!"

"It's from the Skaers," Fang says.

"I know. So what?" asks James. "Dagou invited them. They couldn't make it to the party, so they sent this. It was a gift."

"Is it a gift if what they send is dog meat?"

For a moment, the chattering from the room presses in around their silent little group.

Fang blinks. "Oh shit. I was just—"

There's a sudden hacking cough. It's Eric. He's not coughing; he is gagging.

Brenda touches his shoulder. "Eric?"

Eric stiffens. "Let me get out!"

James jumps up. "I'll take you to the bathroom." He snatches a glass from the table and heads toward the back. Eric follows blindly, coughing into his hands. Everyone turns to watch.

In the bathroom, James waits while Eric throws up in a stall. Eric has eaten a lot of stew, and now, seeing and smelling the half-digested soup of what he has eaten, and knowing what it might be (is it possible?), sends him into another round of vomiting. He retches and retches again.

"Fuck. Oh fuck."

James remembers Dagou unwrapping the paper package of stew meat, aglow over the generous gift. Was it too good to be true?

When Eric straightens up, his face slick with vomit, James turns the taps to warm so he can wash.

"What the fuck?" Eric gasps over the faucet.

James considers what to say.

"Do you think it's true?"

Skaer's Diner is the last of what was once a cluster of family businesses: a bar, two restaurants, and a butcher's. Once, when they were both in middle school, Trey Skaer shoved Ming's face into the toilet at the butcher's. Where did the Skaers get that gift of meat? And where is Alf?

James hands Eric a glass of water. "It's not true," he says. "Fang was just messing with you. Honestly. You feeling better now?"

"I'm getting the fuck out of here."

Eric washes his face, and together they walk back into the dining room. The families with children have departed, and other guests are putting on their coats. Eric heads for the door. James follows him out to the foyer, where he searches the rack for his coat, mumbling. "Goodbye," James calls after him. "Merry Christmas." His call is muffled by the snow. Brenda stands at his elbow. Together, they watch Eric disappear into the snow-surrounded parking lot.

"Thank God he's gone," Brenda says. Her features are severe, her squint crowding her dark lashes close together. She crosses her arms, huffs a cloud of steam. After a minute, a BMW pulls out and turns quickly into the street, tires squeaking.

"Didn't you invite him?" James asks carefully.

"We went out in high school. He just got divorced, has partial custody of a son. Decided I was the one who got away."

"He didn't seem comfortable here."

"No kidding. Well, you win some, you lose some." But she turns back toward the restaurant with an expression of anticipation.

James monitors the consumption of dessert. First, the guests are served a fresh fruit plate with local apples and pears, orange slices, pineapple, and pomegranate. Next comes Brenda's favorite, long-life peach-shaped red bean paste dumplings. Finally, each group of remaining guests is given a big bowl of hot sweet fermented rice broth with smaller dumplings made with sticky rice and black sesame seed paste.

Freedy and his brother enjoy second bowls of the rice broth. They're sitting with Fang and Alice, holding their bowls Chinese-style, with steam rising on their faces. Katherine, who in the last hour has grown increasingly crestfallen and pale, has gotten up to collect the plates. James wishes Ming were here. He tries to talk to her, but she says, "I'm okay," waving him off. She has the determined expression of someone planning to stay until the bitter end.

Leo is now at the bar again, red-faced. "More ice!" he roars at James.

James goes back down the basement steps and hurries into the freezer room, checks again to make sure the key is still on the shelf, and grabs another bag of ice.

When he comes upstairs, almost all of the guests have stumbled into the foyer.

"Fabulous," someone says. This is Jerry Stern's friend Maud, the one who's running for the town council.

Maud is holding Brenda's two hands in her own leather-gloved hands and gushing, as if Brenda is the wealthy hostess of an ornate home, "Brenda, you've become a part of something marvelous here."

And Brenda, as if this woman has ever given her the time of day, gushes back, "It's been lovely to see you, Maud."

"I've eaten myself drunk," Mary Wa is saying. "Let's go home."

In twos and threes, the final dinner guests stroll out into the snowy, crystalline night, relaxed, their eyes shining and their earlobes pink, desiring nothing.

Silent Night

In the empty dining room, Dagou looks victoriously around at the mess. The guests have left wet napkins, crumpled napkins, napkins festooned over the backs of chairs, overturned wineglasses, champagne flutes and soup bowls, fruit peelings and half-eaten fruits, garlands of poinsettias, at least two neckties, and a number of holiday presents piled on the front table.

While James and Freedy collect the trash, Tyrone gathers the tablecloths and napkins. They all work together to collect the dishes. Freedy and Tyrone, who live in her neighborhood, have offered Brenda a ride home. She invites each of them to choose something from the pile of presents, and packs the rest into a couple of shopping bags. Dagou gives them a wad of twenties. He thinks of the sensual happiness with which Brenda passed around the dishes. He's eager to be alone with her. "I'll be there as soon as I can," he says. She smiles at him and steps out the front door.

He passes Katherine in the hall; her eye makeup is a little smudged. He can sense her anguish. He thinks, in her direction: *Please leave.* To his relief, the next time he comes through, Katherine is nowhere to be seen.

Leo directs James to stack the leftover whiskey at the base of the stairs. Later, Dagou sees his father talking to O-Lan. O-Lan is listening with a private, knowing look Dagou has seen before, an expression she wears only when talking to his father. ". . . thinks he's a big spender!" Leo's saying in Mandarin, slurring a bit. Dagou's hands shake. He tries to focus on the memory of Brenda's warm, brilliant voice telling the entire room he was a marvelous chef, the meal was an achievement. He imagines bounding through the deep, white, holy night, weightlessly, up to her door.

"Everything okay?" James asks, emerging from the stairs. Calm enough, but with a faint glimmering about his features that Dagou, heartstrings twanging, recognizes.

"Sure. Listen," Dagou says. "You're gonna get laid tonight. You've got guaranteed admission. I know it!" Pride swells into his mind: perfection. "Listen, you gotta use my apartment."

James blinks, confusion shifting to a bewildered gratitude. "No, no—"

"My pad! It's perfect! Come on, little brother. Your first time!"

"What about you?"

Dagou winks. "I got plans elsewhere. Just use my place! And forget the restaurant. We cleaned; don't bother to set up. You can do it tomorrow morning. Go get her!" he adds, as James begins to protest. "I'm leaving soon."

". . . his Life Savings!" Leo Chao is saying to O-Lan.

"Get out of here," Dagou says to James. "Good luck tonight!"

O-Lan, looking tired and grim, is taking off her apron. It's ten minutes to midnight. "You can go home now," Dagou tells her, and for perhaps the first real time, he wonders if she does have a home.

There's a shout from the stairs. His father has found more leftover vodka. "Hey," he calls out to Dagou, "help me bring this to the freezer!"

His father is hoarding the vodka, Dagou knows, for his own use.

"You're going to miss that bar," he says, hustling past Leo, who is swigging a final finger from one of the bottles.

"Ha!" Leo's guffaw is like a blow. "I haven't sold this place! I was bluffing. Sucker! You believed me?"

Dagou says nothing. His father can take everything else: the vodka, the profits, and the restaurant; yet he won't take one more day of Dagou's life. He loads the final dishes. Once again, rising like hot steam into the crevices and alleyways of his memory, past the windows, past the cornices and roofs and turrets and towers of his reasoning mind, unfurls his dark dream.

"Hey!" His father's roar from below knocks out his breath. "Get those bottles down here. You want to be here until Christmas morning?" Dagou hears, from the basement, the jingle of bells.

"Hey, loser!"

Moving numbly, Dagou picks up a half case. Not feeling its weight, he stands at the top of the stairs. He can hear his father's muffled singing, sardonic, sentimental in his deep baritone voice, exaggerating the held notes.

"Siiiiilent niiiiight . . ."

He hears the creak of the freezer door. The floor is dissolving, as if through the curls of black steam rising from below, and he is falling, falling into darkness. The restaurant is empty and his father is in the freezer. The events unfold themselves to him as they have a dozen, a hundred, even a thousand times: himself, having done what he has long imagined doing, emerging from the basement, turning off the lights, walking freely out into the silent night. All is calm, all is bright.

Carrying the vodka, Dagou descends the stairs.

The Gift

Katherine puts on her coat, alone, but not empty-handed. How did Mary Wa remember Winnie has always given her a Christmas gift? Typically, something unfathomable: a china piggy bank, a Badgers baseball shirt. Once, a set of tiny matching silver ear-cleaners. She and Dagou had a running joke about those presents. Still, she treasured them. It was not precisely the thought that counted, not for Katherine and Winnie—but the ritual of the gift. This year, Winnie no longer believes in material possessions. But Mary Wa has remembered. Clutching her present, Katherine ducks into the bathroom. She's promised herself not to unwrap it until Christmas morning. She'll be in Sioux City, where she and her parents will have piled two dozen colorful boxes under the tree, and she'll have brought with her this one package from Haven. A most likely puzzling, probably goofy reminder of the community, of Winnie. Winnie, alone at the hospital. Winnie, seeking tranquility. What is nothingness like? Dagou is gone. Katherine shuts her eyes. Against her burning lids, she can still see Dagou and Brenda, torch-lit, clutching hands. They are one. In their fleshiness; in their beauty, almost coarse; in their matching physicality of charismatic light: they are one. She is gripped by panic; her heart quails. What is there in all the world? Standing at the sink, she removes one of her mittens. Using a fingernail, she makes a tiny rip on the corner of the package. There's a flash of embossed gold: it's a Bible.

The exploration began more than a dozen years ago, in college. Raised white, by a white family in a white city, she first reacted to Dagou with resistance, even repugnance. She rebuffed his advances in the same way she rejected that unknown part of herself. He rose to the challenge, insisting she meet him at the Asian American Students House for the Lunar New Year party. Why not? he teased. He wasn't inviting her to the Language Club; she wouldn't have to learn Chinese. Was she not curious, did she not want to explore even this watered-down version of Asian culture? Of course, it wasn't only culture he wanted her to explore.

Dagou, funny and self-deprecating, was even then a specialist of appetite and lust. Dagou, with his old-country parents and Haven community, became, over the years, a desire, a fixation.

She gazes at the green jade glowing on her finger. She listens to scraps of conversation: Dagou and his father moving the liquor, Leo Chao bellowing and singing from the stairs. Then quiet. She tucks Mary's gift back under her arm. She wipes her eyes and leaves the restroom, nodding at O-Lan in her puffy coat. She won't go back into the dining room, doesn't want to see the tattered decorations. Doesn't want to say goodbye to anyone; they're probably assuming she's already gone. She's going to leave through the rear door. As she makes her way back down the hall, a light catches her attention. The door to Leo's office is open.

DECEMBER 25

Dagou's Dream

IT'S THREE A.M. when Dagou and Brenda finally hoist the shopping bags of Christmas presents onto Brenda's bed and open everything. There's a beautiful cocktail shaker from Jerry Stern. Mary Wa has given them a ginormous, glossy gold box of chocolate truffles that Dagou suspects must have fallen off a truck, or else they must be fake chocolates, since she never spends an extra cent if she can help it. There's a useless tourists' blue and white china tea set with dragons. There's a stuffed gray mouse, a fountain pen, a ballpoint pen, and a shaver. There's a dragon wall clock from Maud Marcus, who doesn't know the superstition about giving clocks of any kind (that your life is coming to an end), and an elegant designer umbrella from the architect's American wife, who doesn't know the superstition about giving umbrellas (that your life will fall apart). Brenda loves the silk scarf from Corey Chen's shy Taiwanese boyfriend. Eric Braun, who either does or doesn't know the superstition about knives, has given them an excellent chopping knife.

"What was that all about?" Dagou asks.

"I used to sleep with him," says Brenda. "Senior year of high school. I haven't seen him in years. He got rich, got married, had a kid. He fooled around, was kicked out by his wife, and had nowhere to go for Christmas Eve."

Dagou considers this. He understands. In the transformation of the last few hours, his terrible jealousy has released itself into the night. He thinks of James and Alice, in his apartment, and a wild happiness and pride for James fills him. "Do you want one, too?" he asks. "A baby."

"Not right now."

"Maybe sometime?"

"Maybe."

He reaches for her. They have sex again. Brenda sniffs Dagou's hands and seems to find the odor of sesame, surprisingly, a little moving. As he watches her cry out, joy flows through him and into the world, hovering over them both, then releasing into the winter night. It's Christmas morning. They're together, joyful, in Brenda's sweet, glowing bed, and it is like a marvelous dream, his best dream. The world is new at last. It doesn't matter if the restaurant is theirs, or not: there could be other restaurants, whole other worlds, and he is in the center of splendid possibilities. He must forget about the past. He is free once more; the years-long desperation wanes (it doesn't go away, it cannot entirely vanish), but for the present, everything is in its proper place.

Dagou sleeps. The bedroom door opens and Alf appears. He's enormous, the size of a lion, and his round black eyes are as big as eight balls. He leaps onto the bed, planting his huge black paws on Dagou's chest, and licks Dagou's face with a tongue like a washcloth. Dagou puts his arms around Alf's neck, grown as thick as a waist, and feels the comfort of his smooth, warm fur. He's happy enough to weep. He climbs onto the dog's back like a small boy and the enormous Alf pushes his way out of the room, trotting down the stairs. The front door opens and he bounds out into the night.

Down the dark street he goes, then turns the corner, loping energetically southward.

"Where are we going?" Dagou asks, gesturing behind them. "Go back!" Dagou directs. "Let's go get Brenda, Alf! Turn back."

But Alf carries Dagou through a series of alleyways opening away from Letter City, past the Spiritual House. Then, with a great bound, Alf's paws leave the pavement, and they're climbing into the air. Dagou looks down, but the streets have shut beneath him. He can no longer identify the houses.

"Turn back," Dagou commands, but Alf plunges firmly ahead into the night. Dagou, holding on to the fur of Alf's strong neck, can feel the dog's thundering heartbeat. Now they're high above Lakeside, over the penthouse. The city park is somewhere below, with its empty swimming pool, its carousel shut down and tented for winter. Dagou can just see the lights of Haven, at first glittering and then, as they continue on, receding, until below them there's only the wide, dark lake. The lake that existed long before the lights, before the town; the lake encountered hundreds of years ago, renamed by the Americans.

James's Dream

Early in the morning, the distant bells of St. Ludmila ring three times. As he lies in bed with Alice, far above the restaurant, some other, distant sound nudges James awake.

Thump, thump.

James opens his eyes. He and Alice are curled together under Dagou's furry comforter. In the moonlight, he glimpses Alice's elf costume carefully folded on a chair.

Alice stirs. "What is it?" she murmurs.

Thump.

"I thought I heard something." James props himself up on one elbow, but there's nothing. "Maybe it's just a tree branch, maybe the wind."

He hasn't slept in this apartment since childhood; its noises have grown strange to him. Still, he's jolted by the unmistakable feeling of another consciousness intruding on his own, another soul.

Alice pulls him down to her. "It's all right, James."

He listens, struggling to stay awake; it's quiet now.

"It's probably nothing," he mumbles. "Only—"

Only—for some reason, he remembers the sound of knocking from below, in the train station, as he led the old man, the stranger, up the staircase.

"Go to sleep, James." Alice takes his hand.

Thump.

They sleep.

PART TWO

The World Sees Them

WHEN THE NEWCOMERS first arrived in Haven, they found a smallish city near a lake. On the margins of the city, Americans were hard at work, building avenues lined with newer stores, businesses, restaurants. Busy living out their own tragedies and triumphs. Paying little attention. The newcomers were noticeable, with their Asian faces. But their dreams and aspirations were an open secret. Visible, but invisible.

You could say that until the death of Leo Chao, their lives were private. No one paid them much attention.

Now they receive subtle stares when they walk down the street. It's awkward, it is mortifying. After all, they're not the Chaos; the Chaos' shame isn't their shame. It's true their children grew up with Dagou, Ming, and James. They celebrated Christmas with the Chaos for decades, and everyone makes Winnie's recipe for red-cooked pork. And it's true you couldn't help sensing something wrong. Sensing, over the years, a curiosity growing about that house and the three boys. Too much privacy in their smooth faces like shuttered windows. But doesn't every family have its own closed windows and closed doors? Isn't every family a walled fortress of stories unknown even to its neighbors? Disobedience of sons to their mothers, wives to their husbands, and men to their own old mothers?

THREE MONTHS LATER

The Chinese Brothers

IT IS NOW late March. Morning sun slants through the plate-glass windows of Skaer's Diner, reaching the corner where James Chao sits reading with a half-finished plate of scrambled eggs and toast. He glances out from his hoodie. It's the same university hoodie he wore at the train station, but he's no longer a student. He hasn't been on campus since January, when Winnie suffered her second, fatal stroke. At that point, he applied for a leave of absence and moved his things out of the dormitory, back to Haven. His hair is shaggy and more length has come into his hands, but the most noticeable change is in the way he looks out from the hoodie. It's not the expression of a college student.

There's another change. The red-haired server at the diner is watching him. From behind the register, she lets her gaze slide over to his corner of the room. She makes eye contact when she takes his order, and comes back to say they're out of strawberry jam packets but she found one more in the back. James notices her, too, sees the way the small silver cross rests on her freckled chest and moves as she breathes. He knows what her attention is about. In the last few months, he's experienced a transfiguration; a current has run through his body, waking him up. Still, he can't quite understand what she sees in him. In truth, he exists in a liminal space bridging his old self to a future self he can't yet grasp.

He's rereading a website article, "The Curious Case of 'The Brothers Karamahjong.'" It's ostensibly an analysis of the impending trial of William "Dagou" Chao, now known as "Dog Eater," who has been indicted for committing a "restaurant murder set in an insular midwestern Chinese American community," an "ethnic enclave" where an "American girl," a "blond bombshell" (this is Brenda, who changed her hair color senior year of high school) "drove both father and son into a frenzy," compelling the suspect to work out obsessively, then to embark upon a desperate spending spree, leading to a bacchanalian Christmas bash, culminating in the consumption of the family dog, whose fate has become an anti-immigrant flash point. A party followed by the suspicious death of the father, owner of the restaurant.

"They keep to themselves," said Jane Yoder, a neighbor James has never met. "They have their restaurant and their own friends."

A member of Dagou's high school class is quoted as saying, "He was obsessed with her. She was everything—blue-eyed and sexy, on the homecoming court."

James takes a few more bites of scrambled eggs, studying the photos. First, Dagou's mug shot, widely circulated since the story was picked up by the supermarket tabloids: "Suspect: William Dagou 'Dog Eater' Chao." The image is Dagou, and not Dagou: darker than he really is, with fierce, hooded eyes. His gaze challenges James, yet beseeches him, and there's an almost disturbing air of repose in the curve of his full mouth. The website has gotten hold of more images of Dagou: his high school and college yearbook photos, also printed in a manner that make him seem more dark skinned than he is; and one snapshot from New York City, of anonymous origin, showing the twenty-five-year-old Dagou leaning over his bass, his bow low at the frog, his shoulders bunched under his shirt.

Brenda's high school yearbook photo could have been dropped in directly from a 1950s pinup poster. Her blue eyes gleam at James. A wave of ash-blond hair curves against her cheek. She is so fresh and sultry that there could be no question she "drove the immigrant father and his son into a frenzy."

In Ming's photo, he appears more light-skinned than he really is. But the contrast with Dagou is just as obvious in his erect posture, his jacket and tie, his aura of conventionality and exactitude. "The middle brother whose ignorance of the conflict and whose absence from the crime scene clearly exonerates him from the murder, Ming Chao has provided the financial support to release Dagou 'Dog Eater' Chao on $1 million bail."

Under James's photo, the article has reprinted the one quote James gave to a reporter, before Ming texted him to shut up. "My brother and father had their disagreements, but Dagou would never commit murder. My brother is innocent." For some reason, Ming and Katherine don't want James to release any more statements to the press, not even in support of Dagou. They've made James promise not to talk, even though Jerry Stern, Dagou's lawyer, issued no such edict.

In Alf's close-up, he's less than a year old, almost unrecognizably puppyish. He gazes directly at James, head slightly cocked, bat ears unfolded in typical, unceasing alertness. His small black nose is shaped like a heart, the fur on his jowls shimmers, and the blaze on his chest is bright white and fluffy. The image is cropped so that his hindquarters are only partially visible, and a woman's arm (Winnie's) can just be seen.

His mother and Alf are gone now. James puts down his fork and shields his eyes with his hands. It's a few minutes before he can refocus on his screen. There are 294 comments. James scrolls down, then clicks.

Sheri

CA 42 m ago

As a dog lover, I cannot forgive William Chao for callously cooking and serving his father's pet. This is indefensible behavior. I notice the story of Alf's disappearance and the mysterious meat dish, which was earlier reported, has been hushed up. PETA has this under investigation and the truth will out. Animal abuse is criminal and immoral. Justice for Alf!

Jean Hu

Manhattan 38 m ago

The dog dinner is the Juniper-Tree, adult-diaper-revenge-drive detail of this story making it go viral. Without Alf, no one would care. You'd have just another private tragedy of an oppressed immigrant family.

Fang Wa

Haven 36 m ago

As a person who has known the Chao family for many years, I deride the spread of this rumor as false and malicious, not to mention racist, gossip. The entire Chao family was devoted to Alf and was broken-hearted when he disappeared. The dog-meat story began as a joke. This incident has been blown up and circulated by anti-Asian scandal-mongers.

charlotte wisniak

oshkosh 32 m ago

stop the abuse of helpless animals

You Jin

Iowa City 30 m ago

Please see the attached link to a consortium of dog lovers and concerned citizens from many countries who have been able to rescue Asian restaurant dogs and bring them to the US for adoption.

Joe M.

Louisville 8 m ago

I lived in Xi'an for two years. It's where I met my wife. I was able to taste dog meat several times. It's good—a lot like mutton, but with a special savory flavor. I happen to know that the Chinese prize black dogs for their flavor, over any other color.

Jonathan N.

Lafayette 46 m ago

As a Chinese American, I find this entire case an embarrassment to my community.

Keiko

Milwaukee 43 m ago

Your comment is an example of the self-hatred that has led to stereotypes such as the "model minority." Why must we Asians be superior to other groups?

GS Meng

Flushing 1 hour ago

This story is blowing up because of the racism of the white American community. Look to your own families, people, and don't throw stones.

Linda H.

Washington DC 5 m ago

Agreed. In the newspapers, there are articles about a tyrannical world leader driving emigrants away from the borders of a country that was once a haven for refugees; police officers choking our own citizens in cold blood; immoral judges disallowing marriages of life-long lovers; deranged shooters gunning down scores of well-wishers at a rock music benefit; children going hungry in acutely troubled countries whose economies are stumbling from corruption; hurricanes, floods, tsunamis; whales beaching and foundering on the shores; runaway fires streaking down clogged arteries of desperately escaping vehicles. Amidst this turmoil and grief, why Leo Chao? Why did the death of Leo Chao become news? It couldn't just be the rumor of a dog meat restaurant. Perhaps it debunks the myth of immigrant success, and tells the story of a secret from behind the high walls of family and community: that behind a family business, a successful father and a set of handsome sons, prowls, clawed and fanged, a mythical monstrousness of tyranny, hatred, and murderous intent? Or perhaps it's all a desperate need for readers to displace their hatreds, their traumas, the tyrannies under which they suffer, onto a story of tyranny and revenge refreshing and different enough to allow them to believe it is not theirs.

Sylvia Han

Atlanta 28 m ago

Brenda Wozicek is a trashy gold-digger bent upon corrupting the lives of innocent Chinese men, and she has been a poor influence on the three sons, not to mention the father.

5 REPLIES

Saskya 27 m ago

Dagou, I'll make you forget all about Brenda!

Jana 26 m ago

Yes! I heart Dagou!!!

Frannie 25 m ago

James is the one for me. What a sweetie <3 <3 <3.

Nunu 23 m ago

Ming Chao is the hotte$t!

Ed Wong 19 m ago

At last, I've discovered the secret of how to attract women as an Asian male: get indicted for patricide.

The diner door opens and shuts. James squints through the sunlight at the newcomer, who approaches his corner, wearing a jacket and a Mao cap. Skaer's Diner is where no reporters, friends, or even family would go to find James. But beneath the red star and khaki brim, familiar curious dark eyes shine through dirty wire-rimmed glasses. It's Fang.

Fang removes his cap, comes directly to the booth, and stands there, observing him. James shuts his computer. "I thought I might find you here," Fang says. "You ready to go to the Spiritual House?"

"No." James smooths his hair with his fingers. Under his hoodie he's wearing a white dress shirt. In an hour the community will gather for a memorial to mark the final day of the seventh week after Winnie's death.

"Let's walk there together," Fang says. "I have something to discuss with you."

Leaving the restaurant, they turn down the adjacent alley in order to keep their journey private. Since the story in *USA Today*, they've had to make an effort to avoid strangers—"literally yellow journalists," Fang says—camping out in the Holiday Inn, lurking near the restaurant, or attaching themselves to any Asian passerby to ask if they know the Chao family or anything about them. For a few minutes, they don't speak. In the freedom of the alley, James relaxes in silent companionship, letting his mind wander. During these last months, with the tumult of shock and change, time has shifted. He half expects to see his father, alive once more, striding toward them in the alley, a little rumpled, squinting in the morning sun.

Fang pulls out his cap and puts it back on. "Why'd you go to that awful diner?"

"Privacy, I guess."

"I'm surprised you're not driven out by the bad vibes," Fang says. "But listen, I need to talk to you."

They reach an intersection with a medium-sized street and James crosses quickly, head down, ducking back into the alley. Fang trots after him.

"Listen, James. Do you remember what Gu Ling Zhu Chi told your dad?"

"You know I don't understand anything she says. But Dagou told me. I remember."

"Gu Ling Zhu Chi told him he was in danger of a *bad death*. What does that mean? A bad death doesn't stop with the death. It means something in his death is going to be a part of your life. It's going to play out and become *your story*."

Fang's gaze is dark. Although he and Alice appear hobbled by eccentricity, they're also emboldened by it. Their mother is an ordinary person, but somewhere within her, or, most likely, within their lost father, there must have been a great capacity for strangeness. Fang doesn't care what people think. He doesn't lose track of anything he sees, and he won't fail to speak up. Ming says Fang is un-American. He has no ability to adapt, forget; and isn't that what you do in America? Adapt? Forget?

Now Fang says, "Do you remember that racist children's book, the book about the Chinese brothers?"

The words echo in James's mind, but only faintly.

"'*Once upon a time,*'" Fang intones, singsonging, "'*there were five Chinese brothers and they all looked exactly alike.*'"

Now James recalls the image on the cover. Five pigtailed, slit-eyed figures lined up in a row. He'd rather forget it. But he says, "Each of the brothers had a superpower."

"Each of the brothers was a freak. The first could 'swallow the sea.' The second one had an iron neck. The third could stretch his legs like rubber bands. The fourth brother could survive fire. And the fifth could hold his breath for an immeasurable amount of time. Not superpowers, exactly, but distortions. A Western catalogue of dehumanizations. The brothers are interchangeable, yet freaks. And do you remember to what end the freakish powers were deployed? Do you remember, James?"

"No." James wants, needs, to be left alone, but the only way to end a conversation with Fang is to hear him out. "Tell me."

From under his cap, Fang holds forth. He describes First Brother, who used his freakish sea-sucking ability to find valuable, exotic fish. Every day, he plundered the ocean, bringing in a living for the family. Then one day a child asked to go with him, begged to be allowed to search the waterless seabed. The First Brother agreed to let him come if he made one crucial promise: that he return to the shore when it was time. The child promised.

When they reached the shore, the First Brother deployed his powers: he swallowed the ocean. "He literally drank the sea," Fang says. "His head grew, and grew, swelling tightly like an enormous balloon on which his slanted eyes were distorted to tiny slits. With greed and with delight, the child rushed out to search and play upon the rocky bed. While the child ignored his signals to return, the First Brother stood on the shore, suffering, his face turning red, his cheeks bulging with the world of coursing salt water. His head a thousand times its normal size.

"He was a strong guy," Fang says, "but even he could not hold out. '*It is very hard to hold in the sea.*' Eventually, he had to give in. The sea gushed back out of his mouth. And the little boy drowned under the waves. Dead."

"Can't we talk about this later, Fang?"

"The rest of the book is about the consequences of this unfortunate death," Fang persists. "And who tries to do the cover-up? The other brothers. Their gifts, talents, their freakish abilities, have existed throughout time for the sole purpose, in this narrative, of avoiding the consequences of the murder."

James and Fang face each other.

"I know what you're thinking!" James's voice rings through the alleyway. "You think Dagou was holding it in. He's First Brother, and he couldn't take it anymore. He let his suffering and anger spew forth, and he killed our father. But I don't believe it! I think the whole thing was an accident and Dagou's innocent."

His shouts startle the pigeons roosting above, who flutter up and vanish from view. Fang doesn't answer. The pigeons circle back.

"What is it?" James asks, more quietly. "What do you want?"

"I've got to ask you this," Fang says. "I know you testified to the police. I've read the newspapers and news sites, I read about what you told them. But I've been considering every detail. Considering with, let's say, a view from outside the family, an objective view. I want to understand what happened, independent of what Officer Bucek says is true. Or what the jury decides is true."

"Maybe the difference between us is that I believe in the process," James says, folding his arms. "The police and the jury will figure out what happened."

"My question is this," Fang says, ignoring him. "When you went downstairs the second time, close to the end of the party, to get more ice. Did you *really see* the key on the shelf at that time?"

"Yes, I did."

"You're going to testify in court."

"I don't think I can get out of it."

"Because," Fang says, "if you're wrong—if you remembered wrong, and the key was not on the shelf at the end of the party—then your father could have been killed by anybody, and *not* just Dagou. By anyone during the party, or even anyone who happened to be inside the restaurant to sneak it off the shelf in the weeks before the party."

"No," James says. The pigeons above are no longer circling but clucking, cooing, listening. "Here's where we disagree: I do remember seeing the key on the shelf. But, even if I remembered it wrong, I believe someone could have stumbled down there and *accidentally* removed it. It was an accident."

"James," Fang says, "*you* loved your dad. But don't let your love make you so blind you can't see you were the only person who did. Everybody hated him."

"No one hated him enough to kill him."

"How can you say what depths of hatred people keep to themselves? The Skaers, for example. Do we know what the Skaers feel about your family's restaurant, what they think your parents' workaholism has done to drain their family businesses over the years? And there are others."

James doesn't answer. He remembers Dagou's story about Ken Fan, shamed by Leo's behavior at the post office. *My father made them all look bad.*

Fang is still talking. "Did your dad's claim that he was going to sell the restaurant make Dagou angry enough to do it? Is Ming mercenary and bitter enough to do it? Or what if Dagou wasn't alone in this? How about Brenda? Why's she involved with your brother? If all she wants is money, she would start sleeping with an older man. Either she's, one, got yellow fever; or, two, she's hot for your brother specifically. What if she's unwilling to give up having sex with your brother? What future does he have, except his father's restaurant?"

"You've got sex on the brain."

"It takes one to know one," Fang says, raising his brows. "But thanks for giving me credit. Because I can't attract sexual partners, people think it doesn't matter to me." He wards off James's objection with an upraised hand. "Anyway, I'm not sure what it is, exactly, but *something* was going on."

"Well, you're wrong about Brenda. She'd never get Dagou into so much trouble."

"Why *wouldn't* it be an employee? I know JJ was in California, but what about that woman who chops vegetables?"

"O-Lan? She never goes near the freezer. She couldn't read the sign, so she didn't know about the key."

"Then back to Brenda. How did she get hired? Your father usually hires FOBs."

"My dad's hired outside servers before. Brenda's broke, and so my dad gave her a job. As a favor," James adds, although he knows Fang won't believe him.

"You know as well as I do, your father didn't give favors. It was all a transaction for him. And he never made a simple transaction. He made a deal. Listen, I know! My mother is much tougher than she appears, but even she had to pull some stunts in order to do business with your dad. He would've run her out of business if he hadn't figured out it would be too time consuming and potentially risky to buy his 'oriental groceries' on his own. Oh no, he let my mother stay afloat as a calculated cost. He didn't think about anyone except himself. You know it's true."

"It could be true," James acknowledges.

"An *apparent* transaction, James. Just admit that he screwed everyone: women for sex, and men for money. Anyone might have had the motive to kill Leo, might have had an itch they needed to satisfy. Might *still* need."

They've reached the end of the alleyway. They're walking out onto a sidewalk that runs along a broad avenue. Two blocks away, in an older residential neighborhood, is the former school where the Spiritual House is located. James lowers his voice because they're no longer shielded. "What do you mean, *still*?"

Fang peers at James from under his cap. "Well, where's your father's money? There's not a peep in the news that anyone has found any of his money."

A Mysterious Visitor

Winnie Chao's three sons know as much about her as most sons know about their mothers. They remember her smell, sound, and touch; and now, after her death, they can recall a hundred ordinary details; but from these facets the larger story of her life can't be completed. They're well acquainted with the hack of her ironic laugh, but they've never heard the eager giggle of her early youth; they remark upon her appetite for food, but they have no idea that she liked to bite even her husband in the throes of passion. They know only that she hated him and don't understand she'd loved him. They're still nursing their own shame, as men.

For seven times seven days, as Winnie's spirit wandered quietly between the living and the dead, her sons didn't see her: not in the restaurant kitchen, where Dagou gestured at O-Lan from the stove; nor in the dining room, where James reread a note from Alice while Ming and Katherine bent together over a laptop. Katherine looked up, sensing she was being watched, but after a moment she turned back to the screen. Only some of the nuns knew Winnie was there. One evening at the Spiritual House, with bright snow falling outside the windows, Sister Omi paused while heaping cabbage leaves into a stainless-steel bowl. She felt a restlessness pass through the room, into the cabbage, which seemed to hover in her hands. Nearby, Sister Chung-Hung bent over a bowl of rice and vegetables. A large, pensive woman who frequently had visions during meals, she wasn't surprised to see a black-haired Winnie, wearing the same wool coat and plaid scarf from the day of her arrival at the Lake Haven Station, in the middle of winter, more than three decades ago.

Now, on the forty-ninth day, Dagou, Ming, and James, together with her essential people, gather at the Spiritual House to support Winnie's spirit as it makes the transition to a rebirth in the Pure Land. Gu Ling Zhu Chi is here again, with An at her elbow. Also, the nuns; also, Winnie's closest friends among the Chinese families in Haven. Fang and Alice are here, and Brenda. Jerry Stern arrives early, uncharacteristically professional in a suit and tie, and spends some time with Dagou in Gu Ling Zhu Chi's sitting room, making sober conversation. Katherine can't take the day off from work. She has sent an arrangement of plum blossoms and a generous donation.

When the prayers are over, the group stands near the entrance, unwilling to depart quite yet, telling stories. How Winnie came to the U.S. as the paper sister of a distant cousin and met Leo Chao in Chicago, standing in line at a convenience store. Leo, who had somehow managed to make it to the U.S. on his own, and who was already managing a restaurant. (He hired her immediately.) Within a year, they had set out for Haven, "like pioneers," Leo always said, among the first Chinese people ever to live there.

"Do you know, James," says Ken Fan, "that in those early days your mother was being courted by a man named Pu? In the end, your dad said, he had to step in and marry her, to save her from the fate of being named Winnie Pu."

James tries to smile, but he's still thinking about what Fang said as they were walking: everyone hated his father. He imagines Fang now, whispering, *Look at all of these people here for your mother. No one gathered for your father.*

He wouldn't want them to, James silently argues back. *My father didn't believe in any of this. No chanting or incense, no assistance to a future rebirth in the Pure Land. No repenting of his sins, any reunion with his loved ones in Heaven. He didn't believe in anything except the primacy of his own self.*

Exactly! Fang would say. *Your father was the consummate American id, an insatiable narcissist, a shameless capitalist who wanted to screw everyone.*

And what did it mean for the Chao brothers, James now wonders, to be the sons of Leo and Winnie Chao? He thinks of Ming, when they talked at the Other Restaurant, and his torment at being a yellow child in the American Midwest. He thinks of Dagou's radio story of Leo at the post office, mailing gifts to a mysterious recipient, probably a woman. He pictures his mother, wearing herself out working in a restaurant that opened earlier and closed later than any place in town, living ashamed in a community aware of what shamed her; and he, like Ming, is crushed by what this must have been like. How have they been damaged, raised by Leo, who took his sons along the back alleys of Haven on errands of philandering? James considers Dagou, who is sweating, and Ming, standing pale and impatient in his expensive suit. Their father, the immigrant success story. Longtime owner of his own business. What did it mean to all of them, to be raised in this country, promised a life of American achievement, by a man who exploited their labor?

Leo Chao is dead, yet he will always be their father. He has given all three of them an inheritance of himself. And they've all accepted a part of this inheritance. Although he has rejected his father's ambition, Dagou owns Leo's garrulousness, his sexual palate. Ming has rejected his father's Asian-ness, but accepted Leo's ability with math and his goal of a Life Savings. And James?

"No," James says aloud. "I don't want it."

As if she can sense what he's thinking, Alice looks up.

Gazing at Alice, James knows he's also accepted his father's inheritance. That surety of desire, making his hands twitch now as he imagines reaching under her skirt. Over the last few months, he has become attuned to her body in a way he hadn't known was possible. And it's as if this new power—the uncanny ability to detect in others the feelings he and Alice have awakened in each other—has grown into something he can't suppress or ignore. He is changing. For example, he knows from simply standing near them that the stale old sexual feelings between Mr. and Mrs. Fan are enclosed within a kind of talcum-powdered envelope of cordial respect. On the other end of the spectrum, he's strongly aware that Sister Omi and another novice are awash in a passionate magnetism of very recent sexual feelings. Where will his inheritance take him? Gu Ling Zhu Chi said he would have adventures, live in many places. She said love would matter to him, more than anything else. He wonders, not for the first time since leaving college, what she meant by this.

"James?"

Brenda pulls James aside, into the room where the offering table is. She's wearing a simple black dress and has twisted her hair into a dark bun, revealing only a glow of blue at the ends. James can sense she's been affected by the ceremonies marking his mother's death. Yet she's no longer thinking about the prayers. She frowns at him, her lashes thickening.

"You seem a little angry, James. Are you okay?"

"No. I mean, sure, I'm functional, if that's what you mean." James fixes his gaze over her shoulder, at the black-and-white portrait of his mother hanging above the offering table.

Brenda bites her lip. Her teeth are perfectly white and even; her mouth is full and red even though she's wearing no lipstick. James is more aware than ever of his sexual attraction to her, but he understands that whatever flirtatiousness she might have felt toward him is gone. It's been replaced, not by indifference, but by a kind of mutual concern. Family love. He knows she does truly love Dagou.

"James," she says, "you don't have to answer if you don't want to. But I've been thinking this over a lot. About that night—Christmas Eve."

"What about it?"

"Are you sure about when Katherine left the restaurant?"

James doesn't answer. Brenda's question has brought him up short. "Well, no," he says after a moment. "I didn't actually watch her leave. But Dagou and I both know, we're both pretty sure she was gone. Why?" He's still looking at Winnie's portrait. Winnie gazes soberly back at him. For a moment he almost believes she's trying to tell him something. It would be about tranquility, about how to find tranquility.

"Well, this is just stuff I think about when I can't sleep," Brenda says slowly. "But sometimes I get a hunch; I can sense he's bluffing. He knows she was doing something that night, something she maybe shouldn't have been doing, and all of this bluster about what *he* was doing—his whole story about going downstairs, standing at the door, about changing his *mind*—it's just some way of protecting her."

Forgetting his mother, James turns his gaze to Brenda. She is frightened. "Of course he's protecting her," he says, determined both to comfort her and to reassure himself. "He protects her all the time, because he feels guilty about being in love with *you*."

"She's been holding something back for months. She's fighting to control herself, I don't know why."

"She still loves him, but he really loves *you*. That's all it is."

"I hope you're right."

They rejoin the dwindling group; Brenda takes Dagou's hand. Several of Winnie's friends have departed. Jerry Stern is gone. Three nuns stand near Dagou, listening to him patiently, James can see, out of respect for their mother.

"Ma was a singular Chinese mom," Dagou is saying. "She raised us to believe in the value of a spiritual life. She was a devout Christian and a devout Buddhist. Some people have double happiness, but Ma had double spirituality. And she had faith in us, in her kids."

"You were a good son to her," says one of the nuns.

James nods. Even in those terrible days when he was being held and questioned constantly by the police, Dagou sent O-Lan to deliver delicacies to Winnie in the hospital. Now he holds Brenda's hand tightly and uses his other hand to blot his perspiring face with a wad of Kleenex. "She never gave up on me," he says. "She told me to believe in myself, she told me to believe in love. She was a really singular. . . ." His voice trickles off.

Fang steps away to the bathroom, the same bathroom where Alf once put his pink tongue into the toilet.

"So, you chose to have a speedy trial?" Ken Fan rescues Dagou.

Here Dagou glances furtively over at Ming, who refuses to look back. Ming, who's come up with bail. Ming and Katherine, along with Jerry, are in favor of pulling out the legal stops to delay the trial for as long as possible, for at least a year.

"I just couldn't wait anymore," Dagou says to Ken Fan. "I want everything to be over with. So yeah, I opted for a relatively speedy trial."

Ken says, "It will all work out. Whatever happens, it will all work out for the best."

How can he utter that platitude? James wonders. He can't mean that Dagou ending up in prison could be for the best. Dagou doesn't notice. He thanks Ken profusely, perspiring. The day before, he and James went to Target to buy something to wear to Winnie's event, because his shirt and slacks from the winter no longer fit him. He eats continually when he's not in public.

"Listen," Fang says, pulling James aside. He's wearing the keen look James recognizes from the alley. Detective Fang. "There's a stranger in the bathroom. Someone in dirty sneakers."

"Is it a guest?"

"No, that's what I'm saying." Fang hesitates. "It was a stranger, in the other stall. I left the bathroom and waited in the hallway for a while, but they didn't come out. Come look."

They head to the bathroom. James checks inside, but whoever had been in the stall has vanished.

When they rejoin the group, Mary Wa asks James if he'll be going back to school in the fall. James shrugs, and she reaches out to pat his arm. Winnie's death has aged Mary. Her permanent wave is silver-tipped and her irises are faded. Still, she is solicitous to others. She asks Ming if he's been sleeping.

"I'm still catching up," Ming says.

Katherine also worries about Ming. The previous weekend, she pulled James aside to discuss what she called his "manic symptoms," asking James to keep an eye on his brother when she's in Chicago. "He's fragile," she said. "He's much more distressed than he lets on. He should stop drinking coffee. He should stop looking at the internet."

Ming needs to take a few days off, Mary Wa is saying now. This has been a terrible time for him, it is all an awful shock. Stay here with friends, at the Spiritual House, for a few more minutes. Even as she's saying this, Ming slides toward the door. One of Ming's tricks of being an escape artist, James surmises, is that no one expects him to stick around, even for his own good.

James walks Ming to his car.

"Fang says there was a stranger here, in the bathroom," James says. "Someone with really dirty sneakers."

"Yeah, well," says Ming. "It's the paparazzi. We're all famous now." He reaches the door of his car. "Villagers," he mutters. He leans against the shiny black surface, closing his eyes and letting the fresh air stream over his face. "They're coming for me, too, did you know that?" James remembers what Gu Ling Zhu Chi said: Ming is ill.

"Are you okay?" James asks. "You're . . . changing, somehow."

"What do you mean?" Ming barks, opening his eyes to glare at James.

"Nothing—well, you look like you might be coming down with something."

Ming shakes his head, shakes off the thought.

"You need rest. Have you even gotten a full night's sleep since you did all of that driving, Christmas Eve?"

"Listen, I've got to go. I've got a flight to catch."

James listens. Ming is holding his breath. Then he says, "I don't need sleep."

"It's the trial," James says automatically. "It's putting us all on edge."

"It's not the trial," Ming says. "The trial is a procedure, and when it's over, we'll know where we stand. In case of the worst outcome, we'll have the option to appeal." Ming shakes his head again, very slightly. "It's something else," he mutters, not to James. He opens the passenger door of his rental car, puts his computer on the front seat, then circles to the driver's door, still muttering. He doesn't know James is listening, with his special new ability to hear.

"The villagers are out," Ming is muttering. "Following the trail in the snow. . . ."

Ming's door slams shut. James watches the car disappear, turns, and goes back inside.

The Carpetbag

In the entryway of the Spiritual House, Dagou is kissing Brenda. He gives her one last, tender kiss, and leaves for the restaurant. James knows after arriving at work, Dagou will boil noodles and make an enormous batch of pork with scallion strips, chopped garlic, and jiu cai. He'll dish out a large bowl for himself, scoop hot pepper sludge over it, and sit in the corner of the empty dining room, shoveling in the savory, spicy pork noodles. Eating, and being with Brenda, are his best means of steadying his emotions these days.

Most of the nuns return to their rooms or to the kitchen. Mary, Fang, and Alice say goodbye. Soon only James is left to do Gu Ling Zhu Chi's bidding: he's to carry his mother's personal effects to his car and take them home.

As he follows Sister Omi into a storage room to retrieve Winnie's possessions, the irony of what James is doing doesn't escape him. For some time, his mother wanted to leave the house where she lived with his father. She planned and schemed to leave; then, in her final months, she achieved her desire to live in tranquility with the nuns. Now she's dead, and James is transporting her personal effects back to the house she was so desperate to get away from. Still, it makes no sense to take her things anywhere else.

Maybe it doesn't matter, because Winnie had so little, only one box and one bag, the carpetbag Dagou packed with clothes for the hospital. Someone must have brought it back to the Spiritual House after she died.

James goes through the box. Although his mother was able to scale down her belongings in Buddhist fashion, some of her old habits did survive her transition to a life of tranquility. There are very few personal possessions, but there are multiples of each. James counts two small statuettes of the Guan Yin—one gold, one robed in white—and two small incense pots. There are seven strands of prayer beads. Three of these James keeps for himself and his brothers, and the rest he gives to Omi. There are a couple of beautiful old shoehorns. Half-used toiletries, which he throws out, with doubles, which he gives away. Only items of the old country, irreplaceable, are singular. A pendant of Guan Yin seated on a lily pad. An ivory comb missing two teeth. A jade button.

Why had his mother lit incense, all those years? Because of her quarrels with his father? Because of Dagou? Because of the hatred and anger in her house?

When he's repacked the remaining items into the box, Omi picks it up, somewhat unnecessarily, and follows him to the car.

James puts down the bag of clothes and takes out his keys. Omi sets down the box, seizes his hand, and looks up at him, her eyes filled with tears. He's suddenly panicked by the grip of her bony fingers. He remembers hearing someone say that people who become Buddhists begin with too many feelings.

"Winnie was my friend," Omi says.

James understands that the passion he glimpsed between Omi and the other novice is fueled by grief. He's filled with pity and the desire to be alone. "Thank you, Omi."

James opens the trunk, hoists Winnie's things inside. Stooping under the lid of the trunk, he finds himself staring at Winnie's carpetbag.

The bag is burgundy in color. But how is this possible, when he knows, remembers with the vividness of small details in devastating moments, that the bag in her closet at the hospital was blue? He can still visualize the blue carpetbag, which no one ever opened because Winnie, after checking in, never left the unit. She had done everything she could to detach herself from him, but the news of Leo's death was an unendurable blow to her. She never again wore anything except for skimpy, freezing, cotton hospital gowns. Blanket after blanket they spread over her, tucking them around her shoulders, while the bag sat in the closet. Not long afterward, she suffered her second, devastating stroke. James envisions his mother, unresponsive, in the hospital bed. He feels again the recognition that she's let him go. But he has no recollection of what happened to the blue bag.

James unzips the burgundy bag. It's half-filled with clothes packed for the hospital, folded neatly, smelling of incense.

Without warning, he remembers the train station. The old man's melting features. He remembers the concrete and steel, shadows, night falling, cold, the taste of cranberries.

Back in January, while Winnie was still alive, the police questioned him and his brothers about a bag belonging to Zhang Fujian of Suzhou, China. They all denied knowing the location of the bag. Ming had never seen it. Dagou had never heard of it. James described how he'd put it into the cavernous trunk of his father's Ford Taurus. But he couldn't remember taking it out. The police searched the Ford, the house, the restaurant. They never found it.

At the time, James and Fang wondered what connection the police could have discovered between Leo's death and the bag carried by the man in the train station. Were the two cases intersecting? Why did the officers question James so thoroughly, so pointlessly, about a bag of money that, as far as they could see, had nothing to do with Dagou, their father, or the restaurant?

Now James hears an echo of Fang's voice in the alley: *Where's the money?* It doesn't matter whether the two cases intersect. It's his responsibility to report his new discovery to the police.

He thinks back, once more, to December, to his arrival with Ming, in Haven. At the restaurant, he'd transferred Zhang Fujian's bag into his father's Ford. Say he had later that night removed the bag, along with his own luggage, and brought it into the house. There, somebody—most likely his father—could have discovered it. But it was also possible he, James, had abandoned the bag inside his father's trunk, bringing only his own luggage into the house. It was possible Zhang Fujian's bag had been left inside the Ford and Dagou had unloaded it, instead of this burgundy bag, for Winnie, at the hospital. In a haze of anger at his father and in panic over Winnie's sudden illness, Dagou could've removed Zhang Fujian's blue bag from the Ford, confusing it with Winnie's, and taken it to her hospital room. It could have rested in her little closet, in the hospital, while detectives impounded and searched the Ford to recover the bag for Cecilia Chang, the bag that was somehow connected to the investigation. Then, after Winnie died, someone—one of his brothers, or even one of his parents' friends—would've carried the blue bag out of the hospital and loaded it into a car. And then what?

Dagou might remember. Or he might, at least, remember bringing this other bag of Winnie's clothes back to the Spiritual House. But Dagou has enough to worry about now, and, sunk as he would be in a medicating haze of pork noodles and jiu cai, cannot be expected to keep things straight.

Ming isn't much better. Although he's now frequently in Haven, staying at the family house, in his old room, he's in a deep distraction. He's usually bent over his laptop, arguing with Katherine or Jerry over plans for the trial; or else he's sunk into their father's old chair, his face lit by his phone, buried in his Phoenix deal.

James pulls over and texts Ming. *Where is the bag of clothes from Ma's room at the hospital?*

He speeds the remaining half mile and runs into the house, taking the stairs down to the basement two at a time.

Ming doesn't text back. For an hour, James works downstairs, methodically moving every box and suitcase, every duffel. Layer by layer, what he unearths is not a few months old, but years, decades old, from the time when his mother and father were hopeful new Americans, jaunty and light-stepping, filled with qi. Had his father ever worn a fedora? Had his mother ever been slender enough to fit into the qipaos from the red suitcase? James finds three cigar boxes emblazoned with the words *It's a boy!* and pastel blue cutouts of gingerbread children. He raises one of the boxes to his face, sniffs the faded, sweet tobacco smell. He searches every corner of the basement. After an hour, he climbs, more slowly, back upstairs. There's one other place to look. As he approaches the room that was once his parents', his footsteps slow.

The familiarity and strangeness of the room assault him. The wide dresser top his mother once tidied, frantically putting things away, is now piled with clothing and the Chinese newspapers that block the walls, the window, pressing from all sides. The musty air is thick with Leo's stale sweat. His animal substance fills the room. Yet James smells, also—he's sure of it—loneliness, and fear. He turns on the light. First the closet, piled with shoes: he goes through it pair by pair, box by box, to the back of Winnie's corner. Tears smart his eyes. He closes them briefly, then continues to look through the items in the bureaus, under the bed. Finally, conceding failure, James leaves the room, shutting the door behind him.

Unknown

James texts Ming a second time, but gets no response. Then he showers and waits for Alice. Sitting at the unlit kitchen table, he watches for her shadow at the back door. In an effort to stay unseen, surrounded by windows, he doesn't even risk a lit phone to check his email. The lengthening days push back the dusk, requiring the two of them to meet later and later. In her bedroom, in the gathering dark, Alice is shedding her worn nightgown for a black T-shirt and jeans. She's perching on her bedroom windowsill, climbing onto the porch roof, and shimmying down a post, stealing along the ten alley blocks to the house. He's protested her route, worrying she'll be unsafe, but no one frequents the back alleys except for other lovers hurrying to their assignations. She's watched over by Haven's secret-keepers, and by the ghost of Leo Chao. Even during this time in the glare of trial publicity, it's possible, they've learned, to keep an open secret from the eyes of reporters, friends, and all family but Dagou. Everyone smiles over the public knowledge that he and Alice are sweet on one another. But apart from Dagou, no one would approve of what they do together on the nights when Ming is at the restaurant.

James designs his daily plans and conversations to protect their meetings. He's aware now of a depth and cunning he never knew he had. With each successful machination, he stretches the reach of his inheritance: Chao wiliness, Chao secrecy, Chao cunning. Still, he's surprised when things work out. He feels a jolt each time he sees her shadow at the kitchen door. Feels astonishment, in the bedroom, each time he's able to bring her to pleasure. Chao appetite, Chao desire. Alice is less bewildered than he. Somehow, she always knew, in her sketchbook: her elaborate visual imaginings of the underground were early explorations of what lay beneath the visible world. For James, each spark of power and pleasure is a discovery. Their nights together are changing him, changing his life, maybe even more than they're changing Alice. James knows he's in love. He knows he's experiencing a sexual awakening: dimly he understands he won't always feel every moment as intensely as he does now. Dagou has told him. Long ago, Dagou warned him. But he doesn't think about it. This denial is also an inheritance of the Chaos.

Tonight it's warm, and in the creases of her skin James can sniff the sharp and intimate smell of fresh sweat. Their bodies slap together wetly. Afterward, they lie in bed and watch the watery moonlight shining through the window, moving up the wall, glinting against his little group of childhood trophies. Alice reaches over him for her glasses and puts them on. Not for the first time, he's seized with the knowledge, the fear, that she's about to change everything. But when she speaks, her tone is light.

"A funny thing happened," she says. "On the way here. I was in the alley that crosses Kelly Street, and I heard barking from somewhere that sounded just like Alf. Exactly. But when I looked around, the only dog I could see turned out to be a sort of poodle with its nose sticking out of a car window."

"Are you sure?"

Alice nods. "What I really knew, in that moment, was—I was *sure* of it—that Alf is alive, and someone's taking care of him."

"I don't think so."

After three months, James hasn't received a response to his signs, ads, and repeated check-ins with the Humane Society and other local shelters. More than the other confirmed, known losses, the question of Alf keeps him awake at night. Ming is no help. Dagou and Brenda are consumed with worry over other problems; James doesn't want to bother them about it. He has told only Alice; they've spent hours repeating the same conversation.

"Of course, Alf can't have just disappeared," she says now.

James replies with a point he's made a dozen times. "If he was brought to the police department, or the Humane Society, we would know. We had a chip embedded between his shoulder blades. Dagou had it registered. They would call us."

Alice touches the spot between James's shoulder blades. She knows James has called the police department that morning, calls them every morning, so they don't forget to keep an eye out for Alf's body.

"I wish we'd gotten him a GPS collar," James says for the tenth time. "But Ba didn't want to pay for it."

"He wasn't wearing his collar," she reminds him, as she does every time the idea of a GPS occurs to him.

"I think he's dead."

"Well, I think it's possible he *isn't* dead, *or* at the police department, *or* the Humane Society. Someone's taking care of him. Someone who's too busy or upset to bother looking at the news. Or maybe . . ." James senses she's about to say something she's never mentioned in all their conversations. "Maybe they know who he is, know who he belongs to, but they've fallen in love with him and they don't want to give him up."

Alf's secret life. James remembers his father's words, when Dagou proposed buying the GPS collar. "Leave the dog alone," Leo said. "Let him have his secret life!" Leo would know more than anyone. James remembers Alf's familiarity with the route to Letter City. Brenda thought he had a girlfriend there. Alf, keeper of secrets.

Alice says, "Mr. Strycker called the store today."

Simeon Strycker is the prosecuting attorney.

"He wants you to testify for the prosecution?"

"Yes."

James shakes his head. He imagines Dagou talking into the reeds about killing Leo. He sees Ming, his jaw clenched, driving through the snow. And he knows that he, James Chao, Alice's secret lover, is also capable of doing something wild, entirely irrational. It might be an act of heroism or an act of self-destruction. At the moment, he would do anything to protect Alice.

"What does he want you to say?"

"I don't want to talk about it," she says. "I just want you to know. Just you and Lynn and Fang."

"Okay," he says. He curls away from her, on his side. Alice curls behind him and slides her arm around him. But her words ring between them. Why won't she tell him? He tells her everything.

Alice believes in Alf's private life, because she, Alice, has a private life. James knows Alice, has known her since he can remember. Yet she is unknowable.

Invisible Car

Where is the bag of clothes from Ma's room at the hospital?

On the shuttle at O'Hare Airport, Ming frowns over James's text.

He's en route to the East Coast, more than ready to leave—frantic with the desperation that torments him whenever he's been in Haven longer than a day or two, even and especially now that his parents are dead. Time has shifted for Ming as well as for James: as he reads the text, his mind circles, once again, back to December. There was the phone call to the restaurant, about the missing carpetbag. The quarrel with Katherine. The argument with O-Lan.

Why is he preoccupied by his disagreement with O-Lan, a person who, truth be told, repulses him? O-Lan smells strongly of hand lotion but underlying this is an odor lotion can't disguise. There's a term for this in Mandarin, "fox smell." He has found her B.O. repugnant since their first encounter years ago, when he conversed with her in defiance of Leo's callous disregard of this new help, ignorant, clearly without papers (which was one of the ways his father saved money). Even now, out of resistance, Ming continues to talk to her; and, as if she senses his insincerity, she makes their conversations as challenging for him as possible.

That afternoon, December 23, with James trying to eavesdrop in the dining room, she asked him whether he was still planning to fly east. She'd overheard his father telling a customer, one of the Chinese community, that he was leaving town.

"You're flying out today?" she asked. He leaned forward to decipher her Mandarin. "You know you won't be able to come back."

She spoke too quickly for him. He was forced to ask, "What are you talking about?"

She stared, not at him, but at the artwork on the wall. Regarded the cheap Song landscape reproduction with an expression of contempt.

"There's going to be a storm," she said. "The storm, our storm, is moving east. And it will join with another storm, coming up the coast."

"I'll just have to try to go," he said. He wasn't sure of the Mandarin expression for "take off."

She went back to her work on the counter. The kitchen was quiet in the midafternoon, with only a large cauldron of broth simmering on the stove.

"Hey," he said, more harshly than he had intended.

Slowly she turned, in mocking obedience to his command.

"You told me that after I reach New York, I won't be able to come back. What made you think I would want to come right back?"

In her impenetrable expression, he could make out the shape her face would have when she was an old woman. "I'm just saying, young boss, that if you decide to leave this afternoon, you won't be able to come back. You'll be gone for days."

She was forcing him to ask. "What difference does that make?"

"If you were to be needed at home."

"I have a lot of work to do. My mother is out of danger. Why would I come back?"

"You would be the one to know that. He's your brother, young boss."

This remark for some reason lit Ming up with rage, but he only answered, sardonically, in English, "Am I my brother's keeper?"

Because she couldn't understand, he had the last word. She turned back to chopping cabbage in a manner both servile and dismissive. Ming escaped to the dining room, only to bump into Katherine looking for Dagou and to begin *that* infuriating conversation. Then the phone call about the carpetbag. The meeting with James at the Other Restaurant, and then straight to the airport. Like a well-trained athlete, speeding through security and boarding, buckling his seat belt. The flight attendant closing the door.

The moment his plane left the ground, Ming knew he'd made the wrong decision. The certainty gripped him like a sudden claustrophobia. He took out his phone but couldn't focus on the screen.

There was nothing to do. He'd have to wait it out. He adjusted his seat, closed his eyes.

But his mind wandered to the restaurant again, the conversation with O-Lan. "There's going to be a storm." He hated her. Her fox smell, her shovel jaw, the inexplicably familiar smirk. The minutes hobbled by. After some time mulling over this half dream, he became aware of a change in the plane's flight pattern: it was no longer descending, but banking. The plane had slipped into a holding pattern and was making long, sweeping circles around Newark Airport. Pushing up the window shade, he could see the distant flashing lights of two other planes looping below them, waiting. The pilot's voice crackled over the audio system: bad weather, no one allowed to land. Air traffic control was diverting all planes inland to Bradley Airport near Hartford, Connecticut.

An hour later he was staring at the lit grid of the runways, their edges sparkling with light snow. It was now early in the morning, and his eyes hurt. Why, after all, had he thought he could beat this storm? It was the same winter storm that had buried Haven, the snow into which Alf had vanished. And now, on the East Coast, the storm was being whipped up by a nor'easter's howling wind.

He turned on his phone and found a text from Katherine: *Big family fight at hospital.*

He sat in the dark plane for perhaps five minutes with the snow-sparkled runway lights woven around him. He'd said, "I'm not my brother's keeper!" He texted back. *Thank you for letting me know.*

She instantly replied, *Dagou is very upset.*

After a moment, he typed back, *He gets that way.*

He threatened your father. People heard.

As the other passengers deplaned, Ming sat belted into his seat, almost afraid that any movement would reveal something to the sender of this text. He imagined Katherine waiting, also in the dark, her black eyes fixed on her phone, her precise, smooth features reflecting its glow, a thousand miles away now. Could she look through the screen and see his agitation? He must be calm, very calm.

After a long moment, a reply came like a gift into his mind. He typed, *Maybe you should talk to him.* He erased it.

I'm surprised you managed to leave, she continued out of turn.

I was diverted to Hartford. He sat still for a second, then typed, *I'm deplaning now.*

Ming, he needs to talk to someone.

Ming could think of no way to answer her unspoken question, nothing she would accept. Finally, he wrote, *You.*

Wasn't this the permission she wanted? Wanted, for whatever reason, permission to be the strong one, when his brother was weak? For a dozen years now, more mismatched every year, unwilling to let his brother go and take a chance on showing her flaws to someone who was not inferior to her? Ming scowled. And who was he, Ming, to mock her for this? Wasn't he, Ming, also relying on her superiority and competence, leaning on her unnatural interest in his family, and on the unswerving, inexplicable bedrock of her loyalty to them all? Relying upon Katherine to get him out of a situation he couldn't bear. The difference was that he, Ming, *knew* he was being a coward, while his brother was a coward without a kernel of self-awareness.

Katherine didn't text back.

On the tarmac at Bradley Airport, hunched into the collar of his overcoat, Ming took out his phone and began to look up flights back to the Midwest. All flights were canceled for the next two days. Air travel in the entire Northeast was at a standstill.

He would rent a car and drive to New York City. Wait out the storm there for a couple of days, dealing with an electronic blizzard of its own kind, with Phoenix. Ming chose a sport utility vehicle with four-wheel drive, a white BMW. He would blend into the snow. He felt an urgency to hide himself, to reveal his location to no one. Someone could be coming after him. This is irrational, he thought. You should go to a hotel and rest. But he was being perfectly rational: white was neutral, white was invisible, white was innocent.

He'd opted out of all of this. Chosen to live his life away from his family. The stupidity of Dagou, the naïveté of James. The cruelty of his father. He'd done everything he could for them. Had paid dowry to the SH, given his mother what she wanted. Had tried to talk to James, to tell him to get away. There was no way to help Dagou. But he'd warned Katherine, repeatedly. Hadn't he told her to give up? What else could he possibly have done? But he'd left Katherine in Haven while Winnie was sick. (His mother would be all right, she would forgive him. She knew he needed to get away as badly as she did.) Was it possible, had Katherine been trying to tell him, that his brothers weren't as strong as he, that his mother's illness would be especially hard on them? Hard on Dagou? (He'd sent Katherine in his place. He'd left town. Katherine knew he had done this.)

He drove over the metal teeth at the rental exit, steering the BMW through a flurry of snow toward Interstate 91. He would turn south, toward the city.

But when he reached the highway his hand shot out and flicked the signal to the left, toward the north. He stared at the blinking arrow and thought of O-Lan's little triangular teeth, like a cat's teeth. He must follow it, the blinker heading not south, toward New York City, but north, into Massachusetts, where he would reach Interstate 90, which would lead him back to Haven.

The roads around the airport had been plowed. Not until he turned onto the highway did he realize there were at least four inches of churned-up snow on its surface. It took an hour to drive the twenty-five miles north to Springfield, Massachusetts. There he left 91 and slowly followed the white exit ramp onto Interstate 90, a broad, churned snow trail west, into the Berkshires.

As he drove into the mountains, the storm grew worse. Snow fell through the headlight beams in silvery gusts, pouring down on the narrow tire tracks before him, as if someone above had opened up an enormous box of glitter and dumped it over Western Massachusetts. The lone car in front of him crawled along at twenty miles per hour.

Ming pulled in at a rest stop to buy coffee. The parking lot was crowded with shaggy white cars. Making his way between their shapes, Ming slipped. He was obliged to right himself by plunging his arm into the layer of white covering another car. The shock of cold up his sleeve enraged him. His phone fell into the snow. He crouched in the snow, pawing through it until his ice-block fingers bumped against something solid.

In the food court, travelers had hung their damp coats on the backs of their chairs. They sipped coffee and played cards. He checked his phone, then the clock on the wall. His phone said one a.m. but the clock said three a.m. What time zone was he in? Leaving the bathroom, Ming felt a buzz in his pocket. He turned off the phone.

A few of the travelers glanced up. He sensed, with the instincts of someone who had grown up as an outsider, that their eyes rested upon him for a moment longer than they normally would. They were thinking what was he doing here. Quickly, he checked his reflection in the window. Of the three brothers, only Ming, the smallest, favored running and biking. Like all of the brothers, he had their father's high cheekbones, and eyes with strong epicanthal folds and not a hint of a double eyelid. All of the brothers were good-looking, but only Ming had Winnie's pale skin.

When he went back outside, he couldn't find his car. The parking lot was freshly covered, unfamiliar. Back and forth he walked between the rows of vehicles, scraping windows, license plates. Snowflakes sifted down his collar. Finally, he decided on a methodical approach; he clicked his key fob at the beginning, middle, and end of every row. This proved successful. He turned on the engine and heater, used his arms to swipe at the windows. There were no other cars at the pumps. Cowards.

He waited at the entrance ramp and got behind a pickup draped in white. He followed, creeping along, sipping from his coffee. Heavy snow churned under his wheels. Then the pickup turned off the highway. Ming drove on. Here and there were swipe marks where a car had slid off the road; cars lay overturned like dead roaches, and on one of the long inclines near Lenox, several trucks lay on their sides. Police cars twirled their lights. After Lenox, he was able to drive behind a snowplow for dozens of miles, but the plow turned off near the state border and he was alone, the lone car traveling west, an invisible white car in the white storm, traveling secretly past Albany.

There had been a maddening superiority about the corners of O-Lan's mouth. But despite her warning to him that he wouldn't be able to return, he was coming. As for Katherine, who'd called him up for the sole purpose of chastising him for leaving Haven, leaving his brother: he would show Katherine; he would arrive after traveling heroically through the night, and she would be astonished, humbled.

Gradually the snow grew pale; the sun had risen. He hadn't yet reached Rochester. It was the morning of Christmas Eve; Dagou would be preparing for the party.

All day, Ming drove on, stopping for coffee and catnaps in the passenger seat. As he had guessed, the snow gave out near Erie, Pennsylvania; the highways in Ohio were well plowed. At three a.m. on Christmas Day, the sky was clear. He went into a service plaza to stretch his legs. Holding a fresh black coffee, he walked past a man and a boy wearing puffy down jackets. The boy was sleepy but the man and Ming locked eyes for a moment. The man's eyes popped open. Startled, Ming checked his reflection in the window. An alien and yet familiar creature stared back at him from the semidarkness. Its face was that of a stranger: sallow, greenish yellow skin, slits for eyes. The creature was unshaven, his dark mug protruding. Ming raised his arm; the creature raised its arm. He hurled his coffee and a blotch covered the window. The smell of coffee hit the air. Hot dark drops splattered on his shirt.

"Hey!" somebody yelled.

He bolted through the doors and out into the snow, ran to his car, and pulled back onto the highway.

It was afternoon on Christmas Day before he turned on his phone and found several voice messages from Katherine, *Please call.* It was from Katherine that Ming learned his father had died in the cold.

An Imagined Family I Never Had

Sorry to bother you again. Do you know what happened to the bag from Ma's hospital room? I'm about to file a report with the police.

Ming texts back, *Someone else must have unloaded it. Check at the SH.* He pockets his phone and takes the elevator up to his apartment: clean, neutrally furnished, comfortingly bare. He's chosen a high-rise in the Thirties from which he can follow the changing traffic lights straight up the avenue to his midtown office. He swaps out his shirts and underwear; presto, the suitcase is ready for his next trip to Wisconsin. He's experimenting with a direct flight to Chicago. In a week, Katherine will pick him up at O'Hare and drive him to Haven for a meeting to discuss, and hopefully decide for good, whether Dagou is going to testify on his own behalf.

Ming has time for frequent trips to Haven now, because he's no longer sleeping. Katherine insists it's mania, but he can't be so easily pathologized. Someone has to keep an eye on Jerry Stern: someone has to monitor preparations for Dagou's trial, a month away. With JJ and Lulu gone to California for good, someone has to help James and Dagou and Brenda keep the restaurant open. Maybe now that he's an orphan, Ming is finally being the son his parents wanted. Returning to Haven every weekend, helping Jerry plan the family defense. Coming up with the money for bail, not to mention the fee for breaking the lease on that ridiculous penthouse. Working shifts at the restaurant, helping out his brothers.

Only Katherine is Ming's competitor, coming to Haven as frequently as he does. She drives up from Chicago every weekend, staying at a picturesque B&B run by a gay Ukrainian couple who seem to be unaware of who she is (although Ming suspects they know all about the trial and are leaving her in peace out of what he grudgingly calls midwestern decency). She's obsessed with the legal aspects of Dagou's case.

Others don't use the word "obsessed" to describe Katherine's behavior—instead, they say "dedicated" and "loyal" and "devoted." No one has the heart to question why she's still visiting, still wearing Dagou's ring. Once, Mary Wa slipped up and referred to Katherine as Dagou's wife. (Ming pointed out this would mean Brenda, his actual partner, was his mistress.) Ming is the only person besides Brenda who sees Katherine for what she is—a vengeful martyr in a Kabuki mask of dedication. Ming is also the only person besides Brenda who knows how infrequently Dagou actually talks to Katherine—knows (because he's keeping track) that aside from infrequent, strained coffees, Dagou *never* sees Katherine.

At O'Hare, Katherine executes a perfect pickup on the arrivals curb. But the pleasure of being met at the airport is destroyed by her jabbering about family matters. Ming has to bite his lip to keep from rattling out a stream of critique: She's as bad as the most racially deprived white person fetishizing Asian culture. Her interest in Dagou, in the Chao family, is entirely due to her sense of deprivation after having been raised as racially Chinese in a well-meaning but white American family. Can't she get over it? Can't she even be grateful for the total, blissful wipe-out of the self-abnegation, the anxiety, the shameful graspingness, of immigration? Rather than missing out, Katherine has been fast-forwarded; and yet she chooses, stubbornly and idiotically, to push the rewind button by worshipping their family. She's unaccountably sorrowful about the deaths of his parents, even his father.

"Are you sad?" she asks Ming tearily.

He glowers at her profile; she's focused on the road, responsible driver that she is. No one else would have the gall to ask that question of him. Keeping his voice level, he replies that people need to mourn in their own time. He takes out his phone to avoid more talk. But she doesn't notice. Is he getting enough sleep? Is everything all right with his health?

"I'm fine. I need a cup of coffee."

"I'm sure you're fine," she says, after they pull into a Starbucks, "but you look simply awful."

"I've got to take a call," he says, hoping to end the conversation.

"Is it Dagou?" She blushes. "I mean, are you going to talk to Dagou?"

"Are *you*?"

"He's—busy," she says. "My therapist says this is a hard time for him."

In his New York life (his adult life), Ming has the luxury of an even temper, but an hour with Katherine and he can't control himself.

"Does your therapist try to make you forgive him?" He gulps the coffee, burning his mouth. "Does she say it's all a *process*?"

Katherine stops at the car and bends over her sneaker, slender fingers making clean white shoestrings into perfect loops. Ming imagines her as a child, learning to tie her shoes, stubbornly making rabbit ears. The vision fills him with rage. He presses on.

"Why do you idolize him? Why do you idolize *us*?" he asks, wrenching open the door to the passenger seat. "You've got to know by now, Katherine, that just because we're biologically connected, and although we're *one hundred percent Chinese American*, our family is a clusterfuck. We're lost. My parents' marriage was indisputably lost, and Dagou's lost, he's a disaster, and only a genuine miracle will pull him out of it. Even James, his life is going to be lost the moment he grows up enough to know his ass from his elbow. And I—"

"*You* are filled with self-hatred. You're as racist as any extremist bigot!"

She gets into the car, but doesn't start the engine. Instead, she turns and glares at him. He's alarmed, not by what she's just said (she's probably right), but by the sight of her face. Katherine is pale, her eyes filled with tears, and even though he knows she was raised by a husky Corcoran blonde, her emotional palette is not his mother's, not a drop of her upbringing bleeds Chinese; despite this knowledge, he is seized with the kind of pain only Winnie made him feel. It's pain he would give anything—any amount—to escape. *Has* given.

Katherine starts the car and pulls back onto the highway, avoiding his gaze.

"You idolize him," he repeats.

"You *think* I do," she says, her voice shaking. "You think I worship him, and all of you. You think I humiliate myself clinging to an imagined family I never had."

"I've got to get out of here," Ming says. "I can't stand this for one more minute."

"I *have* a loving family," she says.

Ming leaps at this. "Exactly!" he says. "They love you, you all treat each other way better than anyone in my family treats each other!"

"And they *support* my relationship with Dagou, they want me to be connected to my Chinese identity—"

"*What* Chinese identity?" Ming shouts. To his horror, she looks, again, like a little girl. He sees her at six years old, standing on the playground, watching the sun shine on the blond hair of her classmates. He can't stand it. Even though he's been there, is familiar with the origins of self-hatred, *knows* he can't bear it because it reminds him of himself, he can't speak to her any more. He puts his headphones on and turns up the sound.

They meet at Katherine's B&B to discuss the question of whether Dagou should be a witness for the defense. Dagou wants to tell his story. "I just have to explain what happened," he's told each of them. Brenda says he should do what he thinks is best. Katherine, on the other hand, says what happened isn't believable; it's best for Dagou to remain silent. Katherine has called this meeting in an effort to take charge, but she's too bossy and the pitch of her anxiety is too high. Without meaning to be, they're all against her. Ming takes notes on his phone.

Katherine: "We've got to persuade Dagou that not to testify is in his own best interest!"

Brenda: "Won't the jury be expecting him to defend himself?"

Katherine: "He's not required to testify!"

Brenda: "Jerry, is that true?"

Jerry: "It's true."

Katherine: "We need to lay low, be very careful! We have no idea what questions Simeon Strycker would prepare to trip him up, to twist his words, in a cross examination."

Ming (in Charlie Chan accent): "Be vely careful, vely ancient Chinese seclet."

Katherine: "That's not funny."

Brenda (to Katherine): "Simeon Strycker can't twist the truth. I think you're watching too much Court TV."

Katherine: "Strycker's got something up his sleeve. I wasn't going to mention this. But sometimes, when I'm in Haven, I'm pretty sure he's hired someone to follow me—someone must be following us around."

Silence. Ming assumes Brenda has taken Katherine's point, but it turns out she's only pausing for dramatic effect. She lowers her voice. "You don't believe he's innocent," she says. "That's why you think he shouldn't speak on his own behalf."

For a moment, Katherine looks startled. She reddens, as if caught. She recovers herself. "This is about how to win. This isn't about who can *stand by her man*."

"Won't it backfire?" Ming asks, finally coming in on Katherine's side. He launches into his argument: That Dagou has zero impulse control, he could say anything. Isn't this already clear, Ming points out, from all the crazy things Dagou has said to the police, when he had the right to remain silent? Isn't it obvious he'll do the same thing in court? But Ming is too late. Katherine pushes back her chair and runs out of the room. They hear the door slam, her footsteps on the pavement, then the revving of her engine. An empty gesture, driving away in a huff, since the B&B is her lodging, after all. They shrug, and everyone packs up, goes home, to spare themselves and Katherine the embarrassment of their being there when she returns.

Later he feels obliged to pick up her call. Her voice, high and tight, crackles into his ear. "This is insane! Dagou needs a different defense attorney than Jerry Stern! Anne Sloane is the hottest young defense attorney in Milwaukee and she's dying to take the case. You need to help me, Ming! Talk to Dagou."

She's right: Dagou needs a better lawyer. But Ming has spoken to Dagou half a dozen times, and Dagou has refused to work with anyone except Jerry Stern.

"He trusts Jerry," Ming says.

"Then he's an idiot." Katherine begins to sob.

"Come over to our house," Ming says finally. "I'll make dinner."

Ming searches through the family kitchen for supplies. Winnie left them overstocked with canned and dried goods, but the Chao men don't buy groceries. The fridge is stuffed with take-out containers. While Katherine pretends to catch up on emails from work, Ming digs out from the piled-up counter a sprouting yellow onion and some aged potatoes. He dices the onion, and, after digging the eyes out of the potatoes, he cubes them. He watches Katherine's reflection in the picture window. She studies his wiry hands moving with confidence from knife to bowl to pan handle. (At home, he won't use the wok.) He cracks some eggs, deftly, showing off his dexterousness perhaps, and makes a savory Spanish omelet. Dagou isn't the only talented cook among the Chao brothers. The aging cabbage and the carrots from the fridge become, with a few flicks of magic, a salad, dressed with sesame oil and sweetened rice vinegar, sprinkled with sesame seeds. Ming and Katherine sit down at the cluttered kitchen table and eat together, not talking. Although doubtless Katherine would've preferred something "more authentic"—fried rice with eggs, green onions instead of yellow, and stir-fried cabbage instead of salad—the dinner leaves her curiously softened. Waving Ming aside, she takes off Dagou's jade ring and puts it gently on the counter, then does the dishes.

They retire to the living room and continue to fight over the case. Ming thinks Katherine is overmanaging Jerry Stern. Jerry is disorganized, but it's the disorganization of someone who knows what's in each pile of papers. (Katherine, Ming notices, is mentally re-sorting Jerry's piles, which would only leave Jerry in a state of confusion.) Ming argues Katherine should trust Jerry's instincts. Jerry will be the defense lawyer, whereas Katherine will be a bystander, save for the period when she will be a witness.

It's not clear whether Katherine herself should testify. He can't explain why he has this apprehension. She is, in essence, the perfect witness: well groomed, conservatively dressed, reasonable, relentlessly honest, utterly credible. Despite all this, for some reason he has a sense the trial won't go well for her. On this night, fortified perhaps by the omelet, he ventures to tell her.

All of her befuddled pleasure from the little dinner is instantly forgotten.

"How do *you* know anything?" she says. "Who knows Dagou better than I do? Who talked to him every day, while you were off *making your fortune* in Manhattan?"

Ming, pushed into a corner, comes out fighting.

"That's why you should back off," he says, reaching for his superpower of expressionlessness. "This is an emotional trial for you. You could crack under the pressure."

Katherine grows scarlet. Her lower lip swells, and Ming is reminded of Dagou and their father at the Spiritual House. With a *screek*, Katherine pushes back her chair. She grabs her purse and stalks stiff-legged into the kitchen. He hears the jingle of her keys.

This is followed by a long silence. There's no movement toward the door; she's absolutely motionless.

Purse in hand, Katherine stands in the kitchen, rigid fury abruptly slack, struggling to comprehend what has happened.

It is a Chao family foible: misplacing things. You could call it losing things, though they never do call it this. They've lost too much: their family ship balancing bravely on a crest, a wave of losses. Lost money, lost home, lost country, lost languages, lost years, lost ancestors, lost stories, lost memories, lost hopes, lost lives; and there is more, it's clear from their veiled faces, their foreboded happiness, their infrequent, wild laughter. Their extravagance. To balance the losses, poor Winnie stockpiled more sons, more dishes, more emergency supplies. Months after her departure, the kitchen cabinets are still three-deep in canisters of tea, white wood ears, brown wood ears, bottles of fermented rice, bags of dried shrimp.

Is it because of Winnie's crowded counter space that in this moment Katherine can't recall, can't quite even imagine, where she put the ring? (Or is part of it, she can't help thinking, that she's rattled by the little dinner Ming made? The way he cooked, with more reticence and more precision than Dagou, but, unexpectedly, with that same attention?) She wants to leave him in a fury, but she literally cannot leave empty-handed. She breathes for several minutes, in and out, moving her gaze slowly, methodically around a package of dried mushrooms. The space on the counter is empty.

She looks at her naked finger. Then at her other hand, down at the floor, back at the counter. Then into the sink. She doesn't lose things. She keeps them safe. Someone *moved* it; it was moved. Not by her. Did Ming get up, when they were arguing—did he leave the room?

Footsteps behind her. "What's the matter? What're you looking for?"

She turns, flinches at how young and tired he seems. "It's—the ring. I can't find it."

He scowls at her finger, and then, without a word, they begin to search. Systematically, removing every plastic pouch, every canister, tin, container, piling them on the table. Wiping down the counter. Squinting under the counter.

"Are you sure you put it there?"

"I'm sure." Her voice is shaking.

They move everything back to the counter and go over the table. Then the sink again, the floor, the windowsills, the cabinets. They look through Katherine's purse, although she's certain she didn't put it in there. Then the other room. Two hours pass. They're exhausted. She can tell he wants her to leave: if only she would leave!

"Maybe I'm remembering wrong," she says. "Maybe I knocked it into the sink. Maybe we should take the drain apart." She stares, hard, at the empty sink strainer. "No," she says, "I'm *sure* I put it on the counter."

But there's no other possibility. Unless—*would* he, would Ming have done it?

"What is it?"

"*Nothing*."

Could it be? Is it possible that, despite his claims, he's jealous of Dagou because he's the oldest? Does Ming secretly want all of the things Dagou has never questioned being entitled to? Could it actually be—her breathing sharpens—

"*What is it?*"

She snaps. "Did *you* take it?"

She expects him to explode. But he only shakes his head. "Why would I do that?"

"Because you're so competitive!" No, she is the exploding one. There's so much she's been holding back: what everybody thinks she feels; what she truly feels; what she alone knows, or suspects, and cannot even allow herself to think, about Dagou. She *must* hold back. She regains her self-control. "You might want the one valuable thing he has that you can't buy. You might want to be the one—the one to give the ring to the mother of the future family heirs. You might, somewhere, deep down, be as old-school patriarchal, as dynastic-thinking, as your brother, as your father!"

Her words are followed by a resounding stillness. Then Ming says, as quietly as James, "That I might want what he has."

"I'm sorry."

"I might. But I would never take it from you."

She thinks: Because it means so much to me, and not to him after all. But there is something else in his tone, an uncharacteristic, almost unendurable gentleness.

They stand and stare at one another. Her eyes burn with tears. She sees, making its way through months of weariness, grief, confusion, and pain, a spark—definitely, there is a moment when a flicker of Chao desire, which she knows so well, flares into Ming's black eyes. He will—unquestionably—take her into his arms. What does she want? But then Ming remembers who she is. He gathers himself, and says, "You should go home."

Useless Feelings

He doesn't get involved with Asian women. Though Katherine is only genetically Asian. She's been raised by a white family, and her emotions, Ming reminds himself, are white emotions! Still, because of certain childhood scars fused into his psyche, the sight of her discouragement (really, any flicker of upset or disappointment) stirs up in him useless feelings, Asian feelings, that have been pushed away long ago.

Ming can't tell if she still wants to be with Dagou. It could be pride alone that keeps her working on Dagou's behalf. But were Ming to be honest with himself, he believes it's less than fifty percent pride; it's more a profound loyalty and, yes, love. What kind of love is this? he wonders. What is its source? How and why did she attach herself to his buffoon of a brother in such a way that love was woven in so deep?

Ming remembers Katherine on the first Christmas Dagou brought her home. They were in their senior year of college, and Ming was a high school junior, old enough to recognize another socially disciplined introvert. She was pretty—beautiful, really, right from the beginning—but shy. Most likely it was Dagou's casual manners and his natural warmth that first drew her out. (Dagou's beer-faced grin, beaming through the crowd at a college party.) He remembers her meeting Winnie. She wasn't faking the part of the diffident, sycophantic future daughter-in-law; she was truly moved and honored.

If *he* (not Dagou) had been dating her, he would have recognized in that moment, with Katherine looking down at Winnie as if at a long-lost mother, and Winnie beaming back up at Katherine as if at a long-lost daughter, that he'd made a terrible mistake to bring her home. That he, the son and the lover, was now responsible. He would've taken better care of her. Katherine and his heedless, harebrained brother. It's more preposterous every day. How can her love be keeping her bound to him? From what depth of love could come this fathomless loyalty? And how can Dagou fail to see it—fail to see what a priceless, peerless gift he dangled, and now squanders?

Ming's First Visit to O-Lan

Weeks pass. It's two days before the trial. Ming is working on a large eggplant with garlic sauce, the final order of the night, when his phone buzzes at his hip. He sets down the spatula, turning from the sizzling wok to check the screen. It's a text from Rydson, telling him to fly to Phoenix in two days for a series of meetings. "Affirmative," Ming dictates, pocketing his phone, turning back to the stove.

So, he'll miss the first few days of the trial. Fine—he won't be in trouble; he's still basking in the halo effect from ponying up the bail.

Savagely, Ming scrapes singed eggplant and garlic from the bottom of the wok. He flinches as hot oil spits in his face, glaring at O-Lan, who stands at the counter slicing scallions into tiny *o*'s. Ming wonders if she was more communicative when Dagou was working. Since the forty-nine-day ceremony, Brenda and Dagou have spent every possible hour together at her house. Tonight, Freedy is serving; Ming is covering the kitchen while James is off with Alice on a supposedly secret date that has been meticulously arranged in person or by note. Alice has no mobile and it's hard to reach her away from the Oriental Food Mart. Ming has gone to see her there, with Mary Wa in the back room spying hopefully, maybe hoping he might save her daughter from being so eccentric and reclusive. In fact, the opposite is true. Privately, perhaps unknown even to James, Ming is supplying Alice with names and email addresses of potential employers in New York, information with which she may create a faraway, impoverished artistic life, a life even more powerfully private, sealed off from Mary.

Ming's sinuses fill with a pungent, burning odor. The eggplant has shriveled into a scorching mess. Ming wrenches the wok off the flame. He's ruined the order and must start over. Yet while he does this (dips oil into the second wok, throws in the garlic to begin again) there comes a nudge, a recognition working its way up from the deep subconscious. It's several minutes before he understands what caught his attention.

O-Lan's sneakers.

They're ancient Converse boy's sneakers that were once black, with white rubber toe tops, stars, and soles; but the toe tops and the stars are gray-brown with an accumulation of restaurant grease, and the black fabric has faded to a dull gray-brown as well, until black and white are almost the same color.

After closing, Ming waits for O-Lan to remove her apron, wash her hands, and step out of the kitchen, past the office. He waits for her car to leave the lot. He locks the restaurant door, and, keeping a distance of about two blocks, follows as she drives through the tangle of back alleyways.

Past old sleeping porches, garages, and back gardens; through unmarked intersections, close to lighted windows, Ming trails the distant taillights of O-Lan's car. It's an eighteen-year-old Dodge, entirely anonymous, probably unregistered. (After all, how could she register the car? She's not legally in this country. Her car can't be legal, either. Or is that true? He remembers Jerry saying one needs proof of residency to register a car, but that may not be the same as proof of citizenship.) Ming frowns into the dark. Years of driving as carefully as possible so as never to be stopped by the police; years of fixing every headlight and taillight. It's a wonder she drives at all. But they've all taken her and her car for granted. Sending her to the Oriental Food Mart. Roping her into bringing food to Winnie at the hospital.

Now she's bypassing Letter City, driving uphill, past the maze of houses to the neighborhood's inglorious back end, near a shabby warehouse for baked goods.

Ming pulls over a block away, switching off his lights. O-Lan parks behind an old house, emerges from the car carrying a bag over her shoulder, and circles up a fire escape whose black-painted metal threads gleam faintly. Ming waits until a light turns on in the attic. Then he gets back into his own car. He circles the block and finds a parking space, locking the door as he gets out. *Xiaoxin.* He places his feet on the metal steps that lead behind the shabby old house. Climbing, circling silently up and up. The door at the top of the stairs is small. The knob turns easily in his hand; he breathes.

Inside, O-Lan stands two yards away, looking coolly at his face.

"Hi," he says, startled to see she's waiting for him.

"Hi," she echoes the English word, her mouth opening blankly, like a goldfish. There's something unfamiliar yet recognizable in the way she says the word. He'll think about it later.

The room, the narrow footprint of the house, is bare and neat, but not fastidiously clean. The ceiling slants toward the eaves, where the low wall is dominated by a window.

"You're ill," she says, in her odd dialect.

"You were at my mother's memorial service," he says, struggling for his Mandarin vocabulary.

She doesn't answer. Ming walks over to the window and peers down the hill on the collection of chimneys and receding rooftops at the edge of town: dark and shabby, with one steep tin roof. The empty warehouse parking lot spreading like a lake beyond. "It's like a painting," he says. "In the winter, it would be almost like that painting by Bruegel the Elder, with the hunters in the snow."

"Your mind is wandering," she says. "You have been getting worse and worse for months. You should go back to New York and stop flying every week. Your younger brother is here. He can look after your older brother."

"You didn't answer me," he says. "I've never seen you at the Spiritual House before. You're not a Buddhist. Why did you come?"

"I can't pay my respects to the dead?"

"Do you respect the dead?"

"I do."

"You weren't invited," he continues after a moment.

"You weren't invited here."

"Why've you stayed in Haven for such a long time?"

"To you, how long is long?"

Now he's sure she's mocking him. He's flustered, hampered by his language skills, which are barely proficient. "This isn't about me. Long for you is more than two years. None of the other helpers stayed past a year. You have nothing tying you to this place. No real job, no family—"

He stops, inexplicably confused. "Did you have some kind of special arrangement with my father?"

"Yes," she says. "But not in the way you think."

He doesn't answer, worn out by the effort to converse in Mandarin.

"What do you think?" she asks.

Below, a man holding a plastic sack half-filled with aluminum cans searches the dumpster. He moves with measured concentration, stacking bags and pizza boxes to one side.

"It's very inappropriate that you have come here to my room," she says. "You're stranger than I would have thought."

Ming watches the man below. What she says is probably true.

"You're so proud of being able to speak Chinese. Yet you're also proud you're *not* Chinese."

Was that scorn in her voice? "But I am," he protests, surprising himself. "I am Chinese."

"You are a tourist. None of you brothers is Chinese, you least of all."

Ming clears his throat.

"I assumed you understood all this: that you, your brothers, all three of you are lost."

The yellow light fills his eyes as he turns to look at her. Strands of white in her hair, ashy skin still shiny with oil, bags under the eyes. Some fundamental answer encased in her bones. Why did he come? Yes, he wants, needs, to talk to this woman, but why?

She goes on. "And here I thought you understood, understood all along, and acted accordingly. Surely you left town knowing it was going to happen."

"What are you talking about?"

"I thought you knew. The storm. The storm coming to the East Coast. I still believe you knew. You don't want to take responsibility for what you knew was happening. You, and only you, possessed the knowledge and foresight to prevent it from happening. And yet you didn't."

"No," Ming says. "I didn't."

"You knew what you were doing."

"You're out of your mind."

"No, I think it's clear *you're* the one who is losing your mind."

A wingbeat of acknowledgment flicks between them.

"What do you mean, I knew what I was doing?"

"You're too intelligent to not see this. You knew about the freezer. You knew it was possible for someone to be trapped inside the freezer."

"Why would I have thought it would happen? Just because something is possible doesn't mean it will happen."

"But your older brother told you it would happen. He told the entire community, he broadcast it on the radio, that he wanted to close the door."

There's a radio on the kitchen counter. "He was angry, he was raving—"

"You knew how miserable William was, how much he hated your father," she says. He's struck by her certainty, her confidence. Is it because she's speaking the truth? "And you, too, hated him. You hated his embarrassing reputation for being boorish, a womanizer, a lout. But you hated him the most because he was an immigrant, a father who couldn't help you accomplish what you wanted, who could give you nothing to bring you closer to what you wanted to be. He was not only of no use to you, he was less than no use. He was a humiliating, shameful person with no control over his crude passions. He was an embarrassment, it would have been better if he were dead, then you wouldn't have to make excuses for him, hide him, disguise him, disguise yourself. Like your brother, you wished him gone. You know that by leaving town you were approving his murder. You wanted him to die! And so, when we were discussing the storm, we were discussing his murder. Americans love to talk about the weather—it can stand for so many things."

Ming waits: she has more to say.

"You, of all of us," she went on, "are the person who is least certain Dagou is innocent."

His mind moves back to O-Lan's first months at the restaurant. He was home for only a week that summer, her first. Didn't he try to speak to her, near the dishwasher? Wasn't he the least distant of the family?

"You hate me," he says. "But I've done nothing against you."

She does not reply, doesn't need to.

"You hate all of us. You think we're fat, stupid Americans. We're spoiled. But you think there's something *real* about us." She gives him a startled glance, and he knows he has correctly guessed her thoughts. "So you've stayed with us. Even my father couldn't figure out how to get rid of you." He remembers something. "He cut your salary once. I remember it, I saw the books. He cut your salary and you kept showing up." Confusion tumbles his consciousness. "Why did you keep showing up? And why didn't—why—"

"Why didn't he fire me?"

She smiles slyly, a wide smile that turns up at the corners like the Cheshire Cat's. He has never seen her full smile, and it repulses him.

Stumbling over his own feet, he hurries out, shutting the door with force, as if he can make her disappear.

Ming's Second Visit to O-Lan

It's the night before the trial. Ming lies fully dressed on his old bed, listening to the neighborhood dogs barking to one another, yard to yard. His turn now. His eyes are dry and he rarely blinks. He keeps rubbing his left ear and feeling his forehead with his palm and the back of his hand. No fever, but his mind moves from image to image with an uncommon speed, touching lightly and refusing to stop, to focus. He sees his brother Dagou in his pink shirt. "You *asshole*!" Shutting his eyes, Ming can still see vividly his old posters (Albert Einstein, John Lennon), his debate trophies and math team trophies, his stack of *Werewolf* comic books, his old bathrobe hanging off the back of the door. His analog clock radio. Scruffy and generic objects, evidence of a past that shouldn't matter. But, of course, this was the room where it began: where he first read a copy of the *Financial Times* that had been left in the restaurant and understood if he could only become educated in the right way, he could grow rich enough to leave this place behind. Not only this house, but this community, this town, this state; and he would never return, never again be near his father. Has leaving Haven been enough? Is it possible to get even farther from them, from all of this? That is what the fifty million is about.

Ming rubs his ears. He leans over and fiddles with the volume knob on his old clock radio. He's set the radio alarm in case he sleeps, to wake him up in time to catch his flight to Phoenix. But he can't sleep. Some time earlier, James checked in, colorless and anxious, and left the house. Now, at closing time, James must be putting up a sign that says the restaurant will be shut down for the duration of the trial. James and O-Lan are removing their aprons and washing their hands.

How old is O-Lan? She has seemed beyond fertility. Slightly hollow around the eyes, with a few white hairs at her temples, dull ocher of her cheeks, soft flesh under her arms. But is it possible she's only in her forties, less than ten years older than Dagou?

Ming props himself up on his elbow, ears pricked. He checks the radio volume knob again. He gets out of bed, still wearing his shoes, and leaves, locking the door carefully behind him. He drives slowly, pausing occasionally to review his thoughts, until he reaches the house. Soon O-Lan will be returning from the restaurant. He parks two blocks away, waiting, until he sees her old Hyundai emerge from one alley, slowly cross the street, and enter the next alley. He waits until the attic light turns on before opening his car door. At the top of the stairs, he tries the knob. Once more, it turns easily in his hand.

This time she's sitting at the table, calmly eating an orange. He hesitates, then plants himself a few feet away.

She chews slowly, watching him with no expression.

"You're related to him," he bursts out. "To us. You are his daughter."

O-Lan smiles again. He can see it now—the family resemblance, in the very spade-shaped jaw he hates. Why hasn't he seen it before?

"Since when do you care about flesh and blood?"

"You're our half sister." It's obvious now. She's not a small woman; there's breadth to her shoulders, and there's something in the way she cants her hips at the counter. Her feline smile, the shape of her cheeks, can only be Big Chao's. He backs away, his body repulsed even as it knows. She's right: he's never acknowledged his own blood, has never wanted to belong to these people, to his family.

"You don't look well," she says. "The customers are right. You're going off the rails."

"Off the rails?" he scoffs. "I'm the only rational person at the restaurant."

"You *were* rational. I used to think you the most reasonable of the brothers. You were rational until you had a glimpse of the truth—very simple, but distorting your assumptions, blowing them up from the inside."

"Get out of here—get out!" Ming yells.

"This is my flat."

He turns to leave. He feels, from behind, such a force of coldness that he stumbles again. A miasma of confusion and hatred and misery rises over him like a wave. He'll be drowned. Surely all of this hatred isn't about him. It transcends him in time and space, it's something from the past.

He turns again to face her.

"You must hate him! You, too, hate him!"

"I thought we had also talked about this," she says. "We agreed on this: *You* are the one who truly hates him. Because you hate yourself."

"Did he know you?"

"He knew. He denied it, in the beginning, but he knew."

"Tell me the story."

"You're such a strange person," she says. "You want to get away, and yet you keep coming back. You want to forget, and yet you want to know what happened."

"Tell me."

"It's not much, to you. My mother, who was cast aside, and robbed, for the sake of an exit to this country, lived in bitterness and died years later, a ruined woman. It's dangerous to cast people aside. You forget them, unaware they've not forgotten you, unaware of the tremendous spite and hatred somewhere in the world. My mother died without money or valuables, without opportunities, without happiness. She never had a life of her own, she had only me."

"Cast aside—for the sake of a way into this country?"

"You wouldn't know. There was a possibility, with a payment, to enter the United States. But only enough money for one person. A thief." She meets his eye. "And he called himself a pioneer."

He looks away.

Now she's telling him about the shame she and her mother lived in. Poverty and hunger. "One year it got so bad my mother searched him down, tracked him down. She never told me this—she kept almost everything about him a secret from me—but I knew, I guessed, I got the truth out of her. She wrote asking for money, for food. Not for the ring, which he stole from her. But for *food*. And she never heard back."

He's thinking about Dagou's radio story. Six-year-old Dagou with the puffball haircut. The unsent package, packed with dried mushrooms, addressed to somewhere in China.

"To think I've always held you in respect," she's saying. "You got the farthest away. You were able to leave him. You're safe in your office, high up in your skyscraper, totaling up your annual bonuses." How does she know about the hunting blind? Ming waves his hand in a spasmodic gesture. He wants her to stop talking now. "But you're the one he most wanted to be. You're the pillager, the plunderer," she continues. "The most American. Of all his sons, you're most like him."

She lowers the half-eaten orange into her lap.

"So many things . . . now I'm a woman without a country, without a mother, a woman whose father is not my father. Who is most at fault? My mother, who died a bitter, ruined, very ill woman, abandoned by my father? She never had a life of her own, she had only her one desire: to ruin my father, to make sure he would not live, to still that endlessly healthy red blood."

Ming turns again, panicked. He leaves the room and stumbles down the stairs.

THE PEOPLE V. WILLIAM CHAO

Journalism 238: Writing for New Media

Posted April 21, 7:51 a.m.

My name is Lynn Chin. I'm a member of Haven's Chinese American community.

In this blog, I will cover the trial of William Chao as my final project for Journalism 238. My personal goals are as follows: Be clear and fair. Follow the assignment guidelines for blog format:

- Use short sentences.
- Make paragraphs three or fewer lines.
- Use white space.
- Use sentence fragments to enliven prose.
- Use bullet points when possible.

Disclaimer: Computers aren't allowed in the courtroom. I never learned cursive and can't print very fast. I can't vouch my quotes from the trial will be perfectly or even sequentially transcribed. For accuracy, check the court reporter's transcript.

Posted April 21, 6 p.m.

We met this morning in the county courthouse's biggest room, under the rotunda.

It's like a courtroom from a 1960s television show. There is dark wood wainscoting. An American flag. In the front are tables for the lawyers, the judge's bench, and a witness stand. In the gallery are about 150 wooden chairs, with an aisle down the middle.

The courtroom was completely full. The following groups sat in the gallery:

- 26 members of the Chinese American community (rows 2–4), including me and my parents.
- Eight nuns from the Spiritual House (row 1).
- Approximately 120 other members of the public (rows 5–16).

My parents and their friends wore pale blue "DG" buttons in support of Dagou. But a lot of the people seated behind us wore red and navy buttons that read, in white type, "JUSTICE FOR ALF."

My friend Fang sat down next to me. His mother, Ma Wa, was with my parents. "I'm amazed our parents are coming to this," I said to him. "My mom and dad hardly ever use vacation days. Now they've taken a week off to watch the trial."

"We need to be here," Fang said. "We need to know what's going on. If Dagou's found guilty, it'll make us all look bad. This is about Haven's attitude toward all Asians."

Fang is a bit of a conspiracy theorist.

Not much happened to start off. Mr. Stern, defense attorney, requested not to allow the prosecution to refer to the defendant as "Dog Eater." The request was granted by Judge Lopate. Now they're choosing the jury. This is called "voir dire."

Posted April 23, 5:30 p.m.

Just checking in to report that voir dire is over. There are twelve jury members and two alternates.

This is a bit off topic, but one of the jury members is familiar to me. She's a chirpy, stout woman in burgundy boots. I know her. I can't remember from where, but when I watched her answering the questions, I had an unexpected feeling. I felt guilty.

Posted April 24, 12:15 p.m.

I'm alone at Starbucks. Everyone else is having lunch at McDonald's, but I need time to myself. Witnesses for the prosecution start to testify next week, and I have a lot to think about.

In case you don't know, Simeon Strycker is the prosecuting attorney (working with assistant prosecuting attorney Corinne Udweala). He's a wiry, tallish man. He has thin hair and wears little gold-rimmed glasses.

I can't *not* mention this thing Strycker does: In the middle of his opening speech, he'd pause and take a drink from a water bottle he keeps with him at all times. The bottle has a black plastic nipple. While he's sucking it, his eyes roll, or focus, inward. The nipple squeals slightly.

Strycker began: "The evidence in this case will tell the story of familial resentment and the violent end of an American dream." He said Mr. and Mrs. Chao "worked inhuman hours to build their American dream" of owning a restaurant, all while raising their sons.

He defined "the young William 'Dagou' Chao" as a "creative type" who didn't make it in New York City and came home to live off of the family business.

Next, he spent a lot of time setting the scene of the alleged murder and describing the party. He said that:

- Dagou had shoveled the snow into piles so high you couldn't see into the restaurant from the street.
- The restaurant was lavishly and expensively decorated.
- There was an unusual amount of free food and alcohol at the party.

He said Big Chao and Dagou fought afterwards. Big Chao said the party was too extravagant. He accused Dagou of stealing money and Dagou didn't deny it. Then Big Chao threatened to call the police.

Near midnight, Mr. Strycker said, when the last employee left the premises, the father and son were still arguing. The next morning, Big Chao's body was found locked in the restaurant freezer room.

Posted April 24, 6 p.m.

In contrast to Strycker, the defense attorney, Jerry Stern, is a round, frumpy guy. He nodded at jury members like he knows them. Maybe he does. Maybe he's stood in line with each of them at the Red Owl. It's the difference between Haven and a bigger city.

Jerry spoke simply, making a few main points:

- That the prosecution's claims cannot be taken as the truth until he can show evidence to back them up.
- That "precisely *how* Leo Chao became locked in the freezer room is not known."
- That there are no witnesses to his death and nothing was captured on camera.
- That much of the evidence is circumstantial.

He said, "It's the prosecution's theory Leo Chao was killed intentionally. Intention is not a given in this case." He reminded everyone that Dagou is innocent until proven guilty.

Jerry's partner, the assistant defense attorney, is a dark-haired woman named Sara Stojkovic. I haven't heard her speak yet. She's polite, organized, and neatly dressed: Jerry's polar opposite. I'm relieved he has someone like this.

Posted April 27, 9:30 a.m.

It's Monday morning, and court is almost in session. I'm in the bathroom, typing in a stall. I need to be alone.

Here's what happened: When I got to the courthouse an hour ago, there was a line of women in the hall, waiting for this bathroom. I got in line behind a woman with a frosted-blond ponytail. When it was her turn to enter, she glowered at me, opened the door, and slammed it in my face. She wore a JUSTICE FOR ALF pendant on a ribbon around her neck.

Posted April 27, 12:20 p.m.

Starbucks, again. This morning we saw Strycker try to build his "wall of evidence" and Jerry punching holes in it.

The prosecution's first witness turned out to be a woman we all recognized from the Christmas party: the unexpected guest. Her name is Cecilia Chang.

Cecilia's a social worker who's fascinated by her heritage. During the party, she told my parents how she met her grandfather during a semester abroad. She took four years of Mandarin in college, and has been writing to him in Chinese (!) for twelve years.

The Bible readers loved her: my parents, the Fans, Ma Wa, and the others. But it turns out she'd come to the party searching for her grandfather's money and personal effects. They disappeared when he died at Union Station.

She testified that:

- Two days before the party, one of the Chao family—it would be James—most likely took her late grandfather's luggage containing $50,000 from the Chicago train station.
- At the party, people talked about how Dagou couldn't afford such a lavish spread. Jerry Stern made an objection (hearsay) that was sustained. Cecilia was probably telling the truth, but it *is* hearsay.

Strycker backed this up with a police security video of her grandfather, walking through the train station, carrying a bag. She was somewhat discredited in the cross-examination, when Jerry got her to admit she had no written proof that there was money in the bag.

But clearly there was something. Some connection the prosecution was going to make between the disappearance of the money and Big Chao's death.

Strycker then brought in his second witness, Yvonne Winters, a night nurse from Memorial Hospital. She was this gaunt, serious white woman. She says she heard Dagou yell he wanted to kill his dad.

She was professional and persuasive. But Jerry asked a bunch of questions that made it clear she couldn't tell a Chao family member from another visitor. She literally thinks we all look alike. She has what Fang would call cross-racial identification issues.

I also made these notes: "Stanley Pardlo, owner and manager of Haven Fine Wines and Spirits. Morning of December 24 at 9:25 a.m., rang up purchases by William Chao of

- 2 6-bottle cases of Stolichnaya
- 2 cases of Jack Daniel's whiskey
- 1 case of bourbon
- 1 case of white wine
- 1 case of red wine
- 1 case of rosé
- 4 cases of Tsingtao beer
- 1 case Korbel champagne

There was also a package of decorative umbrellas.

The total purchase amount was over $2,000, paid in cash. Exhibit No. 27, identified by the witness, shows the receipt recording this. Pardlo remembers because it was unprecedented for William Chao to pay in cash and because the bill was so unusually extravagant.

This is off topic, but I can't imagine James stealing anyone's money. Can't imagine Dagou using stolen money to fund the Christmas party liquor. Strycker has created a James, and a Dagou, nothing like the people I know.

Posted April 27, 7:30 p.m.

I'm at home in my room, still mulling over the prosecution's evidence. Where *did* Dagou get the cash to buy so much liquor when just the night before, according to a clerk from the 7-Eleven, he was unable to produce enough cash to buy some lottery tickets?

I am also thinking about the woman with the ponytail who slammed the door in my face. This dog-eating story is a lightning rod. It has nothing to do with the Chao family, or with my parents' friends. Or me.

But I'm beginning to see Fang is right: our Chineseness has something to do with the way the prosecutor is presenting this trial. So I've decided to include below some notes I haven't used because they come out to longer than three lines. I'm sick of short sentences and paragraphs, sick of white space. I also hate bullet points, though they are useful.

- There was something in the way Strycker set the scene for the crime during his opening statement last week. Specifically, he described Dagou "laboring," plowing and shoveling the parking lot the day before the party, how he heaped more snow on top of the piles made by the city plows, which, "like a wall around the restaurant, made it difficult for anyone to see inside." As if Dagou made a Great Wall, and the Christmas party was some ancient Chinese secret. As if Dagou had tried to prevent anyone from seeing a transgression about to happen in the restaurant.
- Strycker also spent a lot of time in his statement describing the restaurant on the night of the party, as if it were a movie setting: red lanterns, walls "glowing with scarlet light," and the Christmas tree itself an out-of-place American gesture. His list of party details created a vivid mix of cultural idiosyncrasies: Santa Claus, weird dishes, sea creatures, toasts in Mandarin. I grew up attending the Chaos' Christmas celebration every year. I didn't recognize the party described by Strycker.
- Strycker repeatedly referred to our community as an "enclave." This echoes the language in which the print and online media have referred to us as an "immigrant enclave," an "insular group" that is "culturally self-isolating."

As early as his opening statement, Strycker deliberately distorted the story to make the courtroom (and, more importantly, the jury) find it harder to relate to Dagou.

I just realized I didn't write down the fact that there is not a single Asian person on the jury. Why didn't I write it down? Am I so surrounded by white people, in my Haven public life, that I don't notice? I'm sure they notice me, notice I am *not* white.

It was a smart tactic of Jerry's to use her own cross-racial identification bias against Yvonne Winters. But it makes me depressed.

Posted April 27, 11:14 p.m.

One more thing: I remember where I've met the chirpy juror in the burgundy boots. She is a middle school librarian, and Nesbit Ng and I were mean to her in seventh grade.

She's this prim, heavily built woman with bewildered, light blue eyes. She wears black skirts and draping sweaters. We made fun of her, called her "The Lump"; and once, in the middle of study period, I persuaded Nesbit to program all of the computers to burst out into the Chipmunk Christmas song. She was mad.

Posted April 28, 8 a.m.

No one has any idea what O-Lan is going to say when she testifies today, because nobody really knows her. This is not exactly our fault; my mom says she "makes it her business not to be known." She visits Ma Wa's store, but Ma Wa says she never converses. Only Mr. Fan has spoken to her for any length of time, because he's made it his responsibility to welcome every Mandarin-speaking newcomer to Haven. And even Mr. Fan doesn't know much about her. As far as we can tell, O-Lan has no family and no friends. She seems to need no one.

Posted April 28, 12:30 p.m.

Told Fang and Alice I had to get my own lunch.

This morning, while waiting for the trial to start, I had a fight with Fang about what he calls my lack of focus. (He read the description I posted about Strycker and his water bottle.) He said, "What kind of reporter would spend an entire paragraph in the middle of trial coverage writing a description of the prosecuting attorney drinking from a water bottle?"

Maybe Fang's right. But I might as well give up on trying to write according to the format. To be honest, Strycker is beginning to give me the willies. He's like a ghost. His movements are so light, it's like he doesn't have arms inside his perfect suit jacket. He's, what do they call it—immaterial. And to think he's portrayed *us* as oddities. Is he human.

Also, the Lump loves him. She gazes at him in fascination, with her eyes riveted on his face every time he speaks. Is he casting a kind of racist spell on her? Or, is it somehow my fault? (Our fault: will our seventh-grade mischief, our pubescent cruelty, give her a bias against Asians? We, who judged the Lump, deserve it. But does Dagou deserve it? Will we be responsible for Dagou's fate?)

I am starting to sense that in this trial, the boundaries that have kept separate the various compartments of my life (school, home, Asianness, privacy, and misbehavior) are breaking down, and these disparate parts are being revealed to the world.

Here is what happened in trial this morning:

- A forensic locksmith testified that the freezer in the basement of the Fine Chao was, in Strycker's words, "a death trap."
- He said, once you've entered and closed the door, the only way to leave is to use a key from the inside. There was an old sign (Exhibit No. 2) kept near the shelf with the key, reading, "KEY TO EXIT FREEZER ROOM. DO NOT REMOVE THIS KEY."
- A handyman who's done work on the freezer identified and read the sign. The freezer wasn't up to code—it was grandfathered in, or something.
- O-Lan testified.

O-Lan wore her work clothes: black pants, a dark blue shirt, black socks, and dirty sneakers. She clearly doesn't care. She didn't make eye contact with anyone, stared at the floor ten feet in front of her.

The interpreter was a youngish guy with a shiny forehead who spoke musically but mechanically in Mandarin and English. My mom says it's a Malaysian accent. She wondered if he's new to Haven, but Mr. Fan, who knows everything, says he came out just for the day, from Chicago.

There was a kind of stutter in the beginning of the conversation. Even the interpreter had to get his bearings. I've never heard a Mandarin accent like O-Lan's, thick as a dialect. I never noticed how much attitude she has. I also had the feeling she was frightened.

I was struck by how much of the restaurant work is on O-Lan's shoulders. The Chaos work hard, but she's *their* servant. She unloads vegetables and any supplies. She washes and cuts basically all of the vegetables. During and after the meal, she loads the dishwasher. She runs errands. She cleans the floors and counters, uses the vacuum cleaner, and she also handles garbage and recycling. The cooks are men (Dagou, his dad, and one other cook who was out of town over winter break).

Strycker asked her to describe the events that took place in the Fine Chao between 11:30 and 11:45 p.m. on December 24. Who were the last guests to leave? She said James Chao and the hired help. Also, "that American woman," which could have been Brenda, could have been Katherine. I didn't know O-Lan felt contempt for Americans, but it was in her voice. Strycker wanted to know who was still in the restaurant between 11:45 and 11:59 p.m. She said, Dagou Chao and Leo Chao and herself. She was vacuuming the carpet. During this time, she could hear Leo Chao and William Chao arguing in the kitchen. She says she could hear them because she stopped the vacuum to clean up with a mop.

According to O-Lan: During this confrontation, between 11:45 and 11:59 p.m., Leo Chao claimed Dagou took from his (Leo's) Ford a bag containing $50,000. He called Dagou "a thief." O-Lan said Dagou didn't deny taking the money. Big Chao said the money rightfully belonged to a stranger, and that he (Big Chao) had been planning to turn it in to the police (Fang says this doesn't sound like Leo Chao ☺). He told Dagou he was going to tell the police what Dagou did.

At this point, Jerry leaped out of his chair and yelled, "Objection, hearsay! Objection, please admonish the witness to answer only what she's been asked. Motion to strike everything after the answer to the question!" The motions were denied.

Strycker made O-Lan identify Exhibit No. 7, which is a picture of the door to the freezer room. She couldn't do it. Had she ever been in the freezer room? The basement? No and no. Did she know anything about a key on a shelf inside the freezer room? No. He said, please see Exhibit No. 2 (the sign about the key). He asked her if she could read the sign and she could not.

Oh, and there was one weird thing. When Strycker asked O-Lan if she'd ever been in the freezer room, she said,

> "No. I am a vegetarian. My mother was a vegetarian. That room is Leo Chao's temple."
>
> "What do you mean by 'Leo Chao's temple'?"
>
> "He goes into that room and worships meat."
>
> "What kinds of meat did Leo worship?"
>
> (A pause here, while the people wearing JUSTICE FOR ALF buttons fixed their eyes on her and held their breath.)
>
> "All meats. Every kind of meat."

The assistant defense attorney Sara Stojkovic's questions for O-Lan were mostly about her immigration status. She's been living in Haven for years, but with no papers. Would she confirm she's in the US as an undocumented immigrant? Yes. Did she receive any payment in exchange for testifying? No. Did she ask the State, that is Mr. Strycker, to help her with her immigration issues? Yes. Did Mr. Stryker refer her to a lawyer who would help her with her immigration issues? He did.

That's it for this morning. I'm going to call Fang. This afternoon, more witnesses for the prosecution, including James, who has been subpoenaed.

"I've Got This!"

At the McDonald's, James waits for Fang, watching the rain rush down the gutters to the bottom of the hill. He rereads Lynn's blog. Judge Lopate has ruled witnesses aren't allowed to be part of the audience in the courtroom until after they testify. In order to be near Dagou, James has come every day to sit in the courthouse waiting room. From across the hall, he has no idea what's happening in the courtroom. He knows he's not supposed to read anything about the trial, or talk about the trial with anyone who has been in the courtroom. But he can't help himself.

James rereads, *I am a vegetarian. My mother was a vegetarian.* He rereads, *The Chaos work hard, but she is* their *servant.* He turns off his laptop and stares at its blank screen.

He knows, now, why Cecilia Chang, the stranger at the holiday party, was so familiar to him. Her expression and her hair cut into bangs. She'd been the girl with the beagle from the snapshot he had seen, held in the old man's shaking hand, months ago, in Union Station.

He remembers telling his father, in what now feels like another life, of his desire to be small, to be a part of something larger than himself. Throughout the trial, but especially today, as the moment for him to testify draws near, he has felt like a tiny creature approaching the enormous machine of justice, with its wheels juddering, ready to crush his life as well as those of his brothers. He told Fang he believed in the process. He now sees that the machine of justice, supposedly fair and impartial, is in reality subject to loosened screws, worn parts, and any number of quirks and forces that lie outside of his knowledge.

Fang enters the McDonald's, talking on his phone.

"Didn't he use the word 'inhuman'?" Fang asks. He listens to the voice on the other end. "Doesn't matter. He managed to work it in. You wait," Fang says. "Gotta go. I'm with James now." He puts away his phone. "That was Lynn. She's become hung up on the question of where Dagou got his cash." Fang yanks off his wet cap and lets it drip on the table. "Bag of cash!" he scoffs. "She's *still* buying into Strycker's case. Strycker's all about appealing to clichés: The bag of cash. The *American Dream.* The inhuman laborer. The ambitious and ungrateful son who can't appreciate what's been done for him."

"He said my parents 'worked inhuman hours' to build my dad's American dream," James says. "He did use the phrase in a positive way, if that's possible."

"You, too! You're buying into the prosecution's story," Fang says.

"He says Big Chao is a hardworking, stoic immigrant whose inhuman hours are an investment into the American Dream. He's the quintessential Asian American, the model minority: humble, diligent, hardly a person. He put his sweat and blood into his children's lives like every Asian parent."

"That's ridiculous," James says. He pictures his father: coarse hair sticking straight up, eyes bulging suggestively at Katherine, winking lewdly at Gu Ling Zhu Chi and yelling, "Pork hock!" "*Stoic?* How can anyone believe—?"

"But as it turns out, a lot of random people who've been to the restaurant do believe he's low to the ground, a humble server. The jury was nodding. Here's the other thing," Fang says, taking off his rain-speckled glasses. "According to the prosecution, Big Chao's son William, a.k.a. Dagou, is *not* like him. William is a *bad* minority. He doesn't appreciate the opportunities he's been given in this country. He's lazy and ungrateful, dishonest, a thief, and sexually enamored of a woman not appropriate for him, a white woman."

"That's also ridiculous."

Fang squints with his naked eyes, rubbing at his glasses with a napkin. "Isn't the idea that Dagou would carve and serve up Alf ridiculous? Isn't this *all* ridiculous? Anyway, the prosecution says Dagou is an overindulged, oversexed, shiftless yellow-brown delinquent. He possesses an unscrupulous and insatiable greed. He's a thief. And he wants Brenda, and money, and the restaurant, badly enough to kill. *That's* Strycker's story." He examines his lenses. "What're you eating for lunch?"

"Not hungry."

"Buy something. Come on, you've gotta testify this afternoon." He peers at James through his now-smeared glasses. "Where's Ming?"

"His flight gets in at two o'clock. He's coming straight from the airport. Fang, I need your advice. Last night I was thinking about my testimony. I had an idea about something you said a few weeks ago."

"Let's order."

They order hamburgers, coffee, and for Fang a McFlurry with Butterfingers. Then Fang sits down, touches his hat. Still wet. He picks up his Big Mac with both hands and says, before taking a bite, "I'm all ears."

James sits opposite, and begins. "That children's book, *The Five Chinese Brothers*. You said the book is about the consequences of an unfortunate death. You said there was a cover-up attempted by the other brothers. But it wasn't a cover-up, was it? The brothers don't try to *hide* the murder, but they *sub in for each other's punishments*. The one with an iron neck can't be beheaded. The one with the stretchy rubber legs can't be drowned under the sea, and so on. No one can tell the difference between the brothers, and so they think the First Brother is immortal, and they give up."

Fang puts down his half-eaten burger and wipes his mouth. "The key is that the story *itself* assumes no one can tell the difference. The story only works if the *reader believes* the brothers look exactly alike. And, of course, there are the pictures."

"Right, fine. So what if the world at large doesn't care which brother they get, as long as it's *one* of them?"

Fang takes a long sip from his McFlurry. "You're going to claim it's you? No one will buy it. You can't hide your innocence to save your life."

"It might as well be me," James says.

Last night, as he and Alice lay together in his childhood room, their hearts easing, breath slowing into sleep, James jerked awake, certain it was early Christmas morning. He lay next to Alice, his heart pounding, convinced that they were together half a mile across town in Dagou's bed, up above the restaurant. Hearing the thumping from below. "I remember now," James said. Drowsily, Alice took his hand, but James didn't sleep. The thumping from below—why hadn't he remembered it? He'd been present, almost on the very spot where his father had died. He hadn't told Fang about this. He hadn't told his brothers. The thumping, a plea for help. In that moment, it had been in his power to prevent any of this from happening. What had he done? Turned over, gone back to sleep—in short, nothing.

An image appears in James's mind. It's a memory he has tried, for months, to push away. It comes only when he's least expecting it: The face of his father's corpse as he discovered it in the freezer room. The staring eyes frosted over with the gaze of a stone or marble statue. The expression of surprise, of sudden consternation.

He is not, and can never be, innocent.

After hamburgers and coffee, Fang and James climb the hill. As they reach the courthouse, they see a crowd of people around and under the bus station, holding red and navy signs: JUSTICE FOR ALF! A small group of reporters and photographers disengage themselves from the crowd and rush toward them, into the rain. "*Hiiii-ya!*" Fang yells, bringing his hand down in a chopping motion. The reporters scatter. Fang grins at James and they enter the courthouse, go through security. The upstairs lobby is crowded with scores of wet umbrellas. James looks into the courtroom at a sea of red and navy buttons. He can only glance inside; he's not allowed to enter until it's time for him to testify. He's required to wait for the bailiff in the now-familiar room off of the lobby.

The night before, while lying awake, James came up with a Plan B. Now he sends a text to Dagou: *Meet me in the bathroom.* After checking all of the stalls to make sure the room is empty, he climbs onto one of the toilet seats. Hopefully the bailiff escorting Dagou will only peek under the stalls before letting Dagou into the room. He crouches on the toilet, straightening his tie and waiting for his brother to enter. He hears the door open. "Okay," someone says, and Dagou, monumental in a not-quite-charcoal suit, appears. James gets down, leaves the stall. For many days, Dagou has been wearing an expression James has never seen on him before: careful, frightened.

"You wanted to see me, Snaggle?"

"You still planning to testify?"

"Yeah. I need to tell everyone what really happened."

James squares his shoulders. "Listen, Dagou. I've been thinking. Real quick: If I tell Strycker I can't remember—that I'm having trouble remembering whether the key was really on the shelf, at the end of the party—then no one could say how long it was gone. And that means anyone could have done it, or it was an accident. You won't have to testify. Their case is cooked."

Dagou listens, frowning slightly. "No," he says. "You tell them what you saw. You tell the truth. You don't want to perjure yourself."

"I don't care, Dagou." James can hear the calm in his voice. He knows he's capable of lying. "You're more important to me than that."

"Snaggle. Listen to me." Dagou puts his hands on James's shoulders and brings his face close enough that James can see the wide pupils in his shining, deep brown eyes. "I don't know what's going to happen to me, Snaggle, and neither do you. But no matter what, it's most important for me to hold on to my *idea* of you. I need to think about you the way you've always been. No matter where I end up, I'll know you're still you. Tell the truth. Promise me."

James swallows hard. "I promise."

Dagou puts his arms around James. James leans into his brother's warm, mountainous chest. Dagou chuckles, clasps him in his big arms and rubs his back briefly, then releases him with something of his old lightness.

"And don't worry about my testimony," he says. "I've got this!"

The door flashes open and he's gone, leaving James to stare at his own face in the mirror.

A Look of Surprise

When the bailiff finally escorts James into the courtroom, the place is crowded to capacity, stuffed with observers, umbrellas, walking canes, and sweaters. The air is close, smelling of sweat and damp. Still, there's an echoing quality to each chair scrape, each cough, as they turn to watch him coming. The jurors turn. Alf's supporters turn, their chairs straining. The community members turn their rows of black heads and balding heads and salt-and-pepper heads. Several nuns in their brown robes swivel in their seats; An, with her wax-blond crew cut, is among them. Ming is not in the room.

To the community, James has always been the least troubled of the Chao sons. Protected by his older brothers, he's the reticent product of his mother's generosity and his father's tyranny. Studious and agreeable, a future physician. But as he walks into the room, everyone begins to understand that he will always struggle against his family's shadows.

Dagou sits at the defense table, dwarfing not only the assistant defense attorney, Sara Stojkovic, but Jerry Stern himself. From the stand, James glimpses a view of his big neck, recently shaved, bulging slightly over the edge of his collar. A yellow legal pad and a pen are on the table but he doesn't touch them.

The prosecution begins by showing, for a second time, the security video of Zhang Fujian. James has a direct view of the screen. He was informed that they would show the video. But as he watches now, he's seized by the soundless black-and-white image of Union Station, his imagination supplying the light snowfall from the level above, the nearby roar and cry of trains. The people in the video, strangers in their winter coats, hurry in many directions. Then an old man, quite small, clutching a carpetbag, shuffles onto the screen. He moves at a visibly slower pace than the others, who rush past him, back and forth, as he makes his way across.

Strycker speaks. James struggles to focus on the questions, all requiring yes-or-no answers. He might be strong enough to stand up to Strycker. He understands why Fang said he was incapable of hiding his innocence. But he knows that Fang trusts him too much; Fang is wrong. He lies and says he hasn't read anything about the trial. He won't lie about the key only because Dagou has asked him not to.

"While following you, the man collapsed. You performed CPR. Did you notice he carried a bag?"

"Yes, I did."

"Did you take the bag with you when you left the train station?"

"Yes, I did."

There's a gasp from one of Winnie's friends in the gallery who might have been hoping the carpetbag was a red herring cooked up by the prosecution. Strycker goes calmly on with the questioning. The story is confirmed: distraught, having failed to save the old man's life, not wanting his luggage to be left behind, James loaded the bag along with his own luggage into his brother's rental. When Ming dropped him off at the restaurant, he switched the bag, along with his own luggage, to the trunk of Leo's Ford Taurus. What were his intentions? He wanted to check inside for the man's address, return it to his family. Did he do this? No, he didn't. Why not? He forgot about it. His failure to resuscitate the stranger, leading to a sense of shame; Winnie's stroke; the sudden death of Leo and of his mother: these events had driven the bag from his mind.

Strycker brings up Cecilia Chang's phone call to the Fine Chao Restaurant on the afternoon of December twenty-third. Was James present for the call? Yes, he was in the room when Ming answered the phone. Did he realize Cecilia had called about the bag in the Ford? Not exactly. What did he mean? It had been Ming who guessed the subject of the call and told him to search the trunk of the Ford. Following Ming's instructions, did James then search the trunk? He did not; he'd been distracted, and, later, interrupted by a call telling him their mother was ill. He'd gone to Memorial Hospital. Nor did the police find the bag a week later, when they impounded the Ford, investigating a possible intersection between two seemingly unrelated crimes—Cecilia Chang's theft report and Leo Chao's murder.

The prosecution authenticates the police report James filed stating he believed the bag was moved to his mother's room at the hospital that evening, the night of December 23. Why did he wait months to file this report?

"I might've figured out earlier that the bags were accidentally swapped," James says, "but after the police failed to find the bag in the Ford, I stopped thinking about it." He pauses, struggling to sort through everything that happened. He describes how he discovered the burgundy bag. "That's when I put two and two together, and filed the police report."

Strycker takes a long drink from his bottle. Everyone listens to its squealing sound. When he sets the bottle down, the room is unnaturally silent.

"Did you actually see a bag in the hospital room, or talk to anyone who did?"

"It's the only logical thing that could have happened."

"Answer the question yes or no," says Judge Lopate.

"No."

"You never saw anyone put her burgundy bag in your mother's hospital room, true?"

"It must have sat in the trunk until someone brought it back to the Spiritual House."

"I'm not asking for your speculation, I'm asking for what you personally witnessed."

"No."

"If your theory is not true, is it possible the bag was never put into your mother's hospital room?"

"I suppose so—"

"Objection," Jerry calls out. "Speculation."

Everyone wonders why the old man's bag of money is so important. With the entire restaurant at stake, its past savings and future income—with the crime of a man's death at stake, and, with it, the hullabaloo and hue and cry over Dagou, over Alf, and the entire Chinese American community of Haven—what is the significance of Zhang Fujian's bag?

James stares out into the sea of pale blue and red-and-navy buttons. It's like a public exam. He's finished with the question-and-answer section, and now it's time to ID the exhibits. James identifies People's Exhibit Number 5, a drawing of the first floor of the Fine Chao Restaurant, with the door to the basement marked in red; Exhibit Number 7, a photo of the door to the freezer room; and Exhibit Number 9, a photo of the shelf where the key was kept.

"Now I'm going to ask you some questions about the night of December 24. Did you go downstairs to fetch a second bag of ice?"

"Yes."

"Did you observe the key on a shelf inside the freezer room?"

"Yes."

"What time was that?"

"It was around eleven-thirty p.m."

Strycker gestures to the assistant prosecuting attorney, who makes a note of this. Then he continues. Who was in the restaurant at that time? Fang Wa and Katherine Corcoran. Also O-Lan, Leo, Dagou, and James. Did he see them leave? In what order did they leave? James recites that as far as he can tell, Fang left. Then Katherine left. Then he himself left. "But it's possible," James adds, "that I assumed someone had gone and they were still inside the restaurant. And it's possible that someone came into the restaurant after I left. I wouldn't know about that." Strycker asks to have this comment stricken from the record, and asks for the jury to be admonished not to consider James's speculation about possible scenarios.

"Do you know how it came to be that the key was removed from the shelf between eleven-thirty p.m. and the morning of December twenty-fifth?"

"No."

"When you left the restaurant, where did you go?"

"I went to Alice Wa's house."

"What happened after that?"

"I left the Was' house."

"Then where did you go?"

"To my brother's—to William's—apartment over the restaurant."

"Why did you go to William's apartment?"

"I went because he offered it to me, he offered me the key."

"When did you leave the apartment?"

"Around nine-thirty a.m."

"For what purpose did you leave?"

"To go downstairs and set up for the lunch shift."

"Can you describe what you did outside and inside the restaurant at nine-thirty a.m.?"

"As I came down the outer staircase, from the apartment, I saw the family Honda in the parking lot. I expected my father to be inside the restaurant. I let myself inside through the back door. I called for him. I checked the kitchen and the office. I checked in the bathroom. Then I went downstairs, into the freezer room, and turned on the light."

A photographic slide is projected onto the screen. There is the image—a sturdy, older Asian male corpse, thick trunk and limbs sculpted in shades of ocher and gray, greenish blue from cold, limbs thick and still, the head ornamented by a porcupine coat of thick salt-and-pepper hair. James can't look away. There it is again. The eyes open, the staring of sudden captivation. James has been prepared for this, but the image takes him by surprise, as if he's never seen it.

"People's Exhibit Number Ten. Could you describe this photograph?"

"It's my father's body the way I found him in the freezer."

"Just a few more questions, Mr. Chao, and I'll be finished. What did you do after you found your father's body?"

"I called Dagou on the restaurant phone."

"Did he answer?"

"No."

"What did you do after that?"

"I called the police."

"No further questions, Your Honor."

Strycker's questioning is over. James hates Strycker, has hated dealing with him, dreaded the public confrontation. The worst is over now. It's only Jerry. But Jerry's face is solemn.

Was James present on December 23 at approximately three p.m. when Cecilia Chang called the Fine Chao Restaurant? To whom did Cecilia speak? Was William Chao in the restaurant at that time? To James's knowledge, was William ever informed about the money in the luggage? Did William ever speak about the existence of the bag itself? Jerry asks about FM 88.8. Did James hear William on his radio? How far away from William's transmitter was James when he had tuned in with a simple radio? Did William speak about his conflict with his father publicly on that broadcast? Did he mention, publicly, that it was possible to lock someone in the freezer room?

Jerry Stern moves on to James's statement that he remembers the key on the shelf of the freezer room at eleven-thirty p.m. How can he be so sure what time it was? How can he be so sure he saw the key? Is there a photo, a video, any visual evidence at all that the key was indeed upon the shelf in the freezer room? In other words, how can they know he's telling the truth?

"I'm telling the truth," James insists, and Jerry moves on.

Did Dagou offer him the use of his apartment? Yes, he did. Did Dagou's offer of his apartment place James in the building when and where Leo Chao's death took place? Yes, it did. James senses a trap closing around him. Is it possible that Jerry would accuse him of this?

But he does not, and it's Strycker's turn again. Did James himself enter the restaurant at any time between 11:55 p.m. and 9:30 Christmas morning? He did not. Did he stay in Dagou's apartment the entire night? He did. Did he have a witness—was someone present, could anyone attest to the fact that he had not entered the restaurant that night?

James doesn't answer. He stands, his heart whamming his throat. If he just doesn't speak, if he does nothing—

"Answer the question, Mr. Chao."

"Yes."

"Who was that person?"

Just as he opens his mouth to speak, James hears an echo of his own words to Alice, months ago: *Don't tell your mother.*

"Alice Wa."

There's a disapproving *tcch!* from someone in the first rows of the gallery.

Alice's Secret

Finished with his testimony, James is at last permitted to sit with the others. Fang has saved three seats. Two are for him and Alice. The third is for Ming, who's not responding to texts. Now, as Alice takes the stand, James finds himself in the midst of a community silent with disapproval. On Fang's other side, Lynn is frantically taking notes.

After learning Alice was subpoenaed, Lynn and Fang speculated she might be too frightened to give more than yes-or-no answers. But James knew better. Now, as Alice faces the room with her chin raised, he sees more powerfully than ever that what she will say is unknown to him. He feels a stab of longing for Alice—not physical desire, exactly, but more an echo of desire. He's thrust her into the public; now he's powerless to do more than watch events unfold.

Strycker goes straight to Christmas Eve. He asks her to confirm that James was with her for the entire night of December 24–25. When did she and James enter William's apartment? What time did she leave? What did they do? They talked. About what?

"We were talking about God." There was a collective sound, half laughter and half relief, from the gallery. Alice says, "We were talking about the question of how if God knows all of our pain, and the suffering the world imposes on us, and how we impose it on each other—that if God is compassionate, and all knowing, how is it possible God doesn't make himself known to us?" The judge doesn't ask Alice to stick to the point. Lynn gives Fang and James an odd look. James knows she's speculating about whether the judge is a religious person. He wonders if she might muse about this in her blog.

"Did you and James discuss his relationship with his father?"

"We compared the love of God to parental love."

"Did you fall asleep?"

"Yes."

Alice sighs. She's finished what she came to say. Together, she and Strycker have exonerated James.

But Strycker continues. "Did you hear anything unusual that night?"

A bit of pink flares into Alice's cheeks.

"Please speak up."

She stands stubbornly for a moment. "I told you," she says to Strycker, "I don't want to talk about this. And you said—"

"Please answer the question, Ms. Wa," says Judge Lopate.

There's a pause. Then Alice says, "Yes. I heard something. I thought, sometime very late, I heard a noise—"

"I'll be finished in a minute, Ms. Wa. Can you describe the noise?"

"It was a—faint thumping, or banging. It was on and off, while I fell asleep and woke up again."

"Did you tell James about the noise?"

"No."

"Did he wake up?"

Alice looks at her feet. "Yes. He woke up once."

"Did the two of you discuss hearing the noise?"

There's a strained silence. "Yes."

"Please speak up, Ms. Wa."

"Could he identify the source?"

"I—no, I don't think so. Because he asked me if I thought he should go check. And I told him to go back to sleep." Her voice is higher now, the voice of a child.

"Could *you* identify it, Ms. Wa?"

"I—I thought it was a ghost."

"To clarify: you heard a banging noise and thought it was a ghost?"

"Yes."

Soon after, Alice is led back out by the bailiff. As planned, she returns to the gallery and sits in the empty chair next to James. James takes her hand; it's cold. She doesn't look at him.

Ming's seat is still empty.

Around them, the community listens to the testimony. There's the police officer who responded to the incident at the 7-Eleven. There's the woman Dagou knocked over, pointing a surly finger to identify him. Most significant to everyone is the testimony of Officer Carly Bucek, a petite, sandy-haired woman. Officer Bucek's testimony lasts more than an hour. First she's asked to confirm all of the observations she made in her notebook while investigating the restaurant. She's shown a dozen exhibits, and she identifies each of the photographs she took. The bare shelf on the wall; the sign. The scratches on the metal plate around the lock. The frozen meat the victim placed over the air vent in the wall in an attempt to block the cold. The body. Strewn nearby on the concrete floor are the victim's shirt and trousers, underwear, and socks. Even the watch has been removed and is lying facedown near the left hand. Shivering. Disorientation. A final flash of uncomfortable heat as the body made one final, desperate effort to warm itself. The strewn clothes indicating hypothermia as the cause of death.

No, she did not find a key to the door.

No, there were no recent fingerprints from William Chao on the door.

Officer Bucek's notes taken during her questioning of Dagou are quoted at length by the prosecution, and she affirms them all: specifically, that Dagou said, on Christmas Day when the officers apprehended him at Brenda's house, that he had a motive to kill his father, he had the *right* to kill his father, and the method to kill his father. He said he had *planned* to kill his father; at this, it was decided to take him to the station. Officer Bucek is questioned about the impounded Ford. When was the car impounded? When was it searched? Was it possible a bag could have been removed between the afternoon of December 21 and the week after Christmas, when the car was impounded and searched?

In the cross-examination, Officer Bucek is grilled by Jerry Stern about the way Dagou had been treated before he was brought in for questioning. He had been physically restrained. He had been handcuffed. He had been threatened with a gun. Some are encouraged by Jerry Stern's indignant and thorough questioning of exactly when, and why, additional units had been requested for a simple discussion with Dagou; why such extreme measures had been used; in what way and how long Dagou had been questioned at the station; whether his exact words were that he "would" kill his father; whether the subjective tense warranted a person of interest being taken in for questioning. Jerry wants to hear exactly how Dagou had been Mirandized, how he had refused his right to a lawyer, and how he had been persuaded to sign the paper. Was his mother mentioned; had the officers actually mentioned his estranged parents, implied Winnie was a suspect in the killing, and did they know this was not appropriate, it amounted to threatening; and had he, Dagou, agreed to sign the document because of veiled threats against his mother?

After this long afternoon of questioning, the court is adjourned.

Ming's Third Visit to O-Lan

Later that evening, across town, it's nearly closing time at Skaer's Diner. Ming Chao sits in his booth drinking black coffee and staring at coverage of the trial on his laptop. His barely touched fish sandwich has been pushed aside. His small suitcase is next to him. He came straight from the airport, midafternoon, and has been waiting in the diner ever since.

Ming scans the local newspapers; he lurks on Twitter; he studies Lynn's blog about the testimony of James, Alice, the police. Several times, he takes out his phone and starts texting his brothers, Katherine, Sara Stojkovic, or Jerry Stern. But each time, he puts his phone away before sending. At ten o'clock, he pays his bill. No one points out he hasn't eaten or asks if the food was all right. They're used to him now. Since Leo's death, the Skaers' animosity has ceased; trips to the diner are no longer forays into enemy territory. Ming gets into his rental car and drives to O-Lan's apartment.

He's told no one about his visits to O-Lan. But during his time in Phoenix, he couldn't stop remembering. Thinking, blinking into the relentless sun. Some enormous question running like a complex program in his mind, taking up space there, yet invisible to him, blotting his ability to sleep. It's taking over his mind, like the bleeding from a cerebrovascular accident.

The rickety stairs seem to narrow as he climbs. There's a slit of light under the door. The knob, as before, turns easily in his hand. He stumbles into the room. The bare bulb, suspended over the table, lights the two cold dishes waiting there: a lotus-root salad and a plate of little radishes, lightly dressed. He sniffs: the scent of sesame oil.

O-Lan stands near the stove, calmly transferring vegetables into a small bowl. In another small bowl, dried mushrooms soak in water. Her cleaver lies on the counter.

Ming feels a sudden shift in the air. Is he standing in an empty room in another place and time? No, all is as usual, and yet, as he examines the place, it seems to him there's an ephemeral quality to every detail, down to the greasy sneakers next to the door.

After some time (has it been minutes? half an hour?), he speaks.

"Let me tell you what I think," he says, in English. "You came to this country searching for my father. You had some kind of hint about where he was—"

She replies, also in English, "He doesn't hide himself."

So, he was right. "No," he says. "But there are other Leo Chaos. You might've found a dozen before you figured out who he was. Tell me: How many did you try? You came to our restaurant searching for him, and when you found him—" His mouth is dry.

She gives him an almost pitying look. "Yes, it's true. I tried other restaurants in other towns."

"—you took a job at the restaurant. You pretended you couldn't speak English. But of course you could! How else would you know what my brother said, on the radio? Pretending you had no English was a way of hiding, hiding your secret—"

She laughs, frightening him. He speaks into his fear. "Not at first! At first your lack of English was simply caution, a way of limiting exposure to others. But at some point, in your private explorations of the restaurant, you began to realize that not speaking English would be your protection, your alibi—" It's a struggle to think. "You trained yourself not to understand the language. You *unlearned* it. But you knew a person could be locked into the freezer room and in order to escape they would need to know how to read the sign. You knew if the key disappeared, you wouldn't be taken seriously as the criminal.

"And so you finished him off! You waited for the exact moment, knowing for months, even years, that you must wait for the perfect moment, the perfect opportunity! You settled in, you waited—" He breaks off. "How come you're still in town?"

"I live here."

"You'll be deported!"

"Are you going to the police?"

Her question works on him like a jinx, his thoughts suspended.

"Why didn't you go to them the moment you flew in?" she asks, her voice still mild. "Why didn't you go straight from the airport? Surely if you were going to turn me in, you would have done it already."

"It was you who killed him! You!"

She shrugs. "Do you believe yourself?"

Ming can feel his jaw drop slightly open, a parody of stupidity, and yet he can't close his mouth.

"I," she says, "am a desperate person, an illegal immigrant, an alien whose smallest noticeable action could get her deported. I have only my job and my employer. Why would I do something to put myself at so much risk?"

"You've got nothing to lose."

Ming eyes the food on the table. The red radishes with the faint cracks where she has whacked them with the back of the cleaver. The thin-sliced lotus roots, their crisp white lace of bones.

"You're hungry."

"No."

"Eat with me." She pours a second cup of tea. "You're afraid of my food?" Mocking him. She brings two bowls and two pairs of chopsticks to the table. She pulls the stool from the kitchen and sets it opposite the single chair. "Would I poison you?"

Flushing, Ming sits down. He picks up the chopsticks and raises a radish slowly to his mouth.

"Try it. Hong luobo have enough vitamins to keep the blood moving, even in your veins."

The blue circlet of flame dances on the stove. She moves the wok over the flame, adds the oil, and waits, tilting the wok and watching for telltale rivulets of heat. She adds a few sliced mushrooms, and they sizzle in the hot oil.

"How did you feel when you walked into the restaurant? Finding him, finally." The cracked radish, peppery and crisp, holds enough marinade for surprising flavor. Ming takes another. "Did you—" He stretches his mind toward cruelty. "Then did you want his approval, his love?"

O-Lan shrugs. In this gesture, for a moment she seems not as old—not past her childbearing years. She's healthy, and the nibs of flesh under her arms are, after all, nibs of extra flesh.

Ming needs to say this: "You're not required to live out the wishes of your parents."

O-Lan turns to him. Her lips twist. "You grew up in a country where some people have the privilege to believe this is true. How would *you* know about my relationship to them? To anyone?"

"I have my brothers," says Ming, surprising himself.

"You're ashamed of your brother."

Ming can't stop eating the radishes. There's a sharp sizzle, but controlled, as she adds the other vegetables to the oil. "You may hate my father," he says, continuing his thoughts, "but you have no reason—no reason!—to frame my brother."

Again, she shrugs. "You think not? He was legitimate, the official oldest child in the family, and I was not. He is known, he is acknowledged, and I am not. He's Big Chao's child, and I am not. But I'm many of those things: born legitimate, oldest, and Big Chao's child."

She lets the vegetables sizzle untended for a moment, then faces him. "You yourself think William is an embarrassment. You'd be very happy if he weren't your brother."

"You don't know what I think."

She lifts the lid from a small pot and the smell of cooked rice fills the room. Ming picks out a lotus root; it crunches softly. Suddenly he is ravenous.

"You're still trying to believe I killed Leo Chao?" O-Lan asks. "You'll feel better when you confess. In the deepest, most knowing well in your heart, Ming Chao, you believe someone else is the killer of Leo Chao."

"No, it was you—" He's salivating, choking on his words so the statement is less commanding than he had intended. He clears his throat. "You, Chao O-Lan. Chao O-Lan is the killer of Leo Chao."

"No, it's you, Chao Ming."

She brings the wok to the table and he looks eagerly into it. There is celery and sliced, pressed tofu with mushrooms. Wordlessly, she ladles him a full bowl of rice. He bends toward his bowl, scooping the food into his mouth with chopsticks.

She speaks calmly in English, with little inflection. "I may be a monster to you, but I don't eat like a monster, and you do. You're barely human, your hands are barely warm, you don't hold heat."

She puts rice into her own bowl. "I've seen you checking your pulse, your steps, your runs, your calorie counts. You don't cook your own food, you eat raw vegetables that have been washed by strangers, your condiments come in plastic, you eat meat that has been sitting for days in the refrigerator, stuffed between pieces of bread, and you eat alone.

"You think you can get rid of them? Extract your family from your body if you give up Chinese food? Extract your own blood from your body?"

Ming can't stop eating to speak, so he only points at her with the chopsticks.

"True," she says, "I also eat alone. But I have no one to eat with, and you do. You could be with that Katherine. You only have to let her know and she would recognize her feelings. But you push her away. Your brothers, also."

Ming reaches for more rice.

She puts her chopsticks down. "Why do you push her away? It's because of what she is. You don't want to be with a woman who looks the way you do. What kind of human being are you?" She observes him calmly. "How many times were you warned what was going to happen, and you did nothing?"

Ming's throat closes again. "I was in the Hartford Airport at the time!"

"You were."

"You persuaded me to go. You made me go!"

"No, you chose to fly east. You went even though you knew there was a giant storm."

Steam rises from his rice; Ming wipes his face.

She looks puzzled for a moment. "When you decided to go to New York, in full awareness of the weather, you were acting in full knowledge of what would happen. You *wanted* it to happen."

Ming shovels in food. He's breathing loudly while he eats, like a laborer, a coolie. It's delicious: the white rice, the savory tofu, the tender, slippery mushrooms, the celery, so crisp and yet so easy to swallow, because she has stripped away by hand the tough fibers from the outer layer of green. He has a sudden vision of his mother cutting through a stalk of celery to this layer of green, then, with a flick of her wrist, pulling the long sinew of fiber from the stalk. She removed the fibers only for meals she made at home for them, Monday nights. This was when he was a small boy, before they had risen up against her food and started eating TV dinners. Ming remembers how much he used to despise everything about the pressed tofu: its flavor of anise, its brown skin, its origin in the humble bean.

At last, all of the food is gone. There is only a single radish left, and a fragment of bone.

O-Lan sits watching. His eyes dart away to her narrow mattress with the pair of slippers next to it. A cardigan hangs from the bedpost, and, at its foot, there is an old blue carpetbag.

Ming takes one last deep breath and pushes back his chair. "Goodbye," he says. He hurries out, slams the door behind him, and stumbles down the stairs, shaking, flushed with shame.

Ghost in the Machine

He lies on the bedspread in his old room, staring into the dark.

But not entirely dark. He hasn't lowered the shade, and the moon, now only hours to full, shines in the window, lighting up the objects of the past, making them jump out at him. The posters on the wall. The old clock radio, a familiar hump on the bedside table.

His old room and the old moon that would be full at noon. Soon, the noon moon. The noon courtroom.

The fire escape to O-Lan's room, steel-colored in the moonlight.

(Her canine tooth against the orange peel.)

(She is his father's daughter, and very much like him.)

He now knows the facts. He alone knows the facts. He must call Jerry Stern; he'll do it first thing in the morning. The moonlight falls on Ming's old clock radio. (He hears, in his mind's ear, the sputter of static, then the disc jockey's twang awakening him in the winter morning dark. It's the local pop radio station rousing him out of bed. He's a freshman in high school, being woken in this room on the morning of a debate tournament. No, that was years ago. He lives in New York now.) Tomorrow the trial continues. He and Katherine, Brenda, and Jerry Stern are set to meet before the trial, at eight forty-five a.m. Ming checks his phone. It says midnight, but his clock radio says two o'clock. He must reset the radio.

In the quiet, he hears the neighborhood dogs barking one after another, yard to yard. Then a lone, nearby howl rises over the others. The howl picks up the thin hairs behind his ears; his cheeks grow cold, his fingertips sharpen against his palms. Ming frowns. The dog, seemingly loyal, bottomlessly hungry. The dog, like the sons, not as loyal as the man might think.

Ming turns on the old radio.

The click of the power, then volume. The radio spits softly, a low wet hiss and warble of waves unseen. He soothes the tuning knob between his thumb and forefinger, seeking a station. This knob requires him to turn smoothly, slowly, in order to catch hold. He wonders if the radio has stopped working. But after half a minute, he nicks a brief crackle of static; he rolls the dial back and forth over the place, searching for a catch. Back and forth. Another crackle of static. He rolls even more slowly, carefully, feeling for the place; and then, just when he's giving up, the hiss ebbs, giving forth to a low hum. It's a hum of medium register, full-bodied as a note from an alto sax, but not made of human breath; it is inhuman and as such comforting. He turns up the volume and the hum fills his mind, pushing away thought, pushing away movement. He lies clutching the bedspread, for perhaps five minutes, perhaps an hour, listening to the hum. Then a crackle of static sounds at the edges. Static, hum, static, hum.

A voice is coming in and out. Someone's talking. Ming reaches cold fingers back to the dial, twiddles it, delicately, back and forth. He can hear, below the static, a voice he knows. He's obliged, commanded, to bring it forth.

It's a low, mellow voice, and strong, with a rich tone similar to his brother Dagou's, and yet not at all, because of crags and furrows and a husky rasp of age, deepened and strengthened like a sixty-nine-year-old whiskey that has absorbed the smoke-blackened and gnarled wood of its container; because it stirs up a deep disquiet—no, a fear, so that he has to steel himself against it—a voice so familiar to him it seems to speak from some part of his own mind, and yet it is suffused, saturated, with an unknown country, another world. (A muddy village, a half-filled bottle of smoky oil above the stove. Stones in the river, a basket of fish curled and twitching in the stern of a boat.)

Fine hairs stand out on his neck. His body curls spasmodically on the bed.

Clearly now, the voice speaks. "The *tail* of fear is wagging the *dog* of the son."

"Stop it," Ming says.

"Fear, weakness, cowardice. You didn't get that from me."

"I said get lost."

"You're not happy to talk to me? After I worked like a dog, to feed you, to support you, to buy this house, with a room for you to study? You wouldn't be a high-flying hotshot now without me, kid."

(Mornings waking in this room, this chamber of stark loneliness and desolation. Dagou gone to college now, no more big, sweaty but loyal fool between Ming and the villagers. The crackle of the radio, the smell of an egg frying in oil. Beads of soy sauce sliding from the translucent skin, then the hot, sulfurous runny yolk curdling in his gut. Fear. Longing for the bus, the protection of the driver when they lived farther away from school, in the old apartment.)

Ming reaches for the volume knob, squeezing the voice back into the radio until the knob clicks. Silence. He curls on his side, relaxes, but keeps his eyes open watchfully.

He will not engage. He'll climb into his hunting blind, although somehow he can't climb now, cannot lift himself past the first steps of the ladder—his body has changed shape, and his four feet are on the ground. *He* wasn't working for his father, he wasn't exploited. He never worked for anyone except himself. (Those days of years ago. The runny egg yolk making a hot, sulfurous trail down his throat, curdling at the acid in his stomach. The walk to the distant, hostile middle school alone, the walk changing to a run, to flight, a daily race for survival through the neighborhood of villagers. Past the old butcher shop, with its odor of meat. The school. The bathroom with its metal door, the cold, wet throat of the toilet.)

Ming feels his forehead. He gets out of bed, shuffles to the bathroom, thrusts a washcloth under icy water, wrings it out. He returns to his room. He lies down and spreads the cloth over his eyes. For a moment everything is still. But then he can hear it again: the voice, at first unintelligible and yet fully familiar in its identity.

"This is FM 88.8. Chao Family Network."

Ming puts his hands over his ears.

"Good night, good morning. Earth to Ming Chao, Ergou."

"You don't exist," Ming says. "You're dead."

"Frozen, dead, buried. You all tried to kill me using different methods, like the way they tried to kill Rasputin. I survived."

"Your death has been documented by the police. You don't exist."

"So easy to get rid of me. Just like closing a door, eh?"

"And you can't be Dagou pranking me, messing with his radio. It was confiscated as evidence."

"The old man is allowed to visit his favorite son."

"I'm not your favorite."

"That's out of your control. You can't choose my favorite. You, you're my son, you're my true inheritor."

"I don't—" Ming presses his hands to his ears. "Don't want it!"

"But you are, I gave myself to make you. You can't unchoose me."

"Get the *fuck* out of my head."

"There's something I want you to do. Now, while it's eight hundred thirty-eight."

"You're my imagination. I control you and I want you to go away now. Go *now*."

"I want you to go to the restaurant. Into the freezer room—"

Ming leaps up, seizes the cord to the radio, and yanks it from the wall.

Silence.

Ming never did understand the reason his father kept the freezer room. Surely the occasional money he saved on meat couldn't have covered the utility bills for that room. In all his father's money-grubbing practices, the freezer room was the only one Ming could never make sense of. Leo was simply attached to the room.

Ming plugs the radio back into the wall.

Immediately his ears fill with static. After a moment, the voice emerges, full, triumphant.

"In length and breadth how doth my poodle grow!"

"You can't know Faust," Ming says.

"You *think* I can't. Jerry Stern told me. That Jerry is good guy."

"This is a dream."

"You never took me seriously. I've got smarts. You're ashamed of me, think I don't know anything? I know my English. I taught this old dog new tricks! Listen to this! Hot dog! Work like a dog! Fight like cats and dogs. Call off the dogs. Lie down with dogs—get up with fleas! It's a dog's life. Wouldn't wish that on a dog. Raining cats and dogs. Let sleeping dogs lie. Love me, love my dog. Lucky dog. Top dog. Dirty dog. Put on the dog. Shaggy dog story. Sick as a dog. Dog breath. Put a dog off the scent. Why keep a dog and bark yourself. Go to see a man about a dog. Blind dog in a meat market. Dog sniffing another dog's butt. Dog ate my homework. Dog-eat-dog. Dog-tired. Dog sleep. Dog tags. Chowhound. Beware the dog—"

"Shut *up*!"

"If it's in your head, why'd you plug the radio back in? You don't need electricity."

Ming can't think of an answer.

"Admit it. You plugged in the radio out of need. You need to know something you can't figure out yourself. Something only I can tell you."

He stops, waits.

"I do want to ask you something," Ming admits.

"Now we're getting somewhere."

"I want to ask you about my sister, whatever her true name is. My sister at the restaurant."

"It's before your time. And you know why she's here. Not for her mother. That's just a fancy lie. She came here to get three things. First, money. Then, my life. And finally, the ring. I've been trying to tell you. That's what she's been searching for all along. What is hatred that can't be solved with money? Money and murder. What is getting revenge but getting money?"

(Ming hears an echo of his own voice, in the Other Restaurant.)

"You can measure the size of a man by how much money he wants. You, my son, you're a man. Your older brother, chasing his bullshit ego around, chasing his penis now, he'll always be a nobody."

"And my sister?"

"She came all the way across the world. Not for a large amount of money. Not a fortune. But it was somebody's Life Savings. Enough to purchase papers, transportation, a piece of property, just a small one in a nowhere town—start-up costs for a little business—"

"The restaurant—"

"And now she's got some money. But not what she wanted. Not what she was truly after. So she stuck around, even after I was dead, even after she got the ring. Until she finally had a chance to talk with you, so that one person left on earth would remember who she was, what she did."

Was this true? Did O-Lan have the ring now? "What was she truly after?"

"Ask your brother."

"Dagou doesn't know anything."

"No, ask your little brother."

Ming plunges on. "Don't try to lead me off the scent. What did you do to her mother? You took money from her, didn't you? You left her and her daughter, your own child, and you came to the U.S. What money was she after?"

"I'm saving the profits for you. Your inheritance."

"I don't want it."

"It's nothing to you. You will think it nothing. But you, you're my son, and I want you to keep it."

"Shut up," Ming says.

(At that moment, he hears a familiar but unidentifiable sound from somewhere outside of the room, near the door. He's cramped by an old fear, and his body seizes on the bed.)

"Admit it. You hate me, not because I've done bad things. Not because I know money is exchangeable for love, or life, or God. This is what you yourself believe."

"Shut the fuck up!"

(Footsteps, pursuing him. Ming's gasps come quickly now.)

"You don't hate me for this. Nope, you hate me because you think I'm only a small-timer. If I'd managed to sleep with a woman who had a billion yuan, well, then you would find me a more suitable father. But my scale turns out to be on the level of a small business, something humble—"

"Get out! Get out!!"

("Ming? Ming?")

"I told you—"

Somewhere in the back of his mind, he hears the clock radio turn off. There is a hiss of air. The station is gone.

Ming staggers to the thermostat, adjusts the heat.

A moth flutters by and he sniffs its wings, its radiant dust. He feels an intense physical discomfort. The dry heat presses in on him from all sides, as if he is encased in wool; the room is terribly stuffy. He's gulping for air, he's thirsty. He drops to his knees—that's better. He crawls toward the bathroom, pushing away the image of simply putting his head into the cool wet basin of the toilet, guzzling its contents. Repulsive. Disgusting. He stretches out, rears up, and braces himself upon the sink. Slipping, almost falling, he reaches out for the faucet. (Something's wrong. This is not his hand.) The moth flutters by. Following it instinctively, tracking its motion, he catches a glimpse of something in the mirror. He looks away, panting hoarsely, and then, with a slow, deliberate turn that requires all of his strength, he looks into the mirror again.

He sees a dark beast's shape, brown-black in the face, golden at the ruff, shaped by a long, rounded muzzle and peaked ears. Large ears standing alert, crowned by coarse brown hair. Yellow eyes close-set, eyes at a slant, pupils high over the ring of pale iris. Eyes cold, the eyes of a wolf. Ming cries out, whines, but the yellow eyes do not flicker or change. Then he sees someone coming for him, coming up behind him. The villagers.

("Hey, Chao!" Footsteps thud nearby. They are boys. Hands grab him. He thrashes, swings wildly, but he is pummeling air, only now and then does his fist thud into an arm or belly. He's not strong enough to overpower them, but his true flaw, he knows, lies inside—fear, cowardice, weakness. They're dragging him through the alleys of the village.) He is thirteen years old. It is a brilliant, mellow autumn afternoon. "My dad's gonna butcher you and string you up, gook." Ming thrashes desperately, wildly, breaking free only to come crashing down against the ground. Pain shooting through his left wrist. He screams, and they seize him up again, they hustle him into the back door of a place that stinks of meat. *"Gong bong, ching chong, king kong." "Here, into the bathroom."* His feet jerk out from under him. His whole body swinging like meat on a hook; his head swinging. *Crack*. Colors shoot like stars, close to his face. He tries to scream. Blood dripping, blood blooming red in the water. Thrust into the toilet's mouth, a faraway stench of stale urine and feces under the rim, then cold wetness, choking, coughing, screaming, soundless screaming into water.

(Something is pounding on the door. Ming sniffs: Not James. Who is it?)

Light floods his eyes.

"Ming? Are you all right?"

It's Alice Wa. She grabs his arm, trying to pull him up, her grasp surprisingly firm. "It's nine-thirty, it's morning. I left the courthouse. I promised I would come to check on you. Dagou testifies today."

"Fuck off."

"Ming, are you sick?" There's no gasp of surprise, no show of dismay. Although she is a flake, Alice has some stomach for this. Perhaps she understands, more than the others.

"Fuck off, Florence Nightingale."

"Your voice is hoarse. Ming, you need to get into bed. Or maybe stay there on the floor."

There's the rough wool of a blanket against his chin; he throws it off.

"You look terrible. Wait here, I'm going to get someone."

"No, no."

"Then you need to go to the hospital."

"No." Ming sits up. "I'm going to the trial. Don't try to stop me."

A Character Witness

Straightening her shoulders in her eggshell linen suit, Katherine takes her place on the witness stand. For Winnie's sake, she will be calm. Yet she can feel, emanating from her body, a palpable, shattering anxiety.

She affirms she is an attorney at the Chicago accounting firm Sims, Mauk, and Machado. She was the fiancée of William Chao. How long were they engaged?

"For twelve years."

As the gallery takes this in, Katherine briefly imagines the article in the pages of the *Sioux City Journal*: How is it possible their former high school debate champion, who has succeeded in the world and achieved so much, could allow herself to be bamboozled by a dog eater? How is it possible she could be the unquestioning fiancée of a murderer for *twelve years*? What kind of a character witness will she make? Obviously, she lost perspective on Dagou's character long ago.

Yet Katherine answers the questions without blushing. She ignores the jury, the community, and the people wearing Alf T-shirts. She's focused on her one objective: That she will answer only the questions put forth in the examination and the cross-examinations. This has been her strategy for months, walking a delicate tightrope of the agreement she made with herself, over Winnie's deathbed: that she wouldn't lie to defend Winnie's oldest and beloved son, her own former fiancée; but, for Winnie's sake, she won't reveal anything that isn't asked of her. She'll do what she can to stand up for Dagou—not for the sake of what they once were to one another, but for Winnie.

For several years, she has suspected the futility of her approach to the past. She knows this now: You can't create it. You can try forever; you can fall into the process; you can devote yourself. But it isn't a relationship, it's not a work in progress. The past is gone.

The only option is to move forward and to do the best you can.

"During the twelve years you were engaged, was he ever violent toward you?"

"No."

"Was he violent toward others or did he express violent tendencies in your presence?"

"He was sometimes loud, and very candid, but never physically violent."

"Did he ever talk about a plan to kill his father?"

"No."

There are lies, and lies of omission. She wasn't asked the question: Had he ever wished his father dead? *This* statement she'd heard a hundred times, beginning shortly after his fateful mistake of returning to the Midwest—a decision he'd made for Winnie's sake, and also (Katherine believed at the time) because she, Katherine, had received a very good job offer in Chicago. For years, she'd felt guilty, responsible, for his return to Haven.

Now Jerry is finished, and it's time for the cross-examination. Assistant Prosecutor Corinne Udweala frowns through her glasses. She puts one hand skeptically on her hip for a moment while she's checking her notes.

"Would you say he and his mother, Winnie, had a close relationship?"

Again, this question. "Yes."

"To your knowledge, did she give William cash gifts?"

"Yes." Katherine shifts on her feet. Strycker has been stealthily building an argument involving small amounts of money, but what is he getting at? "If you mean birthday presents. She gave him money for birthday presents."

"How much money?"

"Five hundred, a thousand dollars."

Udweala raises her voice ever so slightly. "In mid-December of last year, did you give William ten thousand dollars?"

A rustle of surprise comes from the front of the gallery. It's James. Katherine can see him from the corner of her eye. He didn't know about the money; Dagou did not tell him. He's staring at her now, surprised, a little hurt. She retrains her gaze on Udweala. "Yes."

"Why did you give him the ten thousand?"

"I knew he needed the money."

"In this conversation, did the subject come up of a ring?"

A murmuring rises, then a *shhhh*.

"Yes."

"Was it an engagement ring?"

"Yes."

"What did you discuss, regarding the ring?"

"He asked me to give it back."

"Was he ending the engagement?"

"I don't know."

A giggle breaks out from somewhere in the back of the gallery.

"He asked you to return the ring. Then what happened?"

"He admitted he was broke. He said he wanted to sell the ring. I gave him some money."

She hears a rustle near the door: perhaps it's Alice, returning with Ming. But it's just someone fumbling with their inhaler.

"Were you paying him to continue the engagement?"

"Objection!" Jerry jumps in. "Irrelevant."

The objection is sustained. It's too late. A high titter rings out, followed by the thunderclap of a loud "Ha, ha!" from a man in the jury. For a moment it seems the room will break apart in laughter.

But in the first few rows, the community holds the line, stonily looking straight ahead. And at this moment it is clear to Katherine, more definitively than it has ever been, that she is beloved. She straightens her shoulders.

"I gave him money," she says steadily, "because he needed it and I wanted him to have it."

"To your knowledge, what did Dagou do with the ten thousand dollars?"

"He bought radio equipment. He put new tires on his truck. He bought new strings for his bass, and a gym membership."

"Did he spend all ten thousand?"

Of course, it's possible Dagou spent all ten thousand. He's not in the habit of saving; he's inherited Winnie's extravagance. New tires, illegal radio equipment. Who knew what else? But if he did spend the money, she's not aware of it. She frowns. It's possible he spent the money on Brenda. But could even Dagou—adding infatuation to his prodigality—make all of ten thousand vanish in a matter of weeks?

"I don't know," Katherine says. More urgent in her mind is the question of why the prosecution is focused on tracing every possible source of income, on nailing down precisely how little money Dagou had. Her testimony is finished; she has permission to sit in the gallery. Mary Wa embraces her. She leans into Mary for several minutes, comforted by the familiar smell of the Oriental Food Mart, troubled by the puzzle of the prosecution's plan, relieved she hasn't been asked to reveal her secret. She takes a few deep breaths. The next witness for the defense is Brenda Wozicek.

The Testimony of Brenda Wozicek

Creak! Chairs protest as people crane to watch her enter, followed by the gray-haired bailiff. Even in the courtroom, she can't control her magnetism. Some actually rise as she passes, as if this is a wedding and she's the bride. She takes her place at the stand. For perhaps a minute, everyone stares at her in silent judgment. Must the fabric of her jacket wrap around her body like that? Must her hair dip in that wayward curl over her forehead? Must her eyes be so vividly blue? And her blouse: it suits her, even Ken Fan can't take his eyes off of her, but must she have chosen a scarlet blouse?

"I'm his fiancée," she's saying to Jerry Stern. For all her physical presence, she speaks quietly. Everyone leans forward, and she turns to them, eyes shining with a righteous light. An uncomfortable whispering arises from the gallery. Only Katherine appears wrapped in calm. "He's also the son of my late boss, Leo Chao," Brenda says.

"How long have you known the defendant?" Jerry asks.

"I knew Dagou—William—in high school."

"Did you know him well?"

"No. Our groups didn't overlap."

"When did the two of you become involved?"

"Shortly after I started working at the restaurant."

"You were sexually involved?"

"Yes."

"Were you officially involved at the time?"

"No." Brenda's lips twist. Her self-possession, her surety would be absurd if it were not for the arresting curve of her mouth.

"Did this change on the night of December twenty-fourth, morning of the twenty-fifth?"

"Yes, we became officially involved. After the party."

"Why that night and not before?"

"Well, for one thing, William had a kind of understanding with Katherine Corcoran. The way he described it, the relationship wasn't sexual anymore and they were just good friends but they had never officially ended their engagement. Because his mother was in poor health, and she was close to Katherine—and because Katherine was like a member of the family. It was kept up out of politeness, but I knew Dagou would end it immediately, if . . ."

"If what?"

"If and when we became officially involved."

"Did you and William ever discuss the possibility of moving in together?"

Brenda shakes her head, bemused. "No."

Jerry nods. "During your time as Leo Chao's employee, did you go down to the freezer room?"

"No. It didn't have anything to do with my job, which was to seat people, bring their drinks, take their orders, bring their food."

Jerry glances through his notes. "Let's visit the morning of December twenty-fifth. Did William Chao come to your house after the party at the Fine Chao?"

"Yes."

"At approximately what time did William Chao arrive at your house after the party?"

"Between midnight and twelve-thirty."

"What was his frame of mind when he visited you during the morning of December twenty-fifth?"

"He seemed relaxed, much happier than he'd been lately."

"Would you say a weight had been lifted from his shoulders?"

"Yes. The party had gone well and that cheered him up. The party was for his mother. He was devoted to her. He'd wanted the party to be special, in her honor."

"Can you tell the jury what was said?"

"Well, he told me his father had only been joking, and he hadn't sold the restaurant."

"Did he say he had shut Leo Chao into the freezer room?"

Brenda frowns. "No."

"Please elaborate on this."

"He told me he'd been so upset with his father—for being so domineering—that he'd created a plan. But he specifically said he didn't carry it out."

"Please describe what he said."

"He said his father had double-crossed him in a terrible way, had promised him the restaurant and then announced he would sell it. And then told him the whole thing was a joke! He'd waited years for the time when he would be able to live his own life. He said his life would begin when his father was dead, and not before. And that after the party when his father went downstairs, all he had to do was to step in, remove the key, and leave, shutting the door. But he didn't do it. Couldn't, didn't do it."

Jerry waits for a moment, looking thoughtfully at Brenda. "How did you respond to this?"

"I told him I was glad he didn't do it."

"To reiterate, William specifically told you he did not shut his father into the freezer room?"

"Yes."

"Do you believe him?"

"Yes, I—"

"Objection: relevance."

"Objection sustained."

"After this conversation, he was in your presence until the following morning?"

"Yes—he was with me all night."

"When did you go to sleep?"

"We didn't fall asleep until after four o'clock. I heard the bells ringing. The next morning, I woke first around eleven-thirty and went downstairs to make some coffee. Dagou was asleep upstairs until early afternoon, when the police knocked on the door."

Jerry examines his notes again. He has just a few more questions, he says. Had William ever discussed inheritance laws with her? Maybe, she can't remember. Does she remember him telling her he understood the law to provide that his mother would inherit everything should his father die? No. Did she herself know the law? Yes. "Did William tell you he was trying to please his mother with an extravagant party so she would give him the restaurant after his father's death?" No, of course not.

"You were aware of Winnie Chao's will?"

At this question, there's a rustle from the second row. Every one of Winnie's friends is surprised. Did Winnie make a will, when Leo had not?

"Yes."

Mary Wa turns to stare at Ken Fan. Lynn's father raises his brows at Lynn's mother.

"Have you seen the will?"

"No. Dagou said she told him about it in the hospital, when she was sick."

Jerry raises his voice. "Do you recall William telling you that Winnie Chao left all of her property to a Mrs. Ling Gu, of the Haven Spiritual House?"

There's a long moment in which time is suspended. "Yes," says Brenda, but the word falls almost unheard into a canyon of amazed silence.

"No further questions, Your Honor."

Cultural Differences

As Corinne Udweala gets ready to start her cross-examination, a clamor of speculation takes over the gallery. The community is on tenterhooks. How could Winnie possibly have made a will, when Leo did not? And how could she leave everything to the Spiritual House, forgetting her own children? Even Fang is surprised. Even Katherine is rattled from her calm. The nuns are whispering and murmuring in their chairs.

Ken Fan muses aloud that Winnie most likely assumed she'd never outlive Leo, with his physical strength and his immortal confidence. She must have assumed *he* would take over all of their property when *she* was dead: "So, why did she make a will?"

Mary Wa lifts one finger, replies, "The will is opportunity to set things right." After decades in the U.S., pursuing profit and family fortune, Winnie would have come to see the property as a burden. She would have sought to rid the family of the restaurant: she might even have believed that the restaurant was founded on greed and dishonesty, that it was a cursed property. She must have wished to try, by letting go, to lift the Chao family out of this whole mess: the greed, the hatred, and the covetousness. To bring them, with her final act, toward tranquility. And now, as a result, Gu Ling Zhu Chi is the owner of the Fine Chao.

"Gu Ling Zhu Chi must have kept it a secret, must have decided to let the Chao brothers stay for the time being," says one of the women from the Spiritual House. "She must be waiting until after the trial to decide what to do with the restaurant." Everyone remembers Jerry's presence at the forty-nine-day ceremony, his sequestered conversation with Gu Ling Zhu Chi and Dagou. But no one believes they could all keep such a secret.

It's Katherine who brings them back to the moment. Jerry Stern has brought up Winnie's will in order to exonerate Dagou from the plot to kill for the restaurant. But Strycker must also have known about the will. This would explain why the prosecution spent so much energy following the trail of smaller cash. Prompted by Katherine, everyone can see it: Winnie's birthday gifts. The money for the ring. And ultimately, the blue carpetbag containing Zhang Fujian's money. The prosecution doesn't need the restaurant to make its case. The prosecution's story takes on weight: On Christmas Eve, following the party, Leo accused Dagou of stealing the fifty thousand dollars, and threatened to call the police. Minutes later, in danger of losing his personal freedom over the only windfall of money he would ever have, Dagou locked his father into the freezer room.

James says nothing. So, the entire trial has circled back again: Back to the moment in the train station, when he had turned at the sound of the old voice. *Please help, young man.* If only he hadn't heard. If only he'd rushed up the stairs, escaped. Or remembered to give the luggage to the EMTs. If only he had handed it over to the lost-and-found. Would none of this be happening now?

He longs to talk to Alice, but Katherine has sent Alice out to search for Ming.

Corrine Udweala begins Brenda's cross-examination.

It's most likely Udweala has been chosen with the jury in mind. Matching Strycker against Brenda might seem harsh, but Udweala has the no-nonsense manner of a vice principal chastising an oversexed teenager. Brenda is in danger, James can tell. Like a teenager, she wears her righteousness too close to the surface.

"You said Leo Chao was a 'domineering' man. Did he ever treat you this way?"

"No. He was different with me than he was with the others."

"Why do you think this is?"

"I think because I wasn't family. And because I'm white."

"But you believe he was domineering toward his family?"

"Yes."

"Did you consider your relationship with Leo Chao to be one of friendship?"

"We would sit and talk."

"Did the two of you discuss his relationship with William?"

"Not specifically. He made general comments about how a child could never know a parent. That was it."

"What did you talk about?"

"Lately he'd gotten to describing his regrets."

"Please explain."

"He talked about how, if he had stayed in China, just 'stuck it out,' he said, he might have been able to get truly rich. That there were too many people in business here already, and it turned out there was a limit to how rich he could get in the U.S., but in Asia things had opened up and it was possible to get rich without constraints. How he'd made this fundamental life mistake. Sometimes he asked me if I thought he was old."

"How did you answer?"

"I just said no, not that old."

"Were you aware at any point that Leo Chao had sexual intentions toward you?"

From the gallery, James studies Lynn's juror. Her eyes are gleaming, her small mouth slightly open. Her expression is sterner, more righteous, than when the other witnesses were questioned. She's judging Brenda.

"No."

"Were you aware at any point of Leo and William vying for sexual access to you?"

"Objection, irrelevant." The objection is overruled.

Brenda raises her voice. "What are you trying to say about me? Are you trying to say, did I lead them on? What are you implying here?"

At the outrage in her tone, everyone is uncomfortable. People cough, people look away, people cross their arms.

"You say you were physically involved with William Chao shortly after you became coworkers. Did you ask William to break up with Katherine Corcoran?"

"No."

"Why not?"

"Objection, relevancy." The objection is overruled.

"That sounds like a leading question to me. And none of your business."

"Ms. Wozicek," says Judge Lopate, "please answer the question."

"If you must know, I could tell Dagou was in love with me, and it didn't matter to me if he was attached. It was I who had the doubts, mostly. Other doubts."

"Why did you have doubts?"

"Objection, relevancy." The objection is overruled.

"Seriously, is this relevant?"

"Were there other things? What were your other doubts?"

Brenda looks at Jerry. "Objection," he says.

"Objection overruled."

Brenda's nostrils flare. "I had reservations, I suppose, about our cultural differences."

"Can you give an example of a reservation about your cultural differences?"

Brenda turns to Dagou. He nods, and she relaxes visibly. "Well, as one example," she says, "I had a schedule and a salary at the restaurant, not huge, but with tips an acceptable compensation, because I wasn't part of the family. I saw the amount of work Mrs. Chao did—and how much work Dagou did—and I wasn't confident they had fair compensation. Mr. Chao—my boss—was a dictatorial man. You could even describe him as tyrannical. And I didn't see how Dagou would ever get ahead unless . . ."

"Unless?"

"Well, unless he was in a situation where he wasn't working for his father."

"So it would be to your personal advantage if Leo Chao were no longer alive?"

"Objection. Relevance."

"Overruled."

"That's an insult, and a leading question."

"Ms. Wozicek, please answer the question."

"If you look at it that way, yes."

"You said you and William became 'officially involved' on December twenty-fourth?"

"Yes."

"That night, did you and William ever discuss a recent windfall of fifty thousand dollars?"

"No."

"Did you and William discuss your plans to move in together?"

"I said, no."

"Did you agree to become officially involved with William even though you both knew another woman still considered herself his fiancée?"

"Yes."

"Did you decide to do this because William's financial prospects had suddenly improved by fifty thousand dollars? Enough to live together, in the Lakeside Apartments, after his father was dead?"

Brenda flinches. Jerry calls out, "Objection! Speculation! Foundation! Assumes facts not in evidence!" The objection is sustained.

Udweala rephrases the question. "You said you had financial reasons not to be 'officially involved' with William Chao. Did you become 'officially involved' on the evening of December twenty-fourth, despite the fact that he had not broken off his engagement with his girlfriend, because William now had fifty thousand dollars?"

"For God's sake, no." Brenda's voice is sharp. "I told you, he never told me about any fifty thousand. What are you implying here? You want to make me out as some kind of slut? A whore? You want the jury to think that Dagou tried to pay me to move in with him?"

Again, James glances at Lynn's juror. Her lips are set, her eyes bright, and James understands that with these blurted questions, Brenda has said exactly what the prosecution wanted.

Dagou Tells the Truth

James knows the history of the defense: How, in the past weeks and months, Jerry, Sarah, Katherine, and Ming have grown united in their belief that Dagou should not testify on his own behalf. That, however carefully they coached him, he would go off message. They all worked to persuade him. But Dagou insisted, with the stubbornness of his father. The jury would expect him to explain. Wouldn't they believe him if he simply told the truth?

Now Dagou, a mountain of gray serge, towers hopefully before the citizens of Haven, his eyes alight with belief that the truth will set him free.

From where he sits between Fang and Lynn, James prays the jury will believe his brother.

"I'm going to begin by asking you about the freezer room," Jerry says. "Please estimate: how often did your father go into the freezer room?"

"A couple times a week. If we couldn't find him, when his car was in the parking lot, he was pretty sure to be down there. We had a joke; we called it his 'third office.'"

"Who else used the key to the freezer room?"

"Just family. My mother and brothers."

"Did O-Lan know about the key to the freezer room?"

"Objection, speculation. Foundation."

"Overruled."

Dagou shrugs. "It's possible." Jerry, focusing on Dagou, nods. "But, to be honest," Dagou bursts out, "it's unlikely." Jerry and Sara look at one another. "See, O-Lan hates raw meat. So the family dealt with the meat. We've arranged our habits so she never has to go into the freezer room. And even if she went in there, there's no way she could read the sign."

Jerry pauses, then asks, "Are you certain she doesn't know about the freezer room key?"

"Yes, I'm certain. I suppose I shouldn't say this, it would help exonerate me to say I was not certain. But I always tell the truth." Dagou straightens, puffs out his chest, exhibiting his honesty. "No one spends more time at the restaurant than I do! And I've never seen her even open the basement door."

"Did you mention the key in your early morning, December twenty-third, radio broadcast?"

"Yes."

"On December twenty-fourth, were you and your father the last two to leave the restaurant?"

"I think so."

"Are you sure?"

"No."

"Did you and your father engage in an altercation that night?"

"Not more than average. He shouted at me, called me a loser."

"Did he accuse you of taking a bag of cash from his car?"

"No."

"Did he threaten to call the police?"

"No."

"Did you take the key from the shelf in the freezer room?"

"No." Dagou's voice is firm.

Jerry nods. He turns toward the judge. "No further ques—"

"There was a moment when I thought about it, to be absolutely truthful," Dagou says.

Everyone sighs, almost groans.

Jerry turns, a little wearily, to Dagou. "Please describe what you mean."

"My father went downstairs and into the freezer room. I also went downstairs."

Jerry's face is expressionless. "You were both downstairs."

"Yes."

"What happened next?"

Dagou stares at his hands, gathering composure, then straight up at Jerry. "When I got down there, the light was on and the door to the room was open. It would have been easy to reach in, take the key, and push the door shut. I actually hesitated."

He turns to the jury. "But I didn't do it," he says. "I don't know if I can explain. What happened was—it was like grace. I felt released. Someone, something guided me to turn around, to go back up the stairs. I turned around." He looks proudly at the judge. "I went upstairs, and I left the restaurant."

"You made the decision not to close the door?" Jerry speaks very clearly.

But Dagou doesn't accept his phrasing. "It wasn't a decision. I simply did not do it. I'm not saying I haven't been angry at my father, that he hasn't enraged me. I'm not saying I hadn't wished that he were gone. I have. But ultimately, I did not do it."

"What did you do after you went upstairs?"

"I left the restaurant and drove straight to Ren's—Brenda's—house."

"Were you at her house until the police arrived at two p.m. on December twenty-fifth?"

"Yes."

"No further questions, Your Honor."

Dagou gives Brenda a shy smile, which she returns. He's finally done it, what he's wished to do since his arrest. He's told his side of the story to everyone. He's glowing, grinning broadly at them all now: rosy, vulnerable, newly born.

Dagou also smiles at Simeon Strycker. He wants even Strycker to like him, James can see—Strycker, his enemy, who emits an untouchable indifference, a reptilian coldness.

But Strycker's tone is casual, almost friendly. "You referred to the freezer room as your father's 'third office,'" he says. "What are the first and second offices?"

Dagou's head bobs with relief. "The first office is the restaurant office, in the back. The second office, that was what we said when he was taking a dump."

"Thank you."

Dagou gives another little smile.

"And do you live in an apartment above the restaurant?"

"Yes."

"Did you pay rent to your father on that apartment?"

"Well, he let me stay there in exchange—"

"Please answer yes or no, Mr. Chao," says Judge Lopate.

"No." Dagou lowers his head.

"Is it true that on December fourteenth of last year you signed a lease on a penthouse apartment in the Lakeside Apartments in south Haven?"

There comes a rustle of surprise from the community. Fang reaches over James and writes on the corner of Lynn's legal pad, *The dog wants a bigger house!*

Strycker is saying, ". . . and paid a deposit plus first and last months' rent, totaling sixty-three hundred dollars?"

"Yes."

"Was the monthly rent on the penthouse twenty-one hundred dollars, beginning January first?"

"Yes."

"On the morning of December twenty-second, did you ask your father if he would make you a partner at the Fine Chao?"

"Yes."

"What was his response?"

Dagou's expression dims. "He wouldn't do it."

"On the evening of December twenty-third, you drove your Toyota pickup to your father's house. You parked the Toyota at the house and switched vehicles, taking the Ford Taurus, your father's car, to Memorial Hospital. Is that correct?"

"Yes."

"Why did you switch from your own vehicle, the Toyota, to your father's car?"

"I left the Toyota at my dad's because the plow was still attached."

"Where did you drive the Ford?"

"I drove to the Spiritual House and packed a bag of clothes for my mother. Then I drove to the hospital."

"Were you on Memorial Hospital's fourth floor at approximately ten-thirty p.m.?"

"Yes."

"Did you threaten to kill your father at that time?" Strycker's voice is low, almost intimate.

"Yes."

Strycker looks at his notes. But he could be pretending. His eyes aren't moving; he's not even blinking. "According to testimony, on the night of December twenty-third at ten fifty-four p.m., at the 7-Eleven convenience store, you attempted to make a purchase of one bottle of Jack Daniel's whiskey and lottery tickets and were unable to complete the purchase of the lottery tickets due to lack of funds. You then assaulted a customer. Is this true?"

Dagou nods. "Yeah, it's true. I want to"—he takes a gulp of air—"apologize to her. I was in a terrible state of mind."

"What did you do after you left the 7-Eleven?"

Dagou looks confused. "I . . . got back into the Ford. I drove around."

"Where did you drive?"

"I drove to Brenda's house. I shoveled her driveway and front path. Talked to her for a minute. Then I got back into the car and went home."

"You say you shoveled her driveway. Where did you find the shovel?"

"In the trunk of the Ford."

Strycker pauses almost imperceptibly. "So, on December twenty-third, at Brenda Wozicek's house, you did look inside your father's trunk?"

"I never knew about the cash! I had no idea!"

The judge says, "Answer the question, Mr. Chao."

Dagou flinches visibly. "I did."

"At that point, did you discover, in your father's Ford, a carpetbag containing approximately fifty thousand dollars?"

"No."

"Did you and Brenda discuss your plan to move in together and use the fifty thousand to help pay the rent on the penthouse apartment?"

"No!" Dagou yells.

"Objection!" Jerry says. "Argumentative. Assumes facts not in evidence."

"Objection overruled—"

"I didn't take any money! I'm not a thief!"

Strycker pauses before continuing, "Let's move on to the morning of December twenty-fourth. Did you use cash to buy eight chickens and twelve ducks from the Shire farm on Highway 30?"

"Yes."

"At approximately nine twenty-five a.m., did you purchase from Stanley Pardo of Haven Fine Wines and Spirits two six-bottle cases of Stolichnaya, two cases of Jack Daniel's, a case of bourbon, a case of white wine, a case of red wine, a case of rosé, and four cases of Tsingtao beer? And a case of Korbel champagne, and a package of decorative umbrellas? Paying in cash?"

"Yes."

"At approximately nine a.m., is it true you bought groceries from the Oriental Food Mart, paying in cash?"

"Yes."

"How much did you spend at the Oriental Food Mart?"

Dagou stares starkly, thinking. "About six hundred dollars."

"Where did you get the cash to pay for the alcohol and the groceries?"

"I had it, it was my money."

"If you had the money, why did you have no cash to pay for the lottery tickets on December twenty-third?"

"Why does it matter? I had the cash all along. I didn't want to spend it. But Ma was sick, and I spent money I had to make a good party."

"Where did you get the money to pay for the party?"

Dagou doesn't speak for a long moment. His lips are pursed, his forehead is rumpled. The gallery rustles with the sound of people shifting their weight.

Finally, he mutters, "It was for the ring."

"Please speak up."

"It was left over from Katherine," he says, red-faced. "I used her money for the down payment on the new apartment. But I still had money left over. I was saving it so I could give it back to her. So we could be fair and square. So I could ask for the ring back. Then I could sell it for more than ten thousand. To pay the rent on the apartment." He levels his shoulders and turns to Judge Lopate. "I may be an asshole, Your Honor, but I'm not a thief!"

"Where were you keeping the money?"

"I had it under my mattress."

Strycker lifts his pale brows. It is like the stab of a knife. "Let's move on," he says, "to approximately twelve a.m., December twenty-fifth. Between approximately eleven-thirty p.m. on December twenty-fourth and twelve a.m. on December twenty-fifth, you and your father had an altercation in the restaurant?"

"Yes."

"What was it about?"

"I said before, he called me a loser."

"Did you fight about anything else?"

There's a moment before Dagou answers. Only a fraction of a moment, but people glance up, noticing. "He wanted to know where I'd gotten the money for the party."

"Did he accuse you of taking a bag containing money from his car, the night before?"

"No."

"Did he inform you he was about to call the police on you?"

"For chrissake, no!"

Strycker pauses, allows the jury to experience Dagou's profanity.

"During this altercation, did you wish your father dead?"

"Yes."

"Did you have these thoughts before this altercation?"

"Sure."

"How often did you have these thoughts?"

"Well, maybe about ten times a day. No, fifteen times a day."

Strycker takes another drink of water. "How long have you been having these thoughts?"

Dagou lowers his voice. "I'd rather not answer."

Judge Lopate says, "Please answer the question, Mr. Chao."

"Oh, well, all right." Dagou gazes out at the back of the gallery. "It started when I was in high school, went away when I was in college, and then, after I came back to Haven, it crept up on me again."

"Can you describe your thoughts?"

James begins to pray again. *Please, God, please watch over him. Please keep him safe.*

Dagou looks straight at Strycker. How he manages to meet the prosecutor's eye, James can't imagine; some great force of will guides him now. Strycker's eyes are colorless, his expression unreadable.

Dagou loosens his tie, takes a gulp of air. "Well, the thing is," he says, "I wasn't the oldest son he wished for: I turned out to be a beta, even with my physical fitness, my personality, and my grades. I could not conquer America for him. I came home with my tail between my legs. But I was also *exactly* the son he wished for: someone he could take advantage of, ignore, disrespect, and underpay, a non human, a dog. Nothing exists for him except himself. I understood this from watching him after my mom got pneumonia. He didn't care as long as I was here to take her shifts. That was when I started *wishing* he was dead. If he were only *gone*." He twists again toward Judge Lopate. "But, Your Honor, there's nothing unusual about wishing someone dead. *Really*. Everybody does it."

There's a loud noise from the defense table. Jerry has dropped his phone. Why he's even holding the phone at that point is unclear. He must have picked it up and dropped it to get Dagou's attention. Dagou's peering hopefully around at the first rows of the gallery. James tries to smile, everyone tries to smile, in encouragement; but instead they grimace.

"Admit it, people! *Everybody does it!*" Dagou's expression is imploring now. "It was like a new world, this picture in my mind—this *vision* of the house, our street, our restaurant—without him in it. New sidewalks, green trees, the houses lined up with their siding all clean and bright in the sun. The real America. The wish to be like a baby—and the world without anything in it: no shame, no hatred or responsibility. A fresh start."

Strycker smiles.

James holds his breath. *Please, God—*

"An imaginary world. A world where he's gone and everything is immediately, and miraculously, safe! And then one day, I realize there's a way this could happen. He could get trapped in the freezer room and never come out. Not violent, see. An accident. The door to the freezer room, swinging shut. The empty nail inside. When I'm angry, instead of punching him, I think of the door swinging shut. That's how the wish becomes a plan. It would be nighttime, after work. We'd be the only ones in the place, we've closed up, and my dad just happens to be in the freezer room and the door just happens to be open, and I just happen to reach in and take the key, then nudge the door shut. I think about it at odd moments. Sometimes even the first thing after I wake up. The door shuts and the world is new again."

There is absolute silence in the room. Katherine is very pale. Her eyes are dark and glittering.

"I request a brief recess," Jerry says.

The judge denies it.

"And then the opportunity reveals itself, after the party. The guests leave. Ren leaves. James leaves. O-Lan is ready to go home. There's just my father and me, alone in the restaurant, late at night. I'm taking off my apron. I'm standing in the hall. My father, still shouting, heads down the stairs. I hear his footsteps. I hear him open the door at the bottom of the stairs, hear him walk into the freezer like I've heard him do a hundred times before. He's telling me I'm a spendthrift, a loser, a wimp. He's telling me I'm too cowardly to ever get back at him. Taunting me! I stand there listening, and, *I want to do it.* All I have to do is take the key, close the door. Then put the key into my pocket. It would be freedom, it would be triumph, and his frozen corpse would be a trophy, the world's biggest Christmas present! So I walk down the stairs. I reach the door. But at that very moment, right when it's all going through my head—right then—you *have to* believe me here—I just—don't do it!"

He is coughing—no, he is sobbing into the hushed room.

Please—

"Maybe it wasn't grace. Maybe I just can't do it. Instead, I turn and walk back up the stairs."

Tears stream down Dagou's pumpkin face.

"I'm a candy-ass, a failure! I can't reach in. I can't take the key. I fucking *can't do it.* I can't close the door and walk away. So I don't do it because I'm a coward. The moment passes. *I didn't do it.* And the world is still here, as messy and terrible as ever!"

Silence.

"Now, looking back, I wish I had done it! If I had done it, then at least I would be proud. I would be a man!"

His voice rings into the gallery.

"No further questions," Strycker says.

No one moves, not even to cough. They're all watching Dagou. His big shoulders are bent, his face is in his hands. He's still sobbing as Judge Lopate dismisses him. Then she dismisses the jury, and the members of the jury slowly stand. The lawyers begin to pack up their briefcases. The testimony is over. James is fixed to his seat when a low chatter begins somewhere in the back of the room. There comes the sound of the door opening. There is the sound of a muttered argument—but no one turns. They're focused on Dagou.

Then a murmur rises from the back of the gallery. A familiar voice rings out. "Call for a break!"

James whips around. It's Ming, with Alice and the bailiff hurrying after him.

"Ming!" James shouts. He tries to get past Fang.

"Shut *up*!" Fang hisses. He and Lynn seize James's arms. Though he twists frantically, he can't get loose.

Ming is making his way up the aisle. He looks terrible. Green skin, jagged cheeks, and black eyes glittering feverishly over his jacket and loose tie.

"Call for a break," he's saying. "A break in the proceedings! I have to speak."

Judge Lopate is on her feet urging the jury to leave the room. They're filing out, staring at Ming like everyone else. Even Strycker is staring.

Ming is halfway up the aisle when Ken Fan leaps up. He puts his hands on Ming's shoulders, trying to steer him back. On Judge Lopate's orders, the bailiff hurries to the jury, shepherding them ahead of him. The judge orders the lawyers to the bench. Ming tells Ken Fan, "I'm here to give evidence against myself. I'm the guilty party."

Finally, with a terrific wrench, James breaks free. He leaps to his feet. The three brothers stand in the courtroom: Dagou staring out at Ming, Ming turning to Dagou, James looking from one brother to the other.

Katherine cries out, "Ming, stop! You were a thousand miles away!"

"I didn't have to be there!" Ming says, squaring his shoulders. "It's the perfect murder, don't you see? Dad was obsessed with that freezer. It was only Dad who could be killed. James is wrong. The key was gone. Anyone could have done it. No proof, no witnesses!"

"Ming, you know you didn't do it," Katherine says. "You had no motive."

Ming smiles broadly. "We all hated him. We were all his bitches. Our motives lie in the past. It's a dark room with the flayed corpses of animals in it. Nobody in their right mind wants to go there."

James is struggling through the crowd to reach Ming. Worming his way between Katherine and Ken Fan and the other community men who have surrounded his brother, trying to grab him by the shoulders.

"Forget Alf! I'm the one who got away. Do you know what kind of person our father was? A terrible person. . . . He knew that about himself. But he wanted power, he needed to keep people around him. So he found a way. The key was marrying my mother, did you know what a fool my mother was? She fell for him, once to marry him and at least three times after that. Three dogs. Dagou is the big dog and I'm Ergou, the second dog. I'm the dog who ran away. I've gone into the wild. More than foaming at the mouth. I've become one of them. I'm a—"

"Ming, stop," Katherine begs. She is sobbing.

"I knew she was my sister! Not in my conscious mind. But my unconscious mind knew she wasn't normal, not like the others. She's a wily one. She's involved me in her drama, her wasted-life drama. The drama of her wasted life. It's true I wasn't in the state." He pulls something out of his pocket. His hands are shaking. "It's true, I have a boarding pass! But that's no alibi!"

Ming turns, speaking to the gallery. "Villagers! Villagers, I arranged to be gone." He turns to the prosecuting attorney. "Strycker, you think your case is watertight. But Dagou broadcast his plan. He isn't the only one who knew about the key. James knew. I knew. I could easily have taken the key with me, flown to New York City, and dropped the key into the Hudson River. I am responsible for Ba's death. I did it!"

Katherine's voice rings out, "No, you didn't! Ming, you didn't."

Katherine stands and turns to Ming, her face contorted with tears.

She squares her shoulders. Then she takes a shuddering breath and says, "I have the key."

For a moment, no one moves. As James, startled, turns in her direction, he glimpses Brenda in the gallery looking daggers at Katherine.

"It's right here in my purse." Katherine opens her purse, removes a key, and holds it up to the judge. The brass key, with its distinctive square head, glints slightly.

Stunned, Ming asks, "Where'd you find that key?"

Katherine says, "In Dagou's jacket pocket. In the restaurant office. I was looking through his pockets, after the party. I—I was very upset that night. I thought it was *her* key."

There is a single hoot of nervous laughter, followed by a shocked silence.

"Yes, it's true. I swear to God, that is where I found it."

"Mistrial," Jerry is saying. "Call for a mistrial!"

Judge Lopate tells the lawyers to show up first thing in the morning. She says she'll decide about the mistrial then. James and Ken Fan, after speaking to the bailiff, escort Ming out of the courtroom. James takes Ming by the arm and Ming, snarling, shakes him off. James takes hold of him again, more gingerly, and Ming doesn't resist.

James's Secret

At the nursing station in the psychiatric wing, James is told Ming needs psychotropic medication. He'll be kept at least a night for observation, and if he's not a danger to himself or others, he'll be released. He was given a sedative and is now asleep, says the nurse. But when James enters the room, his brother is wide awake. Ming sits up too straight, and his eyes are too bright.

"Get me out of here," he says.

"I think it would be good for you to stay here for a night. Nothing's happening out there. Just deliberation by the jury."

"A jury of villagers," Ming snarls. "He doesn't stand a chance."

Ming's bright eyes lock onto James's eyes. James holds the gaze bravely, but Ming's righteous anger sears into his mind.

"Forget it. Just forget the condescending medical bullshit, Mr. Premed. You've got a shitty bedside manner. You don't want me out of here. You've always envied me, wanted to see me put down. Fine, I'll get myself out of here. I know what to tell them. I'll tell them. Get me a cup of coffee."

"Ming, you're not well."

"Let me begin at the beginning, Doctor. She's one of us. Our sister. Dad knew all about it. She has his jaw like a spade. She has his smile like a cat. He never was a dog, you know, as he claimed—he was a cat in dog's clothing. It was she who had the dirty sneakers. I went to her apartment. I talked to her three times. She's spent years in Singapore, I think. She speaks flawless Commonwealth English. She staked us out, she's been living here and working at the restaurant, pretending all the while to be something else. I ate radishes cracked with her cleaver. I ate her lace bones. She told me I'm the murderer." Ming sits even more straight, his hair mussed, but still elegant and oddly compelling in his hospital gown. "It's I who knew it would happen. I foresaw—I knew it would happen! I wanted it to happen, and I didn't prevent it. I let go of Dagou. Dagou took the rap. I let him take it. I thought he killed Ba, I thought he *would* kill Ba, but it was really me because I knew—"

"Back up," says James, shaking his head. "Did you say, do you mean O-Lan is—"

"That's why she never left. I'm pretty sure Dad once tried to fire her, and she wouldn't go. I've got to get out of here, James. I've got to keep her from escaping. She's a flight risk. Green card, indeed. She'd rather kill us all than be a citizen of any country."

"You need sleep and rest."

"I need coffee."

"No more caffeine, doctor's orders."

"I'm getting out of here."

"Ming, you're having a nervous breakdown."

Ming cocks his head and looks up to the left, as if a lamp has turned on in the corner of the room. "That would explain a lot."

"Can I do something?"

"Go talk to her! Keep her here!" Ming, his eyes flashing triumphantly and angrily, recites directions to O-Lan's room. "Now get out of here. Go. There's no time."

As James runs through the fluorescent-lit halls, he considers what Ming has just told him. Weightless, he pumps the length of the building, toward the exit nearest the parking lot. He can't feel the floor under his feet. He can no longer focus on the significance of Ming's words, for his heart is in flight from them.

Around him is the hospital. He has the sense of being in the arteries of an endless, brilliant beast, an organism, its windows glittering in the dark like jeweled dragon hide, a lone phlebotomy cart circulating in its corridors, tiny vials of blood moving along its arteries. The basement bowels, the cafeteria, the offices at the top. The little room where Winnie died—grief-stricken, jolted by the news of his father's death, bound to Leo in love and hate. He had once wished to be a doctor, to know this place. The more he learns about the body, the less he has even the smallest sense of knowledge or control, and the more he understands there is no such thing as knowledge and control.

But he is the youngest brother, and he must follow orders. He recalls Ming's directions, drives through Letter City into the oldest part of town, the shabbiest part. James reaches the house Ming described to him, "cheap white siding, 1920s style, big but with something meanly scaled in all of the proportions." Using his phone as a light, James climbs the outside stairs.

A single door at the top. His fist echoes and he knows—believes—he knocks in vain. He puts his hand on the knob. As he turns the knob, he believes—hopes—the room will be empty.

He enters, closing the door behind him.

Someone is sitting in the dark, near the kitchen. James flicks on the ceiling light. O-Lan wears jeans, a T-shirt, and a denim jacket; at her feet is the blue carpetbag.

"Hello," he says, in English.

She doesn't answer.

"Ming says you can understand me. I'm here to make sure you stay. You've got to stay."

He waits for several seconds; still she doesn't answer. The light casts shapes over her face. He can see it now, beneath those marks of pain and age: that unmistakable vitality, the blood of his father. He looks at her left hand. On her third finger is the blunt shape of the ugly, yet priceless, ring.

When she speaks, her voice holds the rich, mocking fortitude of Big Chao. "Do you *believe* I should stay?"

James struggles against the impulse to recoil from the aggression, and the surprise, of her spoken English. For some reason, he remembers Winnie's voice, *You need to breathe.* He breathes. "I don't know," he says. His mother stays with him, guiding him. "Do you trust anything?" he asks, as she might have done. "Do you have faith, in God, or in the teachings of Buddhism?"

"I've been to see Gu Ling Zhu Chi," she says, surprising him. "I went straight to her temple when I first arrived in Haven. The nuns took one look at me and let me in. They can always tell when someone is truly meant to see her."

"What did she say?"

"She asked me for my story. I told her I had come to town to destroy my father. I told her about his great injustices toward my mother and me. She prayed for me. Then she summoned Leo Chao to the Spiritual House, and she reintroduced us."

So all along, Gu Ling Zhu Chi had held this knowledge over his father. It explained Leo Chao's respect for the old nun.

"I was hungry, homeless, an illegal. She advised him to give me a job. In this way, she thought, he could begin to make it up to me. I would learn to live in peace. And I would serve as a reminder to him, that we must consider the consequences of what we do. She made him promise to employ me. And she offered me lodging."

"Why didn't you take it?"

O-Lan shook her head. "She wanted to keep an eye on me. But she didn't force me to live with her, it's not her way. I took a room here instead. I worked for him. Of course, he didn't improve. He exploited me. Gu Ling Zhu Chi was wrong on both counts. He didn't change his ways, and nothing weakened my determination."

"But Gu Ling Zhu Chi is right," James said. "We must consider the consequences of what we do. You have to stay in Haven now. There'll be an appeal."

"I don't mind if everyone knows what I've done," she says. "Yes, there'll be an appeal, and my testimony will be discredited. But I won't be here. Why would I have stayed?"

James has to think back, slowly, in order to remember. "A green card."

"They assume it's what everyone wants."

Of course, the prosecuting attorneys assumed she'd be held in Haven by the promise of citizenship. But Ming was right. Why would she *want* to be a part of this, or any, country? O-Lan, the Orphan, who had no native language.

"You should all know one more thing," she says. "One more piece of the story."

He nods, he is ready.

"Your mother guessed who I was. Not right away. It happened about a year after I arrived. I told her what your father did to my mother and me. It's why she left the restaurant. Why she left your father and went to the nuns."

Did she guess that he's often wondered why Winnie had left them? Is she trying to comfort him? It's possible. In the set of her lips, and in her neck and shoulders, he reads a stubborn and familiar resistance. There is deep pain in her, as well. He's seized with the recognition, the understanding, that it is even more terrible to be a daughter of Leo Chao than it is to be his son.

"But you're our sister," he says. "We can't just let you go. Where would you go?"

She smiles. "I'm not going to tell you that."

"I'll stop you." James takes out his phone. "I can call 911," he says. "There are only three entrances to the freeway. The police will follow you."

She shrugs. "That's your decision, little brother. You do what you think is right. I'm leaving now. Goodbye."

There are so many things he wants to talk to her about. More than the ring, the carpetbag. But he finds he cannot bear to be rebuffed by her.

"Goodbye," he says. Their eyes meet. She reaches for the bag. He stands in place, in her way, but he doesn't try to stop her. Quick as a cat, she moves past him, out the door, and down the stairs.

James sits down at the card table, holding his phone. She told him to do what he thinks is right. He brings up the screen to dial and stares at the bright numbers. One call, and he will have done the right thing. She'll be caught, and she'll receive the punishment she deserves. But is it right? It is more terrible to be a daughter of Leo Chao—worse to be his Chinese daughter than his American son. What would Dagou want him to do?

James puts his phone back into his pocket. He'll wait for the authorities to discover the room is empty. By that time, his sister will be far away, many hours out of town, possibly states away from Haven, in any direction. Soon, James will go back down the stairs, to the hospital. But for several minutes he sits at O-Lan's empty table, steadying his breath.

The Closing Statements

It's midmorning, and the courtroom has grown bright and warm, before Judge Lopate is ready with her decision on the request for a mistrial. The sun, pouring through high windows, glints off the buttons worn by the waiting spectators. Everyone watches as Judge Lopate takes a sip of water. Then she announces that the jury had been dismissed and essentially sequestered by the time Ming told his story. The witness had also been dismissed. There's no mistrial.

In the first few rows, the community listens with their faces closed, protected. Outsiders might describe them as emotionless and inscrutable. In reality, almost everyone is praying now. By an accident of timing, most of the Christians sit on one side of the aisle today, and almost all of the Buddhists sit on the other side. Katherine is on the Buddhist side. Lynn suspects she chose deliberately, knowing that the temple women wouldn't hold yesterday's words and actions against her. Maybe Dagou will be found innocent; maybe he'll forgive her for betraying him in order to protect Ming. Omi sits on the Christian side. Watching her lips move, Lynn suspects she has switched to Christianity because she believes Dagou is guilty. Christianity provides a concrete action plan for sins, even mortal ones. Christianity acknowledges wickedness but maintains Dagou might still be saved.

Strycker stands to deliver his closing statement. He says the law that a son must respect the father is universal. He quotes the Bible: "'Honor your father and your mother, so that you may live long in the land that the Lord your God is giving to you.'" He quotes Confucius: "'The virtue of filial piety is essential to the establishment and continuance of human society.' Therefore," he continues, "William 'Dagou' Chao has broken the rules not only of the American culture in which he was raised, but of the culture of his ancestors!"

Strycker stares at the jury. "Does William 'Dagou' Chao have the right to walk free as a member of our society? Does a man who has used every method within his means, legal and illegal, to pour his hatred for this man into the ears of family, friends, and strangers; does William 'Dagou' Chao, who has literally broadcast his desire to murder in the exact way this murder was performed, who has admitted that he had murderous intent, have a right to remain free after that murder?

"William 'Dagou' Chao has committed a murder under the laws of our country. *He must be punished for it.*"

As Strycker's high voice penetrates the room, Dagou sits motionless. There is a long hush. Jerry Stern gets slowly to his feet.

Clearly, deliberately, Jerry makes a plea for rationality. "Appearances," he says, "are not the same as truth; rumors are not the same as truth; threats are not the same as murder; an unexplained death is not the same as a murder; and a statement made in the subjunctive, under pressure of police, is not a confession."

Jerry reminds the jury members about their job. That it's the jury's task to judge whether Dagou is guilty *beyond a reasonable doubt.* That the case for Dagou's guilt is entirely unclear. It's only known that Big Chao died of hypothermia. Without evidence that anyone took the key on purpose, it's reasonable to assume this death was a tragic accident. "And while William wears his heart on his sleeve," Jerry says, "while he may have vocalized thoughts that seem to supply the motivation to commit an unspeakable act, there are others who may have had similar motivation to harm Leo Chao. And there is even reasonable doubt as to whether anyone may have *intentionally* taken the key and shut the door."

He straightens now. His voice deepens and carries to the back of the room.

"Mr. and Mrs. Chao brought their lives to America so their family could have certain rights and freedoms. And after all of their hard work, Mr. and Mrs. Chao would want their sons to keep the privileges they have struggled for, the rights they have earned.

"Think long and hard about taking those rights from William Chao," Jerry says. "Would you vote to imprison a man on circumstantial evidence? Would you vote to take away the liberties his parents sacrificed themselves to give to him? Please do not destroy a human life."

Jerry's plea is followed by stillness. Then Judge Lopate straightens her reading glasses and begins the complicated, methodical job of instructing the jury. Dagou's fate is now up to them.

Lynn scribbles in her notes: *The evidence is circumstantial. The jury gets to decide. If they believe Dagou, they'll vote to exonerate him. If they don't believe him, they'll vote to convict. Will the jury believe a flawed but heartfelt Asian man? We shall see.*

The Moment of Return

That night, James and Alice get into his childhood bed. "Please," he says to Alice, "I don't think I can live with this unless I tell you and Dagou. I know, we're supposed to tell the truth in court. I didn't lie even to save Dagou, and I revealed my relationship with you to the police. But please, if you are capable, forget I ever told you this. I disobeyed Ming and let O-Lan go. I let Dagou take the punishment for her, for me, and all of us. We're all guilty. We let this happen under our watch. We let him mistreat her and we let one of us do something unconscionable. All four of us are guilty now."

"I'll forget all about it," Alice says. He knows she won't forget, but she won't tell.

They lie with their heads on the same pillow, looking into each others' eyes. "I let her go," James says. "I let her go even though she killed my father." The old man in the train station. Leo and Winnie. "I don't know how I'll get over this."

"I don't think you will."

"What do you mean?"

"I don't think we can get over what we do."

James reaches for her.

"I can't," Alice says. She draws her knees up, protectively, between them. Her chilly, pointed toes press against his stomach.

"Don't you love me?"

She doesn't answer for a moment. Then, "I do. I do love you."

"Then tell me why not."

"Because," she says, knowing he needs it spelled out, "I can't do it now that I've testified, now that we all know he was trapped that night, dying in the restaurant, just downstairs. We can't pretend it didn't happen. We can't pretend we don't know, and that we didn't do anything about it."

"It's not your fault," James says. "You thought it was a ghost."

"I told you to go back to sleep. And now, after my testimony, you know what I did."

She can't forget it. He can't talk her out of remembering.

They had sex so many times. But until it happens again, it's in the past tense, it's unreachable. Hasn't he always somehow known, even when they are together, that each minute with her is in the fugitive tense? Already escaped and gone forever? Even the night before the trial. The memory waits for him. On the second time that night he somehow managed to outlast her; he was still inside of her, Alice silently and fiercely rubbing against him, and then, to their surprise, she began to shudder and moan. In that moment, when he knew she was about to come, did he shut his eyes to feel it pass through him, did he accept it as only the first of a thousand times? No, he opened his eyes. He pulled slightly away from her in order to watch her face. He wants nothing in the world but to see that again.

Remembering, wrenched with helplessness and fear, he tries to hold her to him, but she clutches her knees to her chest, her body enclosed and private, sealed into itself.

"Alice," he says, "then what will you do now? Will you go to the Spiritual House? Will you become a nun?"

She smiles. "No."

"Then . . ."

She touches her nose to his. "I said I can't ever do it with you anymore, but it doesn't mean I'll never do it with anyone else. Just not with you, and not in this community." At her use of the words "this community," he understands she sees herself as being apart from it. "Not here," she says.

"You're going away?"

"Yes."

She's lying in his bed with him, their heads on the pillow, and she is looking back into his face, her eyes serious and wide, deep pupils, caramel-colored irises. She is eight years old. They are squatting over an anthill on her lawn. Below them, ants boil from the mound, their flat wings tilting, glittering in the morning sun. She is fifteen years old and hunched over her sketchbook, glancing up at him from the back room of her mother's store. She is nineteen. She's standing in the Spiritual House, she drops her purse, their heads almost bump together, and he smells vividly her cheap shampoo. Then the light changes and it's autumn; leaves blow down a broad and unfamiliar sidewalk in an unknown city. She is standing before a plate-glass window of an art supply store, wearing all black, her face a pale oval reflected in the glass. Her hair is cropped in a way he's never seen before, so that it sticks up a little, rough edged like the feathers around a crow's beak. James's vision fades; for a moment he can't see any further into the future. He closes his eyes. With an effort, he imagines Alice standing at a mirror in a smaller, high-ceilinged chamber with a narrow bed, clothes draped over her bureau. She's seated at a drafting table in a painting studio, the northern light from a high window filling the room with spiritual purpose, like the light of a cathedral. He can't make out the outline of her drawing.

In this instant, when James understands he may not see Alice much anymore, he doesn't know this is the moment when time will begin to circle backward. Even though he'll see her before she leaves for New York, although he'll see her, less and less frequently, at the Christmas holidays, he'll never again see her head on the pillow next to his; he won't feel this way again, but will only return to it, over and over, in his memory. And each time he returns, the memory will change, will alter and degrade. Will she be looking into his eyes with the same intensity as now? Or will she not look at him in quite the same way, will she gaze at him with gentleness and yet with a kind of coolness, of distance? No, not even the memory will be the same. At some point, the hundredth repeat, the thousandth repeat, the memory will be lost to time. James and Alice look into each other's eyes. Alice looks away and the moment is gone.

The Verdict

Posted on May 1, 3 p.m.

You've probably heard the jury has found Dagou guilty of murder.

Judge Lopate had thought the sentence through. She acknowledged Dagou was born into an unusually complex, emotionally violent family, an immigrant family that had no choice in our society but to labor under unreasonable hardship in order to establish itself. Also, born the first son of a "difficult man with a domineering and violent temperament."

"In these things," she said to him, "you had no choice. But as human beings, we are not merely victims of fate." She says it's foundational to American society that its adult citizens are expected to exercise free will and to behave in a morally upright manner no matter what the difficult circumstances, no matter what has been done to them.

She went on about how Dagou lives in the United States. "You may believe you remained with your family out of filial piety, the pillar of your culture's vision of family. But you are now living in a culture where you are allowed, even required, to make your own choices, your own decisions," she said. "Your behavior was that of a trapped animal who would kill its keeper in order to escape. But in reality, you were never trapped.

"The jury has found you guilty of second-degree murder. You have been sentenced to thirty years' imprisonment without parole."

Behind us, the gallery burst into applause.

Dagou sat stunned, with his gaze fixed on Judge Lopate like he was expecting her to take it all back. She met his gaze calmly, then looked out at the gallery.

From the first few rows, we all stared back at her.

We were outraged, stunned, anguished; but we did not fight back. We were, by and large, too docile. Too well behaved, too pragmatic, too self-doubting. I sat speechless, like the others, ashamed of myself, and furious that not one of the jury chose to believe a flawed but heartfelt Asian man.

Only Fang stood.

"Appeal!" Fang bellowed, loud enough for everyone to hear. "There'll be an appeal! *Ack*!"

Ma Wa had reached up and thumped the back of his head.

DECEMBER 24

Anniversary

IT'S A MILD winter morning more than six months later. Deep in the Chao house, seated at the old PC in his late father's cluttered den, James waits for Dagou to appear on-screen for a prescheduled video visit from the prison fifty miles away.

For Christmas he's sent Dagou a journal, stationery, and the allowed religious necklace: Winnie's pendant of Guan Yin, seated on a lily pad. He's already purchased credit—paying a hefty fee—for his brother to buy toiletries and snacks. Thanks to video and in-person visits, small presents, Brenda's attention, and daily workouts, Dagou is holding on. He must serve his sentence in prison until Jerry, Sara, and Katherine can prepare for the appeal. They're counting on the likelihood that O-Lan's flight will discredit her testimony, as she herself predicted.

While he waits for Dagou, James rereads Lynn's latest post. She's still blogging, despite the fact that she received a C on the trial assignment, seventy-six out of a hundred points. (Among other factors, she lost credit for each sentence over twenty words and every paragraph over three lines long.) This brought her course grade down to a B for her first journalism elective. Her mother and father are dismayed, but Lynn has decided to keep writing.

Posted December 24, 9:15 a.m.

The big news was announced yesterday: Alf has been found! He's well and happy, living with the Skaers, of all people. That pack of Skaer cousins, after messing with James's phone, later found Alf in the snow and saved him. They thought they'd keep him long enough to upset the Chaos, then return him to Leo. But the cousins fell in love with him and didn't want to let him go. When Leo's death hit the news, they adopted him.

James studies the accompanying image of Zack Skaer, wearing a Christmas sweater, posing with his arms around a fat, middle-aged French bulldog with a white blaze on his chest. A red bow is stuck between his ears.

James has decided not to confront the Skaers about keeping Alf. What argument can he make, considering that his own family lost the dog, let him run out to founder in the snow? The Skaers saved Alf; they had the right to adopt Alf; they deserve to keep him. James will write to thank them.

"Hey, Snaggle." Dagou's image materializes on the monitor.

Dagou looks pretty good. There's the hint of a glow in his face. It could be his shave, in preparation for the day's visit. He hasn't given up.

"I did eighteen sets already," he tells James. "I do twenty push-ups, jog to the end of my cell and back twenty times, that's a set. My plan is to get really ripped in the new year. I've been reading about it. You can lift using the coffee jugs, you can do chin-ups by wrapping toilet paper around the—" There's a delay in the transmission. James is reminded briefly of his brother's broadcasting from FM 88.8.

"You look great," he says.

"—you can eat peanut butter for protein." Dagou never liked cheese. "How are you, kid? You look like shit, to be honest."

James feels his lips twitch. "Thanks."

"When are you going back to school?"

"I don't know."

"Come on, kid, you can't beat me at being the loser of the family. You have to go to school."

James swallows hard. Every time he talks to Dagou, either in person or on video, he worries it might be the last time he'll be able to see him, confide in him.

"I shouldn't take out loans if I don't have goals."

"Fuck goals. You should be in college. And fuck loans. Mingo owes you, big-time. He can pay for your school."

"I always planned to be a doctor," James says. "Since grade school, I never questioned it."

"So don't question it."

He had thought of it as saving lives and helping others. But his failure in Union Station changed all of that—led, step by step, to the moment when he let O-Lan escape and Dagou go to prison. Of course, he's confessed to Dagou about letting O-Lan get away; his brother understood, has forgiven him. But Dagou's forgiveness changed nothing about what he'd done. It's as if one unthinking day he'd set foot on an island with an active volcano. A fissure opened in the ground. Now he's standing on one side, watching his life move further and further away.

"A tiny weed widening a crack in a man's life," says Dagou. "Those thoughts are dangerous, kid."

"I can't help it," James says. "I just keep thinking."

"That was my problem. Take my advice: get back to school. School, it could be like my working out. Keeps the energy contained, keeps your brain from developing unhealthy habits. But—" he drops his gaze. "I'm the last person you should come to for advice."

"You're my oldest brother," says James. "You're the only person I come to for advice."

"We miss Ma," Dagou says. His chest swells in a deep inhalation, then collapses in a sigh. James thinks of his father, shooting sparks in the dark.

"I loved Ma," says James. "Only—"

"Only she had no good advice about getting laid." There's another short delay. Dagou is saying, ". . . before she died, when I went to her at the hospital. I asked about him. About Ba."

"What did she say?"

"You know her, she would quote the Sermon on the Mount. 'Love your enemies and pray for those who persecute you, so that you may be sons of your Father who is in heaven.' It was her favorite verse of the Bible. And then, when she could no longer take it, when Christianity became too much for her, she went to the Spiritual House, where it was about cessation from attachment, from desire. She tried to let go of all of it. But she never did, you know. She never ceased attachment. She told me to love. In the hospital. To love him."

"Maybe she didn't know what she was saying."

"She knew."

For a long moment, neither brother can come up with a response. Then Dagou grins.

"As for getting laid again, you can come to me for advice. I deliver! From behind bars, I can get you laid. I should do a column: 'Dear Convict.' 'Dear Convict,'" he intones, in his best voice from FM 88.8. "'There's this hot girl, and she doesn't know I exist. What do I do? Signed, Horny Bastard.'" Dagou shrugs. "'Dear HB,'" he says, "'You need to get convicted—'"

"That's not funny. And you're not a convict." To comfort Dagou, James has said this before.

But today, Dagou says, "That's not true."

"Yes, it's true!"

"It's true on a *technicality.* I'm being held unlawfully. I didn't commit the crime for which I've been convicted. But if you look at it another way, I deserve to be here. I did a lot of other shitty things, for which I wasn't punished."

James struggles to reply.

"Forget about it. Listen up. I had an idea about another dish for the fantasy party! I know it's too late now, so how about next year? Ma's savory zongzi."

In the last two months, Dagou has been making plans for an ever-more-elaborate fantasy Christmas party. At night, lying awake, he tries to recall every dish his parents ever discussed and attempted: the triumphant reconstitutions of fish dishes from the other side of the world; the salted greens and crispy skins they teased from childhood memories. He remembers even the failed meals. He directs James and Ming to reconstitute these recipes and to feed their results to Tyrone, Freedy, and the most loyal customers, who critique the dishes. Dagou and James spend most visits discussing these experiments. Are they trying too hard with their cao bing? Is their bing too neurotically or timidly sliced, or too evenly stir-fried? Does it miss the crunchy and uneven bits that had graced their mother's celebrated version?

Lately, Dagou has been seized by the idea that if only there were no hunger, humankind would be all right. He means more, he says, than hunger of the body. He believes they're related: Hunger of spirit *is* hunger of body. The answer lies in the stomach.

"I've been writing to Katherine," he says. "She's going to visit me today, on her way out to the party. I'm going to grill her about the afternoon, like, five years ago, when Ma taught us to make her savory zongzi."

Although she's had two video visits, Katherine hasn't gone to see Dagou in person since his conviction. James suspects they'll be discussing more than recipes. "And Brenda?"

"She's coming tomorrow. Christmas visit."

Dagou's features twist. His face is wretched, darkened.

"I can see her mind go back and forth!" he says. "She walks in thinking, *I'm going to dump him, gotta dump him* now! I can see the other guy. He's an accountant. White guy, dirty blond hair, six-pack abs, met him at the Festival Foods"—James knows there is no such person—"and he's coming by to help her with her leaky sink or make himself useful around the house, since there's no man around. Why stick with me? Why be faithful to me, an imprisoned loser? Every visit, I know she's going to dump me, then she walks in here and feels sorry for me. I should give her her fucking freedom back. If I was a better guy, I would. I will. Fuck if I'm going to keep her tied down."

"She loves you, Dagou."

"I've been trying to break up with her every time she walks in here."

"You're just low because today's the anniversary . . . of what happened."

"I'm a shit."

To cheer up his brother, James tells the news that Alf has been discovered with the Skaers. He's even a little fatter than before.

"Ba always said that dog was a whore." Dagou shakes his head, but James can tell he feels better. They've reached the end of the visit. Katherine will be coming to see him at two o'clock. Dagou wishes James a great Christmas party. He also sends a greeting to pass along to Ming, who's left his job in New York and is now living, with James, in what was once their father's house.

The Life Savings

As the earth's axis tilted away from the sun, and as the medications took effect, Ming's inflammatory monologues eased. He's not drinking coffee, and he's promised not to spend more than ten minutes a day on the internet. His native arrogance has made it possible for him to gradually and scrupulously wean himself off of the psychotropic drugs, the anti-anxiety drugs, the sleep-inducing drugs, and the antidepressants. He goes to the gym and visits occasionally the talk therapist prescribed for him. But the psychosis has opened a window in his mind, and he now has extra insight that comes from an experience in another world. He's as fierce and critical as ever, but he struggles with vivid dreams, and he doesn't tell most of them to anyone, not even his brothers.

Ming and James used most of the bail money, plus some of James's savings, to buy the house and restaurant back from Gu Ling Zhu Chi. It was right that the property should go back to the Chao family, Gu Ling Zhu Chi said. She'd received a visit from Winnie's spirit before the forty-nine-day ceremony; Winnie was troubled about the will after her death. And of course the old abbess wouldn't refuse the money to endow the Spiritual House, where their mother and their half sister had sought refuge. After sending the money to the Spiritual House, Ming wasn't yet at ease. They had more to pay back, for the past and for the future. And so the money left over has been put into an account to pay for health benefits for Brenda, as well as for Tyrone and Freedy, who're working part-time while they save up to start their own restaurant.

When James comes looking for him, Ming is waiting in their father's old chair, watching a soap he secretly enjoys, set in Wyoming, about a ranching family that owns a llama, Thelma, with an IQ of 155.

James says hello, sits in Winnie's old chair. "Did you have anything for lunch?"

This is the anniversary of Ming's drive through the snow: of the texts from Katherine, of his unshaven muzzle in the window at the service plaza. No, he hasn't had lunch. He stares at the TV, ignoring James, and glowering at Thelma, who's playing a trick on her human owner, Macy, involving a mailbox and a locked gate.

But during the commercial break, he mutes the sound. The old house stands around the brothers, hushed, as the winter sun moves up the sky.

For months now, he's been holding back on James. He's been taking things one day at a time, biting his tongue. But on this day, the anniversary, he must speak. "I thought you were different," he says. "I thought you were on higher ground. I told you go search the car. But instead you got distracted and went off like any one of us, off to sniff some tail. While you're making out with Alice, Dagou cluelessly drives away with the money in the trunk and everything goes to hell."

He stops and waits for a reply, but James doesn't try to defend himself. Most likely he knows Ming is right.

Ming goes on. "It's just a guess, but I'll bet you a bundle that Dad *saw* Dagou brought the wrong bag to the hospital. That he *knew* the money was in Ma's room, and probably even *checked on* it, but for some reason he decided to *leave it in the room* where *anyone* could have gotten to it. He *knew* about it, so why didn't he put it somewhere else immediately? Why not put it in the house? Or in the restaurant office? For crying out loud. Fifty thousand dollars. Fifty thousand, and he lets it sit in a hospital closet."

"Maybe he thought O-Lan would steal it if he left it in the office."

Ming has already considered this. Leo would have known O-Lan also knew about the bag, he says. She would have learned about it from her bilingual eavesdropping. She'd be expecting it to turn up sooner or later. "So he leaves it where he assumes she won't think to search. But he never gets a chance to retrieve it. Dies first. Not knowing that O-Lan might actually have some connection with Ma."

James says, "Maybe he *wanted* her to have the money."

"No. No way. He simply overlooked the possibility that O-Lan and Ma might have had their own relationship. That she'd feel *gratitude* for Ma's decency when she was starting out. That Ma might guess who she was, but not hold it against her. That she might *want* to deliver food to Ma when Dagou's being questioned. So, at some point, when she's bringing Ma *soup*, she eyes the bag. Takes it right out of the hospital room and puts it into her trunk. Although of course she doesn't leave town. Not yet. She's watching and waiting, waiting to get that ring. She follows Katherine, back and forth. To the restaurant. To our house. She's spying through a window when Katherine takes off the ring and puts it on the counter."

"Why didn't she leave town then? After she got the money and the ring?"

Ming hesitates. "She was waiting to talk to me."

"You've got it all figured out." James tries to placate him.

But James can't possibly understand; because of the false language barrier, he never had a conversation with O-Lan. He's never eaten her food. For a moment Ming can almost taste the red radishes, the thin white lotus like the lace of bones. With an effort, he trains his mind back to the conversation. "Of course," he says, "that still doesn't solve the question of where Dad was planning to put the money after retrieving it from the hospital. There's the biggest mystery: What was his real way of hiding money? He left the money in the hospital and died planning to get it back and bring it to his secret hiding place. You know he was sitting on a pile of cash, years and years of cash. His Life Savings."

"You think he was loaded."

"I *know*. Some people, they go through life, and what they have to show for it is money. I know Ba was that way." He finishes the thought. "It takes one to know one."

They sit silently in front of the TV. Ming is aware of Christmas Eve oppressing them. James checks his phone. He's about to leave for the restaurant, to set up for the party. They must both be at the restaurant soon. James puts his phone away, and Ming senses something he's never felt around his younger brother before—not love, not exactly. Comfort, gratitude, and trust. He knows he must take a risk and bring up the matter he's been keeping back, something that's been growing in his mind. He stares at the screen's bright, meaningless images.

"I suspect you're another one," he says. "I think you've got a taste for treasure, James."

There is a tick of quiet between commercials.

"Ming," says James, glancing over, trying to meet his eye. Ming looks away. "So, it's about the freezer room. I don't think Dad's stash is invested out in the world. I think it's at the restaurant, in the basement."

Ming keeps his gaze trained at the television.

"You were going on about a lot of stuff, when you were sick. I had a hunch—so I went and looked it up. Eight hundred thirty-eight thousand dollars, that was the going price of a bar of gold, last winter."

So the old nun was right, and James is, indeed, cannier and more relentless than they've been giving him credit for. "You fucking well know Dad wasn't talking to me from the spirit world. That was just a crazy fucking hallucination, James."

"Listen, Ming," James says, "I went downstairs last week, to check it out. The room seems like it's falling apart. The south wall, in the back, it's like part of a brick wall was halfway taken down. There are at least three skinny bricks, recently painted."

"Stop."

"He told you about it," James persists. "He must have wanted you to go find it. He must have trusted you not to waste it."

"No, no, thanks. I don't need it and I don't want it."

They sit together in silence. "We can leave it down there," James says. "In case one of us needs it in the future. For the restaurant. Or for more legal costs, or—"

"All right."

When James is gone, Ming heaves himself out of his father's chair and goes upstairs to get ready for the Christmas party.

What the four of them (Ming, James, Brenda, and Katherine) rarely mention is the fact that they're keeping the restaurant open for Dagou, who will need the place after the appeal is successful and he's out of prison. This is the advantage of a family business, Ming thinks, as he gets into the shower: it can employ an ex-convict as a matter of policy.

Anyway, they have time on their hands. Business has become less steady after the verdict. The Haven regulars haven't abandoned them, but the peripheral customers have stayed away because of the persistent rumor about dog meat. The rediscovery of Alf might help somewhat. But people are cautious: the restaurant is now marked, or marred. It's no longer an upstart business founded by new arrivals, but a local institution with a history and tragedy of its own.

Are the Chaos immigrants anymore? Ming wonders, as he searches for his reflection in the steam-covered mirror. Are they still an immigrant family, now that their mother and father are gone, and after all the passion they've spent, the transgressions they've committed in Haven? He remembers the luncheon at the Spiritual House: Leo shouting, Alf pressing his butt against his shoes, he himself retreating safely into his hunting blind. He can't pretend he's innocent, can't protect himself anymore. If the past year has been about anything, it has been about their recognition—his, Dagou's, and James's—that they are Americans now. This country is the place where they have made their ghosts. It's home.

The Portal

The midday sun, unseasonably warm, shines through the last oak leaves that drop into James's path, as he rides his bicycle, without haste, down Cosgrove Avenue, toward the restaurant. At a long traffic light, he digs his hand into his pocket and discovers the piece of sesame candy given to him a year ago by his mother, at the Spiritual House. He unwraps the sticky candy and eats it slowly, enjoying the sweetness, popping the seeds between his teeth.

Arriving at the restaurant, James skids to a stop to avoid the small figure of Mary Wa, emerging from the station wagon in which she sometimes makes deliveries. She's insisted on delivering the supplies for the party.

"Let me help," says James, leaning his bicycle against the restaurant. In the front seat of the car, Alice is sitting with her sketchbook. James's heart pummels his chest. He hasn't seen Alice in almost four months.

"Where's Fang?"

Mary opens the back of the station wagon. "Fang is still asleep," she says. "And what are you doing, awake?"

James shrugs, smiling slightly.

"You never used to be this way, James Chao. Keeping my son up until three o'clock in the morning, drinking and talking about who knows what. Fang says you and Lynn make him apply to Madison. But what about you, James? You're not going back to school? You don't want to be doctor anymore?"

"I don't know, Mrs. Wa. I'm taking a break."

"Just because your brother is not allowed to live his life, it doesn't mean you don't live yours," she says, with an uncharacteristically sage expression. "You get on with your own life." She puts a hand on his shoulder. "You're getting strong," she says. "Well, you need some time. Time to get over everything, and time to get used to the fact that Winnie is no longer on this earth."

James says nothing, but it is comforting to have a motherly hand on his shoulder. After a while, he moves away, toward the entrance.

"You're not locking up that bike?"

"No one's going to steal my bike."

"We need something to eat," Mary says unexpectedly. "Come on, Alice."

Alice gets out of the car. Together, they walk through the red double doors, under the banner that has been up for three months and is beginning to fly a bit loose on windy days, GRAND RE-OPENING.

The sun streams into the dining room, lighting up the same old booths upholstered with red vinyl. Yet there are notable changes. The lampshades are new. The place looks cleaner than before, and the air is less sticky, as if someone has personally wiped the decades-thick film of cooking oil from every square inch of every table and booth. Someone has. The walls have been repainted smoothly in "Himalayan Paw," a matte golden color chosen by Katherine. An enormous lucky bamboo, which Katherine purchased for an unreasonable sum, stands near the door. There's a flock of framed black-and-white photographs on the walls, snapshots of the Chao family members over the last dozen years: James and Dagou, when James was in middle school; Dagou posed with his instrument; all three brothers; the brothers with their parents. Near the register, there's a photograph of Alf and Winnie, taken sometime in the year before James left for college. Winnie kneels with her arms around Alf, who's beaming at the person behind the camera. Someone has gone to the trouble of removing the glow of the flashbulb from his eyes.

"There's no need to hide anything," Katherine said, on the day when she brought over the stack of framed photographs wrapped in brown paper.

In the kitchen, the old counter has been replaced. The office has been cleaned out. The bathroom has been remodeled, and, downstairs, the refrigeration in the freezer room has been disconnected.

Mary Wa asks to be seated. "Alice needs something to eat. All she would have this morning was orange juice. Dumping cold acid into her stomach, first thing."

Nervously, James gestures to a table.

"I'm okay, Ma," says Alice. She sits down in a resigned way and looks at the menu.

She's dressed characteristically out of season, wearing an arsenic-green cotton print that emphasizes her long, thin arms. The dress is the kind another girl might have bought at a vintage store, but James guesses it came from an old suitcase in the basement. He remembers the smell of her skin. He wants to run his hands up and down her arms, to make her shiver.

Alice asks for tofu and mushrooms; she must have decided to continue with her plan to stop eating meat. Is she getting enough protein? James adds extra tofu and a beaten egg into her soup. From the kitchen, he watches her profile as she eats. He wants to take a photograph but he's sure she would be disturbed by that, and it does seem voyeuristic. Still, how else to imprint in his memory the exact slope of her forehead, the long curve of her nose against the gold wall of the restaurant, glowing in the winter light? As he stands there watching her eat, each moment stretches into a translucent pool of time—endless, and yet over in an instant.

He has to leave her alone. Still, he interrupts her as she makes her way to the bathroom. "When are you going to New York?"

"I told them I would start on January fifteenth." She's taking a job in Brooklyn as a babysitter for one of Ming's old coworkers, sharing a studio apartment with one of Lynn's classmate's sisters.

"So, really soon," he says.

He's afraid he's guilt-tripped her, but she studies him somewhat gently and asks, "How are you?"

James shakes his head. "I miss you," he says quietly, but her mother is hovering. "I'll see you tonight, at the party."

Alice nods. James stares at his sneakers. After the verdict, Alice said it made sense for them not to be alone together for a while. Of course, they'll always be friends, but why bring back old feelings? James wonders now. Have the feelings Alice once felt for him vanished in the same way so much of Dagou's anger and hatred for Leo Chao have gone?

After emotions are felt, expressed, where do they go? Is there a place where spent passion collects? Surely it can't simply vaporize, disappear like smoke. There must be a secret hiding place. For every old love affair, a locked room.

Now Alice is leaving with her mother. He waves from the door as they get back into their car. It's hard to be the one left behind.

He's staring at Mary Wa's vanishing station wagon when he senses the opening of a portal. Hears Dagou's deep, husky voice. *I forget you have such bad Chinese. You'll live a big, important life, you'll grow up into a powerful man. You're going to have adventures—expansive, challenging adventures; you're going to live in many places.* Maybe, when the appeal is successful, he'll say goodbye to Dagou, and to the restaurant. Maybe he'll go out into the world. He could have other lovers, perhaps many more. And he'll be all right financially, he'll find a job. Didn't Ming say he, James, had a nose for money like their father and like Ming himself? Didn't Gu Ling Zhu Chi say he would remember everyone he ever knew? It's possible that, somewhere out in the world, he'll meet up with Alice, and they'll be together again.

Family

By five o'clock the restaurant tables are rearranged in preparation for another, much smaller Christmas party. Instead of long rows, the tables are set up in a square, with chairs along the outside. There are red tablecloths and napkins, and in the center there is another table with a very tall vase that Katherine has filled with red roses, holly, and fancy white mums. For Christmas the brothers have planned a menu of sea bass and vegetables—nothing grandiose this year—although, to honor their parents, they've also stewed a large kettle of pork hocks.

Around four o'clock, Jerry Stern enters the restaurant and sits down in his usual booth. James, wearing an apron, waits on him.

"Talked to Dagou yesterday, about the appeal," Jerry says genially. "How about a beer?"

While James gets the beer, Jerry picks up one of the restaurant menus and flips through it. The plastic cover and the laminated pages are smooth and glossy. James wiped each of the menus with Windex one night when he found it impossible to sleep. The menu is also fat with new inserts reflecting ideas Dagou dreams up and persuades them to try.

"How did Dagou feel about the appeal?" James asks, returning with the beer.

"Of course, discussing it made him a bit anxious, but—" Jerry frowned at the "Chef-at-Large Menu," an orange sheet of paper. "Bird's nest soup? Think the chef-at-large might be getting you in over your head?"

"You tell him."

Jerry says, "I've suggested to your brother that he find someone else. There's an attorney from Milwaukee Katherine wanted to bring in—"

"She was just anxious, Jerry. You know Dagou would never agree to be represented by anyone else."

"Katherine is a big help to me and Sara," Jerry says. "For an attorney at an accounting firm, she's showing a real gift for litigation."

"She told me she's thinking of quitting her job and becoming a public defender."

"Talk her out of it." Jerry squints at the menu again.

The door bangs open, and they hear a throaty shout, "Haven't I been patient enough?"

Brenda stalks into the restaurant in a fiery tantrum. She strides past the tables and chairs, flinging her jacket and purse across the seat in her booth.

"She needs to get the hell out of Haven!" Brenda shouts. "She needs to detach! This isn't hers anymore, she needs to get over this and go on with her life!"

Along with her purse, Brenda carries a laptop computer. She has begun to take accounting classes at the community college. She's wearing blue-rimmed glasses that emphasize the color of her eyes. She looks prettier than ever to James, especially now as she stands with feet planted, knees slightly bent as if ready to attack from the haunches.

"What happened?" James asks, although he knows very well what happened.

"She's been to visit him!" Brenda's eyes glitter with outrage and resentment.

"He needs visitors," James says. Since Katherine revealed her muddled loyalties and stood up for Ming in court, she has truly become family—and he can't tolerate another loss of family. "He's an extrovert. He needs distraction, cheering up."

"Why does she need to see *him*?" Brenda rages. "They're broken up. They've been broken up for a year. And how could he let her visit? Doesn't he remember she betrayed him? She doesn't believe in him. She stabbed him in the back!"

"They were best friends for a long time, Brenda."

"He says she apologized and begged his forgiveness! Why should he even talk to her? Why should he even give her the time of day? But he did. He *did*. She was there a full hour!"

"Did he tell you all of this?"

"I made the guard tell me some of it."

"You did?" James can't help asking. To cover, and to feign innocence, he adds, "Did he forgive her?"

"He wouldn't tell me. So I know he did!"

It's so typical of Dagou to succumb to Katherine's apology and then to be unable to hide this fact from Brenda.

James suspects the scene was stormy and they forgave each other in mutual prostrations and exclamations of love. He suspects Katherine got on her knees and Dagou burst into tears; and although they didn't go back to their college days, there was undoubtedly a kind of passion, far more than Brenda would have considered necessary or appropriate. But this makes perfect sense, is somehow comforting to James.

"Why doesn't she move on?"

James smiles. "Why don't any of us move on?"

His words shake Brenda out of an internal labyrinth. She fixes her gaze on James with maternal concern. "Are you thinking of leaving town, James? You have your whole life ahead of you—you're not going to spend another year here in Haven, are you?"

James doesn't answer.

More times than he cares to admit, he's rewatched the station video online, lying in bed with his screen flickering. The black-and-white train station, the strangers in their winter coats, the old man clutching his carpetbag, shuffling across the screen. James has seen the video so many times he knows each dip and sway of the bag. Too soon, the man who was briefly his grandfather disappears.

I'll memorialize him, James thinks. *I'll talk about him tonight at the party. I'll ask everyone to raise a glass to Zhang Fujian.*

He thinks, *I am James Chao, son of the late Leo and Winnie Chao, brother of Dagou and of Ming, once lover of Alice. . . .*

"Sometimes I think she's not interested anymore," Brenda is saying. "Maybe she's just waiting for Ming to come around. They're made for each other. They'll end up together; it's just a matter of time."

It will only happen after they have all survived the present moment. For now, the world is holding still. Appeals can take years to prepare. And yet, for Ming, something has shifted: he is no longer opposed to dating Asian women. This he ponders in the kitchen, chopping ginger to make their mother's favorite sea bass. He's soaking two giant tubs of pea greens according to the nun Omi's instructions. As a penance to his brother, he is slowly mastering recipes from the Spiritual House, as well as trying out the dishes Dagou dreams up in prison and wants so badly to be making himself.

On certain days, Ming feels certain he and Katherine loathe each other, and that this hatred is so specific and well founded, so based on things each has said or done, that there is no way they could ever transcend it. They're two highly compatible people fated to speak only about one subject, and, if Dagou were to be released from prison and Katherine to abandon Haven for good (with less guilt, and diminished attachment to this momentous, and hopefully successful, appeal), they might talk less and less, until they're just friends on social media (perhaps, for this purpose, Ming might rejoin social media). Katherine will meet a more deserving man—maybe a fellow lawyer. She'll give up her daydream of becoming a public defender. Ming will return to New York, throw himself into his work, and finish making his fifty million.

At other times, Ming can just as clearly envision the two of them clutching hands before a justice of the peace. He can see their enormous airy old apartment in an august building along the lakefront in Chicago. Together, more than they would alone, they'll be able to move forward from the present. They'll cycle through Bavaria and eat their way through France. They'll bicker constantly. They might even make a pilgrimage to China: to Katherine's orphanage and Leo and Winnie's ancestral villages. And eventually they might have the Han children Katherine once wanted; they'll raise a new dynasty of Chaos to conquer the restless, shimmering vision of the world Leo Chao dreamed about, the vision that led him to this unlikely place.

They have one snapshot from Katherine's phone. In the image, Dagou fills the kitchen doorway in his smudged white apron, grinning carelessly at the photographer. O-Lan stands behind him, working at the counter, slightly out of focus. Whenever a Chinese newcomer visits the restaurant, Ming shows them the photo and asks if they've seen anyone resembling her. No one has. Of all their contacts, only Gu Ling Zhu Chi might have an inkling of where she is. Ming and James have tried several times to reach the old abbess. They know they must speak with her soon because her time is coming to an end. But on their most recent visit to the Spiritual House, they were stopped at the door by An, who examined them with her blue gaze; and they were told that, in her dotage, Gu Ling Zhu Chi was dozing through the afternoons. No one must disturb her rest.

The New World Hotel

Far away, the sun is setting over the desert. The sky behind it deepens to royal blue. Under this there lies an infamous and extraordinary city, and near the city's edge stands the New World Hotel, a glowing palace of debt and fancy.

When it's well past dark, a Chinese woman leaves the hotel through the side door of the lobby, skirting the cars lining up for valet parking. She's a plain woman, with canniness and discernment in her gaze; she could be anywhere between thirty-five and fifty. She strolls down the strip, past a kaleidoscope of lights. She passes sparkling trees, reindeer, sleighs laden with gifts, life-sized, psychedelic gingerbread houses. There are also palaces, monuments to what she knows are lesser desires: fake country villages, fake European landmarks, false worlds. But the art inside the New World Hotel is real. There is a Constable, a Shishkin, and, she's almost sure of it, a Brueghel the Younger.

She walks to the hotel almost every day. It's possible to go inside and view real paintings. To win a little money, stroll the sculpture garden, then slip out and make her way down to the anonymous room where she is living. This city, more than anywhere she's been, is a mix of exaggeration and routine. Every day, the same and new. In the mornings, sunrise. There is a world here, and there's the underbelly of the world. There is the desert, where it's possible to bury the past in shifting sands. Her father would have loved this.

She glances down at her finger, at the green jade glowing faintly in the dusk. Seen through the window, abandoned on the counter. In the end, the ring was easy to reclaim. She'd simply slipped through the back door, into the kitchen with the stealth of a cat. She has the ring now, and she has her birthright. She has her real name: Chao Ru.

She came to America resolved to make herself an orphan. In doing so, in carrying out her plan, she found a family. Deep in the interior, toiling at that shabby restaurant with its neon sign: there, she found three brothers. She has no desire to call or write to them. But it's something to know they exist, living their own flawed, desirous lives. That her blood is shared. The blood of the thief, the pioneer and the marauder, the yearner and the usurper.

She looks out at the desert and its dream of tranquility.

ACKNOWLEDGMENTS

As A WRITER tunneling through midlife—as a mother, administrator, and teacher—I would have found it impossible to complete this novel without the support of the residencies that hosted me generously and repeatedly despite my not showing many external signs of creative progress. My profound gratitude goes to these organizations and the people who make them possible: the American Academy in Berlin, which generously supported this project in its later stages; the Corporation of Yaddo, especially its leader Elaina Richardson; MacDowell and the James Baldwin Library; and my Midwest residence-away-from-home, Ragdale, especially Jeff Meeuwsen, Amy Sinclair, Laura Kramer, and Chef Linda Williams. Many thanks to Write On, Door County, and director Jerod Santek. I owe much to the radical hospitality of Hedgebrook and its founder, Nancy Skinner Nordhoff, as well as Vito Zingarelli and Amy Wheeler.

The Iowa Writers' Workshop has been a truly meaningful place to work for the last fifteen years. I am extremely lucky to have the luxury of working with Sasha Khmelnik, a literary and tactical genius who is brilliantly and diplomatically guiding the program toward modernity. I am profoundly grateful to Connie Brothers, an extraordinary person, for our daily conversations over many years. Many thanks to Deb West and Janice Zenisek for saving my skin on countless occasions; and to Kelly A. Smith and Leah Agne. Many thanks to Charles D'Ambrosio, James Galvin, and Mark Levine for serving as Acting Director. I'm also indebted to my superb colleagues Jamel Brinkley, Ethan Canin, Ayana Mathis, Tracie Morris, Marilynne Robinson, Elizabeth Willis, and especially Margot Livesey.

The University of Iowa made it possible for me to complete this novel. I am deeply thankful to CLAS deans for supporting my writing: Linda Maxson, Raúl Curto, Joe Kearney, Steve Goddard, Sara Sanders, and Roland Racevskis. I owe much to the provosts of the last fifteen years, especially Barry Butler and Kevin Kregel. I appreciate Carol and Gary Fethke for their support of the Workshop and its writers. I am indebted to the support of Bruce and Mary Harreld. I would also like to give profound thanks to the University of Iowa Center for Advancement, where the inspiring Lynette Marshall and Jane Van Voorhis work to provide stability for our program and its faculty. Generous friends of the Workshop have made it possible for faculty to write, especially the Meta Rosenberg Foundation, Marly and Laura Rydson, and Mitchell Burgess and Robin Green. I appreciate the support and friendship of Louise and Alan Schwartz of the Truman Capote Literary Trust.

Iowa City has been a home to me and my family for fifteen years. I would like to thank our beautiful independent bookstore, Prairie Lights, and its owner, Jan Weismiller. I'm also grateful for the Preucil School of Music, Willowwind School, and the Iowa City Community School District. Thank you, Iowa City Parks Commission, for unanimously approving the naming of James Alan McPherson Park.

I owe much to the community at the Warren Wilson College MFA Program for Writers, where I first heard Charles Baxter's lecture about writing a scene in which a character shouts that he wants a cup of coffee. Many thanks to Debra Allbery, Peter Turchi, and C. J. Hribal. I am grateful to Debra Spark and David Haynes, who read early versions of this novel and provided important feedback.

Warmest gratitude to the community at the Napa Valley Writers' Conference, where patient attendees have heard me read from this novel-in-progress half a dozen times. Thanks especially to Angela Pneuman, Andrea Bewick, Nan Cohen, Anne Matlack Evans, Iris Jamahl Dunkle,

Catherine Thorpe, and Charlotte Wyatt; and to Andy Weinberger at Readers' Books of Sonoma. I also appreciate wonderful time spent at Aspen Words, the Bread Loaf Writers' Conference, Tin House Summer Workshop, and Kundiman.

Many thanks to the generosity of Clydette and Charles de Groot and the American Library in Paris. I would also like to thank Hugues and Claude de Rocquigny for their hospitality and friendship. I am indebted to Carolyn Kalhorn and the real Alf. I am deeply grateful to the residents of Les Cerqueux-sous-Passavant, especially Yanan Par and Pascal Métayer and his family, as well as Huguette and Gilles Couteleau of L'Eraudier, with fond memories of René Couteleau.

I am grateful for the friendship of Yiyun Li, whose love of Russian authors has sustained so many readers and who encouraged me by laughing during a reading of an early version of this manuscript many years ago in Napa. A thousand thanks to Bennett Sims for sharing his virtuosity in an inspiring letter, and for "The Brothers Karamahjong." I am indebted to Kevin Brockmeier, extraordinary writer, friend, and reader; and to Tom Drury for his kind, expansive reading of the manuscript. I'm grateful to Jess Walter for his visionary advice guiding me toward omniscience. James Han Mattson provided significant feedback. My deep appreciation to Ada Zhang, for her generosity and insight, and for finding the church, the courthouse, and the restaurant.

To Eileen Bartos, Andrea Bewick, Nan Cohen, Craig Collins, and Dr. Elizabeth Rourke: I am truly grateful for your generosity and friendship. My deepest thanks to all of you, especially Eileen, for reading my work.

Robert Stauffer and Kathi Hansen philanthropically provided hours of pro bono consultation. They are not responsible for any of my legal errors in the book.

I'm indebted to all of my students over the last fifteen years. They have been profound, gifted, and kind. I appreciate their patience with me and their acceptance of my shyness, bluntness, and inadequacy. My thanks for understanding the necessity of getting work done.

I would like to thank Tameka Cage Conley and Derek Nnuro, for their friendship; Sarah Frye and Alex Madison, for my wonderful ten-year party; Garth Greenwell, for inspiring passion about reading; Jorge Guerra, for advice and support of diversity at the Workshop; Ben Hale, for his aesthetic capaciousness; Arna Bontemps Hemenway, for his correspondence; Evan James, for looking at ants with Tai; Carmen Maria Machado, for generousity years ago; T. Geronimo Johnson, for friendship and support; Ben Mauk and Carleen Coulter, for introducing me to Berlin; Belinda Tang, for her inspired work during the pandemic; Tony Tulathimutte, for "diaperfilling"; and Kevin Smith, for music and tai chi.

Many thanks to Mary Ellen Gallagher, for teaching me to love Paris. Many thanks to Pauline Ryan, for friendship and generosity to the Writers' Workshop. My deep appreciation to Jean Kwok, especially for encouraging me to drive to Wisconsin to see my dad. For important readings of the cards, I am grateful to Rebecca Makkai and Xochitl Gonzalez.

Many, many other people inspired me and helped me complete my work over the last fifteen years. I would like to thank Jen Adrian, Alexia Arthurs, David Baculis, Jr., Charles Black, Tyler Brooks, Janet Skeslien Charles, Lauree Christman, Joy Chung, Dr. Tony Colby, Tim Conroy, Christina Cooke, Victor Diamondfinger, Iracema Drew, Steven Fletcher, Dr. Mbechi Erondu, Angela Flournoy, Claire Fox, Allan Gurganus, Paul Harding, Adam Haslett, Matthew Henerson, Sarah Heyward, Michelle Huneven, Riley Johnson, Matthew Kelley, Dimitri Keramitis, Yu-Han Kuan, Elaine Lai, You Jin Lee, Chris Leslie-Hynan, Peter Lessler, Cristóbal McKinney, Rachel McPherson, Kyoko Mori, IfeOluwa Nihinlola, David Wystan Owen, Amy Parker, Doris Preucil, Tianhao Shao, William Shih, Sara Stojkovic, Brandon Taylor, Alden Terry, Frankie Thomas, Vauhini Vara, Kris Vervaecke, Monica West, Liz Weiss, Rachel Williams, and Mako Yoshikawa.

I am exceptionally lucky that this novel has found a home at W. W. Norton. My deepest appreciation to Jill Bialosky for her wisdom and her belief in this project. Thanks also to Drew Elizabeth Weitman, Erin Lovett, Michelle Waters, Kelly Winton, and Ingsu Liu.

A thousand thanks to Sarah Chalfant and Jin Auh for years of patience and support.

I feel very grateful to my three sisters, Tai Chang Terry, Dr. Huan Justina Chang, and Ling Patricia Chang.

I would not have finished this novel without the humor and generosity of my brilliant and loving husband, Robert Caputo, who has been truly supportive of me and my work. I must also thank my wonderful daughter, Tai Caputo, who has been deeply kind to an imaginary book-sibling throughout her fourteen years, never once complaining while her mother devoted unreasonable time and attention to its make-believe people and their problems. Thanks also to my humane and wise mother-in-law, Katherine Caputo, and her chicken soup.

The following supporters of this novel are no longer living but are remembered frequently with love and gratitude: Scott Johnston, Joe and Genie Patrick, Eavan Boland, James Alan McPherson, James Caputo, Helen Chung-Hung Chang, and Nai Lin Chang.

ABOUT THE AUTHOR

LAN SAMANTHA CHANG is the award-winning author of the collection *Hunger* and the novels *Inheritance* and *All Is Forgotten, Nothing Is Lost*. Her work has appeared in *The Best American Short Stories*. A recent Berlin Prize Fellow, she has received grants from the National Endowment for the Arts and the John Simon Guggenheim Foundation. Chang is the first Asian American and the first female director of the Iowa Writers' Workshop. She lives in Iowa City.

CPSIA information can be obtained
at www.ICGtesting.com
Printed in the USA
LVHW101759310322
714931LV00024B/767/J